AMOS OZ

Born in Jerusalem in 1939, Amos Oz is the internationally acclaimed author of many novels and essay collections, translated into over forty languages, including his brilliant semi-autobiographical work, *A Tale of Love and Darkness*. He has received several international awards, including the Prix Femina, the Israel Prize, the Goethe Prize, the Frankfurt Peace Prize and the 2013 Franz Kafka Prize. He lives in Israel and is considered a towering figure in world literature.

ALSO BY AMOS OZ

Fiction

My Michael
Touch the Water, Touch the Wind
Unto Death
The Hill of Evil Counsel
Soumchi
Where the Jackals Howl
A Perfect Peace
Black Box
To Know a Woman
Fima
Don't Call It a Night
Panther in the Basement
The Same Sea
A Tale of Love and Darkness
Rhyming Life and Death
Suddenly in the Depths of the Forest
Scenes from Village Life
Between Friends
Judas

Non-fiction

In the Land of Israel
The Slopes of Lebanon
Under this Blazing Light
Israel, Palestine and Peace
The Story Begins
How to Cure a Fanatic

AMOS OZ

Elsewhere, Perhaps

TRANSLATED FROM THE HEBREW BY
Nicholas de Lange
in collaboration with
the author

VINTAGE

1 3 5 7 9 10 8 6 4 2

Vintage
20 Vauxhall Bridge Road,
London SW1V 2SA

Vintage is part of the Penguin Random House
group of companies whose addresses can be found at
global.penguinrandomhouse.com

Penguin
Random House
UK

This edition reissued in Vintage in 2016
First published in hardback in Great Britain by
Martin Secker & Warburg in 1974

penguin.co.uk/vintage

A CIP catalogue record for this book is available
from the British Library

ISBN 9781784704933

Typeset in India by Thomson Digital Pvt Ltd, Noida, Delhi

Printed and bound in Great Britain by Clays Ltd, St Ives plc

Penguin Random House is committed to a sustainable future
for our business, our readers and our planet. This book is made
from Forest Stewardship Council® certified paper.

In memory of my mother

Do not imagine that Metsudat Ram is a reflection
in miniature. It merely tries to reflect
a faraway kingdom by a sea, perhaps elsewhere.

Contents

CONTENTS

PART ONE
Over Against the Fishermen

1

A Charming, Well-organized Village

YOU SEE before you the kibbutz of Metsudat Ram:
Its buildings are laid out in strict symmetry at one end of
the green valley. The tangled foliage of the trees does not break
up the settlement's severe lines, but merely softens them, and
adds a dimension of weightiness.

The buildings are whitewashed, and most of them are topped
with bright red roofs. This color scheme contrasts sharply with
that of the mountain range, which completely blocks the view
to the east, and at the foot of which the kibbutz lies spread.
The mountains are bare and rocky, cut by zigzagging ravines.
With the sun's progress their own shadows spill gradually
down these folds, as if the mountains are trying to relieve their
desolation with this melancholy shadow play.

Along the lower terraces on the slope stretches the border
between our land and that of her enemies.

This border, prominently marked on the maps with a thick
green line, is not visible to the observer, since it does not
correspond to the natural boundary between the lush green
valley and the bleak, bare mountains. The soil of Israel over-
flows the limits of the valley and spreads up the lower slopes
toward the barren heights. So the eye and the mind – or, more
precisely, geology and politics – come to be at odds with one

another. The kibbutz itself stands some two miles from the international frontier. We cannot define the distance more precisely without entering into the bloodstained controversy over the exact location of this line.

The landscape, then, is rich in contrasts, contrasts between appearances and reality and also inner contrasts within the appearances. These can be described only by the term 'contradiction.' There is a kind of enmity between the valley, with its neat, geometrical patchwork of fields and the savage bleakness of the mountains. Even the symmetrical architecture of Kibbutz Metsudat Ram is no more than a negation of the grim natural chaos that looks down on it from above.

The contrast inherent in the landscape naturally plays a prominent part in the works of Metsudat Ram's own poet. Sometimes it takes the form of a genuine symbol, as we shall see if we look at the poems of Reuven Harish. For the time being, let us borrow the poet's favourite contrast and apply it to matters that Reuven Harish does not write about.

Consider, for example, the striking contrast between our village and the typical village, which arouses nostalgic feelings in the hearts of city dwellers. If you are accustomed to the sight of ancient villages, their roofs soaring on high in convoluted northern shapes; if in your mind you associate the word 'village' with horse-drawn carts piled high with hay and with pitchforks stuck in their sides; if you yearn for crowded cottages huddling round the rain-swept spire of an old church; if you look for cheerful peasants with brightly colored clothes and broad-brimmed hats, picturesque dovecots, chickens busily scratching in a dung heap, packs of lean, vicious dogs; if

4

you expect a village to have a forest round about and winding dirt paths and fenced fields and canals reflecting low clouds and muffled wayfarers heading for the shelter of an inn – if this is your mental picture of a village, then our village is bound to startle you, and it is this which has compelled us to introduce the term 'contradiction.' Our village is built in a spirit of optimism.

The dwellings are absolutely identical, as is demanded by the ideological outlook of the kibbutz, an outlook that has no parallel in any village in the world. The well-known lines of Reuven Harish convey the essence of the idea:

> In the face of a foul world bent on doom,
> And the lascivious dance of death,
> In the face of sordid frenzy,
> In the face of drunken madness,
> We will kindle a flame with our blood.

The houses, as we have said, are brightly painted. They are laid out at regular intervals. Their windows all face north-west, since the architects tried to adapt the building to the climate. Here there is no agglomeration of buildings clustering or ramifying haphazardly down the ages, nor blocks of dwellings enclosing secret courtyards, for the kibbutz does not have family homes. There is no question of separate quarters for different crafts; the poor are not relegated to the outskirts nor is the center reserved for the wealthy. The straight lines, the clean shapes, the neatly ruled concrete paths and rectangular lawns are the product of a vigorous view of the world. That was what we meant when we stated that our village was built in a spirit of optimism.

Anyone who draws the shallow inference that our village is stark and lacking in charm and beauty merely reveals his own prejudice. The object of the kibbutz is not to satisfy the sentimental expectations of town dwellers. Our village is not lacking in charm and beauty, but its beauty is vigorous and virile and its charm conveys a message. Yes, it does.

The road that joins our kibbutz to the main road is narrow and in bad repair, but it is straight as an arrow in flight. To reach us you must turn off the main road at a point indicated by a green and white signpost, skirt the potholes in the road, and climb a pleasant small hill not far from the kibbutz gates. (This is a green and cultivated hill, which is not to be seen as a finger of the mountains thrust violently into the heart of the valley and lopped off, since it has nothing in common with the menacing mountain heights.) Let us pause for a moment and engrave the striking colored picture-postcard scene on our memories. From the top of the hill we can look down on the kibbutz. Even if the view does not inflame the heart, still it pleases the eye. The open iron gates, a sloping fence, and, nearby, a tractor shed. Agricultural implements scattered about in cheerful disorder. Buildings crowded with livestock – chickens, cattle, and sheep – constructed on the latest plan. Paved paths branch out in various directions, and avenues of bush cypresses trace the skeleton of the over-all shape. Farther on stands the dining hall, surrounded by well-kept flower beds. It is an outstanding modern building, whose size is relieved by its light lines. As you will discover, its interior does not belie its façade. It radiates a delicate, unpretentious elegance.

Beyond the dining hall, the settlement is divided into two separate blocks, the veterans' quarters on one side and the young people's on the other. The houses wallow in cool greenery, overshadowed by trees and surrounded by lush lawns pricked out with brightly colored flower beds. The soft sound of rustling pine needles is ever present. The tall granary to the south and the tall recreation hall to the north break the uniform lowness and add a dimension of height to the settlement. Perhaps they can compensate to some extent for the missing church spire that, whether you admit it or not, is an integral feature of your picture of the typical village.

To the east, at the farthest corner from your vantage point, is a collection of huts. This serves as a temporary home for training courses, work camps, and army units, anyone who comes to share our burden for a limited span of time. The huts bestow a pioneering character on the whole picture, the air of a border settlement ready to turn a resolute face to impending disasters. So does the sloping fence that surrounds the kibbutz on all sides. Let us pause here for a moment to evoke your admiration.

Now let us look toward the fields of crops all round the kibbutz. A heart-warming sight. Fields of bright green fodder, dark orchards, cornfields echoing the sunshine with a blaze of gold, banana plantations with a tropical air of overpowering vitality, vineyards spreading right up to the rocky heights, the vines not sprawling untidily but neatly arranged on trellises. The vineyard, delightfully, makes a slight inroad into the mountain terrain, which is indicated by the gentle curve of the ends of the rows. We shall refrain from reciting yet another of the poems of Reuven Harish, but we cannot conceal our modest pride at the marked contrast between the cultivated plain and the grim heights, between the blooming valley and the menacing mountain range, between the confident optimism below and the unruly glowering presence above.

Take your last photographs, please. Time is short. Now let us get back in the car and complete the final stretch of the journey.

2

A Remarkable Man

LOGICALLY, REUVEN Harish should have bitterly hated the tourists. The man who wrecked his life was a tourist. It had happened a few years previously. Noga was twelve and Gai was about three when Eva left her husband and children and married a tourist, a relative, her cousin Isaac Hamburger, who had been spending three weeks with us that summer. It was a sordid affair. Ugly instincts came to the surface to torment and destroy. Now Eva lives with her new husband in Munich. They run a night club there in partnership with another fine Jew, a sharp, shrewd bachelor by the name of Zechariah Berger, Zechariah Siegfried Berger. We must claim the reader's indulgence if we find difficulty in describing the event and its heroes without giving vent to our own moral indignation.

Logically, Reuven Harish should have hated the tourists. Hated them bitterly. Their very existence reminds him of his disaster. To our amazement, Reuven has seen fit to take on himself the regular task of showing the tourists round our kibbutz. Two or three times a week he gives up some of his free time for this purpose. We have become used to the sight of his tall, lean form leading a motley procession of tourists around the farm. He expounds the rudiments of collectivist ideology to them in his friendly, intimate voice. He is not tempted into facile reasoning, nor does he shy away from theoretical principles. He never tries to satisfy the exotic expectations of his heroes. His resolute straightforwardness cannot tolerate compromise or circumlocution. In his youth he was fired with blazing enthusiasm, which in later years evolved into a different kind of enthusiasm, a sober enthusiasm without arrogance but with a strict self-discipline of unrivaled purity. He is a man who has known pain and is bent on reforming the world, but who knows that the twists of life cannot be reduced to simple formulas.

It is a fine thing for a man who has known suffering to aspire to reform society and to strive to remove suffering from the world. There are some sufferers who hate the world. They spend their lives cursing it destructively. We, in accordance with our philosophy of life, are against hatred and against curses. Only some kind of mental perversity can make a man choose darkness in preference to light. And it is as clear as daylight

9

that mental perversity is the opposite of right-mindedness, just as day is the opposite of night.

At first we were surprised by Reuven Harish's dedication to the task of receiving the tourists. There was something strange and illogical about it. Gossiping tongues tried to explain the instincts at work here. It was said, for example, that people sometimes want to remind themselves of pain, to turn the knife in the wound. It was said that there are different ways of hiding a feeling of guilt. There was even an outrageous suggestion, which we reject absolutely, that he wanted to seduce a young girl tourist to wipe out his humiliation with a fitting revenge. And there were other explanations, too.

Whoever objects to such gossip betrays his own lack of understanding of our collective life. Gossip plays an important and respected role here and contributes in its way to reforming our society. In support of this claim, let us recall a statement we have heard made by Reuven Harish himself: the secret lies in self-purification. The secret lies in judging one another day and night, pitilessly and dispassionately. Everyone here judges, everyone is judged, and no weakness can succeed for long in escaping judgment. There are no secret corners. You are being judged every minute of your life. That is why each and every one of us is forced to wage war against his nature. To purify himself. We polish each other as a river polishes its pebbles. Our nature notwithstanding. What is nature, but blind, selfish instinct, deprived of free choice? And free choice, according to Reuven Harish, is what distinguishes men from animals.

Reuven speaks of judging. Gossip is simply the other name for judging. By means of gossip we overcome our natural instincts and gradually become better men. Gossip plays a powerful part in our lives, because our lives are exposed like a sun-drenched courtyard. There is a widow in the kibbutz, Fruma Rominov by name, who is steeped in gossip. Her judgments are severe, but not cold-blooded. Those of us who fear her caustic tongue must overcome their weaknesses. And we, too, judge the widow. We accuse her of excessive bitterness and we cast doubts on her commitment to the ideals of the kibbutz. So Fruma Rominov in turn is compelled to overcome her nature and to refrain from excessively malicious remarks. Here, then, is a concrete illustration of the image of the pebbles in the river. Gossip is normally thought of as an undesirable activity, but with us even gossip is made to play a part in the reform of the world.

After Eva's marriage to her cousin Isaac Hamburger, she settled in Munich with her new husband and assisted him in his entertainment business. The news that reached us by roundabout ways announced the appearance in her of unsuspected talents. Our reliable source of information, which will be revealed shortly, added that her sensitive taste brought an unusual character to Berger's and Hamburger's cabaret. Customers flooded to it for a rare entertainment which captured the imagination. Decency constrains us not to describe it in detail.

Eva had always been energetic and practical, and she also had a brilliant imagination that was forever seeking an outlet in some form of artistic expression. Such qualities as these in

11

a faithful wife are a stimulant for the intelligent husband. And Eva Hamburger had been blessed, even as an adolescent, with a graceful, deerlike beauty.

Long ago, Eva used to copy out Reuven's early poems in her slanting handwriting. In a special album she used to collect the cuttings from the kibbutz-movement papers in which they appeared. The album itself she decorated with delicate pencil drawings. A warm grace infused everything she did. Despite her unfaithfulness, we cannot forget the devotion and good taste with which she used to lead the meetings of the classical music circle of our kibbutz. Until a demon entered into her.

Reuven Harish bore the blow with remarkable self-control. We had never suspected that there lurked in him the determined resignation which he displayed in the moment of crisis. He did not neglect for an instant his work as a teacher in our primary school. His pent-up despair was free from any hint of animosity. His grief endowed him with a certain radiant sensitivity. Here in the kibbutz he was ringed with a halo of general sympathy.

Toward his motherless children he displayed a discreetly moderated devotion. See him walking in the evening along the kibbutz paths, wearing a blue shirt and a pair of threadbare khaki trousers, with Noga on one side of him and Gai on the other, stooping to catch every one of his children's words, even their most idle chatter. The girl's eyes are like her father's, large and bright green, while the boy's are like his mother's, dark and warm. Both children are endowed with a rich inner life. Reuven is careful to remain close to them, without trampling on their inner thoughts and feelings. He exercises a father's authority and a mother's attentive love. Moved by his love for his children, Reuven began writing children's poems. These were not the verses of a childish adult but those of a grown-up child. There is no heavy mockery in them, but subtle humor and a pleasant musical quality. The publishing house of the kibbutz movement had the splendid idea of producing a collection of his children's poems in a beautiful edition. The book was illustrated with drawings made by Eva, long ago, before the flood. These drawings were not originally intended to accompany children's poems, and they did not correspond to the text. But there was a kind of harmony between the drawings and the verses. This is a puzzle to which there is no simple solution. The congruence might be explained, of course, by saying that Eva and Reuven were still, fundamentally, et cetera, et cetera. There may be another explanation. Or there may be no explanation at all.

However that may be, Reuven's poems are not comical amusements for children. His children's verses, like all his poetry, present a poetic commentary on the world in simple language and appealing imagery.

Now we shall reveal a little secret. Indirect contacts have strangely been maintained between Reuven Harish and his divorced wife, between Eva Hamburger and her abandoned children. Isaac Hamburger's business partner is in correspondence with one of the members of our kibbutz, the truck driver Ezra Berger. Occasionally, Eva Hamburger adds a few lines in her sloping handwriting in the margins of his letters, such as:

It is four o'clock in the morning, and we have just got in from a very long journey through forests. The scenery here is very different from yours. The smells are different, too. Is it terribly hot there? Here it is cool and slightly damp, because of the northeast wind that blows at dawn. Could you send me, say, a napkin embroidered by my daughter? Please. Eva.

The gossip maintains that behind these snatched lines there lurks a warm affection. Our opinion is that they can be read in different ways, ranging from warm affection to cool indifference. There are those who firmly maintain that one of these days Eva will return to the bosom of her family and her kibbutz, and that the signs are already apparent. Fruma Rominov, on the other hand, has been heard to remark that it would be better if Eva never came back. We used to think that Fruma said this out of malice. Now, on second thought, we are not so sure.

Reuven Harish, as we have said, has redoubled his love for his children. He is a father and also a mother to them. Sometimes, if you go into his room, you find him busy with wood and nails making a toy tractor for Gai or drawing pretty patterns on pieces of material for Noga to embroider.

He has also redoubled his ideological zeal. His serious poems, those that are not intended for children, emphasize the contrast between the mountains and the settled land. It is true that they are unpretentious, but they do display a faith in man's power to rule his destiny, and they are not mere versified slogans. If we approach them without preconceptions, we can find in them sadness, hope, and love of mankind. Anyone who scoffs at them betrays his own inadequacy.

> The turbid torrent rushes into gloom:
> Can man, so stunted, pitiful and weak,
> Reach up to snatch a firebrand from the sun
> And smile to see his fingers black and scorched?
> Has he the strength to build a mighty dam
> To stem the torrent and to tame the flood,
> To leave behind him grim subservience
> And paint his life a peaceful shade of green?

Reuven Harish throws himself wholeheartedly into his teaching, which endears him to his pupils. Even his dedication to the task of receiving the tourists is, when all is said and done – and leaving aside the malicious insinuations of the gossips – a sure sign of his devotion to the ideal.

The restrained poetry of his language, his intimate way of talking, the gentle pathos without a hint of insincerity, all these things endear Reuven Harish to us. A man of learning and at the same time a peasant, a man whose life has been enriched by suffering, Reuven Harish is one of our most remarkable men. And yet he has a certain simplicity. Not the simplicity of fools, but a clearly defined simplicity that is virtually a conscious principle. Let idle men of little faith mock him; we will mock them in return. Let them mock him to their petty, futile hearts' content. Mockery of him condemns itself and betrays the tediousness of the mocker, who will end up alone, bogged down in his own captiousness. Even death, about which for some reason Reuven has been thinking deeply today, ever since he saw the tourists off, even death will be more bitter for them than for him. They will face death empty and bare, whereas he will have left his slight mark on the world.

If only it was not for the loneliness.

The loneliness is agonizing. Every evening after coming back from Bronka Berger's room, Reuven stands alone in the middle of his own room, tall and thin as a youth, and stares in front of him with a surprised, insulted look on his face. His room is empty and silent. A bed, a wardrobe, a green table, a pile of exercise books, a yellow lamp, Gai's box of toys, some pale-blue pictures left behind by Eva, congealed bleakness. Slowly he undresses. Makes some tea. Eats a few biscuits. They taste dry. If his tiredness does not get the better of him, he peels some fruit and chews it without noticing its taste. He washes his face and dries himself on a rough towel, which he has forgotten to send to the laundry again. Gets into bed. Hollow silence. A wall light which is not fixed properly and will fall down on his head some night from force of gravity. The newspaper. The back page. A supplement devoted to problems of communication. Dear fellow citizens. The sounds of the night steal into the room. What day is it tomorrow? He turns the light out. A mosquito. He turns the light on. Mosquito vanishes. Turns the light off. Tuesday tomorrow. Mosquito. Finally, damp, uneasy sleep. He is tormented by nightmares. Even a pure man of sound principles cannot control his dreams.

*

We have dwelt so far on Reuven Harish's virtues. It is only right that we should also say something about his faults. Not to do so would be to neglect the right to judge, indeed, the obligation to judge, which, as we have said, is the secret of this place. But propriety and our sympathy for Reuven Harish combine to make us limit ourselves to mentioning one specific matter as briefly as possible, and indirectly.

A man in the prime of his life cannot go for long without a woman. Reuven Harish, who is exceptional in many other ways, is no exception to this rule.

A platonic friendship had existed for some time between Reuven Harish and a colleague in the kibbutz school, Bronka Berger. Bronka, too, is one of the veterans of the kibbutz and was born in a town called Kovel on the Russian-Polish border. She is about forty-five, and so a few years younger than Reuven. If we were not aware of her good qualities we would say that she is plain. To her credit it must be said that she is a sensitive woman with strong intellectual leanings. What a pity that the friendship of the two teachers should not have remained pure. Some ten months after the flood – that is to say, after the upheaval of Eva's departure – gossip informed us that Bronka Berger had found her way into Reuven Harish's bed. We must stress our disapproval of this immoral affair, because Bronka Berger has a husband, Ezra Berger, the kibbutz truck driver. Ezra Berger is the brother of the celebrated Dr Nehemiah Berger of Jerusalem. Furthermore, the object of Reuven Harish's affections is also the mother of two sons, the elder married and about to become a father, and the younger son is the same age as Noga Harish. So much for the negative side of Reuven's record.

We seem to have mentioned the names of the three Berger brothers already in passing. This was not how we ought to have introduced them. Since it has come about accidentally, let us take the introductions as made. Siegfried Zechariah Berger, the youngest of the three brothers, is the partner of the Hamburgers in the cabaret in Munich. Ezra Berger, a man of fifty or so, is the father of Tomer and Oren Geva, the deceived husband of an unfaithful wife. Dr Nehemiah Berger, the eldest and most distinguished, is a scholar of modest reputation and lives in Jerusalem. If our memory does not deceive us, he researches into the history of Jewish socialism. He has already published a number of articles on the subject, and one day he will collect his scattered studies into a book that will contain all the sources of Jewish socialism from the time of those great reformers, the prophets, up to the establishment of the kibbutzim in the revived Israel.

The three brothers have thus followed diverging paths. They have moved away from each other and from their origins. All three, however, have experienced hardships and sufferings. Those who believe in an ultimate justice hold that even suffering is a sign of divine Providence, since without suffering there is no happiness and without hardships there is no redemption or joy. We, on the other hand, who yearn for a reformed world, do not believe in this kind of justice. Our aim is to eradicate suffering from the world and to fill it instead with love and brotherhood.

3

Stella Maris

REUVEN HARISH does not chase after barren fireworks. Only action can bring warmth to a heart touched by icy fingers.

He wakes at six o'clock in the morning, gets washed and dressed, picks up his brief case, and walks over to the dining hall. Many of our members begin the day with a sour and sleepy look. Reuven starts his day with a smile. As he slices a tomato or chops a radish for his breakfast, he makes light conversation. His tone is cheerful. See him telling Nina Goldring about the organization of a regional orchestra, discussing the price of grapes with Yitzhak Friedrich, the treasurer, or arranging with Fruma Rominov the earliest possible evening for the next meeting of the education committee. On Monday Mendel Morag will be away; he is going to Haifa to take delivery of a consignment of timber for the carpentry shop. He is sure to stay the night there with his sister. What about Thursday? Mundek Zohar won't object. Thursday, then. How is Tsitron, by the way? I know they're going to visit him in hospital at lunchtime, and I very much wanted to go, but there was a phone call last night telling us to expect a party of Scandinavian tourists then. Hey, Grisha, the barber's coming today or tomorrow. Or have you decided to let your hair grow long, like a beatnik? I can't stand soft tomatoes. Grisha, would you have a look on the table behind you – is there a good firm one there?

At half past seven he goes to the school and waits for the bell to ring. Today I'm going to give you your exercise books back. Some of your essays were a pleasure to read. Some of you, on the other hand, still don't know where to put a comma. That is intolerable in the full sense of the word.

Now let's try to find the central idea in Shimoni's *Memorial*. What is the poet trying to say? Self-sacrifice, yes. But what is self-sacrifice? That's the question.

At twelve o'clock school is over. A hasty lunch. The tourists are due at half past one. My name is Reuven. Reuven Harish. Welcome to Kibbutz Metsudat Ram. Well now, we can talk quite freely.

At a quarter past two the tourists leave. There would have been nothing exceptional about this group if it had not been for the strange remark of the old Dutch colonel. When that goy had the nerve to say – stressing his great military experience – that the mountain was about to fall on top of us and crush us, I couldn't think of an answer. A phrase that would stick in his mind, for him to hand on to his children and grandchildren. What ridiculous arrogance. 'As an expert.' I know what I should have said: The mountain will not fall on top of us, because your expertise is only valid elsewhere. Here we observe a different law of gravity. As for death, of course it is true that we all die eventually, but some people are dead even while they are alive. A slight difference, but a decisive one.

What a pity that Reuven Harish is not good at giving instant ripostes, that he needs time to think of a clever answer. To his credit it must be admitted that he is industrious. Having seen the tourists off, he goes home to his empty room, gets

20

undressed, has a refreshing shower, puts on clean clothes and settles down to his marking. There is nothing casual about his work. The red pencil deals ruthlessly with the children's scripts, pouncing on spelling mistakes, filling the margins with comments, firmly but carefully expressed, to avoid discouraging their young minds. Reuven does not consider himself above arguing seriously with his pupils' views. Just because they are only ten or eleven years old, it is wrong to crush them with dogmatic, authoritarian statements. Mistakes, Reuven is in the habit of saying, are not a monopoly of grown-ups. His pencil never draws a red line without specific grounds. That is why his work is not mechanical.

His mind is alert, as always. His sharp green eyes are equally alert. Here is an absorbing subject, for instance: the difference between the work of the children of the members born in Germany and that of the little Russians. It could provide the material for a subtle study. The former express themselves in carefully balanced phrases. Their writing is neat and tidy. The latter let their imagination run riot. The former frequently suffer from dryness. The latter – from absolute chaos.

Of course these are gross generalizations. We must not rush to deduce from them such dubious notions as a 'Russian soul,' an expression of which Herzl Goldring, who is responsible for the upkeep of our plants and gardens, is fond. No. After all, both groups were born here. Little children are not presented to one to work on like potter's clay. A true artist perceives the form hidden in the block of stone; he does not force his material, but releases the hidden form. Education is not alchemy. It is a subtle form of chemistry. Not creation from nothing, but creation from something. If you don't take heredity into account, you are beating your head against a brick wall. But it is even worse to make heredity the be-all and end-all. That line is bound to end in nihilism. That Dutch officer wanted to know if I don't long for adventure. What greater adventure could there be than education? Even just a father, a man with children. But he said he didn't have any children. That is why he spoke like that about death. A barren tree!

These thoughts supply the rough draft of what he will say to Bronka tonight.

Between two-thirty and three o'clock Ezra Berger prepares his truck for a long journey. Twice a day, at six in the morning and three in the afternoon, he leaves for Tel Aviv with a ten-ton load of boxes of grapes. We are now at the beginning of the harvesting of the early grapes. Since the beginning of the grape harvest, Ezra has taken on a double job, which occupies him from six in the morning to nearly midnight.

Everywhere else, if a man works a double shift, it is because he is short of money. With us, of course, it is different. Why has Ezra Berger decided to take on the work of two drivers? The question has no answer in material terms. If we believe the gossip – our collaborator in this story – Ezra's excessive industry is due to the relations between his wife and the poet and teacher Reuven Harish. This explanation, which we heard from Fruma Rominov, is undoubtedly sound; only its formulation is, naturally, a little oversimplified.

Anyway, Ezra Berger's powerful body can easily cope with the extra effort. It is a thick-set body, hirsute, and somewhat pot-bellied, with thick, heavy limbs. His muscular shoulders support without the intervention of a neck a dark head with thinning hair. A coarse-featured, solid face, half hidden by a gray cap, the other half staring out at the world with a blank expression. His appearance neither attracts nor repels. What is remarkable is the thick gold ring he wears on the little finger of his left hand. This kind of ornament is commonly worn by truck drivers, but it does not become, in our opinion, a driver who is a member of a kibbutz.

Ezra Berger does not belong to the intellectual circle in our kibbutz. His place is among modest, straightforward men of action. Do not jump to the hasty conclusion that the kibbutz is neatly divided into two categories. No. Ezra Berger himself would refute such a rash idea. He is not young any more (his younger son is already taller than he is), but he still clings to the world of ideas. True, he is not a great reader, nor is he well up in the classical writings of the kibbutz movement. Nevertheless, he is fond of the Bible, and on Saturday, his free day, he reads the Bible. And he reads all the articles of his brother, the scholar. We must not be quick to judge him if he is not one of our regular debaters. His views, which were formed in his early youth, are clear, well defined, and easygoing. This, too, is part of his integrity, which is secretly envied by several of those who outwardly mock it.

There is a peculiar charm in Ezra's remarks. They are spiced with sayings and proverbs. That is why you never know whether he is talking seriously or only pretending to be serious. He is a withdrawn man. His affected gravity is a barrier between him and us. He surprises us by joking without smiling or smiling when it is not right to smile.

A man like Ezra Berger does not collapse because of a woman's unfaithfulness. True, he suffers. But his suffering is restrained. Pruina says he is restrained because he is coarse. We maintain that there is something noble about his restraint, if you can call moderation and self-control noble.

First of all, he ties a thick rope to the base of the side of the truck and expertly winds it round a bracket. Taking three steps backward, he raises his arm and hurls the coiled rope over the top of the cab. Then he walks round to the other side of the truck, where the end of the rope is waiting for him. He takes hold of it and pulls with all his weight until the wooden sides groan submission. When it is quite taut, he winds it round the iron hook again and repeats the process three times, until the sides of the lorry are well tied with three loops of rope. Finally, Ezra spits into his big hands, rubs them together, spits again on the ground in a vaguely angry way, and places a cigarette between his lips. He lights it with a gold-plated lighter, a present from his brother (his brother Zechariah Siegfried, in Munich, not his brother Nehemiah, who lives in Jerusalem). After taking a few phlegmatic puffs, he plants his foot on the running board and uses his knee as a desk while filling in the docket.

What next? To the kitchen to collect coffee and sandwiches. Ezra will be on the road until after midnight. We have a saying: Ezra without coffee is like a Leyland without fuel. It may be a trite saying, but it expresses an undeniable truth. Nina Goldring, the kitchen supervisor, pours the boiling coffee into the yellow thermos flask, just as Ezra, in his thick rubber soles, comes creeping up behind her. He puts his hand on her shoulder and says in his deep voice:

'Your coffee is like a soothing balm, Nina.'

Nina Goldring is frightened by the rough touch and the rough voice. A burning black drop falls onto her arm. She lets out a loud, startled cry.

'I frightened you,' Ezra says, stating, not asking.

'You . . . you took me by surprise, Ezra. But that wasn't what I wanted to tell you. I wanted to say something important. You made me forget what it was. Oh, yes, now I remember. You've been looking very bad these last few days. I've meant to tell you several times. With such bloodshot eyes you drive at night. For drivers, lack of sleep is very dangerous, especially for a man like you, who . . .'

'A man like me, Nina, does not fall asleep at the wheel. Never. With the help of Him who gives strength to the weary, as they say. I think about selected subjects or drink some of your coffee, or else I sleep and my engine gallops home like a horse who can smell his stable. I can do the last stretch of the journey with my eyes shut.'

'You just remember what I'm telling you, Ezra. I say it's dangerous and . . .'

'What does it say in the Bible? . . . God favors fools. According to that, I should come out of any trouble all right. If I'm a fool, nothing can happen to me. And if anything does happen to me, that'll prove that I wasn't a fool. They can carve my name next to Ramigolski's – he and I were friends, you know – and Harismann can write an elegy about us, dear departed friends, et cetera. What's the time? My watch is always slow – is it three yet?'

'Yes, it's five past,' said Nina Goldring. 'Here, smell this coffee. Strong, eh? Don't you rely too much on those sayings. Charms and promises don't do any good. Take care.'

'You're a good woman, Nina. It's very kind of you to spare a thought for others, as they say, but there's no need to worry about me.'

'Yes there is. A man can't live without someone to worry about him.'

Good-hearted Nina regrets her words almost before they are out of her mouth. They may not have been very tactful. Goodness knows what conclusions he might have drawn.

Ezra Berger puts the thermos, the sandwiches, and the triangles of cheese down on the empty seat beside him and puts his head out of the cab window to maneuver his machine backward out of the loading bay and onto the road. She's a good woman, Nina Goldring. Only rather short and plump, like a goose. A feast fit for a king for Herzl Goldring. There is a kind of order in the world, as the philosophers say, a kind of logic: intelligence doesn't go with kindness, and kindness and good works do not walk together. Otherwise, one person would be perfect in every way, and another would be a swine's snout, as they say. That's why it is ordained that a beautiful woman should be vulgar. Now, that one is going to be a beautiful woman some day. But there's another side to the coin. She's the poet's daughter. 'Yes, young lady, what can I do for you?'

Noga Harish is a girl of sixteen, tall and slender, like a boy. Long, thin legs, narrow hips, and slim thighs half-covered by

26

a large man's shirt. Her thick, fine hair streams down over her shoulders and halfway down her back. Her build is sharp and angular, which gives the faintly showing signs of womanhood an untamed air. Her face is tiny, lost in the cascades of hair. Noga's hair is dull black. It frames her cheeks and forehead like the ring of soft shadow round a candle flame. Her eyebrows are fine, as in old pictures of the Madonna. Only the eyes are so large that they break the essential harmony, and in them there lurks a flash of green. The eyes of Reuven Harish set in Eva's beautiful face. Ezra Berger looks down on her from his cab window, and nods his head as if he has just been made aware of some secret truth. A moment later he shifts his gaze to the windshield and lets out an abrupt 'Well?'

'Tel Aviv, Ezra?'

'Tel Aviv,' he answers, still not looking at her.

'Will you be back late?'

'Why?'

'Will you have time to do me a favor?'

Ezra plants his elbows on the steering wheel and rests his chin on his shoulder. He throws her a tired, slightly amused look, empty of sympathy. A warm, flattering smile widens Noga's fine lips. She is not certain that Ezra has quite understood her question. She leaps up onto the running board, presses her body to the scorching metal door, and smiles her coaxing smile into the man's face.

'Will you do me a favor?'

'Fortune favors the fair. What do you want?'

'Will you be a dear and buy me some embroidery thread in Tel Aviv? One reel of turquoise.'

'What's turquoise?'

This was not what Ezra had meant to say, but for once he let the words out without thinking. He looked away from her again, like a foolish schoolchild.

'It's a color. Turquoise is a pretty color halfway between blue and green. I'll explain to you where to get it. They're open till eight o'clock. Take this bit of thread with you as a sample. That's turquoise.'

Noga's feet are not still. They perform an inner dance on the running board, without changing positions. Ezra can sense her body clinging to the outside of the cab door. How often I've seen this girl before. But now what. Noga interprets his silence as a sign of refusal. She tries to win him round by pleading:

'Ezra, be a dear.'

Her voice tails off into a whisper. Since Ezra Berger is the father of two sons, both older than this little thing, he allows himself to rest his rough hand on her head and stroke her hair. Normally he doesn't like girls who act like little women. This time he feels a certain affection. He removes his hand from her head, takes her tiny chin between his thumb and forefinger, and announces with good-humored solemnity:

'All right, young lady. Your wish is my command. Turquoise it is.' The girl, in return, places two dark fingers on his hairy, sweaty hand and states:

'You're sweet.'

Taking into consideration the difference in their ages and the girlish tone, we can forgive her this remark. But for once we cannot plumb the depths of Ezra's thoughts: Was there any reason for his sudden release of the clutch pedal, so that only

Noga's extreme agility enabled her to leap off the moving truck in time? Is there any explanation for his unusual haste? He is already disappearing in a cloud of dust. Have a safe journey. Don't forget my turquoise thread. Of course he won't forget. He's sitting huddled in his cab, pressing hard on the steering wheel, thinking about women. First of all, about the girl. Then about Eva. About Bronka. Finally, his thoughts come back to Noga. Such a tiny little chin. Your father would go out of his mind, little Turquoise, if.

The kibbutz is fainting in the sunshine. The concrete path is so searing hot that scorched bare feet hop from the pathway to the grass verge. A gentle hop. An inner dance. Little beads of perspiration sprout on the suntanned brow. Soundlessly, wordlessly Noga chants to herself a gentle tune that clouds her eyes:

> Pomegranate scents waft to and fro,
> From the Dead Sea to Jericho.

In the shade of the gnarled carob tree she lingers, resting a thoughtful hand on the bark of its trunk, shielding her eyes with the other, and gazing up toward the mountains, where light mists drifting relieve the menacing mass. The damp heat attacks the vapor. There the rocks overflow, silently, motionless. Only in the winding gulleys sheets of shade remain, as if the mountains are amusing themselves with some strange game.

On the edge of the lawn a chirruping sprinkler whirls. For fun Noga runs between the jets of water. Perhaps because of

29

her slight build, perhaps because of her tight little mouth, or her dark hair, there is something saddening about the girl, even when she is having fun. She is all alone now on the empty lawn, in the white brightness. Backward and forward she leaps on her long legs, challenging the jets of water. Without any aim, without a smile, she plays with a vague concentration. Blurred sounds waft on the air. If you take the trouble to sort them out, you may identify the growl of a distant tractor, the mooing of a cow, women arguing, and the sound of falling water. But the sounds flow together into a single vague unison. And the girl, so far as the eye can judge, is now totally absorbed in herself.

I didn't want him to joke with me. I wanted him to notice me. Can he really have had no idea what turquoise is? Turquoise is a color halfway between blue and green. A very special color, even if it is a bit loud. He always talks in proverbs instead of words. I say, 'Will you do me a favor?' and he says, 'Fortune favors the fair.' I'm not sure he meant anything by it. He just throws these sayings out so as not to have to answer questions properly. I thought that it was only to me he spoke in proverbs, but he does it with everybody. 'Your wish is my command.' He wasn't quite serious when he said that. He wasn't quite serious when he stroked my hair, either. He stroked my hair as if he was doing it unintentionally, but he did it intentionally. Women can sense these things. But there is something about him I like. He always seems to be saying one thing out loud and something quite different deep down inside him. Anyway, when I asked him to get me the thread, it wasn't just an excuse for stopping him for a chat. I really do need it urgently. Still, I thought he might talk a bit. He's not tall and he's not all that good-looking. Daddy's Bronka's man, but he's very strong. You can tell. Stronger than Daddy. There's one thing I'm thinking of about him. It's a good thing Herzl Goldring can't see me running around on his wet grass. He doesn't shout, he just waves at you to get off, but what a look of hate he gives you. It's four o'clock. Time to go to Daddy's room. Sometimes I want to be very ill so that Daddy will have to look after me day and night, or sometimes I imagine that he's ill and I have to look after him day and night, and then I cry so much that everyone knows that I love him much more. If you're very sad, your heart can break. But you only get broken hearts in books. There's no such thing, really. Isn't it hot.

Noga goes into her father's room, agile, barefoot, on tiptoe. From the entrance hall she peeps secretly into the room. Reuven Harish does not look at her. Reuven Harish looks at his watch, removes the exercise books from the table, puts them in his brief case and shakes his head from side to side, as if arguing with himself. The bird face appears to the girl in pointed profile. He hasn't noticed her yet. With the lightness and agility of a startled animal she runs up behind him, leaps on his back, and kisses the nape of his neck. He jumps with surprise, turns round, and seizes his assailant's shoulders with his pale hands.

'Little cat,' he stammers, 'when will you stop creeping into the house like a thief? It's a bad habit, Noga, I'm not joking now.'

'You were frightened,' the girl says warmly, stating, not asking.

'I wasn't frightened, I was just . . .'

'Just a bit frightened. What were you doing? Writing a poem? Did I frighten your Muse away? Don't worry, Daddy, she'll come back.'

'Who, E–?'

'The Muse – whoop, I've caught her by her hair.' (A quick, fascinating movement of the hand: arching through the air, closing on an imaginary prey.) 'Do Muses have hair, Daddy?'

'Dear Stella,' Reuven Harish says, and kisses his daughter on the forehead, close to the roots of her hair. 'Darling little Stella.' Noga breaks free from her father's clasp and moves her hips in her usual inner dance.

'Have I told you about the performance? No? My class is putting on a show for Shavuoth. Sixteen days to go. A dance sequence combined with readings. I'm dancing the vine. You know, one of the seven kinds of fruit. Symbolic movements. And . . .'

'Stella,' her father says again, and reaches out to stroke her hair. The girl senses the gesture and slips away with a movement of the shoulders. She's already filling the kettle.

Stella. It was a name that Eva had often used. It was no ordinary nickname. Eva's mother had been called Stella. When Noga was born, Eva wanted to call her Stella after her poor dear mother. Reuven argued that he hadn't come all the way to Palestine to give his children non-Jewish names. The name 'Kochava' was suggested, as the Hebrew version of Grandma Stella's name. Eva pleaded for the sake of euphony that the name 'Kochava Harish' was too harsh and guttural. Eva's opposition was decisive, as happened with everything that aroused the gentle objection of that delicate, black-eyed woman with her thin, tightly pursed lips. Reuven agreed to the name 'Noga,' which was a kind of compromise between Eva's musical sensitivity and his own straightforward principles. Noga is the name of a star, and so 'Noga' hints at the name of poor dear Grandma Stella.

Grandma Stella died in a respectable suburb of Cologne a few months after the death of her husband, the banker Richard Hamburger (Eva's father and Isaac's uncle), and two years after her only daughter had joined the pioneers and gone off without her blessing to Palestine, where she had married without her blessing a simple man, born in Germany admittedly, but the son of a simple slaughterer from a remote Podolian hamlet.

As luck would have it, Grandma Stella died at the end of the good old days and did not survive to perish in a concentration camp. An official order arrived canceling her widow's pension from the Petty Trade Bank of Cologne, and Grandma Stella died of shame. In a roundabout way, Noga Harish preserves her memory. It would be overpious to claim that the girl resembles her Grandma Stella. Richard Hamburger's granddaughter walks about barefoot most of the day like a simple peasant girl. On the other hand, Noga may have inherited Eva's outwardly gentle obstinacy, which Eva in turn inherited from Stella Hamburger.

At happy moments Eva used to call her daughter affectionately 'Stella,' and sometimes she called her 'Stella Maris.' There was no explanation for the addition. If we are to believe Fruma Rominov, it reflects a predilection of Eva's for charcoal-drawn seascapes: a solitary white-sailed boat on a misty horizon, waves lightly rippling, a canal lapping against greenery, all in a somewhat old-fashioned, slightly sickly taste. Some of these drawings were included in the volume of Reuven Harish's children's poems, even though they do not correspond to the subjects. But we seem to have wandered rather; we only wanted to explain the name 'Stella Maris.'

The kettle is boiling. Noga makes some coffee for her father, tea for herself, and cocoa for her little brother Gai. We won't say that she acts absent-mindedly, but her eyes don't seem to follow her hands as she works. Her big eyes seem constricted as if they are looking not outward but inward, into her own mind. I think he was trying specially hard not to look at me. Why do I find the thought so enjoyable?

Reuven sits at the coffee table, his hands spread out in front of him. He is looking at his daughter. He is not happy. She's a little girl and she's not a little girl. So far she hasn't said a word about Bronka. Really, it's up to me to start a serious conversation. Suppose she anticipates me and comes along one day and asks, asks me a question, what will I tell her? What will I say if she asks today, for instance? Now. This minute. What will I?

Gai Harish opens the door and forgets to say hello. Reuven rebukes him.

'All right. Hello. But I don't want any cocoa.'

He drops straight down on the rug, as usual, and without a pause or a preamble proceeds to say something very disturbing. This is the gist of it:

34

'This afternoon, after the geography lesson, Bronka explained to us about the Arabs. What ideas she has! Just like a little girl. She thinks they shoot at Jews without meaning to, or something like that. She says they don't hate us at all, they're just poor people and their Secretary in Damascus tells them to fight, and we mustn't hate them, because they're workers and farmers like us. So who should we hate, eh? And she says they'll make peace with us soon. Phooey! What I say is, it's not very educational to tell children in Class III things that aren't true. The fact is, we fire at them, not at the ones in Damascus. And then they curl up and keep quiet. We won't have any peace till there aren't any Syrians left – isn't that right, Daddy?'

'Look how filthy your face is,' Noga says. 'Get to the washbasin at once. I'll wash it for you.'

'Be quiet. Can't you see I'm busy talking to Father?'

'Well, just you talk to me and listen to what I'm telling you,' Noga demands sharply.

'Noga, when grown-ups are talking, women shouldn't interfere.'

Gai Harish is good-looking, but in a different way from his sister. Little Turquoise is dark, while Gai is fair-haired, with a matching complexion. A mop of blond hair falls carelessly over his high forehead. A broad army belt binds his clothes to his lean body. His features are strong and angular like his father's, but a dark warmth animates his eyes. What a fine picture father and son make sitting together at the desk. While Noga puts the food away and washes the dishes, sighing deliberately like a busy housewife whose work is never done, the men stick stamps in the album. The album is arranged in subjects, sport, flowers, space, animals and, to our sorrow, war. Reuven uses the hobby as a means to teach his son a sense of order and discipline. Meanwhile, Noga has finished her chores and picked up a little recorder. The tunes she plays are long and graceful, like her fingers quivering over the holes. She is curled up in the old armchair, her knees drawn up to her chin, her back curved, her eyelashes lowered, her mind full of images. Going out early in the morning before sunrise, wandering barefoot by the fish ponds and watching. Slipping into the old stables, where there have been no horses for years, but where rough walls still harbor an odor of moldering hay. Shouting inside the stables. Listening to the echo. Going out. Singing in the breeze. Lying awake at night in a winter storm, while the rain cries and the thunder laughs at it. Going on a journey by boat. Being a woman somewhere faraway.

Once, in the autumn, at this time of day, I came in here to have a shower in Father's shower. I took off my smelly working clothes (I'd been milking in the dairy). I turned the tap, but no water came out. I had to go to the common showers. But I didn't want to get back into my filthy clothes. In the closet in the shower room I found a kind of fine blue dressing gown, with buttons up the back. It was Mother's. It must have got left behind. I put it on and picked up a towel and soap and my hairpins, and went across to the showers. I had my shower. I was on my way home. Suddenly, Ezra Berger came toward me on the path. That time, too, he turned his head away and didn't look. But before he turned away, he stared at me. Not at my face. If only Rami was different, I'd have told him. I wouldn't tell Rami anything like that. He'd get the wrong idea about me. And he'd go off and tell that old witch Fruma. Once he told me that his mother said I was like my mother because an apple doesn't fall far from the tree. I felt like going and slapping Fruma's face. But then I thought a bit and I realized that if I got angry it would show I felt insulted, and in fact it wasn't an insult at all.

Later on, when a slight west wind ruffles the treetops and brings relief from the parching heat, the Harish family go out into the garden, onto the lawn. Reuven Harish devotes this time to the perusal of the newspaper. Gai conscientiously waters the roses. Noga, with her back to her father, embroiders daintily and beautifully. Suppose she turns her head suddenly and asks a question, what can Reuven say. Her long legs are folded underneath her. Her hair falls across her left shoulder and cascades over her breast. Her lovely fingers move quickly across the cloth. A picture of dainty gentleness. Let us store it up in our hearts. If things turn out well, it will prove that love is stronger than hatred. If badly, we can conjure up the soothing image as a source of comfort and to take the poison out of the sting. Things can happen. It's a disturbing mixture, Noga's girlish looks and her womanly manner. An evil eye, a glazed, ravenous eye, is going to fasten on our enchanted little deer. There is a terrifying story about a little girl carrying a basket through a huge forest. Even Gai is old enough now to make light of this German children's tale. Reuven Harish, on the other hand, will tell you that if you read the Grimm brothers' fairy tales with your eyes open, you will see how the Germans became a nation of bloodthirsty wolves. And he is right. But our eyes are on little Turquoise, on Stella Maris, and we fear for her.

4

Bronka Hears Shooting

> Our valley, where the Jordan sings and splashes,
> Is filled with sounds of labor and of hope,
> Ablaze with brilliant fires of power and vision,
> A green flame lapping up a rocky slope.

THESE LINES from a famous poem by Reuven Harish are familiar to every child. They have been set to music and are frequently sung. At kibbutz-movement congresses and assemblies of pioneering youth we have often seen a line or two of the poem adopted as a slogan, in letters formed of plaited cypress boughs, sometimes even in letters of fire: *Brilliant fires of power and vision*, or A *green flame lapping up a rocky slope*. This is no mere rhetorical figure but a heartening reality. If the words meet with a cynical smile, they will fire the shafts of mockery straight back at the scoffer. A brilliant vision spreads before us now, now when the harsh white glare is subsiding, when the first signs of night arouse sweet dreams in our hearts. At noon the sun beats down cruelly on the well-kept valley. Now, at evening, the view can be seen in a more favorable light.

Kibbutz Metsudat Ram nestles in a long, narrow valley, near the bed of the River Jordan. The valley is a tiny stretch of the greatest rift on the surface of the earth. It starts in the north of Syria and runs down through desert gorges and across broad plains, divides the Lebanon mountains from the Anti-Lebanon, until it becomes the valley of Ayyun on the border of Lebanon and Syria, near the little town of Banias. Here these gentle streams come together to give birth to the lovely River Jordan, which cascades softly into the northeastern corner of the land of Israel, a region of unparalleled beauty, dotted with white buildings of kibbutzim, villages, and little towns. The Jordan then flows on southward, with the hills of Galilee rising gently from its west bank and the bleak ranges of Hauran, Golan, and Bashan to the east. The water collects gracefully in the Sea of Galilee, Lake Tiberias or Kinneret, a sapphire in the setting of the land. It was in this region that we settled and founded our kibbutz home.

From Lake Tiberias the Jordan flows on to lap against the base of the dark Mountains of Moab, to fall finally, exhausted, into the arms of the Dead Sea, from which it never escapes, except in the form of a scalding vapor. But the gigantic rift stretches on southward, riverless now, along the valley of the Arava, from which rise the mountains of Edom, slain in a blood-red magic that at sunset takes on a purple hue. By the new town of Elat on the shores of the Red Sea the primeval fissure adopts the form of a lonely tongue of sea, bounded on both sides by the desert, with no strip of verdure to intervene between the water and its thirsty foe. This gulf is a slanting arm of the Red Sea, itself the extension of the monstrous rift, as its long thin shape testifies. Beyond the Red Sea the fault flows on through the tropical forests of East Africa, and farther still, beyond the equator. As if some dark power had tried to cleave the earth asunder with a mighty ax blow, but changed its mind before the deed was completed. A convulsed power seized by deep gloom in mid-action left this scar with its wild beauty.

In the course of its travels the gigantic rift encounters a variety of climates and landscapes, but for the greater part of its length it is bounded by mountainous deserts, which is why it is all hot and humid. We live at one of its deepest and warmest points. Its geological structure almost entitles our valley to call itself a canyon. For a thousand years the place was a total wilderness, until our first settlers set up their tents and made the desert bloom by the latest agricultural methods. True, a few Arab fellahin dwelt or wandered here before our arrival, but they were poor and primitive, in their dark robes, and easy prey for the hazards of the climate and natural disasters, floods, drought, and malaria. No trace remains of them except some scattered ruins, whose remains are gradually fading away and merging, winter by winter, with the dust from which they came. Their inhabitants have fled to the mountains, from where they hurl their baseless, senseless hatred down at us. We did nothing to them. We came with plowshares, and they greeted us with swords. But their swords rebounded against them. In the span of a single generation we brought about a forceful and spectacular revolution, but we paid dearly for our land in blood, as is testified by the memorial to Aaron Ramigolski, our first victim, who left his family and his home in Kovel, on the Polish-Russian border, to be killed here by plotting enemies. There is an allusion to his name in that of our kibbutz. But the secret of success is not to be sought in the heroism of our founders. Far from it. The secret is, in the phrase of our comrade Reuven Harish, purification. That is why we invite you now to stand with us at the entrance to the pleasant dining hall and examine the faces of the men and women assembling there.

They have washed away the traces of dust and sweat in a cold shower, and now they are gathering in little groups, dressed in simple, clean clothes, for the communal evening meal. Most of the old men are not good-looking. Their sunburned faces are battered and furrowed, but their general appearance is one of strength and physical well-being. They are tanned, their features are open and forceful. Some are bulky, like Ezra Berger, others, like Reuven Harish, are tall and lean. Some, like Mendel Morag, the carpenter, and Israel Tsitron, the banana man, have a distinguished head of gray hair. Others, like Mundek Zohar, head of the regional council, or Podolski, the mechanic, who also draws up the work rota, are more or less bald. All of them, however, radiate a feeling of security and contentment. You will hardly find among them the typical peasant face, with that dense, closed look which comes from grinding toil. On the contrary. In their faces, and in their gait, as well, you see the signs of a lively intellect. They are lively men. As they come close, we can hear their confident voices raised in friendly argument, reinforced by animated gestures.

Let us turn now to their companions, the older women: Esther Isarov, who is still commonly called by her maiden name, Esther Klieger, despite her seven children; Hasia Ramigolski, wife of the kibbutz secretary Zvi Ramigolski (the brother of the late Aaron Ramigolski); Bronka Berger, Gerda Zohar, Nina Goldring, the cook, and the rest of them. Their appearance is saddening, if only for an instant. For ideological reasons the kibbutz does not allow its women members to preserve their looks by means of cosmetics, and this policy has left its mark on the older women. You will detect no sign of dyed hair, rouge, mascara, or lipstick. But in the absence of artificial aids to beauty, their faces have a simple, natural appearance. At first sight, though, these women have a rather coarse look. All things considered, they look very much like the men, with their wrinkled faces filled with controlled strength, the stern network of furrows round their mouths, their dark, undelicate skin, their gray or white or even thinning hair. Some of them are bulky, others thin and angular. Their gait, however, like that of the older men, expresses a strong inner sense of security and confidence. Do not make the mistake of thinking that some of them have a cruel look, like that rather bored woman over there. The expression which you interpret as one of cruelty is really one of asceticism. The one you pointed out is a widow called Fruma Rominov, who is in charge of the infant school. Her son, Yoash Rimon, was a young officer who was killed in the Suez campaign, and his name is inscribed on Ramigolski's memorial. In future, stranger, you will be advised to refrain from hasty judgments that mistake suffering and asceticism for cruelty. Fruma's surviving son, Rami Rimon, is due to be called up for his military service in a few weeks' time. Let us pray that he will return safe and sound, because apart from him his poor mother has nothing left to live for.

And now the younger people are coming. Look at them. Aren't they a credit to us? Look how tall they are, the girls as well as the boys. They are all good-looking. Any exceptions there may be simply prove the rule. They are endowed with all the positive qualities we noticed in their parents, without the hardness. Their walk is agile, their movements are graceful and lithe. They have been brought up from early childhood to physical labor, saturated with sunshine and fresh air, toughened by long, arduous expeditions, exercised with sport and games. All of them are sun-tanned, most of them are fair-haired. Their hands are strong and well formed. The hubbub of voices radiates cheerfulness. Though some of them may suffer from an excess of poetic aspirations, they know how to keep them well under control. Let us follow them into the dining hall, not to let them out of our sight. In any case, we are beginning to attract attention by standing here all this time by the swing door, scrutinizing everyone who comes past on his way to supper. If we linger here any longer, our intentions will supply welcome grist for the mill of gossip.

The dining hall is brightly lighted. The air is warm and damp, and full of din and bustle: the clatter of cutlery, the murmur of conversation, the squeaking of food carts, the rattle of pots and pans from the sinks on the other side of the open partition. The tables are covered with brightly colored formica. The walls are adorned with landscapes, with symbolic representations of labor and with portraits of the founders of the kibbutz

43

movement. On each table there is a tray of crisp brown bread, a dish piled high with fruit, colorful receptacles for salt, pepper, oil, lemon juice, and mustard, bowls of butter and cheese and home-made apple preserves, and a gleaming stainless-steel teapot. In the middle, a big bowl for rubbish and leftovers, and next to it a jam jar full of water with a pretty arrangement of flowers and greenery.

At our table there are six people. That's the rule. No new table is to be used until all the seats have been taken at the previous ones. That way it's more orderly.

Herbert Segal, a short, compactly built man wearing rather old-fashioned steel-rimmed glasses, belongs to the German party. (There are two groups in the kibbutz, those from Germany and those from the area around the Russian-Polish border, which used to be Poland but is now in Russia.) Segal is in charge of education in the kibbutz. This work, however, occupies only his spare time. His profession, which he has followed for twenty-seven years now, is dairy farming. He is a man of exceptional talents and a broad outlook who spends his evenings reading Marx and Hegel, Proudhon, Duhring, Lassalle, Saint-Simon, and Rosa Luxemburg. This kind of farmer you will find only in a kibbutz. In his youth Herbert Segal published large numbers of articles before he stopped writing. If he had embarked on a career of communal service, he would have shone among the bright lights of the kibbutz movement. He did not do so, partly because his outlook is slightly to the left of that of the movement, partly because he is a man of firm principles who spurns fame. Instead, he has given himself now, since Eva Harish's departure, to the running of the classical music circle. He himself plays the violin, in an amateur way. If only fate had supplied him with the right wife instead of leaving him a bachelor, we would say that he had managed to strike a perfect balance in his life. This balance is apparent in his measured way of eating, with formal table manners that years of manual labor have not overcome. His shy, fleeting smile has charmed us completely. If ever we have to face moments of pain or embarrassment, we can rely on Herbert Segal to come to our help, out of a spirit of true, quiet, uncalculating friendship. His sensible, sensitive tact is universally recognized and appreciated in the kibbutz.

While he eats, Herbert carries on a discussion with his neighbor, Grisha Isarov, a large man who is in charge of our fish ponds. Grisha has seven children, of both sexes, who are ranged according to age in the various children's houses. In the Second World War Grisha joined the Jewish Brigade and performed a number of remarkable feats in the Western Desert and in Italy, which he is fond of describing.

Grisha's table manners are appalling, and, what is more, his discussion with Herbert Segal has turned to subtle problems in crop rotation, which are really beyond his comprehension. Let us turn our attention, therefore, to the young people at our table, to Tomer Geva and his attractive companion Einav.

Tomer Geva is the elder son of Ezra and Bronka Berger. We are not taken in by the change of surname, because Bronka's bushy eyebrows, which meet in the middle, adorn her son's face, too. Tomer's features are not particularly regular. He has a large nose, thick lips, and broad, strong jaws, and black hairs protrude from his ears and nostrils. We are making his acquaintance over supper. If we could watch him at work, half-naked in a hayfield, glistening with sweat in the sunshine; if we could see him dancing, whirling furiously, defying gravity, his dark eyes under those bushy brows ablaze with vitality; if we could observe him on the basketball court, feinting and weaving light-footedly among his opponents, shooting with deadly accuracy – then we would understand what the girls see in him. A few months ago Tomer surprised us by deciding to marry one of his admirers. Einav is a quiet, pretty girl whose beauty is slightly marred by a limp. Einav's figure is not quite as it was: a slight bulge has already begun to distort the neat lines of her figure, and accentuate her limp.

Tomer is wearing his evening clothes, but they are not clean. His blue shirt is stained with mud and motor oil. Presumably, he has just been out to the fields to turn the irrigation taps on or off, perhaps to clear a blocked sprinkler. He lacks refinement, but his manner is friendly and captivating. Watch him cutting a slice of bread for Einav, leaning across the table to pass her a morsel of pickled herring or cheese, smiling at her stealthily from time to time. Einav responds in kind, and eagerly prepares him a rich, finely sliced salad.

Now let's wash down our meal with a hot or cold drink, whichever we choose, and nod farewell to the others at the table. We pause for a moment at the bulletin board, which is covered with announcements and lists of duties, glance at the headlines in the newspaper over the shoulder of Isaac Friedrich, the treasurer, and leave the dining hall. We can relax on a green bench on the edge of the lawn and contemplate the setting sun.

The twilight softens the scene and flatters the objects scattered around the kibbutz. Delicate shadows shift between the buildings, giving a heavy look to the trees and softening the sharp angles of the functional layout of the place. The lawns look less regular now than they are. Even the concrete paths, thanks to the subtle interplay of shadows, have lost their usual aggressive straightness. Round about stretch meadows and gardens, relishing the fresh breeze and responding to it with a sigh and the suggestion of a seductive tremor.

If we look up toward the mountains to the east, we will find them still bathed in sunlight. The dazzling light, driven away from where we are, has taken possession of the hilltops and entrenched itself there. As a result, they seem farther away than they really are, as if storming new heights. The sky has lost its daytime color, a yellow gray, and turned a startlingly clear shade of blue.

The air is laden with faint sounds. A silence settles on our village, as if a stately caravan were noiselessly crossing the village, a caravan that we cannot rightly name but whose presence we can sense in our throats, full of sorrow and hope and unspecified yearnings.

What a pity the twilight disappears so quickly in these parts. Our sun sets abruptly. The hills to the east are already growing dark. They are vanishing, deserting us, disappearing behind a dark screen. Their summits still hold a dimly capering yellow-purple light, but that, too, grows fainter every moment.

Now huge blocks of shadow come falling down the hillside. They fall in total silence, observing some strange law of gravity. The mountains are trying to bury us alive in an avalanche of shadows. The last rays catch some metallic objects for an instant, a flashing sign of the menacing presence of enemy positions on the mountainside. Little yellow and green lights appear in the enemy camps. A hostile, menacing, terrifying presence. That is why at this moment powerful white lamps go on all round the perimeter of our village. That is why the searchlight on top of the tall water-tower starts lashing the surrounding fields, groping undecidedly, challenging the hillside with a hungry beam of quivering brightness. Another searchlight comes on opposite, and slithers all over us, pawing us with its vicious bright fingers. The suspicious, unfriendly dialogue continues without a word being exchanged.

Eventually, you know, everyone dies, good and bad alike. Those who work for what is right and the wicked ones who destroy everything, and those who are simply degenerate, too. Everyone. They collapse, stop breathing, die, decompose, stink terribly after three or four days. Don't be angry with me for speaking tritely. I'm a soldier. Sometimes I say vulgar things, and then I'm cross with myself afterward. Yes.

It was the Dutch colonel who said this to Reuven during the tour, and he was speaking the truth. There's no denying it. Facts of life. But facts of life can be unfair, and unpleasant. And men must hate unfairness and unpleasantness, and wage war on them always.

Reuven Harish goes with his son Gai to the children's house. Before lights out he amuses the child by reciting some of his poems. Then father and son chat for a while about stamps and tourists, arms and agricultural implements, championships and roses. A kiss, a strong hand gently stroking a mop of blond hair, good night, good night.

Noga has a busy evening. At eight o'clock, a rehearsal for the dance sequence combined with readings, to celebrate the feast of Shavuoth. Noga is dancing as a vine, one of the seven kinds of fruit. At nine o'clock, a meeting of the editorial committee of the youth magazine. Noga is responsible for the 'free expression' section.

Later on, the young people gather noisily in their own part of the kibbutz. Some collect round the radio to listen to the latest hits. Others sprawl on the grass and sing songs, making up their own bawdy lyrics. Finally, later still, between ten and eleven, Noga has an adventure of her own to look forward to. Gossips, be on your guard.

Noga's father takes a short cut across the lawn. Herzl Goldring, the gardener, catches sight of him from his veranda and says to his wife Nina under his breath:

'No wonder the children. Look at their teacher walking on the grass. No education, I tell you. Education isn't just a question of clever talk. It's a way of life. Here, Nina, they're savages.'

'You're exaggerating,' his wife answers sadly.

'I'm not exaggerating,' Herzl whispers furiously.

*

Reuven pauses for a moment in the shadow of the carob tree, tucks his shirt into his trousers, and with a couple of youthful bounds he leaps onto the veranda of Ezra Berger's house. Ezra, meanwhile, is steering his heavily laden truck along dark, winding roads. He won't be back before midnight at the earliest. Bronka is alone in the room. Reuven greets her and smiles briefly. His voice is deep and controlled, as usual. Bronka smiles back, but says nothing. She looks up at him, dark-skinned and tired. She is sitting in an armchair, wearing a sleeveless gray dressing gown. Her legs are drawn up underneath her, emphasizing the clumsy heaviness of her thighs. The room is simply furnished, like all our rooms: one bed on wheels placed under another, higher bed to save space. A light gray bedspread with dark gray stripes. At the head of the bed, a chest of drawers, on top of which is an old radio set. A brown table covered in blue formica. A philodendron in a pot, climbing up a bamboo frame almost as far as the ceiling. A greenish carpet, ancient and threadbare. An empty armchair, Bronka's armchair, and three stools upholstered in a fabric matching the armchairs. A picture by van Gogh: a mysterious great cypress tree, a stormy sky, and two tiny figures walking along a path. A shelf with a few books, a dictionary, picture albums, some textbooks, and journals containing articles by Nehemiah Berger. Another shelf with little pot plants and cheap ornaments. Coffee cups decorated in gold laid out on the table. A dish of cookies baked by Bronka.

Reuven stretches out on the bed, where an open book lies upside down: *The Intellectual Development of Young Children.*

*

'Tired?'

'Yes.'

'I saw you with the tourists this afternoon, by the clothes store. Why do you have to do it? Mundek or Tsvi Ramigolski could show them round. You could lie down and rest instead of running around in the heat of the afternoon.'

'We've discussed all that before, Bronka. Let's drop the subject. Ezra?'

'As usual. Midnight, one o'clock.'

'Coffee?'

'Right away. The kettle's been boiling for five minutes already. I was too lazy to get up.'

'Lazybones.'

'Like all grandmas.'

'Why do you have to keep saying that all the time, Bronka?'

'I'm sure Einav's going to have a daughter.'

'You mean you hope she will.'

'I mean I can sense it. I don't make light of that kind of intuition.'

'Does Ezra want a granddaughter, too?'

'Ezra. Ezra wants to be left alone. He's always tired.'

'Has he said anything recently?'

'No. He hasn't said anything. Him? Never!'

'He's a strange man.'

'Strange? I could think of a different adjective. Never mind. Drink your coffee now, before it gets cold. Sugar's in. You have to get to know Ezra, but it takes time. Have a cookie.'

*

Coffee. Cookies. A few grapes to wash them down. Too sweet. She puts too much sugar in, as if you were a child. Spasmodic conversation, forced smiles. Fingers fidgeting involuntarily round the cookie dish. Listen to the news. Will there, won't there be any shooting tonight? I think they're hatching something. I don't think anything's going to happen for the time being, for two reasons. In the first place . . .

'What are you knitting? A sweater? For Oren?'

'Bootees for the baby.'

'Einav ought to do something about that leg of hers. I've heard of some new exercises they've devised . . .'

'You know, Tomer's changed a lot since he's been married.'

'About Noga. I know what I was going to tell you. It's as if she was struggling with some resentment. She's a little girl, and yet she isn't a little girl. She's so secretive. She never used to be so quiet with me. And she doesn't seem to take an interest in anything these days.'

'It's an awkward age. Oren's the same. Oren refuses to be called Berger. He calls himself Geva. They say it was he who organized the disturbances on Seder night. Every day I hear fresh complaints about him.'

'And Ezra?'

'He won't get awkward. Keeps out of it. Anyway, he never talks much.'

'What's the music tomorrow night? Mozart?'

'Bach.'

'Segal adores Bach. I don't enjoy his music. Too serious. I know it's an unpopular view, but it's true. Mozart's another matter. But Bach, really . . .'

'By the way, there was a letter from Germany today. From Zechariah.'

'What does he say?'

'Nothing special. The usual sort of thing. Siegfried Berger and Isaac Hamburger are opening a branch in Frankfurt, and they're thinking about Berlin. They're expanding.'

'Curse them both.'

'You hate them, don't you?'

'I hate debased Jews. They debase themselves and all of us. Will you show me the letter?'

'Not now, Reuven. Why now? Later. Afterward.'

'Is there?'

'Yes. As usual. A few lines. She doesn't say anything. Incidentally, there was a letter from Nehemiah today, too.'

'From Jerusalem? Today?'

'Yes. Quite a coincidence. Letters from both brothers the same day.'

'What's he got to say for himself?'

'I'll show you his letter afterward, too. He may be coming to stay for a week or two.'

'Will we . . .'

'Don't worry, man, he won't interfere. I don't think he's going to come, though. Every year he threatens to come for a long stay, and in the end either he doesn't come or else, if he does come, he leaves after a couple of days. That's the way he is.'

'What's he up to these days?'

'The same as usual. Researching. I don't know what in exactly.'

'Researching?'

'Yes. Do you want some more coffee?'

'Later, later. Turn the radio off. Is it Stravinsky? I don't like it. It's too violent.'

Bronka thinks about her body. With a feeling of disgust. She puts her knitting down and lets her hands fall to her thighs. She can almost feel, through the material, the swollen veins, the ugly black hair on her legs, the red rash. They say beautiful women find old age hardest to bear. I was never beautiful. I was always broad. I never had a figure like Einav's. But years ago I didn't think about my body like this; now I think about it, and I don't like it. It's like someone else's body. A stranger's. At night, when I can't sleep, and Ezra hasn't got back yet, I sometimes have the feeling that a strange, ugly woman is sleeping in my bed. I can smell her body. She sweats. She has a nasty, smelly discharge. She's not well. She smells unhealthy. She has something wrong inside her. There's a revolting dampness. There are some things I can't talk to Ezra about. Even in the early years. How strange that he was embarrassed with me. He didn't like looking at me, and he didn't like me to look at him when we were together. He wasn't generous with those eyes of his. As if he was doing his duty but without enthusiasm. No, that's not right. He was very enthusiastic, but he wasn't concentrating. His heart wasn't in it. Reuven is very gentle. He's careful, even in physical matters. As if he's handling something fragile. A woman needs strength, too. And violence. Neither of them is violent. Not completely. Right to the end. There's always something that holds back, that doesn't take part. And that's terribly humiliating for a woman. Father had an enormous body. Even without touching him, you could sense that he was very strong and warm. When he was about to kiss you goodnight, you could feel his weight. Even when he was old: maybe because his long beard didn't go white even when he was sixty, when the Germans. He hardly ever beat me, and yet I always used to feel that he was on the point of beating me, flaying me alive.

'Reuven.'

'Yes. What?'

'My father. I was just thinking about him. He was a book-binder. He was always the treasurer of our branch of the movement. He wanted me to come here, but he also wanted me to be a pianist. For years and years a man calls the daughter of his old age "Katzele," little kitten, and then all of a sudden she's an old woman, a mother, a grandmother. She gets fat and she doesn't like her body; she doesn't recognize her own body; she dreams at night about Katzele, and her body is get-ting wrinkled and dried up and decayed. It's terrible.'

'Bronka, why always harp on that theme, why . . .'

The coffee I make is always tasteless; I've never learned how to make good coffee. He never says anything. He's so gentle. But I don't love him very much, either, because there are things I can't say to him and won't ever be able to say to anyone and they're just the things that are so important and in a few year's time I'll be dead and buried. Bialik says, 'They say love exists, but what is love?' They're grand words, but the ques-tion has to be asked. Love is when you can say everything.

When there's no holding back. When you don't have a red rash. On the other hand, how can one be such a romantic fool at forty-four? Forty-five, actually.

'The coffee was tasteless, Reuven. Don't be embarrassed to tell me the truth. You must always be frank with me. That's why you don't want another cup, isn't it?'

'What are you talking about, Bronka? It was marvelous coffee. Really. Truly.'

'Have some more grapes. They're slightly tart, just the way I like them. I can't stand soft ripe fruit, or vegetables, either, for that matter. A soggy banana makes me want to throw up. What are you teaching your class?'

'Shimoni. *The Idylls*. I marked their essays today. There were some excellent ones. You know, it's struck me how different the German children are from the Russians. The only explanation I . . .'

He is tormented by nightmares. Even a pure man of sound principles cannot control his dreams. Bronka Berger and Reuven Harish are both grown-up people. A pure friendship has existed between them for many years, a friendship with a firm intellectual foundation. Even though Reuven Harish is of German origin while Bronka comes from Kovel, the two of them are united by a common outlook; they share the same attitudes to education, the same love of nature and mankind. A friendship of this kind cannot suddenly be transformed into violent, sensual love. Even if they do not surrender completely to one another, well, younger couples, too, united by a bond beyond reproach, do not always give themselves totally to each other without holding anything back. The love of Reuven and Bronka is subdued and sparing, and the physical element is not uppermost.

In the old days Eva had a place in the friendship between Reuven and Bronka. In her usual way, with her lively little smile, she used to make a small (but pointed and perceptive) contribution to their conversations. She enriched their conversations with an air of gentle intimacy.

After Eva had left, because she had left, Bronka, naturally enough, felt herself to be responsible for Reuven's well-being. In the early days she spent long hours with Reuven in his room, to prevent him from feeling lonely. She took over such vexing little tasks as ironing his shirts, darning his socks and making fair copies of his poems.

Ezra did not encourage her in these acts of kindness, but neither did he discourage her. Ezra Berger withdrew silently into himself. If anyone approached him to gloat and drop hints, he responded with ambiguous sayings and scriptural verses. Rumor informed him, too, of the change that had come about in the couple's relationship. Ezra Berger did not make a scene, like a hot-headed youth. He redoubled his devotion to his work and took on the work of two drivers. His simple-minded lack of imagination prevented his jealousy from getting the better of him, we believe. Not that he subjugated his feelings. But a man is made of flesh and blood, and flesh and blood is not myrrh and frankincense but, as the ancient sages have it, 'a drop of stinking fluid.'

*

Ten months or so after Eva's departure Bronka responded to Reuven's starved need. Reuven did not run after Bronka, nor did he try to seduce her. That would be hard to imagine. Bronka herself recognized his need and indicated her willingness of her own accord. It was not desire that drove them into each other's arms (whatever prurient skeptics may say) but pure fellow feeling. We do not say this to justify them. There is no justification for adultery. We say it simply to appeal to your compassion.

Reuven gets up from the divan and perches on the arm of Bronka's chair. He places his hand on hers and tells her about the colonel's curious remarks.

'Suddenly, when the rest of the tourists were already back in their bus, he made a sign to me to come closer. As if he wanted to tell me a secret. He was a middle-aged man, but solidly built, almost athletic-looking. He had a mustache and a cigar, and he was carrying a splendid stick. He looked the picture of an honest citizen enjoying a well-earned retirement, if you know what I mean. I went over to him. He fixed me with an odd look and asked me if I had any children. Then he advised me to get out of here, or at least to send my children away. Why? Because from the military point of view we haven't a hope of surviving here. So he announced. "The mountain will fall on top of you." He didn't omit to point out his professional standing, his rank, his military experience. The mountain will fall on us, according to the rule of logistics. Nothing more and nothing less. I told him that we observe different laws of gravity. Perhaps he understood. He said good-bye with exaggerated politeness. I'm not telling you all this to boast, obviously, but to show you the delightful sort of things that happen to me in the course of my favorite pastime.'

'All right,' Bronka said, 'you answered him very well. But what I say is that you take too much on yourself. You're not well. You're not all that strong, and . . . if you were only to rest for an hour every afternoon . . .'

Reuven Harish smiled but didn't answer. Only his fingers gently stroked Bronka's wrinkled hand. For a few moments they sat in silence. Bronka rested her head on his shoulder. He kissed her. From a great distance there came the sound of a single shot. The echo resounded all around, then merged with the chirping of the crickets, with the murmur of the wind in the trees, with the ever-changing noises of the night that never really change.

Let us avert our eyes from their love-making. There is nothing spectacular about it. It takes place without words, without sounds, without frenzy. A gentle caress, a brief overture, a strained silence. A groan. A relaxed silence.

The night is neither relaxed nor silent. Not our night. The distant motor of the small cold-storage room throbs like a heartbeat in the darkness. It blends with the vague despondent muttering from the hen houses. From time to time there comes a heavy lowing of cattle like a stifled groan. The crickets chirrup without a pause, some with a soft persistent dullness, others with a startling shrillness, starting up and suddenly dying away. From the enemy positions to the east comes the hoarse judder of an engine, and cries, perhaps of men, perhaps of night birds. A jackal's eerie howl rends the air and raises a wild melee of sounds all around, as of a dark ocean swelling up ready to dash its great breakers against our trail houses. Sorrows, delights, and derision merge in a long-drawn-out wail, a sad, sad dirge. Hesitantly, Reuven touches Bronka's face and finds it drenched with tears. He gropes for the light switch. She stops him. You frightened me. It's nothing; you wouldn't understand. How can I understand if you don't tell me. You can't understand if I don't tell you, that's the awful thing. What's awful, Bronka, what have I done to you, why are you. You haven't, only I hope I have a granddaughter, yes, a granddaughter, that's what I want. I would have gone to Father's grave to pray for a girl, only there isn't any grave to go to. You're odd, Bronka, how can anything I do make any difference to that. Perhaps it's not too late, give me a daughter. I'll marry you if you'll give me a daughter, please, please, I can still, I only . . .

The searchlight beam bursts into the room. It traces distorted shapes on the walls in a spellbound game. Suddenly it moves on elsewhere. The woman wipes her face silently. The man gives an embarrassed cough. He wants to put things back on an even course, but he doesn't know what to do. Finally Bronka puts on her wrinkled dressing gown and turns the light on. Without looking at Reuven, she hands him the letters, first the one from Nehemiah Berger.

He asks if it would be convenient for him to come and stay with his family for a few days. His work has come to a dead end. He has put it aside and is getting on with some translating, to earn his bread and butter. He translates to live and he lives to translate, the old vicious circle. But a change of scene would do him good. So he would like to come with a few books and his jumbled papers. If it's an awkward time, they mustn't hesitate to put him off. Finally, dear brother, when does Einav intend to make you and Bronka grandparents?

The very same question opens the letter from Zechariah, the youngest brother. He scans the world press anxiously for news of the serious border conflicts in the region of Metsudat Ram. It looks as if the Jewish destiny hounds the Jews everywhere. He hopes everyone is well. As for his own news, Hamburger and he are starting up a branch in Frankfurt and even putting out feelers in Berlin. Berlin is not, happily for us, what it was in the days of its glory. The fat-faced, thick-headed Berliners are terrified of the Communist blockade. By and large, there's nothing to complain about. The prosperity here in Germany is really astounding. The Jewish worm has turned, and the Krauts are bursting with rage. There are a thousand and one ways of humiliating them. We bought the building in Frankfurt, for instance, from an ex-Nazi official who's been sentenced to a few years in prison. He had to sell quickly, at half price. I made such fun of him and his wife during the sale that their eyes nearly popped out of their greasy faces. There's no difficulty these days in humiliating them, and, as you know, that's a pastime I find enthralling. Isaac, though, doesn't see things in quite the same light. He's content to get rich quickly and isn't concerned to avenge the humiliations. Eva is drawing a lot, as usual. Isaac, of course, has built her a beautiful studio in the attic with a view of the lakes she adores.

They don't have any plans for visiting Israel in the near future. But I am considering making a brief business trip to sign up some Israeli artists for a little German contract. Israeli artists will be a great success in Germany, for rather complicated reasons.

Reuven glances briefly at the contents of the letter, then peers intently at the two or three lines added in the margin in tiny slanting Hebrew letters. He would like to put his nose to the page and sniff it, but he refrains for fear of hurting Bronka.

Dear Bronka and Ezra, Tomer, Oren, and Einav. I think of you often. I am well and have nothing to complain about. Of course I miss my children terribly. My little Stella Maris must be quite grown up by now. I wonder if dear Reuven would send me a photo of her. Could you possibly ask him? Yours, Eva.

This letter is intended for Reuven, though not addressed to him. Pensively, he folds it up. She doesn't mention Gai at all. He puts it back in the envelope. Then he carefully removes the stamps for his son. He puts them in his shirt pocket. He stands for a while, doing nothing, saying nothing. Finally he remarks:

'Of course I'll send her a photo. What a question!'

Bronka says:

'She'll come back.'

'No, she won't,' Reuven answers. 'I know she won't ever come back.'

Bronka looks at him sideways, without saying anything. Reuven looks down at his fingertips. He mutters something to himself. Bronka sighs aloud, once and then a second time. Reuven looks up and smiles at her sadly. Bronka hands him his shirt, which is draped over the arm of the chair. Reuven puts it on absently and smiles like a fondled child. He does the buttons up wrongly. Undoes them and starts again.

A shot in the distance. At once three more shots ring out, much closer at hand.

'I hope we can get through the night without having to take the children down to the shelter,' Bronka says.

'Yes. Let's hope so,' Reuven replies, still absently. 'He'll be back soon,' he adds.

'I'd better tidy up the room. I don't want to stab him in the eyes. He gets home so tired he looks like a sleepwalker.'

Reuven kisses her and goes out into the night with glistening eyes. A dull pain stabs him momentarily in the chest. It may be physical, it may not. In the fields nocturnal creatures howl, as usual.

5

To Be a Woman

RAMI RIMON was born and brought up in our kibbutz. He is well equipped, therefore, to distinguish between positive things and negative ones. The death of his father and then of his older brother, and his mother's excessive bitterness might have had a disturbing effect on his personality. But Rami Rimon is not an effeminate youth, even though his mother declares that he is a sensitive boy who loves plants and animals. Rami Rimon is not much of a talker. Words are sticky. To do or not to do, that is the only question which becomes a man. Girls are the problem. Despite yourself, you find yourself in deep water, and you end up hating yourself. Women are not men, and they don't let men be men. That's their nature. On the other hand, you can't avoid them without incurring the contempt of others, and even of yourself. This dilemma Rami Rimon finds hard to overcome, but he cannot get out of it because he is Noga Harish's friend, and because a boy of eighteen has to have a regular girl friend.

Rami stands all alone on the edge of the clump of trees by the swimming pool. He is waiting in the dark for Noga. You can never rely on her to be punctual. Two days ago we arranged to meet at ten, and she arrived at eleven. Yesterday we arranged to meet at half past ten, and she came early, at ten, and we had an argument. Why did I make her wait alone in the dark when I knew perfectly well she was afraid of the dark. How could I know, how could I guess that she would be early. Answer: when you are in love you should feel inside you when someone is waiting for you. I asked her whether, apart from telepathy, she also believed in ghosts and gremlins. Answer: she certainly does. How can we possibly get on with each other.

Noga has had a busy evening. She has taken part in a long rehearsal for the Shavuoth show (how powerfully she dances, with her boyish body), attended a meeting of the editorial committee of the youth magazine, hastily prepared her school-work, made her bed up, smiled secretively at Dafna Isarov, her plump roommate, and made her way to the clump of pine trees by the pool. Rami was there waiting for her, with his shirt provocatively unbuttoned and a cigarette sticking casually to his lower lip. Noga saw him before he could catch sight of her. She has the sharp night sight of a bird of prey. She crept up softly behind him, her sandals making no sound, her green check robe, too large for her, distorting her outline. She covered his eyes with her icy hands. He started violently. Noga was almost sent flying. She laughed as softly as she could. Rami seized her and tried to kiss her on the lips. She slipped out of his grasp, tweaked his ear lightly, and fled among the trees.

'Throw away your cigarette,' she called from her hiding place. 'I hate you when you smoke.'

'I'm glad you hate me. Come out of there.'

'Horse!'

Rami grinds his teeth in fury, stung to the quick by the insult. The widow Rominov's surviving son has a long face, heavy jaws, and an unusual number of creases round his mouth for his age.

He wanders around for a while till he discovers where Noga is hiding. He fills his lungs with smoke and blows a pungent jet in her face. Noga delivers a sharp slap on his neck. He tries to catch hold of her, but she is more agile than he is. He runs after her, angry and humiliated.

'Just you wait till I catch up with you.' He tries to pretend that his anger is good-humored and amused.

'Go to the army, Rami. Then you can frighten our enemies.'

She lets him catch her, and adds in a sad way that has nothing to do with the game:

'You'll go into the army, you'll find someone prettier, you won't want me. But I don't need you at all.'

Deep in the shadow of the trees they embrace. His lips leave a warm moist trail on her cheek.

'You. Of course I'll want you. I'll want you when I'm in the army. I'll want you even more.'

'Why?'

'Because you're pretty.'

'Tell me another reason. That's only a little reason.'

'Because you excite me.'

'Lecher.'

'Because . . . because you're so.'

'So what? What am I? Tell me. Can you?'

'So graceful. Like a gazelle. Just like a gazelle.'

'Is that all? Can't you think of anything else to say?'

'There is another reason.'

'What?'

'You haven't given it to me yet. Give it to me.'

'Horse!'

The rustle of the pines draws them deeper into the darkness of the trees. They stretch out on a bed of dead pine needles, thinking, not touching.

'Your father.'

'What about my father?'

'He's a strange man. My mother says he's not as great as he tries to appear. He has more weaknesses than he lets on.'

'Tell your mother she's a bitch.'

'You're angry. That proves I was right.'

'Rami, when you're in the army, don't always rush into trouble. We've had enough heroes. If anything happened to you, it would kill your mother. Me, too, a bit.'

'You mean what happened to Yoash?'

'Maybe that's what I mean, but you're a horse. You don't have to say everything you mean.'

'Yes, you do. You and I must tell each other everything. Everything.'

'No, we mustn't.'

'Yes, we must.'

Silence. Still they don't touch. The boy is stretched to breaking point. He has kissed and fondled and groped; now he curses his humiliating fears and plans to take her by force. Oh, sensitive little boy, who loves animals and plants, he eggs himself on scornfully. Noga suddenly tickles the inside of his ear with a pine needle. Gives a deep, warm laugh. Rami puts his hand on her hip, which responds with a gentle movement, a kind of inner dance. Now he tries to cling. His movements are exaggerated, his grip clumsy and painful. Noga does not resist his embrace. Only her laugh billows up convulsively, and she says strangely:

'Little boy, get off. Leave me alone.'

'What's so funny? Don't laugh, I tell you. Don't laugh.'

'It's not funny. But you are.'

'What?'

'Funny.'

'You're not a woman, Noga. You don't even know how to be one.'

'But I don't want to. I hate it. I don't want to.'

'To what?'

'To be a woman.'

The first shot, which we have already heard somewhere else, forces the couple apart even before Rami has managed to get over Noga's laughter. Hell, the buttons are too big for the holes. He leaves her alone and says knowledgeably:

'It's starting.'

But nothing starts. The shot dies away and is lost in the sounds of the night. Rami's knowledgeability is in vain. If he were clever, Rami would not try to attack indirectly. But Rami is not clever. This is not meant disparagingly. He is hard-working, honest, unpretentious, and, when circumstances demand it, self-sacrificing, all noble virtues, which spring ultimately from his straightforwardness. It is his disarming straightforwardness that moves him now to consult his friend about a problem which has been weighing heavily on him.

'You know, Noga, I think I've managed to win my mother round slightly.'

'About volunteering? Really?'

'Yes, about being a paratrooper. The trouble is, if she won't sign I can't go into the paratroopers. I'm entirely at her mercy. Because of Yoash's death I'm officially considered as an only son, and they won't take only sons without a signed form from the parents.'

'And you've managed to get round her?'

'Yes. We had a row. I had it out with her. That I'm not her little baby and that what happened to Yoash wasn't my fault and that what was good enough for Yoash is good enough for me and that not everyone in the paratroopers gets killed and that I'm not prepared to live my whole life in the shadow of what happened to Yoash because my life is my life. Everybody's always making unfair comparisons.'

'Well? What did she say?'

'She didn't answer my arguments. She couldn't. She just called me a fool.'

'And what did you say?'

'I called her a bitch.'

'And what did she say?'

'She didn't say a word. That's why I think I've managed to win her round.'

'I hope not. I hope she sticks to her guns, and doesn't sign.'

If Rami were not so naïve, he would not be so shocked now. What appalling treachery! What a sticky situation. You can't trust any of them. His anger made him say something cruel.

'You can't be relied on. You're just like your mother.'

'Filthy old horse!'

At this a furious quarrel broke out in the quiet wood. Rami hurled all his vexations straight at her, and Noga, either from perversity or from the malicious pressure of her subconscious feelings, answered him sharply, with a honeyed voice and a smile of ice.

What a pity that they are deaf to the rich sounds of the night. Amid the gentle music of the night they pace nervously, round the swimming pool and back toward the houses. With a thousand beautiful sounds the night tries to charm them, but they barricade themselves behind their rancor. In the light of the lamp on the fence Rami stands, his large hands on his hips, a fresh cigarette in his mouth, trying to puff smoke in his girl friend's face. His rage exaggerates his horselike expression. Noga's little face is lowered. The hair falling over her cheeks hides the tears welling in the corners of her eyes.

Nearby, behind a privet hedge, Israel Tsitron, the night watchman, cranes his neck in an effort not to miss a word. He discreetly refrains from revealing his presence. On the other hand, if it were not for him, the two of them would be beyond the reach of gossip. And if it were not for the gossip, Fruma would never find out about her little ally, who is anxious about Rami and tries to prevent him volunteering for a dangerous task, and Fruma's sad heart would not experience that flush of warmth. As we said before, there is a praiseworthy side to gossip. It must not be condemned out of hand.

Sadness? Yes. Naturally. Our gaze follows Stella now as she steals, stooping slightly, back to her room in the children's house. The house is shrouded in sleep. She tiptoes into her room, without turning the light on. Slips between the sheets.

How old is Noga Harish? About sixteen. She will be crying now. Whispering the name of her mother far away. A square of cold moonlight on the wall. Outside the window, dark cypresses sighing in the breeze. What was it like, years ago, when I was little? How she used to hold me and terrify me. How she used to hold me cry say things to me in another language frightened I used to cry with her no one could see Mummy stop it I'm frightened of you Stella Maris if only you'd never been born Mummy I'll go wherever you are I'm yours I'm like you if only you could die if only we both could. It's black why is it so black.

6

Another Sadness

EZRA BERGER'S arms rest on the steering wheel. His eyes gape at the road caught in the headlight beam. The road tricks the headlights with imaginary protrusions. Ezra's thick neck is sunk deep between his hairy shoulders. He doesn't feel tired. Not tired. But a kind of numbness weighs heavily on him and confuses his thoughts. His thoughts wander. Bronka's not alone now. In my room. In my bed. Grandma. Big hips. Thinking about her body. Hair. What a belly. 'Belly like a mound of wheat' – huh! Old dumpling. Turquoise is so slim. Little devil. What a nerve, to say, all of a sudden, 'You're sweet.' If she weren't the poet's daughter, I'd hope that Oren would get her. He could, too. The same way Tomer won Einav. Conquered her. The Bible says 'knew her.' 'And Adam knew Eve his wife and she conceived and bore a son.' Knew. Clever word. Don't think the commentators understand it properly. Don't believe knowing a woman just means fucking her. Must be some difference. Maybe knowing is only when they get pregnant. If there's no difference, it's all just a drop of stinking fluid. Just like what Tomer did to Einav: first he courted her then he slept with her then she got pregnant and then he married her out of a sense of responsibility. Whores, the lot of them. Bronka. Eva. Einav. Turquoise?

Ezra touches the packet of embroidery thread lying on the shabby passenger seat beside him. Now I've learned something new: turquoise is a color halfway between blue and green. A bright color. A cool color. There are warm colors and cold colors. I used to know. Poetic subtleties. I'm going to tell you a little story, Turquoise, a little story but a true story. From real life. Once upon a time there was a princess. . . . No. I was only joking. Once upon a time Ramigolski and I were working over the hill. Aaron Ramigolski, the one who was killed, not our secretary Tsvi Ramigolski. Ramigolski talked to me about the poet's girl. The one he brought from Germany. Yes, your mother, little Turquoise. It was in the 1930s. The poet was still called Harismann, in those days, not Harish. A beau-ty, Ramigolski said. He drew the word out long and smacked his thick lips. I knew Ramigolski well. His father used to pray with my father. We were born across the road from each other, in Kovel. He was a coward. He was very strong, he was a cheerful lad, but he was a coward. He had his eye on the poet's girl. She was so graceful. Like a gazelle, like you, Turquoise. A daughter always takes after her mother, so they say. But Ramigolski didn't dare. He was afraid. Afraid of whom? Afraid of me. Afraid of Mundek Zohar. Afraid of what Fruma would say to Bronka and Bronka would say to Esther.

'I find woman more bitter than death,' the Preacher said, and he knew what he was talking about That's why Ramigolski didn't dare. But he wanted your mother. And he might have been able to take her from Harismann, if he'd dared. She was graceful. Refined. Delicate. But she was a whore. What's she doing now in Germany with that Hamburger of hers? Running a night club. A brothel, more like. A plague on all women. You hear that, little Turquoise? Make a note: 'A plague on all women' – Ezra Berger's motto. I've told you a true story, from real life, to teach you something about real life. Take another example. What did I say to Tomer? You've got someone in trouble? Yes? Einav? All right. Now have a good think. True, you could marry her. But you don't have to. There are other ways. What did Tomer do? He married her, limp and all. 'A wise son makes his father rejoice but a foolish son brings grief to his mother,' King Solomon says, and he makes a very fine distinction. It was Bronka who brought Tomer up to have a conscience. Now Bronka is going to be a grandma, and Ezra Berger is going to be a grandpa. And your father's going to have a grandma for a mistress. Huh! Congratulations. Where does it get us all? Look at Bronka. She's an educated girl. Clever. 'If you've drunk the water, don't spit in the well,' as they say. And me – I may be a pretty simple sort of chap, but I'm clever, too. Only I don't talk much. And talking is half the trouble. 'Speech is silver, silence is golden.' Thirty years ago, Ramigolski and I were working in the fields. Listen carefully now, Turquoise. The Arabs started shooting at us. We were unarmed. I jumped in among the maize quickly. Ran away. Hid. 'Delivered my soul from destruction,' as some poet says grandly somewhere.

And Ramigolski? Ramigolski stood where he was and started talking to them. 'Teaching the bear to be honest and fair.' He got what was coming to him. He screamed. I crawled back and dragged him to the kibbutz. Yes, me. And I'm no biblical hero. He didn't utter a single edifying remark. On the contrary. He cursed us all and he cursed Palestine and he even cursed the Zionist movement. Right to the end. It's the truth, Turquoise. Isn't that what they taught you in your class? No? Bronka? The poet? No. You don't speak ill of the dead. Of course, you can say what you like about a man while he's alive. But the dead are sacrosanct. What's the conclusion? What the sages say: 'Remember what you came from and what you are going to. What did you come from? A drop of stinking fluid. What are you going to? A pit full of worms.' But I'm not Nehemiah Berger; I don't work with premises and conclusions. And I'm not Zechariah Berger, either; I don't make war on the whole human race because the Jewish worm has been trampled underfoot. I'm just an ordinary mortal, thank the good Lord. Do you understand what I've been saying, Turquoise? And if you dare say to me once more 'You're sweet,' I'll give you a clip round the earhole. What do you think I am – a little boy?

Tiberias. He stops to drink a cup of coffee with the fishermen. Marry a fisherman, Turquoise. Fishermen are real men. They don't write poems, they don't spout proverbs, but once they get hold of a woman they keep her for life. 'Till death us do part.' How many times must I tell you not to look at me like that with those green eyes of your father's. It's just as well you're not here to hear what I'm thinking. And I've not finished yet. There's more to come. No, they're not green, your eyes. They're blue-green. Turquoise. Greetings, O Abushdid. Do you have a cup of coffee for Ezra Berger? Great. I nearly fell asleep at the wheel. But I have a system. I think of girls, and it keeps me wide awake. We have a saying: 'A woman is either precious and rare, or a grizzly bear.' It's all a matter of luck.

The fishermen are fond of Ezra Berger. Every night he makes a stop in Tiberias to sip coffee with them and exchange gems of wisdom and dirty stories. Even here he does not talk much. But his sensible outlook, his slow way of talking, his heavy hands curled round the grimy little cup, his impressive broad shoulders, all these combine to secure him a position of respect here. This is not to imply that we do not respect Ezra Berger in the kibbutz. We respect him as a man of action, and for his rough good humor, which always, however, retains a serious element and never degenerates into cheap buffoonery. We are almost tempted to detect a noble quality in his roughness – as indeed there is, if, once again, you can call moderation and self-control noble.

Around midnight Ezra leaves to cover the last stretch of his journey from Tiberias to his home. He still doesn't feel tired. Not tired – but a kind of numbness confuses his thoughts. Ezra covers this last stretch at great speed. The road runs close to the border. Needless to say, at this time of night the road is completely deserted. The headlights pick out fields, signposts, solitary shrubs, little nocturnal animals dashing across the road.

Near the turning to the kibbutz, at the foot of the little hill from the top of which our tourists usually get their first general impression of the place, Ezra hears the sound of a distant shot. He pricks up his ears. He tries to fix the direction of the shot. A green flare rising suddenly in the eastern sky helps him. He drives quickly through the gate. Parks his truck next to the tractor shed, which is lit inside by a yellow lamp. Spits in his hands. Stretches his cramped limbs.

Israel Tsitron, the night watchman, darts up and chats for a moment or two about this and that: a premature birth in the dairy herd, a loud quarrel he happened to overhear between Fruma's Rami and his girl friend, a few shots from the northeast. There's trouble brewing. No, there won't be anything. Good night, Israel. 'Night, Berger.

Outside his room Ezra pauses and quietly removes his shoes. He tiptoes into his room. His eyes strain to pierce the darkness. He sniffs the air quickly, apprehensively, trying to absorb the alien smell into himself. His chest rises, falls, rises. His mouth is slightly open. His heavy head is inclined, listening intently. His arms hang down by his body. His hands are large.

Bronka is wrapped up in a blanket. She doesn't move. Ezra Berger is tired. His mind is wandering. Even so, he can sense for certain that his wife is not asleep. Bronka knows that he knows, and he knows that she knows. Everything is known. Stiffly he gets undressed. His bed is made up. There is a cup of tea waiting for him, covered with a saucer to keep it warm. Everything is as he likes it. Everything is as usual. He stands in his sweat-soaked underwear, staring at the shadows of the shutters cast by the searchlight on the flickering wall. Suddenly he leans over, places a large, dirty hand on Bronka's blanket, and says:

'Grandma.'

She doesn't move. He straightens up stiffly. Fingers the hair on his shoulders and his chest. Crawls in his underwear between the white sheets. Turns his face to the wall. He tries to return to his musings and even murmurs softly: Well then, Turquoise, the fishermen.

Sleep comes on the man suddenly. Like an ax blow. Like a woman.

7

A Painful Sorrow

THE THIRTIES – unforgettable years, years we shall boast of for ever! Metsudat Ram: a tiny terrified encampment, lost in an empty expanse, braving the menacing mountains. A wooden tower, a double barbed-wire fence, dogs barking at the moon. Gray tents and dirt tracks, with billows of dust, four parched huts, scorched tin roofs, brackish, reddish water, smelling rusty in the common showers. A tumble-down shack with a few rickety tables. Frail saplings drooping in the heat. Tormented nights, filled with wild sounds, bathed in harsh moonlight, swarming with horrible movements. Strange noises from the Arab village nearby, the smell of smoke, damp vapors, our cheerful shouting in the middle of the night, wild dancing, party songs full of joy, full of sorrow, full of longing, a mixture of unbridled ecstasy and desperate orphaned sobbing.

Eva.

The time: two years after she first arrived in Reuven's tent. Almost two years after the death of Aaron Ramigolski, our first victim. That autumn we bought a small truck. The first. And at the end of the festival of Hanukka we made our first expedition to Haifa, to see a production of the Habima theatre company. Not all of us, of course, but fifteen of our members, selected by ballot. Fifteen was the total number the primitive vehicle would carry. Eva and Reuven went, and Fruma and Alter Rominov, and Herbert Segal, and Mundek Zohar, our first driver, took the wheel. There were guns hidden under the driver's seat, even though there hadn't been any trouble lately.

It was a clear winter's day. The roads were washed and watered. Patches of bright green flanked the road in places. The sky was a rich, deep blue. And there was the excitement of the new truck. They sang songs and joked. They even made fun of serious things.

After the performance, back in the ice-cold lorry, Alter Rominov opened a discussion.

'Here we are building a new world, living a completely new life, and Habima still keeps harping on these ghetto themes.'

The road was dark. The sky overcast. Not a star to be seen.

In the discussion that ensued, Herbert Segal took a similar stand to Alter Rominov, only, of course, he expressed himself in different words. (It was Herbert's remarks on that occasion which gave rise to his article on culture, still remembered among our veterans for the repercussions it raised.) Reuven disagreed with Herbert. There is a necessary connection between our new life and the old life in the ghetto.

78

Eva, not usually one of our ardent debaters, took part for once in the discussion. She raised her head from Reuven's shoulder and uttered a single sentence, which could only with difficulty be connected with the subject under discussion.

'It's the simple, great themes which ought to be portrayed, like passion and death,' she said, and laid her head once more on Reuven's shoulder.

At this point the conversation was in danger of becoming heated, since no one, not even Reuven, was likely to let these words of Eva's pass unchallenged. Feelings ran deep in many hearts those days, and Eva's warm, languid voice naturally excited deep feelings. But, just in time, a hoarse shout came from the driver's seat:

'Don't talk, friends, sing!'

Two or three voices responded with a burst of song, which smothered the conversation and soothed the passions. We were young in those days, and we put our hearts into our singing. So we sang, and Eva sang with us.

As we approached the valley the darkness became deeper, the roar of the engine more intense. The wind howled in the flapping canvas. Songs of joy gave way to songs of sad longing. Suddenly we ran into a torrential downpour. Jets of icy water came in through the opening at the back, and the passengers huddled deeper inside. Eva laid a pale hand on Reuven's knee.

'You'd think we were somewhere else,' she whispered.

'A ghastly journey through a night of horrors,' Herbert Segal said, to himself rather than to the others. And Alter Rominov, as usual, made a weak joke:

'Noah's ark. And we're the animals.'

Alter's voice did not sound jocular, though.

Eva whispered to Reuven.

'Do you remember? Do you remember?'

And Reuven, the gesture is etched permanently in his memory, shrugged his shoulders.

The brakes screeched desperately as the road fell steeply down into the valley. The yellow headlights peered vainly through the rain and the fog.

Eva whispered.

'On a night like this I'd like to die.'

Reuven shrugged his shoulders again. He was twenty-four, a pure-hearted, bright-eyed youth. What did his bright eyes see, what could they see when they looked at Eva? A girl with a romantic imagination. Fond of sickly stories of love-smitten heroes dying young of consumption. Of Gothic horror stories of forests and wizards and chaste maidens offering themselves to the fierce tempest. He was a pure-eyed youth. How could he imagine.

'It's cold and wet,' Alter Rominov said. 'We might get home on a gondola, we certainly won't get there in this truck.' He was the only one to laugh at his joke.

Podolski said:

'It's all right. We finished sowing a fortnight ago. So what's the matter. It's good.'

And Herbert Segal, under his breath:

'The tents will be carried away.'

Fruma opened her mouth for the first time:

'When I was a little girl, I thought rain was the nicest thing in the world. And it's true when you've got a nice warm house. But in a tent . . .'

Reuven put his scarf round Eva's shoulders. She might catch cold, he said, while he was less delicate and was not afraid of the damp. Eva, strangely, appeared sad and offended.

'You want me to die, deep down in your heart. You want me to die of pneumonia in this intolerable country.'

Reuven was shocked, and emphatically rejected her charge. Eva gave a soft, bitter laugh.

'Death can be so beautiful. Death can be happy.' (Everything she said she whispered softly to her partner.) 'Once I dreamed I was dead. The air was full of black birds. It was twilight. What a beautiful scene it was. Bells were ringing nearby, and further off, and far, far away, to the end of the world, and the black birds whirled around. What happiness. How beautiful.'

Reuven stroked her hair. He whispered that she was a silly little girl. He will never forget that conversation. He remembers the words he chose then. Eva, placated, agreed with him, and said almost joyfully:

'I'm Little Red Ridinghood, I'm Little Red Ridinghood. But you're not the wolf, you're my lamb, my little pet lamb.'

Reuven said nothing. The engine howled like a wounded animal. The wind whistled delightedly, maliciously. There was a sadness. Reuven Harish remembers that sadness. Now, years later, that journey seems to Reuven like a fading dream. But through the mist he can see something clear as a crystal, something nameless but crystal clear. Reuven contemplates it and feels weighed down with despair. What was it, dear God, what was it? Far, far away it shines, crystal clear, blended with the sound of bells and a painful sorrow.

8

Elsewhere, Perhaps

EZRA BERGER wears a thick gold ring on his finger, like many truck drivers, but unlike truck drivers who belong to a kibbutz. Ezra silences the engine of the truck, shakes his large hands, gets down from the cab, and goes to look for a thick rope. The rope he uses to secure his load is missing. Stolen, for sure, by the gang of young delinquents now cruising suspiciously silently round the kibbutz yard, plotting mischief.

Ezra wanders round the motor shed, looking out for a length of rope. Ten to three. Should have got moving by now. Still, yesterday I left at three. But yesterday I was delayed. First by Nina Goldring and then by Turquoise. She still hasn't come to pick up her turquoise. But then, when could she have come? I got back in the middle of the night, left at six this morning, and got in again at one o'clock. She's sure to come up any moment now. If she starts saying 'thank you, thank you' in that ingratiating way of hers, I won't be able to stand it. There's something ingratiating about her. A woman shall compass the man, as the Prophet says. On the other hand, I can't move till I find a piece of rope.

A revolting smell of engine oil hangs in the air. The afternoon air is hot and heavy. A hazy sun beats down furiously on the tin roofs of the sheds. On the edge of the banana plantation opposite a tiny figure is busily unloading sacks from a battered cart. Ezra recognizes Israel Tsitron by his red shirt. Who else, in the blazing heat of the afternoon, would be crazy enough to work in a red shirt? Of course, there isn't a rope here, confound them. I can't imagine why I thought for a moment that there might be one. If I catch one of them I'll wring his neck, so help me. The question is what to do now. Ah, Noga. I thought you'd come. And here you are. You wouldn't like to go and get some cold water from the refrigerator for a weary soul, would you? In this mug. Of course I brought the thread, what a question. What did you expect? It's inside on the seat. Yes, the right-hand side.

'Of course I'll fetch you some water. Why not? Tell me, though, why haven't you left yet? You . . . you weren't waiting for me, were you? I thought I'd be too late. That you'd have gone by now.'

No, Ezra Berger said, he hadn't been waiting for her. They'd stolen his rope, and that was why he hadn't left yet. While he was in the kitchen collecting his coffee and sandwiches from Nina Goldring, the little so-and-sos had come and pinched it. So now he was looking for another rope. Noga suggests with a shy smile that he may not have to look very far afield for the stolen rope. Ezra ask if she means his younger son, Oren. Noga replies that that may be what she means, but that she doesn't necessarily say everything she means. Ezra says he will punish the culprits, his own beloved younger son included. But Noga knows that he won't do a thing. Even when he is angry, it's impossible to tell when he is serious and when he is only pretending to be serious. Anyway, he really did bring the thread. The very same day. That's a fact. Now I'll go and

83

fetch him a mug of cold water. What's so strange about his asking me to fetch him a mug of cold water. There's nothing strange in his asking me to fetch him a mug of cold water. It's hot. That's all.

It's hot. Ezra Berger squats in the shade of the truck, takes off his battered cap, and mops his face and neck. Sticky sweat pours at once from every pore. He hasn't shaved, and his face seems twice as gnarled as usual. He stares into his old cap and peers at the plastic label with the name and address of the makers on it. Can it really be that this is the very first time he has noticed the label? Noga returns, holding the full mug out in front of her with both hands. That's not the way to carry a mug of water. That's how you carry something precious, a baby or a fragile piece of china or a dish of sweetmeats. Ezra distends his mouth and pours the water in without putting the mug to his lips. The trick does not come off. The water splashes onto his chin, trickles down his neck and past the open shirt to vanish in the thick, graying hair on his chest. Noga sees the water spill. She smiles, but to herself, not at the man. Her expression is very attentive. Her eyes glisten greenly.

Ezra pulls a face. The water was cold enough, but it had a sour taste. He opens the cab door, picks up a yellow thermos flask, pulls out the stopper, and swallows a mouthful of coffee. The coffee is intended for the nighttime, but there's nothing to stop him having a mouthful now to take away the sour taste of the water. The taste doesn't go, and Ezra takes a second gulp and a third.

Ezra says:

'The water tastes sour.'

Noga says:

'That's not my fault.'

Ezra says:

'True, but we still haven't solved the problem of the rope. I can't leave without tying something round the load. It'll all collapse.'

Noga says:

'I think there's a length of rope in the old stable opposite the cattle pen. It may have rotted too much, but it might just do. Shall we go and see?'

'Let's go.'

'Tell me something, Ezra. Don't you get bored on these long trips?'

'If I get bored, I think thoughts. Let us follow our thoughts, as Jeremiah says. But then a prophet is without honor in his own country.'

'Do you think about the Bible all the time?'

'Not all the time. Only sometimes.'

'Give me an example. A sample.'

'Well, take our mother Rachel, for example, and her sister Leah. Leah had a lot of sons, but Rachel had only two. All the sons became tribes of Israel. All the tribes of Israel are equal before God. But it seems as if Rachel's sons are more equal than Leah's, because Rachel we call "our mother Rachel," but Leah we just call "Leah." Without the "our mother." No wonder she was "tender-eyed." "Leah" in Hebrew can also mean "tired." Is this stable locked?'

'No, it's open.'

'Is this the rope?'

85

'Yes, that's it.'

'Splendid. You certainly know the ropes round here. Wait a moment. Don't go just yet.'

'The ring on your finger is glowing in the dark. It's very dark in here, Ezra. Let's go outside.'

But Ezra Berger stays where he is, slowly coiling the rope round his forearm and staring straight ahead of him with an intense, surprised look, like a man who has forgotten some vital password, or whose body has betrayed him and suddenly stabbed him with a piercing pain.

It is cold and dark in the confined space of the old stable. Look, there are mice in here. A sinister scratching sound behind the piles of debris. The pungent smell of peacefully rotting saddles quickens the breath.

'Well, then,' says Ezra.

'Let's go now,' says Noga.

Ezra walks back to his truck. The girl accompanies him, with no apparent purpose. Podolski pokes his head out of the motor shed surprisedly and asks why he hasn't left yet. Ezra absent-mindedly answers that he hasn't left yet because the kids have stolen his rope and he is looking for another one. Podolski is even more surprised at this, because he can see a rope coiled round Ezra's arm. Most surprising of all is the presence of Reuven Harish's daughter.

'Want a lift as far as the gate, Turquoise?'

'Yes.'

'Get in.'

'Ready.'

'Here we are, young lady. You'd better get out now.'

'Why here, Ezra? Why not somewhere else?'

'You'd better get out.'

'Why not somewhere else?'

'Out with you.'

'Have a good journey,' the girl says as she gets down.

'Same to you,' replies the man absent-mindedly. But Noga Harish is not going anywhere. She stands by the gate, all alone, tapping the dust with her bare foot, looking not at the truck but at the bunch of grapes that has suddenly appeared in her hand.

9

Plants and Animals

O UR NEXT episode is about rain. Rain on the first of May. Rain out of season, and the more welcome for that.

The characters, in addition to the narrator: Ido Zohar, a sensitive boy of fourteen. Mundek Zohar, his father, head of the regional council. Gerda, his mother, a member of the German faction in our kibbutz. She suffers from varicose veins and wears a thick elastic bandage on her leg. Izia Gurevitch-Gilead, a member of the central kibbutz committee, a devoted member of the movement. And a woman of forty named Hasia Ramigolski, with a dumpy figure and four sons.

It was the first of May when the rain fell.

As usual on May Day, we had put up the flags of Israel and the party round the big lawn, erected a small platform and laid out a lot of wooden benches facing it. The benches were thronged with our members and young people. The platform was decorated with red and white bunting, with a slogan in the middle, 'Workers of the World Unite,' written in red on green and framed with cypress boughs. There was a table of cold drinks on the edge of the lawn. Izia Gurevitch-Gilead had been sent from the central committee to deliver the party message. He stood up on the platform and spoke briefly. A light breeze ruffled his graying hair and also made the flags dance.

There were dark clouds in the west. As twilight approached, the clouds took on colors of startling brightness. The sun has a habit of setting the clouds on fire before retiring for the night.

Anyone with a feeling for the weather could tell in advance that rain was imminent. The previous week we had suffered from a heat wave. But the beginning of the week had brought a change. A discerning eye could see the signs. A nervous tension filled the air, and ominous signs began to appear on the western horizon. On Monday evening the setting sun was soaked up by a bank of cloud. The sunset was purple. Even the temperature dropped somewhat. On Tuesday morning the color of the sky changed, if only slightly. The pale, whitish blue gave way to a deep rich blue, as if the sea had risen to hang upside down in the air over our tiny roof tops and far beyond to the peaks of the distant mountains.

On Wednesday the air became heavier, and the dusty cypresses seemed even more tense than usual. And on Wednesday night, an hour before midnight, the wind arrived. As yet, a soft, tentative breeze, whispering secretively to the trees shading the paths of the kibbutz.

Some said:

'It'll rain by the end of the week.'

Others said:

'It's the wrong time of year for rain. It hardly ever rains so late in the season.'

But some said:

'It may be the last rain of spring.'

At daybreak on Thursday the sea turned stormy. Ripples and waves appeared faraway to the northwest. All day long ragged clouds scudded eastward.

On Thursday night lightning flashed in the north, without a sound of thunder. There was activity in the sheds and barns and storehouses: even the more practical men had begun to smell rain and got busy moving sacks, machines, and agricultural tackle under shelter.

Finally, on Friday, which was May Day, the wind pretended to make peace with us. Insidiously, that morning, it played the part of an ordinary spring breeze.

The celebrations were opened at five o'clock in the afternoon by Mundek Zohar, who spoke of Labor Day as a symbol of the fellowship of workers all over the world. He himself was standing in, he said, for our comrade Reuven Harish, who had been taken ill with a slight cold, and he was sure we all wished him a speedy and complete recovery.

Next, a diminutive girl in a blue skirt and white blouse read out from the newspaper the message from the Secretary-General of the labor movement. The assembled company sang the party anthem and one or two more favorite songs of the movement. Then Mundek stood up again and announced that Izia Gurevitch-Gilead, a veteran worker for the party and the movement, whose devotion to the cause in the early days we all still remembered with pride and gratitude, would now convey to the gathering a message from the movement.

Izia Gurevitch-Gilead began by saying that we were going through a difficult time. He explained briefly why we were going through a difficult time. He went on to talk about the relevance of Labor Day at this moment in time. There was a noisy disturbance, as a tractor made its way round the edge of the gathering, taking a cartload of sacks from one place to another.

The disturbance was short-lived. The tractor passed on, and we sat back once again to drink in the speaker's words.

'Great changes have taken place in the world,' Izia Gurevitch-Gilead said, 'since the *Internationale* was composed. Nevertheless . . .'

The twilight deepened. A dark veil intervened between the sun and the earth. Hasia Ramigolski said:

'It's turned cold all of a sudden.'

Young Ido Zohar, who was sitting next to her, thought aloud:

'It'll start raining before he's stopped speaking.'

Hasia said:

'Don't exaggerate.'

And Izia Gurevitch-Gilead:

'It is very easy to have faith in times of faith. True faith, comrades, emerges in times of doubt, like today. Everyone imagines now that organized society has solved all its problems and that any outstanding problems can be overcome in a moment. They don't seem to realize that the greatest problems of all, the problems of survival, remain to be grappled with. What we need is faith.'

*

Ido steals a glance at the woman sitting next to him. Hasia's body is plump, her legs stout and covered with fine down. Her gray skirt has slipped up. Slowly, stealthily, the boy moves his thigh closer to Hasia's. His imagination runs riot. Stricken with alarm and remorse, he withdraws his leg, striving to avoid the slightest contact with his neighbor. But his fingers are shaking. He looks away, fixing his gaze on one of the flags flapping in the breeze. It won't calm down.

There is no doubt now that it is dark. Izia Gurevitch-Gilead is almost invisible. Only his outline shows on the platform. A brisk gust of wind makes the skin stiffen. Tears of shame well up in Ido's eyes. He breaks his mental vow and squints again at the uncovered knees. They are white, he sees, and gently curved like the rows of vines when they reach the lower slopes.

Izia Gurevitch-Gilead lowers his voice and stresses one word after another:

'The prophets of Israel were the first men to give the world the concept of social justice.'

He is hemmed in now by electric lights. His silvery hair shines like an ancient warrior's helmet. A night bird suddenly screeches nearby, and the orator starts, because it sounds just like a woman screaming.

Hasia leans toward Ido and says anxiously:

'Aren't you cold?'

And answers her own question:

'Of course you're cold in a thin shirt like that. Would you like to put my sweater on? I'm wearing a flannel shirt underneath. I won't be cold. Well? Don't be shy.'

And Ido:

'You . . . you don't need to give me anything.'

He chews his lower lip, and adds:

'Actually, I . . .'

'Yes, you'd like the sweater after all? Take it, take it; you're shivering with cold.'

'No, no, thank you, I don't need it.'

'But you just said . . .'

'Me? I didn't say anything. It's the other way round. I thought you said something. I didn't.'

And the speaker:

'The concept of social justice does not recognize national boundaries. On the contrary. Its aim is to eradicate false frontiers and to set up true frontiers . . .'

At this point the clouds burst. The rain did not start gradually: it came like a sudden blow. The thunder pounded us like a fist in a woolen glove. The first drops, unnaturally warm and thick, splashed on the dusty ground. The dust at first proudly resisted the inevitable and swallowed the water. But as the ferocious torrents continued to pour down, the dust surrendered and fled in confusion and panic into the depths of the drains. The trees were caught in a damp vapor, which closed round the lamps and played strange games with their light. A metal gutter chanted a melancholy tune.

The crowd, naturally enough, fled in disorder for shelter. In the confusion, without any prior intention, two bodies touched. With burning cheeks the boy ran after the woman, calling out:

'I'm sorry, Hasia, it was an accident.'

The woman, who had felt nothing and was surprised at the cry, shouted as she ran:

'Sorry about what? What's happened?'

The rain was so sudden that, despite the rush, everyone was drenched.

On the platform, too, there was a flurry of movement. Izia Gurevitch-Gilead picked up his notes and tucked them away in his pocket.

'At this point I must stop, as it is raining,' he said, but by now he had no audience.

Mundek Zohar, bent double by the downpour, added:

'*Force majeure.*'

Then he linked arms with the speaker to help him down off the platform, since he was not as young as he used to be.

When they were assembled, dripping wet, in Mundek's small room, Gerda Zohar said:

'Just imagine. Who would have thought it. Ido, take your shoes off. You'll spread mud everywhere.'

Mundek Zohar remarked that he had never known it to rain on May Day in all the twenty-nine years he had lived in Israel.

'This morning there wasn't a cloud in sight,' said Izia. 'The rain came on very suddenly. In fact, though, it's not all that amazing. I can remember rain as late as Shavuoth.'

'Don't tempt fate,' said Gerda.

Ido did not say a word but made his way to the sofa, where he stretched out, resting his head on his hand.

Gerda said:

'I've put the kettle on for tea.'

'My wife may be from Germany,' Mundek said, 'but I've taught her to make real Russian tea.'

'Don't put yourselves out on my account,' said Izia.

Gerda opened the built-in cupboard and took out three neatly ironed shirts, three pairs of khaki trousers, and two vests.

'You'd all better change,' she said. 'You're soaking wet.'

Izia, uneasy, refused out of politeness. Gerda asked if he preferred to catch his death of cold. Izia replied that he didn't want to put her to any trouble. Gerda insisted that it was no trouble. Izia yielded and changed. Mundek enthused sentimentally about the tattered rags they used to wear in the good old pioneering days. There followed an exchange of memories.

Izia said:

'Your pride and joy is remarkably silent.'

'Sometimes he is, and sometimes he isn't,' Gerda replied, and smiled at her son. Ido, however, did not return the smile. He may even have grumbled under his breath.

Mundek dropped the subject of the good old days and asked Izia for news of the wide world. Izia said that every last drop of strength would have to be mobilized for the political campaign that was imminent.

Ido was thinking ugly thoughts. He was curled up on the sofa, with his knees drawn up to his chin. A procession of images passed through his closed eyes.

Gerda served tea. She pointed to the thick white bandage that was wound round her leg from knee to ankle and explained that she was suffering from varicose veins. It's old age, she added. Izia ventured to remark that none of them was getting any younger. Even he had been suffering from certain pains. He didn't like to talk about them. What good could talking do, anyhow? The kettle boiled again. They drank their tea. Outside there was nothing to be heard except the falling rain, which had become no lighter and no heavier, but kept up its steady, ruthless pounding. Gerda closed all the windows. The drops played a monotonous tune on the glass panes. Mundek advised Izia to stay the night: it was madness to risk our rough road in such wet weather, not to mention at night. From the security point of view, too, it wouldn't be wise to leave now. Izia refused, out of politeness. Finally he yielded and agreed, and thanked his host and hostess for their kindness. Gerda said there was nothing to thank them for. On the contrary. Mundek would be only too pleased to have an opportunity to reminisce about the good old days. They had another cup of tea (all except Ido, whose father called him an 'angry young man'). They decided not to have supper. It was too wet to walk across to the dining hall, and anyway Gerda had a larder full of cakes, sweets, fruit, and – of course – unlimited supplies of Russian tea.

They talked about the prices of agricultural produce. They all agreed that many ordinary kibbutzniks did not realize the importance of political power.

Mundek asked his son in passing why he didn't get a book to read. Ido said he was listening to the conversation. But he was not telling the truth. Ido was not following the conversation. He was thinking about a girl, a girl two years older than himself. Noga Harish. Noga is like me only different. She's much, much more. More what. Feminine. No. Wild. No. There's a nice word. Heady.

About Noga, yes. I like her smell. Hasia has it, too, but too strong. Exaggerated.

Isn't it good in the rain. The rain washes the earth, and the earth drinks the rain. There's a nice word, 'sodden.' The earth is sodden. Noga hasn't got varicose veins. When she bites her lower lip, she looks like a wolf. The wolf is a frightening animal because he is thought of as a cruel beast of prey. When it rains, the wolf runs and hides in his cave. The wolf's cave is closed and secret and warm and dark. The air then is full of strong smells. The wolf curls up and goes to sleep and isn't afraid of anything, because the wolf is a frightening animal not a frightened animal. Wolves live in lairs in the forest The word 'lair' is one of the nicest things about wolves. Under the rocks high up in the thick dense forests, those forests with the beautiful, bittersweet name 'virgin forests,' where no man's foot has ever trodden. Only wolves' feet and foxes' and other silent animals'. Not feet, paws. The wolf has thick gray or brown fur. Now, when it's cold and rainy, the wolves huddle together to keep warm. And the wind howls in the woods. Pine tree howls to pine tree in the wind in the dark in the wet. Noga's mother Eva is like the she-wolves. Among the pine trees. The water pours down in torrents, streams even into the lair, and what will the she-wolf do then? Where will she go?

Then the thunder. Roaring thunder. Everything trembled. I trembled. Noga trembled there. Hasia. Eva. Everything. Then something very soft. Something lean and supple. Like fur. Like a she-wolf. Like a lair in the rain flooded with quick strong little spurts, streaming through every crack. All in pitch blackness. Soft and light and floating.

When Gerda Zohar served the third round of tea, Ido, too, accepted a glass. He even volunteered to go next door to borrow a blanket for the guest. Izia Gurevitch-Gilead inquired what he was studying at school. Ido explained fully and clearly. Izia jokingly said that up to five minutes before he had thought the boy was dumb. Of course, he had only thought it as a joke. Gerda said that boys of his age were liable to sudden changes of mood without any apparent reason. Izia said that a boy who was taught by Reuven Harish was bound to be sensitive. Mundek challenged the generalization but agreed in the present instance. Gerda served savory biscuits. The guest said that it sounded like the flood outside. Mundek said that by the sound of it the rain intended to go on for ever. Gerda said that ever since she was a small child the sound of rain on the windowpanes had made her feel sad. Mundek said that the summer crops would benefit but that the orchards would suffer. At half past ten they went to bed, not before sipping a fourth round of real Russian tea.

The next day, Saturday, the second of May, the sun shone brightly in a clear blue sky. Even the mountains seemed less forbidding. The Zohars took their guest for a walk round about the kibbutz, because a wonderful spring day like this is only ever seen after rain, and also because it is good for us to foster a spiritual link with animals and plants.

10

Blessed Routine

A FEW days ago, in the early afternoon, we stood at the top of a pretty little hill and looked at the distant view of Kibbutz Metsudat Ram. We were impressed by its strictly symmetrical plan; we observed the contrast between the smiling valley and the glowering mountain range; we made a rapid tour of the kibbutz grounds and heard a brief description from Reuven Harish of the principles of life adopted by him and his fellow members.

A few days have passed. May Day has gone by, with its unexpected rainstorm, and the festival of Shavuoth is approaching. We have recorded various events, here and there, but the events are non-events. Unwillingly, we must admit that nothing has happened. We have met some of the members of the kibbutz, we have looked at a pretty girl, and we have been informed by gossip of a curious lovers' tiff. Here and there the names of the Berger brothers have cropped up, Nehemiah Berger of Jerusalem and Zechariah-Siegfried in Germany. We have made the acquaintance of the fundamental tenets of kibbutz ideology and have not refrained from hinting at a few deviations from them; we are writing about human beings, after all. Even Ido Zohar's unhappiness is not beyond our comprehension. As the kibbutz truck driver puts it, people are flesh and blood, not myrrh and frankincense.

The festival of Shavuoth is not far off now, and getting closer day by day. The dancers meet every evening for a long and thorough rehearsal and practice seriously for their performance at the festival. Noga Harish is the star attraction of the dance of the seven kinds of fruit. She is a slender, enchanting vine. Her hands tremble gracefully to represent the little vine shoots. Her fingers are twining tendrils. Her body is a bunch of ripening grapes. The reader must excuse us: we, too, after all, are flesh and blood, not myrrh and frankincense.

After rehearsals, Noga slips away to her secret assignation in the wood by the swimming pool. Dafna Isarov, her plump room-mate, observes her jealously. Noga thinks that Dafna is asleep when she gets back, but Dafna, lying with the sheet pulled up over her head, is tense and alert in every pore.

Rami Rimon has still not managed to win her over. The girl shrinks from becoming a woman. Rami wonders what he has done wrong and can find no answer. He supposes that he must press harder than he has pressed so far. It is well known that women admire strength. 'The more you beat them, the better they be,' the proverb says. He curses his weakness. He certainly won't get anywhere by talking. Talking is tricky. She can outtalk him any day. Even his mother can outtalk him. He has still not managed to convince her to give her written consent to his service with the paratroopers. Tricky subject. I'm not a baby, and what happened to Yoash wasn't my fault. Why does my whole life have to be determined by what happened to him? My life is my life. Mother and Noga are in some sort of league against me. I'm sure they get together behind my back and talk, perhaps even laugh. Still, he laughs longest who laughs last. That's what the proverb says.

Fruma Rominov and Noga Harish do not get together behind Rami's back, but there is no denying that there is something between them. We would never have thought Fruma capable of displaying such affection. The widow has a soft spot for Noga Harish. Once they happened to sit at the same table in the dining hall, and Fruma smiled at Noga and even said to her:

'You can eat as many potatoes as you like. You've got nothing to be afraid of. In fact, you could do with putting on a bit of weight. You'd be even better looking than you are.'

And one day Fruma went to Noga's and Dafna's room while they were out and left a dish of homemade cookies on Noga's bed. She hasn't got a mother, after all, so there's no one to give her an occasional treat.

Fruma's cookies are justly celebrated. Not a hint of her bitterness can be tasted in them. It was Dafna Isarov who ate most of them, but it's the thought that counts. There's no doubt at all about Fruma Rominov's thoughts. Israel Tsitron told Hasia Ramigolski about a quarrel he overheard one night when he was on duty, and Hasia did not refrain from passing the good news on to Fruma.

Every Wednesday evening the music circle meets in Herbert Segal's room. A subdued atmosphere of culture dominates these meetings. Segal's room is lined with crowded bookshelves:

philosophical works and economics books in German and Hebrew, and even in French, albums of reproductions of works of art, various periodicals, and, of course, treatises on animal husbandry and dairy farming. There is also an upholstered rocking chair and an automatic record player. The latter is the property of the cultural committee of the kibbutz, but its home has been in Segal's room ever since the stormy departure of his predecessor as convenor of the group.

The room is full of smoke. Members are seated on the chairs, on the solitary bed, on the Oriental poufs, and on the plaited straw mat.

Segal opens the evening with a few well-chosen words: the composer's historical background, the themes, the structure of the work, the interpretation in the present performance.

Briskly, the record is deposited on the disk of gray felt, the needle lands gracefully at the beginning of the groove, the first solemn notes ring out. A feeling of fellowship descends on the gathering. Some of the women have their embroidery in their laps, but their work does not distract them from the music; on the contrary, it helps them to relax and succumb to the gentle ripples of sound. Some of the men beat time with their feet. Their concentration prevents them from noticing Herbert Segal's disapproving looks: rhythm is the fundamental element in creation. By beating time they show that their experience of the music is more basic. There are different layers in music, one inside the other. Some people can reach only the outermost layer. Curiously enough, it is these whose faces quickly take on a rapt, ecstatic expression. Herbert himself sits with his head drawn into his narrow shoulders, his back rounded, his mouth open, his hands to his temples, completely surrendering to the music. He is somewhere else.

The older members, who were born in Germany or in Russia, can see the far-off streets of their childhood, lashed by dark rain, perhaps, or shrouded in gloomy fog. Even the younger people, who were born here, feel a sad longing for far-off places, unknown, unnamed places that are far, far away and full of sadness. Silent sorrow settles on every face. They are human beings, tillers of the soil. They are weary. Their eyes are closed. Sorrow clasps their hearts. And our own love, which we have condemned to cold oblivion.

In the interval between two works Nina Goldring and Bronka Berger serve tea. Herbert Segal, as a bachelor, is not expected to act as host, in any case, he is busy at the moment, blowing a speck of dust off a gleaming record.

Three or four times a week Reuven Harish has to present himself in the square in front of the dining hall to receive tours. He greets them in his usual friendly voice. Explains briefly the fundamental principles of the kibbutz ideology. Points out the symbolic contrast between the valley and the mountains.

These last days Reuven has been suffering from dull pains in his chest. They come only once or twice a day, and they may not be due to some physical cause. Certainly overwork and tension play their part. He has been unable for some time to put a single idea into verse. He walks as if he were carrying a heavy load. This is apparently why a slight change has come about in his relations with Bronka. One evening he told her he felt tired and sick and left her earlier than usual. Bronka did not try to stop him. It is possible that the weight which has been pressing on him is the cause of this slight change that can be detected in Bronka. Or perhaps it is Bronka who is responsible for his feeling it. Noga has observed all this. Reuven is observant, and he has seen Noga eyeing him in a strange way, as if she is glad to see him suffer and anxious on his behalf at the same time.

On Saturday evening she sat on the lawn with him and stared at him so pointedly that he could not stop himself asking:

'Why are you staring at me like that? Did you want to say something to me?'

'Pardon?'

'I said did you want to tell me something?'

'Not at all, Daddy. I thought you had said something.'

'No, I didn't say anything,' Reuven replied, surprised.

'Strange,' said Noga, without explaining the remark, and without explaining what she thought was strange.

In the evening everybody, young and old, crowds into the dining hall, dressed in light evening clothes. Einav, clearly pregnant, makes no effort to conceal her lameness. Tomer, her husband, lavishes signs of affection on her. Black hairs protrude from his ears, as from his father's. His tanned skin has the tone of dull copper.

At night the enemy soldiers fire nervously into the darkness. From time to time they light up the valley with colored flares. Even in the daytime they do not leave us alone. In the next sector, to the north of us, a man was shot and wounded in the shoulder while working in the orchard in broad daylight. We, too, have had an incident. One evening a stray shot was fired at Grisha Isarov as he was spreading the nets in one of the fish ponds by the border. The incident was not entirely unprovoked. Grisha Isarov had cultivated a strange habit of bawling Arabic curses in the direction of the enemy positions. Hardly an intelligent action. Grisha is not a child. We hope that in future he will restrain his marked love of adventure.

If Grisha, who is not a child, behaves so irresponsibly, is it any wonder that Gai Harish, who is a child, has introduced a distasteful game among his friends? They play at wars. All afternoon the kibbutz paths re-echo with their noisy games. Armed with stout sticks, they wreak havoc and carnage on the enemies of Israel under the orders of their young commander. Needless to say, many of us are critical of this innovation and are furious at the teachers who do not put a stop to it. Reuven does not know what to do. He does not believe in threats. He advocates patience. Grown-ups, he has a habit of saying, do not have a monopoly of making mistakes. In the course of these days, Reuven handed Bronka a photograph of his two children, for Bronka to send to her brother-in-law in Munich.

In fairness to little Gai it must be admitted that he and his friends do nothing more than make a great deal of noise. The case of Oren Geva (who refuses to be called Oren Berger) is much sadder. He and his gang of hooligans are always up to mischief. They appropriate property and damage it, wreck Herzl Goldring's meticulously kept flower beds and answer his protests with coarse sneers, break into the larders and make off with sweetmeats intended for the little children, start up tractors and roam with impunity all over the valley, throw vulgar looks at the girls of their own age, and even at older women, and bully their juniors. If you go out in the evening to take your clothes to the laundry, there they are holding a council round a small bonfire from which there wafts a smell of roasting flesh. If you come back around midnight from a film show in the dining hall, you can hear whispered conversations and unpleasant laughter in the bushes. In the middle of the afternoon you look up at the tall water tower and see a strangled cat hanging from the topmost railing by a length of truck driver's rope. The case of Oren and his gang has already been discussed in various committees. According to Herbert Segal, an ill wind is blowing from the towns and corrupting our youth. According to Bronka Berger, the roots of the trouble are psychological. Dirty books protrude from their pockets. They smell of stolen cigarettes. Around this time an extremely serious incident roused the kibbutz to an angry ferment. One morning Herzl discovered an empty land mine with Syrian markings in the shrubbery. It was supposed that Oren's gang had been out on a nocturnal foraging expedition in no man's land. It was a miracle that no disaster had ensued.

Bronka suffered agonies of shame and sorrow. Ezra Berger said nothing. When questioned, he shrugged his shoulders and smiled drily. Pressed to answer, he said:

'I'll punish the whole brood of vipers, including my own beloved younger son, as the saying goes.'

Urged on to act, he remarked:

'Give him time. Some lame girl will get hold of him and turn him into a lamp stand. Time wounds all heels, as the wise man said.'

There are thus a number of things that are not running quite smoothly. But if we overlook the exceptions and consider the general picture, we will see that our lives flow smoothly on in their orderly routine way toward the approaching festival of Shavuoth. In the morning the members go off to work as usual. At midday they return to the dining hall, which welcomes them with jugs of chilled lemonade. After a brief rest everyone goes out to the fields again to finish the day's work.

The working day ends at five o'clock. From every house comes the splash of shower water, mingled with sounds of singing. The smell of coffee wafts from the verandas, shaded with shrubs and climbing plants. The lawns are suddenly dotted with deck chairs and groups of people, lazily leafing through the morning paper or snatching forty winks. Some cultivate their gardens, watering, hoeing, weeding, and pruning. Others indulge in their favorite hobby or pastime – stamp collecting, coin collecting, photography, tennis, pet cats or dogs, an aquarium. Some do it alone; others include all the members of their families.

Herbert Segal, for example, walks up and down the concrete path with Reuven Harish. If you must know, they are discussing the latest trends in Israeli literature. Herbert is of the opinion that the young writers are blind. They are living at the height of a national, social, eschatological revolution that is unprecedented in history, and what do they see? Nothing. Storms in teacups. They have no positive message to offer, or even a negative one, for that matter. Reuven thinks he can explain this phenomenon.

'Very well then,' says Herbert, 'let's hear your explanation.'

'It's a matter of optics. They are the pupil of the eye. And the pupil of the eye, biologists say, is blind.'

Even everyday matters take on a new light at this time of day.

Isaac Friedrich, the treasurer, is sitting on a bench under a tree with Tsvi Ramigolski, the secretary. They are deep in complicated calculations. If you eavesdrop, you can catch references to compound interest, credit, contracts, guarantees. But both men look completely relaxed. Not because the financial problems do not affect them personally, but because they, too, are touched by the calm of the time and the place.

Later, somebody brings two or three copies of the evening paper. The livelier members get together to look at the headlines over each other's shoulders. The papers soon disintegrate, the pages passing peacefully from hand to hand. If an occasional discussion blows up, it never develops into a heated argument, because fundamentally we all share the same outlook on the world.

The heat gradually evaporates. The quavering notes of Herbert Segal's violin are answered by Herzl Goldring's accordion.

On the basketball court loud shouts break out. The Metsudat Ram team, top of the kibbutz teams in the valley, is playing a practice match. A small band of spectators huddles round the court. Each successful move is greeted by a burst of cheering. In between cheers the only sound is the silken padding of rubber soles on the concrete. Tomer Geva makes a slight movement with his hips. The opponent who has been set to mark him is taken in by the feint and misses Tomer's actual movement. A totally silent pass. Suddenly the ball is in Rami Rimon's hands. Rami does not hesitate for a split second. He sends the ball straight back to Tomer, who in the meantime has zigzagged like a snake through the defenders' lines. Tomer glances left to mislead his opponents, twists to the right, and, with a spectacular leap, puts the ball through the hoop. A grimace, which is not a smile, plays over his face and vanishes. His mouth is wide open. His face is streaming with sweat. Without a word, with a sharp wave of the arm, he collects his men and places them in readiness for the enemy attack. His team responds like musicians obeying the gentle wave of the conductor's baton. It is not words that count here. We are compelled to admit it. Not words. Here it is muscles and lungs and deadly cunning that win the day. Gleaming bodies weaving a narrow passage. Quick wits and powerful vitality. Razor-sharp reaction. That is what counts here. Perfect control of every sinew and fiber. We are not fond of this place. We are lovers of words. Our responses are too slow.

Sometimes in the evening thick clouds of dust billow among the houses and settle broodingly in the trees. But the breezes soon tire of their quarreling. A light westerly wind caresses our brows and fills us with longing.

After the game Rami picks up his shirt, wipes the sweat off his body with it, and goes to Fruma's room. At this time even Fruma is not her usual sullen self. She is sitting on her veranda, wearing a flowered apron, pressing grapes into a jug. Rami stays with her for a quarter of an hour or so. Nibbles her cookies. Quenches his thirst with grape juice. Helps his mother to hoe and weed her garden. Fruma struggles to put his impending departure out of her mind. Occasionally she sighs. Rami hears her and grimaces.

Opposite, on the other side of the lawn, the Harish family are relaxing. The father is leafing through a book. The daughter is deep in her pretty embroidery. Even Gai, the prodigal son, has returned to the bosom of his family for a few moments. If it were not for the curious tin helmet on his head, we would find no fault with him.

On the dust path Bronka Berger and her daughter-in-law, Einav Geva, are taking a stroll together. They are deep in women's talk, about things a pregnant woman mustn't do, how to tell the sex of the child, good and bad things to eat. Bronka wants a granddaughter, Einav wants a son. So they disagree about the signs. Mutual affection shows on their faces. Their stroll, like everything around us at the moment, is calm and peaceful. Oh, how good it would be if we could make time stand still, if we could finish our story at this point with a shrug of the shoulders: and they all lived happily ever after. Anyone who looks forward to complicated happenings betrays his own perverse inclinations. But time flows heedlessly on, on its unseen course. The sun is about to set. Points of light appear on the mountain heights opposite, beyond the border. The men and women of the kibbutz patiently fold up their deck chairs and get ready for the communal supper. Herzl Goldring asks Nina if it is seven o'clock yet. Nina says it is. Herzl says he has to go and turn off a sprinkler behind the armory before supper. Nina asks him not to be too long. He promises, and keeps his word.

One Friday night, after the festive meal, which had opened with the lighting of Sabbath candles and the hooting of owls, Rami Rimon slips out and makes his way alone to the water tower. Quickly he climbs it. He moves up rung by rung till he reaches the top of the tower, squeezes his body against the iron railing and over onto the observation platform. Even an unromantic youth may well feel sad and seek a moment's solitude. From his lofty lookout post a strange, hazy scene meets his eyes. The sky has turned a dark gray. Beyond the gray screen the dying sun writhes convulsively in a mist of purple, yellow, violet, and gold.

In the enemy positions there is some movement to be discerned. For three or four days now they have been massing their forces. Rami screws up his eyes, the left eye especially, to see better. Military vehicles with six double wheels crawl around, surrounded by dim human forms. Yoash used to say: 'Those people understand only one language, the language of violence. They interpret restraint as cowardice. And they're right. Our old men can't understand that, because they're still Europeans even here in Asia, and because of the time-honored Jewish love of peace. But one day their pressure will make life here unbearable for us, and we'll get permission to smash the Arabs, and after that the map of Israel won't look like a bent sausage any more.' I was only a small child then. I didn't understand what he meant. In those days I was impressed by external signs, by Yoash's uniform, his green battle dress with its camouflage markings, his red beret, the badges. But now I understand what it's all about. Father always used to say: 'Israel must be the opposite of the ghetto. If we're going to live in a ghetto here, we might as well have stayed in Europe. At least there we didn't have the *hamsin*.' Father was such a little man, a little Jew, pale and sick and always humming Hasidic tunes, but deep down he wasn't a Jew, he was a man. That's why Yoash and I grew up to be men. If I'm killed, Mother will become a martyr. They'll all walk round her on tiptoe. And Noga will know. She'll curse herself for laughing at me. And for what she didn't give me before I was killed.

Rami curls his lips. There is no one here now to make fun of his horse's face. Even if there had been anyone here, he would not have dared make fun of him now that he is so upset. He thinks about the tough life in the army, which shows up the true man among the flock of spoiled chatter-boxes. His chest fills. His future feats and exploits throw his mind in a whirl. You'll see. I'll show you. Yoash. Everyone. The lot of you.

He hears the sound of singing, long-drawn-out and poignant. Our kibbutz is welcoming the Sabbath with the slow, solemn melodies of the traditional table songs. The distance blurs the tunes and imbues them with a mournful, incantatory tone: *Come, beloved, to greet the Sabbath. Sabbath descends on the Vale of Ginosar.* Rami does not think about the words of the songs, but weaves from their threads a tissue of dreams.

He thinks about women. He has read somewhere recently that a woman's heart is a riddle that no man can solve. Women really do live in a different world. A more colorful world. Even when they are with you, they are not really with you. But the fault is yours. You let her fix the rules of the game. There is an expression 'to conquer a woman.' Like an enemy stronghold. Like fortifications. If you are like a woman, no woman will ever surrender to you.

Rami tosses his head. He hears a light throbbing in his temples. His sadness gives way to a firm determination. An end to all that. Once and for all.

Full of resolution he climbs down from the tower and turns his steps toward Noga's room.

No more beating about the bush. Straightforwardly. Simply and straightforwardly.

11

Force

THAT EVENING Rami Rimon tried to beat a new path to his friend's heart, a simple, straightforward path. Heedless of mischievous tongues, he went into Noga's room. Dafna Isarov could not restrain a soft exclamation of surprise.

Noga is in, lying on her stomach, her tiny chin propped up between her elbows, her body smelling sweetly after her Sabbath shower, her beautiful hair still damp and heavy. She is engrossed in a volume of poetry by a young poetess.

Rami made a sign to the plump Dafna: Would she mind excusing them? Dafna blushed fiery red, as if caught in the act, and fled from the room, without a backward glance. Rami crossed the room. Sat on the edge of Noga's bed. Put his hand on her shoulder.

'Put the book away.'

Noga inquired if that was an order.

'Maybe. I want to talk to you.'

'I thought you were going to attack me.'

'I want to talk to you.'

Gently, lazily, the girl changed her position. She had been lying on her stomach. Now she turned on her side. She cast a lively green glance at Rami.

'I'm listening.'

'I've been thinking, and now I've decided. That's what I wanted to say.'

'Is that all?'

'I've decided I don't want to join the paratroopers. I'll go into the infantry. Not like my brother. I'll start the hard way. In an obscure fighting unit. Wherever they send me.'

'Why? Don't you . . .'

'I don't care,' Rami interrupted, his Adam's apple bobbing up and down rapidly. 'I want to do it the hard way. But you'll see, both of you. First the infantry. Then I'll do a course and be a section commander. Then an officer. And then I'll come back here.'

'To be near me?'

'To fight here.'

'Child.'

Rami grabbed Noga's ribs and squeezed them till she cried out in pain. Outside the door a stifled sound was heard. Evidently Dafna, listening at the door, had broken down and was struggling with her laughter. Rami swore loudly, and the eavesdropper fled. Now he pressed his broad hands against Noga's breasts until she let out a soft groan.

'What's the matter with you, maniac?'

'I've told you. I've come to a decision.'

'Maniac you're a maniac leave me alone maniac, it hurts, you don't know anything you're a maniac.'

There is a cruel expression on the boy's face. His eyes are protruding, his features distorted. Noga finds him repulsive. He's ugly. Why have I never noticed before how ugly he is?

Suddenly she stopped moving, relaxed all her muscles and said icily:

'Leave me alone, please. Now go. Go away.'

The boy froze instantly, searched her face with a glazed, unrecognizing look, and once more clung to her with his tense body. It was not desire that drove him mad. It was humiliation. A sudden sob burst from Noga's throat. She had to struggle to control her groaning body, which threatened to betray her. Rami was panting. Let us look more closely at his eyes. Believe it or not, they are full of tears.

It was Ezra Berger who intervened at the critical moment to rescue the girl from the unbecoming struggle. While the pair were wrestling, they suddenly heard footsteps coming toward the door and then a loud knocking. Rami retreated, scarlet-faced, to Dafna Isarov's bed. Noga, meanwhile, adjusted her dressing gown, rolled onto her stomach and said, 'Come in.'

What is Ezra Berger doing in Turquoise's room after dinner on a Friday night? Ezra Berger is bringing Noga a packet of embroidery thread. These last weeks the girl has made frequent call on the driver's good nature and exploited him to do her shopping for her. At first she used to reimburse him out of her meager savings. More recently he has been paying out of his own pocket. In return, Turquoise has made him a little bag to carry his sandwiches in, with the figure of a bear embroidered on it. In the early afternoon, between Ezra's first and second trip of the day, she goes to the motor shed to chat with him for a quarter of an hour. They have already snatched a number of such conversations. Not, of course, about serious topics, still less, needless to say, about the painful affair that affects them both, but just lighthearted banter. Ezra, in his usual bluff, friendly way, answers his little friend with proverbs and metaphors, while Noga answers him childishly, as she always does when she talks to people who are much older than she is. That is not to say that she is trying to captivate the man. Not at all. That is simply the way she always talks to people who are much older than she is. There is nothing wrong with these meetings, we must insist, except for one detail of which we do not approve, namely the driver's habit of putting his hand on Turquoise's head and stroking her hair in a paternal sort of way, and even tickling her neck a little. Noga is not a child any more. Is it possible that Ezra Berger has chosen to overlook the fact?

*

'Good Sabbath to you, young lady. See what I have for you.'
Ezra comes in and holds the packet out clumsily toward her.
Noga smiles and holds out both her hands. Ezra catches sight
of Rami lying curled up with his sullen face turned to the wall.

'Ha, my little warrior – you here, young Rominov? Have you
been sent home from the army? What? Not called up yet? Capital!
Meanwhile, you're keeping watch over your sweetheart's bed,
eh? Like Solomon's bed, surrounded with sixty warriors.'

'Good Sabbath, Ezra,' replied Rami, curtly.

'Why aren't you with your mother? It's not nice to leave
her all alone on Friday night. You can court young ladies any
night. But if you'll take an old man's advice, you won't court
them at all. Wait for them to come to you. "A woman shall
compass a man" – that's what the Prophet says. And he wasn't
a prophet for nothing. By the way, why do you suppose there
were "threescore valiant men" round King Solomon's bed?
Wouldn't two or three have been enough? The answer is in the
text: "threescore valiant men, of the valiant of Israel." That's
why he needed sixty of them. You see, the Bible isn't meant to
be declaimed aloud. You have to read it carefully and think
about it. Then you can hear a kind of undertone of, what shall
we call it, of faint self-mockery. What do you say to that?'

Rami shrugs his shoulders. The old bear has chosen a fine
time to pester us with this nonsense. Why doesn't he go away?
Nothing ever goes according to plan. To hell with him.

'Well, Rominov, when are you off to make your name as a
hero?'

'I'm going to the army in ten days,' said Rami, with another
shrug.

'And you're leaving behind a broken heart, eh? Have you ever heard the old Jewish story of "find or found"? No? Then I'll tell you. In the old days they used to ask a bridegroom the morning after the wedding night one simple question: "Find or found?" If he said "found," it was good. If he said "find," it was bad. Very bad. Why? Both words refer to Biblical sayings. One is "He who has found a wife has found a good thing." The other is "I find the woman more bitter than death." Witty, eh? They were wise old men, our ancestors. Every word implied ten more. You mustn't be angry with me, Rominov, because you're a bright lad, and you realize that I'm saying ten words so as not to have to say one. That's the way of jokers, Rominov, and jokers aren't happy people. Sometimes they say unpleasant things. It's not easy for them to control themselves, but they have to control themselves, because if they don't, how can you tell the difference between them and plain bad men? Why do I stay here boring you? As the wise man says, "The best thing I have found for a body is silence." But what the wise man forgot to add is that not everything which is good for the body is good for a man. Good night. Forgive me, Rominov. You've already forgiven me. You're a good lad.'

'Good night,' Rami answered, sullenly. But Noga cunningly frustrated his plans by saying suddenly, with a flattering smile:

'Don't go yet, Ezra. Stay with us for a bit. You're talking so nicely this evening.'

And Ezra Berger?

You can never predict human behavior. We should have expected Ezra to stop talking and go. But Ezra didn't stop talking, and he didn't go. He gave Noga a long, amused look.

Then he sat down carefully on the only chair, between the two beds, turned his rough face toward Rami, and rolled his eyes, like a clown.

Rami lit a cigarette and impatiently blew out a thick puff of smoke. By the light of the match we can observe something we have never noticed before: Rami Rimon has a slight mustache. Not much of one, it is true, hardly more than a pale, fuzzy shadow on his upper lip, but nevertheless.

Ezra, too, pulls out a cigarette and lights it with a gilt lighter. He closes one eye and opens the other wide, staring fixedly at the gold ring on his little finger. Then he raises his eyes and looks the boy over carefully, from head to foot and then back again, from his feet to his head.

'Golden head. What a pity, Rominov, that you're being snatched away from us to take the king's shilling, as they used to say.'

Rami says nothing. He shoots the older man a fierce look of unveiled hatred.

For a moment Ezra flinches as though struck across the face. But instantly he readopts an expression of amused sympathy.

'You have no choice, young Rominov. You must dress up in uniform and go leaping on the mountains, skipping on the hills. But sometimes, my boy, sometimes, on Sabbaths . . .' Ezra closes his eyes and makes a juicy sucking sound with his lips. '. . . on Sabbaths my beloved will have a short leave, and then . . . then my beloved will come to his garden and eat its choice fruits.'

And Turquoise? Turquoise laughs out loud in sweet ripples of sound, her green checkered dressing gown, too large for her, buttoned carelessly over her body, vaguely suggesting the curves of her figure, slipping up above her knees. She does not avert her green-flashing gaze from the boy.

'That's enough, Ezra. Stop it, for Heaven's sake. Let him be. Look, he's gone all red. Why do you tease him? He's smaller than you are.'

There is a flirtatious lilt in her voice as she speaks. She is urged on by cruelty, but even her cruelty is – if we may be forgiven for saying so – so faint and gentle that our heart goes out to her. Besides, she has spoken the truth. Rami Rimon is indeed blushing. He looks down at the floor to hide the extraordinarily horselike curl of his lips. Is it any wonder that Noga redoubles her laughter, and in a shabby gesture hurls the packet of embroidery thread at him?

'Head up, Rami, don't hide, fight back. I want to see you fight.'

This remark fills Ezra with a dejection that accords ill with his words. He lays his hand on Noga's bare knee, then withdraws it, and puts a finger to his eye as if he has got something in it. Turning to Rami, he says, in a changed voice:

'You see what I mean, my boy. Let's play a new game now. Let's play at being brothers.'

Rami gives a look like a beaten horse, gets up, leans toward Noga and hisses.

'Snake. Just like your mother. Poisonous little snake.'

On his way out he almost collides with Dafna, who has crept back to spy on the room from behind the door. In his fury he slaps her face. Her tears bring him back to his senses. His eyes, too, redden.

Meanwhile, inside the room, nothing has happened. Ezra is still sitting silently on the only chair; all he has done is to drop his cigarette end and stamp on it, covering his eyes with his hand. He drags his words out slowly:

'Don't worry. He'll be back. He'll behave himself now. You have to deal firmly with them sometimes. A man must remember where he comes from and where he's going, as the saying goes.'

As he talks, he strokes his young friend's hair with his fingertips and sinks back into his silent ponderings. If she hates me now, she'll be his, and it'll be better for both of them. If she doesn't hate me, it's a sign that really. That I must. That it's fated. Everything is written, for men and beasts alike. And it is written: 'One who is alone when he falls has not another to help him up.' And in the same book: 'Their love and their hatred and their envy are now perished.' I wanted to know. I wanted to force a decision. Now.

'Now I'm off, too, Turquoise.'

'Stay.'

'No, I won't stay. You need to be alone now.'

'You're not nice, Ezra. You're not . . .'

'Of course I'm not nice. Good night, Turquoise. I'm not nice, but . . .'

'But what?'

'Nothing, Turquoise. Good night.'

Rami did not go back to Noga's room that night, or the next day, or during the days that followed. Three days before the festival he took his leave of his widowed mother and set out to make his name as a hero. Oh, how painful were those last hours for Fruma Rominov! She tried with all her strength not to break down and cry, but her strength was hardly up to the effort. She put all her loving care into her son's kit bag, as if it was the kit bag that was going off to face danger. In her devotion to her only remaining son she ironed his underwear, his handkerchiefs, and even his socks, a completely unnecessary action. She packed a tin of home-made cookies in the bottom of the bag, and a brand-new toilet set. She embroidered flowers on the toilet bag with her own hands. Even though she abhorred tobacco, she put in ten packets of special cigarettes that she had recently asked Isaac Friedrich, the treasurer, to buy for her, not the usual cigarettes that the kibbutz provides for its members. She did not overlook the slightest detail: bootlaces, bandages, plasters, three sorts of pills, talcum powder, the last photograph of Alter Rominov and the last photograph of Yoash Rimon, resplendent in officer's uniform, and even a picture of herself as a young woman. She also put in some writing paper, envelopes, and stamps. When she had packed everything, she unpacked it all and ironed the bag itself.

Rami did not repay his mother's affection in kind. His movements were cold and curt. He turned the kit bag upside down, poured out the contents, and extracted whatever was superfluous. He was particularly scornful about the stamps: every child knew that armed forces' mail didn't need stamps. To his credit it must be admitted that, after tearful pleas and sighs, he consented, though with a bad grace, to take the cookies with him. On the other hand, he refused even to bargain about a bag of grapes. They would be bound to get squashed and make everything else in the bag dirty. And, anyway, he'd be ashamed to turn up at an army camp all laden with goodies like a child going to kindergarten. The only thing lacking was for his mother to wet his hair and arrange it in pretty curls. The widow showered her son with advice and warnings. Rami nodded his head and smiled a rude, heedless smile. She embraced him and kissed him on the mouth. The boy did not resist her hugs, but neither did he respond to them with any sign of affection. Fruma tried to persuade him to go and say good-bye to his girl friend, Noga. Why wouldn't he make it up with her before he left? They must have quarreled about something quite trivial. There was no doubt that she wished him well. The boy scowled and cursed. He'd never go and see her, even if she came grovelling on all fours. The widow bit her lip.

Finally Rami relented and forced himself to kiss his mother. His kiss broke down all their defenses. She burst into uncontrollable tears. How touching she looks when she cries, like an elderly baby. Her ugly weeping sears us. We feel like forcing Rami to have pity on her and fling himself on her neck. Good-bye, Mother, I'll write to you. Look at my boy, isn't he handsome, look at him, curse you, look how fine he looks, he's a sensitive boy, if you only knew, he loves nature, only he's reserved, but I know that he's a poet at heart, my fine son.

Rami shoulders his kit bag and leaves. On his way to the car he makes a detour to the cow shed. This is where he has been working for the past year, and he has to say good-bye to the other workers. But how silly of me to forget; there's no one here at this time of day. Only the bull stares at Rami

122

Rimon with his bloodshot eyes. Rami puts his hand through the railings and slaps the bull's jaws. The bull responds with a gust of warm, damp breath. You're a great bull, Titan; don't let them slaughter you. Give them a *corrida* when they come to get you. Olé, olé!

He puts his hand through the bars again and fondles the ring in the bull's nose. The bull answers with a hollow moan. Goodbye, Titan. Rami loves you truly, because Rami has a sensitive heart.

12

Three Paths

Rabbi Naphtali Hirsh Berger, the father of the three Berger brothers, was the cantor in a synagogue of peddlers and waggoners on the outskirts of Kovel. He was a little man of almost unnaturally clumsy proportions, with short, stout legs, a pot belly, and no neck to intervene between his strong, bulging shoulders and his huge dark bull head. His expression was one of drowsy gravity. These features are reflected in the face of young Oren Berger. What was surprising to observe was the almost complete absence of eyes: two tiny slits in a dense network of deep wrinkles, but both sparkling an amazing blue. Another surprise was the pure, strong tenor voice that would burst suddenly from the powerful chest through the thick black beard. He would stand for two or three hours on end in the stone-paved square of the suburb, quite motionless except for the rhythmic chewing of his huge jaws on a quid of tobacco and an occasional jet of yellow juice. It was said that no one had ever seen him happy or sad; he was always just the same, going about his business but with his mind apparently on other things. His business was that of cantor and to some extent that of synagogue treasurer. He performed his tasks without enthusiasm, but without carelessness. His thoughts may have wandered or they may have been concentrated; either way they were always somewhere else, never where he was. There were other men like him in our town; we knew how they earned their livelihood, but we never knew what motivated them, or what they thought about. He always seemed to be daydreaming. Whether or not he actually dreamed, even his three sons, his own flesh and blood, did not know. The Germans came and took him and roasted him in the furnaces of Sobibor. That was long after his wife had died, long after his sons, one by one, had severed their links with their father. His sons all traveled long paths. Sometimes, though, they still recall the tiny blue sparks lost in the rugged contours of his face.

At times, when the roaring crowd acclaims the impressive agility of Tomer Geva on the basketball court in Metsudat Ram, or when we watch Oren wrestling with one of the boys, subduing him with icy rage, then we, too, think thoughts that we conceal in our breast and do not try to share with any stranger.

The first to break away was the eldest brother, Nehemiah. There was a boss-eyed rabbinical student in Kovel, who was something of a politician, something of a womanizer, and something of a philosopher. He it was who persuaded Nehemiah to escape from his father's house to Lvov and to make his way on to the university there.

Ezra was swept away, like so many young men and women, by the youth movement. He and his friend Aaron Ramigolski went up to Palestine together, to become founder-members of our kibbutz. The rest is well known.

Zechariah was banished because of the dogs.

It happened during Passover week, when he was still a young boy. Some gypsies came to Kovel and set up their tents on some land just outside our quarter, to the east. Each night from their camp there came the sounds of melancholy singing and loud bursts of coarse laughter. The nomads had dogs. Wild, starved dogs, of a savage disposition but also given to obsequious fawning. Zechariah made their acquaintance and won their favor with tidbits that he threw them. He took an unwholesome pleasure in playing with the dogs and lavishing caresses and other signs of affection on them.

Occasionally he observed them mating. At night he was consumed by an unnatural urge. Zechariah was a solitary boy, and from his earliest days all his actions had displayed an isolated arrogance.

On one occasion his father caught him playing with the dogs. Perhaps one of the local boys, one of his many childhood enemies, had informed on him. A terrible thing happened then: the father beat his son soundly, and the son, sobbing and hardly knowing what he was doing, set his allies the dogs on his father. The nomads' dogs, for all their obsequious fawning, were of a savage disposition. The whole neighborhood was shocked. The cantor's two eldest sons had already broken with their father, and now the youngest, too, was going to the bad.

Zechariah left his father's house under a curse, and became a bitter man. At first he went to Rovno, where he worked for a Polish farmer, but after a month the peasant dismissed him in a panic. His bearing had called to the man's mind an incident that had happened some years before, when a young Polish lad had taken to firing haystacks from political motives. Zechariah's eyes at times emitted grim flashes.

From Rovno he went on to Warsaw and took a job as a printer's apprentice with a well-known Jewish newspaper. At that time he had a non-Jewish girl friend, a pretty, hysterical girl who lived with him. Then the Germans came and imprisoned him in the ghetto. He escaped and traveled widely: he went to Russia; he may have gone to Sweden; he spent some time after the end of the war in a displaced persons' camp in Italy; from Italy he traveled with a widow to Atlit, and from Atlit to another camp in Cyprus. He returned to Atlit again in 1949, and from there he went, without the woman, to Ramla and then on to Jaffa. In Jaffa he found a partner and went into business for a year. After that he took his leave of his brothers and returned to Europe, to say a prayer in Kovel. He never reached Kovel. He made a detour to Germany, made various representations, and secured some reparation money. In Munich he met Isaac Hamburger, and established a flourishing partnership with him.

As for Nehemiah, he had a bitter struggle. He finished his course at the University of Lvov in abject poverty, taught general history in the Jewish gymnasium, emigrated to Palestine a few weeks before the outbreak of war, and came to Kibbutz Metsudat Ram. Ezra and Bronka did everything they could for him, but the physical work defeated him. He suffered the same fate, he often says, as Yehezkel Hefetz and Yitzhak Kumer in the stories by Brenner and Agnon. It was only to be expected, he adds with a faint smile, since the whole pattern of his life exactly matches that of the unfortunate heroes of the Hebrew novels of the last generation.

Ezra Berger, then, is unique among his brothers. Ezra Berger married and had children, and helped to establish Kibbutz Metsudat Ram. His life is not doomed to sterility. There is a moral in this: men are not condemned inevitably to an accursed, tedious life of sterility. With an effort of will a man can avert the curse and hew out a path of his own.

13

Blindness

FINALLY, AFTER a hard struggle, Reuven Harish's poem:

> Chilly night with arms of metal
>> Settles slowly on our groves:
> Black and scowling in the fields,
>> Menacing, the night wind roves.
>
> Brief indeed is night's dominion:
>> Glaring searchlights pierce the gloom,

Criss-crossing on barbed-wire fences,
   Scattering the birds of doom.

Sleep holds our beleaguered village,
   But the watchmen never sleep;
Vigilant, they clasp their weapons,
   While around the jackals weep.

Though the barren mountain threatens
   To engulf us with its might,
Yet we have a strong protection
   In our adamantine light.

Reuven had to go to Tel Aviv, to see the director of the publishing house of the movement and discuss with him the details of a new volume of his poems. He left the kibbutz early in the morning. By half past nine he was in Tel Aviv and by ten o'clock he had concluded his business, since the head of the publishing house was an old friend. They quickly reached complete agreement about the details of the publication, shook hands on the deal, and had a friendly chat over a glass of iced grapefruit juice. At a quarter past ten Reuven wondered whether to go to Jerusalem to look up some friends of his there. But at the central bus station a curious incident unsettled his plans. Things never turn out quite as one expects.

The bus station was thronging with noise and bustle. The hawkers raised their loud voices in competition with each other, having no care in the world beyond money-making.

Reuven walks slowly along the narrow streets around the bus station, now looking down at the pavement, now taking in the noisy street scene. His time is his own, and he enjoys his pensive stroll. He is detached from the nervous bustle all around him, untouched by the feverish activity. His clear forehead wears a lively look. His green glance roves from the brightly colored stalls to the faces of the passers-by, to the cars rumbling heavily through the narrow streets. His gait is calm and measured.

Reuven is wearing a neatly ironed white shirt over his blue trousers. His black leather brief case weighs next to nothing, containing as it does a few pages of poetry, a newspaper, and two sandwiches wrapped in brown paper. His face is gaunt, his forehead high, his eyes full of lively curiosity. Now and then he pauses to glance at a stall covered with colorful erotic magazines, or at a peddler carrying a tray of crude, cheap knickknacks. Sometimes his eyes linger on a well-built woman tripping along on high heels. Everyone dies eventually, as the crazy Dutchman said.

'He's right,' Reuven suddenly says, so loudly that a nearby shoeblack looks up and asks:

'What?'

'No, it's all right,' Reuven answers absently. 'Thank you very much.' At once his glance rests on a little boy in tears. A boy of five or six, standing between the fresh-fruit-juice stands and sobbing like an orphan. Nobody is taking any notice of him. Reuven hurries across the road. There is nothing more distressing than a lost child.

'What's the matter, sonny?'

The child doesn't answer but bawls even louder.

'What's your name?'

The boy opens his red eyes for a moment, then closes them again, and lets out a sound like the shrill wail of a beaten dog.

'Don't be frightened, there's a good boy. Have you lost your mummy? Your daddy? Tell me. I want to help you. Don't be frightened.'

Reuven overcomes a feeling of repulsion for a moment and stretches out his hand to stroke the boy's head. The child, baring his teeth like a wolf cub, kicks him in the shin and turns to run away. Reuven grabs hold of his arm and stops him.

'Perhaps he can't talk,' Reuven addresses his words to no one in particular. 'Perhaps he's dumb, or an imbecile.'

This last thought shakes him. He grips the boy, who struggles as hard as he can to escape. Reuven blinks and tightens his hold. If I let him go, he'll rush straight onto the road and get run over. On the other hand, what can I do? A policeman, perhaps. I won't leave him until his parents turn up.

Reuven pulls the child toward him and lifts him up. The boy howls and kicks, and dirties Reuven's white shirt front. He clasps him forcefully to his breast. Sharp little teeth bite his cheeks and hurt him terribly. He lets out an involuntary gasp and pulls the child's hair to get the teeth away from his face. The boy, released from his hold, falls to the ground and gives a loud shriek. Suddenly our poet feels a hard blow on the back of his neck and another in his ribs.

'Are you mad, damn you! Leave my son alone!'

'Who . . . who are you, friend? Are you the . . .'

'I'm going to break every bone in his body. Lunatic. Look, look what you've done to my little boy,' the juice seller shouts, his large mustache quivering with rage. His hard fist thuds into Reuven's ribs a second time. A curious crowd of grimacing, unfriendly watchers gathers in a tight ring around the quarrel.

'This madman picked up my little boy and threw him on the ground. The boy hadn't done anything to him, nothing at all. He almost killed him. This madman.'

'My friend,' Reuven stammers, 'the boy seemed . . . I only thought . . .'

'You thought no one was looking, eh, you scum? You thought you could get away with anything here, huh?'

'No, I didn't . . . I just saw a little boy without any . . .' Reuven tried to gain the sympathy of the mocking crowd. 'I wanted to . . .'

'Next time you mind your own business. Stay at home with your wife. Don't stick your nose in other people's affairs or you may get it punched in. Don't cry, Tsion, don't cry, sweetheart, Daddy'll kill the bastard on the spot if he's broken a bone in your body. Daddy'll kill him.'

Briskly the man set to work feeling his son's body. The boy, though hurt by his parent's rough squeezing, did not dare make a sound, but yielded his body obediently to his hands, looking at Reuven Harish the while, calmly, curiously, almost amicably.

'Lucky for you there's no damage done,' said the juice seller, concluding his hasty examination. 'If I'd found anything broken I'd tear you limb from limb, so help me, as sure as my name's Alfonse. Spit at the nasty man, Tsion darling, spit at him, that's right.'

*

131

Reuven Harish walked slowly on and turned into one of the many gloomy cafés in the narrow streets around the bus station. He staggered over to the filthy washbasin in the corner. He wetted his handkerchief, and tried to sponge the muddy stains off his crumpled shirt. Then he sat down, exhausted, at a table. He hid behind his newspaper and ordered a coffee without sugar. 'Scum,' he muttered to himself, biting his lip. 'Dregs of humanity.' The black coffee made him feel a little better. He was evidently agitated. His face was white as death. The hand holding the coffee cup was shaking. What should you do? You should take it calmly. Be composed. Be calm. Laugh at the man, my darling, my sweetheart, laugh at the beaten, kicked man. It hurts. It hurts here. And here.

He put his left hand to his chest. Tried to stifle the pain. Fierce spasms stabbed his chest. With no rhythm, no regularity. No fixed place. A wild orgy seemed to be breaking out in his body. His fingers felt numb and heavy; they were reluctant to obey his orders. Rebelliously they clenched themselves, relaxed, clenched again. In his left leg, too, in the ankle, he could feel a light, rapid pulse, as if the ankle were trying to tell him: I'm not attacking you yet, but remember that I'm alive, too, and that I hate you.

His vision was clouded, his throat felt strangled. His whole body was rebelling against him, giving vent to its base, treacherous hatred.

Reuven licked his lips: tongue and lips seemed alien. He instinctively wiped his eyes with his handkerchief. The mist did not clear. He remembered the mud on the handkerchief; he had probably rubbed it into his face now. Nausea gripped his stomach. A sickening lump rose in his gullet, caught there. He belched, and a bitter taste filled his mouth. The pain was still there, but far away, as if a thick screen separated the man from his pain. His head dropped with a thud onto the table, both hands clasping his temples.

A short, freckled waitress rushed over and asked if he felt ill. Reuven raised his head slowly, and stared at her like a child who wakes in the night and finds a strange face where he expected to see his mother.

'Another cup of coffee, please,' he said in a strangely soft voice.

The waitress nodded, but stayed where she was, looking at him as if she expected him to say something else. Reuven said:

'No. I'm sorry. Not coffee. A glass of water, please. Tap water, not from the refrigerator. Yes, I'm all right. It's nothing serious. Thank you.'

The pain was passing. The nausea remained. A strong feeling of gratitude washed like a hot wave through every fiber in his body. The waitress's concern affected him so powerfully that it was all he could do to hold back his tears. They're not all wolves. A powerful urge to kneel. To say a prayer. To be solemn.

What was it? What happened to me? The pain – mustn't, no, mustn't call it that terrible name. Just a rather powerful physical reaction. That's all.

When the waitress returned holding a lipstick-stained glass of water, Reuven turned towards her and said with a forced smile:

'So kind of you. Thank you very much indeed.'

Have a bit of a nap. People come. And go. Live their lives. And then go far away. Pretty country. Dams, canals, lots of flowers, windmills on the chocolate boxes, clouds, rain, white headdresses, bicycles. Far, far away. *Gott im Himmel,* how tired I am. It's terrible. A real man wouldn't behave like this. He'd behave differently. He'd have smashed that lecher Hamburger's face in. A fist. A knife. An alley. At night. Alfonse. Stella Maris will tell me why. My little daughter. Why isn't your father like a knife? Why isn't he Alfonse? Stella Maris because I'm not. Bronka because Stella. Ezra because Bronka. There's a formula, an equation. Very close. Written up behind a paper-thin wall. Lean on it. You'll break through it. Like a hero in a film. It all fits together somehow. Let's try again. From Eva to Bronka, then Noga. Bronka and Ezra. God, it's like a nightmare. Noga, Eva, Ezra, what. Where am I? Here. *Mein Gott,* why am I so calm, it was my heart Why pretend? *Aber was.* How silly.

A deep, familiar voice, a voice from somewhere else, interrupted his reverie. Could it be? Yes, it was.

'Incredible. Who'd believe it – Harismann himself, in person. Fancy seeing a man like you in a place like this.'

Reuven stood up. It was a meaningless gesture, politeness from another world. He greeted Ezra with exaggerated cordiality, as if (how absurd), as if he was the headwaiter of the place.

'Well, well, look who it isn't. Our Ezra. What a small world. This is quite a . . .' He hesitated for a moment. 'This is quite a meeting. Truly.'

'Amazing!' said the truck driver. 'A week ago I came in here at this sort of time, and who d'you think I suddenly saw?

Yitzhak Friedrich. Over there, at that table. And now today I come in, and who do I find sitting here? Harismann. Good morning, Harismann,' Ezra suddenly added in a different voice, as if to cancel everything that had been said so far and start the conversation afresh. Reuven showed no surprise; he accepted the change and simply said:

'Good morning, Ezra. I'm glad to see you.'

'Feel like a drink, Harismann?'

'Perhaps . . . if you . . .'

'Just the ticket; let's act first and hear the explanations later. You see before you, my good woman, two thirsty peasants. Fruit juice. Iced.'

'Ezra.'

'At your service.'

'Are you driving home now?'

' "And no one to take them home," as it says in the Book of Judges. But I, Berger, shall take you home, my dear Harismann. My truck shall be your truck. I still haven't discovered what a good man like you is doing in a filthy hole like this.'

The two men were sitting opposite each other, one slightly built in his filthy best clothes, the other massively built in an overall that was presumably gray. Ezra had come in here by chance, in search of a cold drink. He was rather amused by the chance encounter. Reuven, for his part, was pleased to see Ezra and did not try to analyze the reason why. It had not escaped the truck driver's attention that something had happened to his companion. He had a nasty wound on his cheek, and he was covered with mud all over. But Ezra was not one to pry. The conversation died out. Both men drank in silence. A little blue vein stood out on the back of Reuven's hand and beat with a rapid, unhealthy pulse. Ezra rolled a half-smoked cigarette between his fingers. It had gone out, but he did not try to relight it. Funny thing. Here we are, Harismann and I, and yet I don't. Something's happened to him. I mustn't look at him. If I look at him, he'll shut up. But he wants to tell me. And I want him to.

'Ezra,' Reuven began, but stopped without finishing his sentence.

'I'm listening. Speak on.'

'I . . . Are you in a hurry?'

Ezra shook his head without answering. His expression radiated sympathy, even though his eyes were still surrounded by fine wrinkles of amusement. Reuven fixed his glance on his empty glass and spoke in a monotone. Logically he ought to be laughing at my misfortune. But no. He's listening without gloating. What is he.

'They insulted me.' Reuven came to the conclusion of his story. 'They insulted me terribly. I might have sat here all day. If you hadn't come along. You think I'm exaggerating. You do, don't you? You think one ought to laugh off an incident like this, treat it as a joke. But . . .'

'You know what I'm going to say to you, Harismann?'

Reuven raised his eyes and looked for the first time into the other's.

'I say: come on. Let's get in the truck and go home. I've had one of those days, anyway. First I had a blockage in the fuel supply. Wasted time at a garage. And meanwhile my battery went flat. Out of the frying pan into the fire, as they say. Never mind. I'm not making another trip today. The truck will have to do without that pleasure for once.'

'We've got used to traveling at night, haven't we?' Ezra said to his truck, as he put his foot on the running board and opened the door for his guest. 'Open the window, Harismann. Why swelter in this heat? No, man, not that handle, that's the door handle. Are you trying to do the leap of death? The other one. That's it. She's not so young any more, this buggy. Once every handle had a label saying what it was, so there was no chance of making a mistake. Over the years they've worn off. Be careful next time.'

'I'm sorry,' Reuven apologized with a wan smile. 'Forgive me. I'm tired. I didn't do it on purpose.'

Ezra released the hand brake and maneuvered his way out of the narrow street. Reuven stared blankly ahead. Laboriously the truck made its way through one crowded street after another, halted from time to time by the threatening glare of a traffic light. Both men were silent, the one concentrating on driving, the other pressing his slight body against the door, trailing his arm out of the window. A greasy, sticky stench filled the cab. Now and again there came a welcome gust of cool sea air, which vanished almost as soon as it arrived. Ezra stuck his head out and swore at another driver. Reuven let the oath pass, out of fatigue. Once the brakes squeaked too sharply. The passenger's head hit the windshield. He let out a low groan. Ezra did not look round, too absorbed in the complicated journey through the crowded outskirts of the city. Eventually, the truck escaped and settled down to roaring in an even rate along the wide, flat road. It was Ezra who opened the conversation, a point we must note to his credit.

'Listen, Harismann, if you want a drink of coffee, there's a yellow thermos on the left. Your left, not mine. Have a look, there's a thermos wrapped up in newspaper. Go on, drink some, you'll feel better. By the way, exactly a week ago I happened to go into that very same café, and found – are you listening? – Friedrich. Funny, eh? Drink some coffee, go on. It's Nina Goldring's. Excellent coffee. Have some.'

Reuven refused with a shrug of the shoulders. Ezra, not surprisingly, failed to catch the answer. It is a natural mistake of someone who has never driven to answer a driver's question with a gesture.

'Are you asleep, Harismann?'

'No, no, I'm wide awake. Thanks all the same, I don't want a drink.'

Through the roar of the engine the driver misheard his reply.

'If you don't want to think, you can talk. I'm listening.'

'What? Oh, no, I didn't say "think," I said "drink." '

'Go on, drink some. Why not.'

'I'm sorry, we're talking at cross-purposes. I said I don't want anything to drink, thank you.'

Ezra gave him a sideways look and said in a surprised tone of voice:

'Well don't, then, if you don't want to. I'm not trying to force you.'

Reuven Harish said nothing. He tried to read his paper. The swaying of the truck made it difficult. And he felt sick again. He eyed the thickset driver and felt a sadness rising in him, which gave way at once to a different feeling, one of shy affection, such as thinkers sometimes experience in the company of men of action. To be more precise, he felt a kind of need to be liked.

The peaceful scenery of the plain of Sharon sped past the window. Neatly tended fields, new villages with their red roofs, fenced pasture lands, avenues of trees shading the road, water towers on the hilltops. Well-kept orchards, white-carpeted flower beds with their network of gleaming metal pipes. It should have been a soothing sight. But the harsh sun, the glass-blue sky, the fierce early-afternoon light, the straight road like a gash in the flesh of the green fields, for once all these depressed Reuven Harish. A man born in the gentle light of northern climes can never resign himself to the stark bright glare of this country. Even patriotic poems merely betray the poet's continual longing to come to terms with this cruel light.

For half an hour neither man broke the silence. Ezra Berger's heavy arms rested on the steering wheel. His body pressed almost lifelessly on the worn leather seat, giving off a smell of sweat. His cap covered half his face. Only his gnarled jaws were visible to the covert sideways gaze of his passenger. His face looked like a half-completed sculpture. His mouth hung slightly open. By the Netanya junction, Ezra drew two cigarettes out of his overcoat pocket, put one to his mouth and offered the other to Reuven.

'No thanks, I don't smoke,' Reuven replied, raising his voice to avoid another misunderstanding. Ezra grinned. After a moment or two he threw his cigarette out of the window.

'You're right,' he said. 'It's no good smoking when you're driving. It tastes funny, and you get no enjoyment out of it.

And if you don't enjoy it, why smoke, as the sages would have said if smoking had been invented in their day.'

Reuven had said nothing of the sort, but he did not trouble to explain. He was afraid that the noise of the engine would distort his words yet again. It was only as they were approaching Hedera that he felt a resurgence of that feeling of shy affection, or the shy need to be liked, and he tried to start a simple conversation. 'Ezra.'

'Yes. I'm listening.'

'Don't you get bored, driving all the time? I suppose . . .'

'No. Not at all. I always think when I'm driving. Let us follow our thoughts, as the Prophet says. Thinking isn't only the prerogative of poets.'

'Inner life,' Reuven said enthusiastically. 'True wealth consists in having a rich inner life, that's what I say.'

'That's right. The wise man has eyes in his head, as the Bible says. I'm not a wise man, but I do know how to think. If you think the same thought a hundred times, it ends up by being very refined.'

'It can lead to melancholy,' said Reuven vaguely.

'It can lead to anything. But if you think systematically, it always leads to the same thing.'

Reuven cast an anxious glance in his direction. What is he getting at? Not that. He shouldn't have said anything. Not that.

'One thing and one thing alone: that we're not getting any younger, Harismann, you, me, the others. The best part of our journey's behind us. You understand what I'm talking about. We all have to die some time. When we were young, we used to think that one dies only once, and that one should die gloriously, as they say. Now we've reached the age. You remember how Ramigolski went? He was a good friend of mine, but I think we've made a kind of false saint of him. I know they say never speak ill of the dead, and all that, but we've come to celebrate his death like a carnival, as if it was good that someone should have died early on, good from an educational point of view, as it were, do you understand – are you asleep? No? Well, at our age, we must realize one fact: the important thing isn't to die gloriously, it's to die as late as possible. Another ten years, another twenty years. My father was already dead when he was my age. So what? So it means I've gained something. "It is better for me to die than to live," "would God I had died for you." Those verses may be allegorical or something, it's not my field, but they're not true. Am I right, Harismann?'

'Let me explain,' Reuven began, but stopped when Ezra laid a heavy hand on his knee.

'Wait. I haven't finished what I was saying. Yesterday, at the Megiddo turning, I saw a shocking accident. You see terrible things every day on the roads.'

Reuven bit his lip and said nothing.

'Are you tired? Do you want to have a nap? Wait. I'll tell you. On the hill going down to the turning for Megiddo there was a truck parked, with a long load of iron rods. Those rods they use on reinforced concrete buildings. Apparently the driver was sitting having a rest. Up comes a giant semitrailer, knocks into the back of him, and pushes the rods through the rear window of the cab. Spitted him like skewered meat. Through the neck. He didn't have a chance. So you can get killed even

141

without doing anything wrong. That's what really shakes you, when you suddenly see how fragile we are. It's terrible.'

'Terrible,' echoed Reuven. Ezra went on talking, strangely, compulsively.

'Now, listen. Sometimes at night you're dazzled by someone's headlights. You drive by instinct. You can't see anything. You're entirely dependent on your instinct. Now tell me this, think carefully and tell me: What is instinct? What is it? It's something capricious, something irrational, completely mysterious. And don't forget: you can't see anything at all with your eyes. You're blinded. Are you asleep, Harismann? No? Still listening? Blinded. *Smite this people with blindness*. For a few seconds you're entirely dependent on your instinct. If it lets you down, you'll die blinded. Then you'll find out just how fragile you are. Like losing in a lottery. Like . . . like tearing paper. Like water.'

'Tell me, Ezra, do you think . . .'

'But it's not just when you're dazzled, not just when you see a fatal road accident. You find yourself thinking that kind of thought any time, for no apparent reason. When you see a skeleton, all bare and white, in a film, you're scared, aren't you? Yes, of course you are. But a skeleton just like that goes with you everywhere. Do you want to have a drink of coffee from the thermos? No? When you eat, when you write, when you laugh, even when you shop, there's always a white skeleton with you, with white ribs, with a skull and teeth and gaping sockets instead of eyes, as in all the pictures. When you have a woman, for instance, it's really just two skeletons grinding together. And if you can't hear the terrible noise which would

142

turn the whole thing into a macabre joke, that's just because there's still a soft layer in between. But it's only temporary, Harismann, it's perishable, it's made of a moist substance that rots easily. It's a very frail wrapping, do you see. You're probably half asleep, aren't you? I just wanted to say that we're very fragile. Amazingly so. If only . . . at least . . . But what's come over me? You're tired, and I'm talking on and on. I'm sure everything I've been saying is written in books. I've probably tired you terribly. "Speech is silver, silence is golden," as they say. You can go to sleep now. We've got another hour and a half's drive ahead of us. You're very tired. You're worn out. I want you to sleep. Sleep. I promise not to drive the truck down the mountainside. Sleep peacefully. I'm not carrying iron rods this time. You can rest assured, as they say. Yes.'

14

Mounting Evidence

DURING THE days preceding the festival, gossip reached fever pitch. If the signs were to be believed, something very strange and disturbing had happened in our kibbutz. One night Israel Tsitron, who was on duty as night watchman, overheard a quarrel. From him we learned that all was not well between Noga and her boy friend, the widow's son, Rami. This was confirmed by the evidence of Dafna Isarov, even if there were some who disputed the details of her disturbing story. According to Dafna, one evening, one Friday night, Rami Rimon had burst into the room that she and Noga shared and attacked Noga by main force. Later, Ezra Berger had appeared and had clashed with Rami, at first with words but later with blows. Eventually, Rami had burst out of the room, looking, Dafna said, very strange. A strange friendship had certainly come into being – so testified the widow Fruma Rominov, between Reuven Harish's daughter and Bronka's husband.

Of course. Now that this news has come to our notice, we connect it with what we have seen with our own eyes but not thought much about. For some days now we have observed the man and the girl chatting together in the early afternoon by the motor shed. Up to now we have seen nothing wrong in these conversations. If the rumors are true, we have been very naïve. It is alleged that Ezra Berger buys his little friend embroidery thread over and above the kibbutz ration and pays for it out of his own pocket. In return, the girl has made him an embroidered bag for his sandwiches. Nina Goldring, who supplies the sandwiches, has seen the bag with her own eyes. It has a bear embroidered on it.

Is it right or proper for the two of them to meet in broad daylight in the middle of the yard, in the shadow of the huge truck, and for the older man to finger the girl's chin and mutter his pointless proverbs to her? Is it right for her to respond with musical laughter, and even slap him on his hairy shoulder? No, it's not right, it's not proper, it smacks of licentiousness.

If we are to believe Dafna, things have gone even further. Noga has got into the habit of getting up in the middle of the night and stealing across to the shed behind the laundry building to meet the driver on his return. Admittedly, Dafna is suspected of exaggerating. It would only be natural. But there is no denying that the affair has gone too far. There is more to it than meets the eye. We are cautious of our judgment. We base our opinion not on Dafna's evidence, which is not universally accepted, but on that of Mundek Zohar, who is a reliable witness. His evidence is decisive, and we shall record it presently. Of Noga Harish it was said that her mother Eva's hot blood flowed in her veins. Of Ezra Berger, Herzl Goldring said, 'Is it any wonder that his Oren is a delinquent? The apple never falls far from the tree.' There were some (Fruma Rominov seems to have been the first to voice this alarming idea) who said that this was Ezra's way of having his revenge. And so on.

For some days we scrutinized the faces of Reuven and Bronka, looking for signs. 'He who sows the wind will reap the whirlwind,' said Grisha Isarov, parodying the truck driver's cryptic style of utterance.

Einav, quietly waiting for the end of her pregnancy, said to her husband Tomer one evening:

'He's in the news, your father.'

Tomer shrugged his shoulders and said nothing.

'I think you ought to do something about it. It's your family, after all.'

But Tomer, whose young body had no rival in the arduous work of haymaking, gave his wife a sneering look, spread out his massive arms and said:

'Why me? I'm not his father. If the old man wants to make a fool of himself, good luck to him. Mother's not much better than he is.'

*

True, Bronka is no better than her husband. It was she who started it all. But this fact does nothing to relieve her present unhappiness. Often, in bed, she turns her face to the wall and cries. Reuven bites his lip and does not talk about it. What can he say? He strokes her cheek affectionately and says nothing. His heart is heavy. He has not changed his habits, though. Every evening he crosses the lawn to Bronka and stays with her until just before Ezra gets back. But for some days now he has resumed the habit of the early days of their friendship, when it was still pure and intellectual. He is content to sit with her, drink coffee, munch grapes, talk awkwardly about art, until Bronka buries her face in her hands and collapses into long fits of sobbing.

If there is a letter from Zechariah-Siegfried in Munich, Bronka gives it to Reuven so that he can read his wife's brief lines. Then they sit side by side on the divan, holding hands. Reuven is as silent as a boy who is in love for the first time. Bronka, too, is silent. She is knitting a hat for her future granddaughter. Sometimes he brings a book with him, and they read it together, as in the good old days. Once Bronka gazed at Reuven's lips and said:

'What's going to happen? Tell me, tell me.'

'It's going to be bad,' said Reuven.

Still the worst did not happen. It is true that Noga sometimes woke up in the middle of the night and slipped through the darkness behind the shrubbery to meet the man on his return. But Ezra, with clumsy affection, rested her head on his sweaty

146

chest, stroked it consolingly, and sent her back to bed. Once he even kissed her. Mundek Zohar, who was on duty that night, saw it with his own eyes and is ready to swear to it, and Mundek is a reliable witness. But it was so dark that the watchman could not see the girl's hot tears, and so he misjudged the nature of the kiss. It was a warm-hearted, paternal kiss, the purest thing in the world.

15

Woman

AT THE end of the week came the *hamsin*. From the mountain range in the east a murderous dryness flowed down to engulf us. The sky was gray, as if the desert had risen to float upside down over our tiny roofs. The heat tore at our vitality with its cruel claws, bringing desperate weariness, tormenting the body and oppressing the soul. Hens died by the dozen, despite the elaborate cooling system. Obstinacy took hold of the cows, and Herbert Segal was reduced to driving them into the milking shed with a whip. The trees grew gray and whispered drily. Scorched yellow patches appeared in the lawns. The men and women of the kibbutz quarrelled violently over trifles. Decency restrains us from relating the words that Fruma Rominov hurled at Bronka Berger on one of these terrible days. But this much we may say, that Bronka, shaken, arrived at Reuven Harish's room during the afternoon, beckoned to him to come outside, so that the children should not hear, and announced breathlessly that she could not put up with any more of it, and that it was up to him, for God's sake, to do what any real father would have done long ago.

And so it was Fruma Rominov's judgment which brought about, even indirectly, the conversation between father and daughter that up to now Reuven Harish had tried to avoid.

They were strolling together in front of the kibbutz office. It was eight o'clock in the evening. The air was dark and stifling. They spoke softly.

'I wanted to ask you if you think, Noga.'

'What sort of question's that, Daddy? I don't understand what you mean.'

'If you think. If you've thought a single thought these last weeks, or if you've given up thinking altogether.'

'I'm not the tourists, Daddy, so please talk frankly to me, don't beat about the bush.'

'I'll talk, Noga. I'll talk. I'll talk in a moment. I won't beat about the bush. And I want you to talk to me, too, completely openly. Sincerely.'

'Don't I always?'

'Perhaps. Tell me, Noga, do you know what people here have been saying about you recently?'

'What have people here been saying about me recently, Daddy?'

'You know very well what they've been saying. Gossip. Nasty gossip.'

'It's always unhappy people who say unkind things.'

'I . . . I want us to understand each other, Noga. Don't force me to say unkind things, too.'

'Why, are you unhappy?'

'Why are you fighting against me, Noga? It hurts me. I don't want us to fight. I want you to be happy.'

'It's hot, Daddy. I'm hot. We're all hot. It's the *hamsin*. Why do you want to talk about gossip now? Why do you think that life is all about talking? There are other things. Not just words. Words aren't everything. Why must you always explain everything? Why has everything got to be explained? The sky won't fall if something isn't explained.'

'There are things . . .'

'Yes. I know. There are things. Fruma said something nasty to Bronka. I know, Dafna heard it and told me. I hate words. It's because of those words that you've come to talk to me now, when we're so hot. That's enough. Let's stop.'

'Never mind about Fruma and never mind about Bronka. I want to talk to you, Noga. About you.'

'You want to talk and you talk all the time but you don't really talk.'

'I am talking. I'm talking about your new . . . friendship, to call a spade a spade. I only want to know one thing: if you think at all.'

'Friendship?'

'Yes.'

'Ezra?'

'I . . . yes. Ezra.'

'Tell me, do you feel . . . embarrassed? Do you find it diffi-cult to ask me things straight out? I've got to keep away from

Ezra because Bronka . . . Oh, it's simple, it's simple. Daddy, so simple, and you're walking on tiptoe as if I was made of glass. I'm not made of glass. I understand. It's simple. Either you and Bronka or me and Ezra, and you were first, so you have first claim. It's so simple, Daddy.'

'Noga . . . Stella, listen . . . Why do you . . . Why do you have to put it . . . Listen to me for a moment.'

'I'm listening, Daddy, I'm listening to every word, all the time. You don't have to ask me to listen. I'm all ears.'

Reuven Harish is a little perplexed. In his embarrassment he tugs lightly at his upper lip, searching for the right words. The heat blurs his mind. The perspiration from his hand smudges his face, and the perspiration from his face sticks to his hand. A strange stabbing stirs in his chest but dies down before it becomes painful. Stella, meanwhile, a naughty little deer, turns her back on him and paws the earth with her foot. On her face is a grimace, which is almost a smile. Reuven tries to stroke her neck. She moves out of reach.

'Let me put it another way, Noga. Look. You're not a child, right? I'm not trying to interfere with your private life. But I don't want you to ruin your life. That's all. That's the only thing I'm talking about.'

'You're sweet, Daddy,' Noga says suddenly. 'You're really sweet.'

Her face shines in the dark. But her teeth, strangely, chatter as if she is ill. He's suffering. He's suffering, and now he's going to start talking about Mother. Oh, poor Daddy, silly Daddy, if only you realized that I'm on your side, only I can't say so because . . .

Reuven is suffering. This is not how he imagined the conversation. She's eluding me. I talk to her, and she dances circles round me. What is she thinking? You can never tell what they're thinking. They dance. You talk and they dance. They're both the same. Outwardly they look calm, but inside, a raving demon. But not her. I won't let her. She's mine.

Affectionately, half-jokingly, Reuven asked:

'To come to the point, Stella, what demon's got into you?'

Affectionately, half-jokingly, Noga answered:

'A wonderful demon, Daddy. A sad, wise demon, full of love. Sometimes he's frightening, but he's a gentle demon. A tired demon.'

'Now I'll tell you something,' Reuven said. 'Something about your mother.'

'No,' said Noga. 'Not that. I won't listen.'

'Yes. You will listen. You must listen,' said Reuven Harish, pressing home to the full his unexpected advantage.

'No. I don't have to. I won't listen. I won't listen to anything.'

'When that wretch Hamburger came, your mother loathed him. I'm not exaggerating: she loathed him, but she behaved politely. He was a close relative; they had grown up in the same house together, but apparently the war corrupted him. That was what your mother thought. She said that he wasn't himself. He wasn't the little boy who had been betrothed to her when she was a little girl. He was someone else. A clown imitating the speech and manners of that dead boy. Well, then. Actually he spent the war in Switzerland, making money by speculating. I'll tell you about that, too, some time. Your mother said she hoped he'd leave soon. Tomorrow. At once.

I was the one who urged her to behave politely toward him. After all, he'd had a hard life. He'd suffered a lot. But your mother hated him. He was clever. He used to say things like "tame partridge" and laugh a slimy laugh. Your mother asked him to shut up, for heaven's sake. He would wink and say, for instance, *"Gold und Silber"* or *"Raus, raus, Dichter."* These remarks hurt your mother terribly. He talked a great deal about women, by the way.'

'I'm not listening.'

'I looked after him most of the time because your mother didn't like to be near him. I took the wretched creature to Jerusalem, Sodom, Elat. Every place, every sight, every name reminded him of some obscenity or dirty joke. He made a point of spending a lot of money on me. Tried to be friendly with his great toothy horse smiles. He had enormous teeth. He talked about women. And he winked.'

'I'm not listening.'

'Once we were coming out of the dining hall, he and your mother and I, and he asked with a wink if it was true that we practiced free love here. The smile showed all those teeth of his. Your mother was so disgusted she ran off. When she came back, he sang some German nursery rhyme about Franzi the gardener peeping into the cellar and watching the prince's children praying. Make him go away tomorrow, your mother said that night, make him go at once. Tomorrow. He didn't stay with us long. Perhaps a fortnight. Then suddenly . . .'

'I'm not listening to a word you're saying. You're talking to thin air.'

'Then one day I went to Tel Aviv, Stella dear, one awful day, and the next day I came home and there was nothing left. Some madness had taken hold of your mother. She went off with that swine. But in her heart, Noga my darling, in her heart I know she regrets it all. Her infatuation ruined me. Me. Us. She wrote me a long letter from Europe a month later, pouring her heart out. Her Isaac was a little angel once; they used to play duets together on the piano when they were little, read poetry, write, draw, but suffering had corrupted him, and she felt it was up to her, and her alone, to purify him. That was how we lost your mother. You were just a little toddler then.'

'Daddy, don't say any more. Be nice. Please, please stop, Daddy.'

'Her infatuation ruined everything. I'm not beating about the bush now. I'm telling you straight out, Noga.'

'You did the same to someone else.'

'No, I didn't. How can you compare it? Bronka and I . . .'

'You and Bronka. Me and Ezra. That's life. It's not made of words. It's ugly. I want you to stop now. Stop talking.'

Then, for no reason, the girl dragged her father over to the shadow of a nearby tree and kissed his face, uttering as she did so a sob that sounded like a smothered laugh or a puppy's crying. Reuven stifled his words and gently stroked his daughter's hair and murmured, 'Stella, Stella,' and whispered to her to be careful, and Noga – in the soft low voice of another woman – told Reuven that she loved him now and always, while the *hamsin* raged relentlessly, unmoved even by powerful emotions.

Noga went to the abandoned stable to wait for Ezra's return.
The darkness and the ancient smells of decay frightened her
for once, and so she waited at the entrance to the stable. She
sat down on a dark, rotting board and thought. Suffering corrupted him, and she felt it was up to her, and her alone, to
purify him. This is where we found the rope. It wasn't very
long ago. It's a long time since there were horses here. Horses
aren't used any more. They've had their day. A horse is a splendid animal. A horse is a powerful animal. There's a contradiction in a horse. He can be wild, and rush over the plains.
A horse has a wild smell when he sweats. I feel dizzy when I
think of a horse's smell. He had enormous teeth, like a horse,
Daddy said. A galloping horse is the most beautiful animal in
the world. He spent the war in Switzerland, making money by
speculating. Speculation is wrong. Franzi the gardener, what
did Franzi the gardener see, what were the prince's children
doing in a dark cellar? And what did he mean by 'tame partridge'? How clumsy he looked when he poured the water I
brought him down his throat without putting the mug to his
lips, and the water splashed onto his chin and trickled down
his neck and vanished into the hair on his chest. How strong.
When he's driving, he thinks about the Bible, about Rachel,
and Leah, for instance, and their children. 'Leah' can mean
'tired' in Hebrew. That's pretty, but sad. He didn't even know
what turquoise was, but I taught him because I'm responsible
for him. What does *Raus, raus, Dichter* mean? I wish I knew.
Outside it's hot in the stable it's nice and cool I'm frightened to
go inside don't be frightened Franzi the gardener is a good man
he won't tell on the little princess. Mummy was prettier than

me. Her light blue dressing gown I wore once and he met me on the path and said *Gold und Silber* and looked at me not at my face then he turned his head and looked away. Daddy's sure she regrets it all in her heart. You don't regret in your heart. Only in literary language. He asked if we practiced free love here. Mummy wanted him to go away. But I'm Daddy's daughter, too. Green eyes. It's true. Now listen carefully, Ezra, there's one thing you've got to remember. I love a horse because he's wild and I have to purify because I'm responsible. It's almost midnight. Not long now. Soon you'll. Old Franzi, the gardener, shame on his peeping eyes. And, you know, there's a contradiction in the color turquoise: it's blue and it's green, like a horse, which can be mild or wild.

Ezra spent a long time tonight with his friends the fishermen in Tiberias. He got home to the kibbutz at one o'clock in the morning. Noga had leaped up onto the running board before the truck stopped. She put her head into the cab and smiled, and her teeth chattered. She must be ill, flushed with fever. Go to bed, little girl, you're trembling all over, are you crazy. Yes, Ezra, yes, yes. You're not well, little one, get moving, Turquoise, forward march – to bed, do you hear, little baby, don't argue now. No, I can't hear, Ezra, I can't hear a word. You're ill, silly, you've got a temperature. *Little bear is feeling ill, stayed up late and caught a chill.* Don't talk, Ezra, I don't want you to talk, I want you to put your arms round me and explain to me what 'tame partridge' means and two more words I've forgotten. No, you're confused, Turquoise, you don't know what you're doing. I do know. I know what I want. I want you to put your arms round me and not talk and not talk in proverbs. And not talk.

Ezra took hold of her thin arm and tried to take her to her room. Noga wouldn't let him. She fought back. She stood rooted to the spot. Ezra didn't want to take her to her room by force. Perplexed, he paused and looked at her, desperately tired. The night air was still thick and oppressive. In the distance dogs howled wildly, and the jackals howled in answer. The night was full of dim anger. Trembling all over, Noga clung to the man's powerful body. He tried to prise her loose. She gripped his clothes with her nails. Delicious kisses on his hairy, sweat-matted chest. Backward she dragged him step by tiny step into the thick darkness of the myrtle bushes. Who taught her tongue to lick his salty neck so tenderly? Or her fingers to play so cleverly on the back of his head? Overcome, he fell, his heavy hands on her shoulders. His voice betrayed him, no longer forming words, only dry groans. Noga was terrified. She regretted it now and tried to escape. His grip was heavy, frightening. Her eyes flickered and went out. Her body awoke and filled with sweet gushes. Warm shudders flowed from one sweet part of her to another. Her breath came in pants, her mouth stretched wide open, her tiny teeth dug again and again into the blind flesh. The ground beneath her stirred, sending quivering ripples through her. On spreading ripples her body floated. Torrents flooded over her, bursting out strong and cruel from forgotten lairs. Wave after wave after wave. The confusion whirled in a cycle, in a burning rhythm. Boiling water battered her body. Boiling oil. Burning poison. Sweet seething poison slicing down into the marrow of her bones.

An imprisoned scream, flash after flash swept away into the water, the waves were not black, they were gleaming, dazzling flares capering in the water, a streaming jet swept her sick body toward roaring waterfalls.

Two or three hours later. Dawn light outlining the slats of the shutters. She turns between her sheets. Strange, secret sensations. Her body curls up compulsively, her knees drawn up to her chin, pressing against her breasts, her fingers caressing her skin. Drop by drop, like rain in a gutter, a song dripped inside her:

> From the Dead Sea to Jericho
> The pomegranate sweetly smells,
> A pair of eyes, a pair of doves,
> And a voice like the sound of bells.

She can hear them in her skin. She can hear the bells.

16

Hatred

FOR SIX more days the *hamsin* oppressed us relentlessly. If you reached out to touch a bench, a wall, an irrigation tap, a stair rail, the inanimate object responded with incandescent hatred. Reuven Harish found relief from the oppression – incredible though it may seem – by casting it in a poetic mold.

Blazing heat, down you beat
On scorpion's lair and snake's retreat.
Leaving your arid desert seat,
The home of Genie and Afrit,
You stamp the plains with scorching feet,
Stifling everything you meet.
Panting souls find no retreat,
Strongest men admit defeat;
Gasping voices beg, entreat
Relief from yellow, parching heat.

Meanwhile, the enemy's provocations intensified. Frequent shots were fired into our fields, by day as well as by night. There were no casualties, however. The enemy were careful not to overstep the mark. They were content to harass us, and remind us that they were there, bent on our destruction.

At the end of the week a small army unit dug itself in the vineyards and pointed machine guns at the enemy positions installed halfway up the slope, on the territory that was the bloodstained subject of dispute between the two states. Our troops had orders not to provoke the enemy. If the enemy launched a serious action, if a stray tractor was cut off by firing, they were to cover it and extricate it. But they were forbidden to return random fire, so as not to aggravate the prevailing tension. They also had orders to dig some trenches, so that people working in outlying fields could take cover if attacked. Digging trenches during the stifling *hamsin,* even at night, is not the most pleasant of tasks. Our soldiers found assistance from an unexpected quarter: Oren Geva and his friends appeared one afternoon to offer their help. Before the commanding officer had managed to dismiss the intruders with a reprimand, they had already dug two or three magnificent trenches. The officer shrugged his shoulders and showed them where and how.

This new problem provoked conflicting opinions among the schoolteachers on the kibbutz. According to Herbert Segal, in addition to the obvious danger to which our children were exposed, it would also encourage militaristic attitudes. It was the forceful opinion of Reuven Harish, curiously, that swayed the balance. In the first place, he said, who could stop them. Second, it would provide a constructive outlet for their excess energies.

For several days the lads threw themselves into their work with a will. They worked well, and they were handsomely rewarded: a pat on the back from the commanding officer for Oren Geva, the satisfaction of being in the front lines, some rich additions to their vocabulary, the privilege of secretly handling the gleaming weapons, and even – pray that no word of it reaches hostile ears – unofficial permission to clean and oil a submachine gun.

In the dining hall after supper small groups gather to discuss the situation. Some decipher and interpret the signs; others hold that the enemy is simply out to demonstrate his presence; others maintain that we are witnessing the prelude to a big show, such as we saw three months ago, when they began by ambushing a tractor and ended up battering a kibbutz with heavy gunfire.

The other topic of conversation is the question of reprisals. Most of the older members think that it would be better for us not to heap coals on the fire. So long as the enemy refrains from launching a real attack, argues Mundek Zohar, head of the regional council, we are better off showing our contempt by maintaining a dignified silence. Podolski looks up from the work rotas to agree with Mundek Zohar and adds that we mustn't allow ourselves to play into their hands by doing what they want us to do.

The youngsters think differently, as is only natural. Tomer Geva lays a large hand on Podolski's lean shoulder and says: Podolski, Podolski, I'm very sad to have to inform you that the dear Arabs haven't read Tolstoy or Rosa Luxemburg, and I'm afraid they're not too well up in Mahatma Gandhi, either. But there's one language they're perfectly at home in. Without a crushing blow, a really juicy blow, as they say, we'll never stop the bastards and their blasted nuisance.

Grisha Isarov, though not a young man, has a youthful temperament. He endorses Tomer's sentiments and remarks: Prevention is better than cure, Mundek, and your fine ideas can cost lives. As for you, Podolski, you've nothing to fear. They're brave when they scent weakness and cowards when you show them a fist. I've known them for thirty years now. They haven't changed and they'll never change. Once, in '46, I went out to set an ambush for a gang of them. Not an ordinary ambush, though . . .

Meanwhile, the military authorities maintained a total silence. One Friday evening we had a visit from a group of high-ranking officers. We received them in the dining hall with cold drinks and fruit. They answered all our questions with a smile and a shake of the head. Afterward, they strolled around outside for twenty minutes, exchanging a few words in an undertone, while an undersized captain ran around energetically rolling and unrolling maps for them. At the same time, he made signs to the curious youngsters to keep their distance. Gai Harish's young gang observed the visitors from a respectful distance, their mouths agape, their heads cocked, their fair hair falling over their foreheads, and wonder blazing in their eyes.

Grisha Isarov's prestige took a mighty leap that night. Among the senior officers he discovered an old comrade from the days of the Jewish Brigade. They fell on each other and exchanged hearty bear hugs, while the youngsters looked on in amazement. Grisha was even allowed to join the officers for the last few minutes of their conference, but unfortunately he did not manage to adapt his voice to their hushed tones but expressed his opinions at the top of his voice. The seven Isarov children, including Dafna, basked in a halo of glory that night.

On Sunday another small group of officers visited us, this time a group of lower rank. They inspected the shelters and the trenches, and looked rather apprehensively at the telephone wire that emerged from the kibbutz office and ran along the lawn on a series of rough wooden poles. One of them detached himself from the group to peer into the surgery and examine the nurse's supplies. Finally, they sat down at an isolated table in the dining hall to jugs of fruit juice and baskets of fruit. They invited Tsvi Ramigolski, the secretary of the kibbutz, to join them, together with Grisha Isarov, with his tousled mustache and his wading boots, and two or three younger men, such as Tomer Geva, who had served as officers in the army.

What a pity that the latter haughtily refused to pass on to us the gist of that fascinating conversation. In reply to your questions they merely shook their heads secretively. If you persisted and pestered them and swore yourself to secrecy, they relented enough to dismiss you with a half-sentence such as:

'It's going to be hot.'

Oren's gang, too, in their usual sly way, were prepared to inform you:

'It's going to be a big show.'

The youngest group, Gai and his friends, promptly translated the hints into action. On Monday evening the kibbutz yard was full of shouting and bustle, scampering footsteps and sounds of battle, and at nightfall the little hill that faces the kibbutz gates to the west was stormed, and the Israeli flag planted on it with great pomp and circumstance.

Even to someone like ourselves, far removed from military matters, it was perfectly obvious that something was afoot, in the stifling heat of the *hamsin*. Grisha Isarov, who was responsible for security, had already taken several hours off his work in the fish ponds and enlisted the help of two or three other members in cleaning out and putting straight the shelters and the trenches.

Grisha Isarov, a man of forty or so, was not one of the founders of our kibbutz. He joined us two years before the Second World War. When war broke out, he volunteered for the Jewish Brigade and reached the rank of sergeant major in

Her Majesty's Armed Forces. After the war he returned to the kibbutz, heavier, mustached, and with an inexhaustible fund of anecdotes. No wonder that Esther Klieger, a nursery-school teacher with an amazing knack for carving abstract sculptures out of tree stumps, succumbed to his charms. Grisha did not rest quietly for long. Within three or four months of returning from the war in Italy, he had succeeded in getting Esther with child, marrying her, and joining the underground army. His exploits as a company commander in the struggle for independence he will be happy to recount to you till midnight, and if he is busy in the fish ponds, then you can hear the stories either from his plump daughter Dafna or from any one of his six other children, who are all as heavily built as their father and all marked, boys and girls alike, with a fine down on their upper lip, which Grisha jokingly refers to as the badge of his unit.

If it had not been for a certain unfortunate incident, Grisha might have risen to high rank in the army; he might have joined the group of senior officers that Friday night in his own right and not as a favor. The details of the misdemeanor that put a premature end to Grisha Isarov's promising military career are not known for certain. According to our old ally, gossip, it concerned a punishment inflicted on one of the men under his command, which exceeded the bounds of military regulations. According to Grisha himself, the modern Israeli army is better suited to tin soldiers than to fighting men. A man of his caliber would not waste his life and talents in an army of halberdiers and gay hussars commanded by chocolate-box admirals.

Anyway, a couple of years after the end of the War of Independence Grisha returned to Metsudat Ram for good and shouldered the arduous responsibility of the fish ponds. His bluff, hearty manner endears him to all around him. His numerous progeny, too, give rise to good-humored jests. Grisha Isarov also manages the security of the kibbutz with whole-hearted enthusiasm, though not without a hint of frivolity. Occasionally, for instance, he straightens his massive back, lays down the fish nets, and hurls vehement Arabic curses at the enemy positions. Or sometimes he sways his hips at them like an enormous belly dancer and gives a hideous laugh. But he is not the kind of man to overlook such trivial tasks as repairing a torn stretcher, taking stock of the ammunition, or his recent effort of cleaning out and putting straight the shelters and trenches.

It was a difficult period for Herzl Goldring. He hardly had time to play his accordion. Because of the heat the plants needed to be watered at least twice as often as normally, and even that did little good. There were not enough rubber hoses for the job. Time and again he had pestered Yitzhak Friedrich, the treasurer, for a small sum to buy plastic hose pipes, but each time Frederick the Great had fobbed him off with excuses; either it's the beginning of the month, and how can we tell whether we'll have enough cash to see it out, or else it's the end of the month, and who has cash to lay out at the end of the month. If he'd asked for a large amount, he'd have got it by now. But if you need a small sum for a vital purpose, they fob you off with one excuse after another. It's symptomatic of the whole place. So Herzl Goldring grumbles to his wife Nina as they sit on their little veranda in the evening, with the light out.

All round the kibbutz grounds you see plants drooping, withering, fainting with the heat. Before you've fixed up the hose to water the flowers on one side of the kibbutz, those on the other side have started to wilt. And Herzl Goldring is a man who feels physical pain at the sight of a dying plant, because he loves his work.

Herzl Goldring's dedication to his flower beds is a byword in the kibbutz. He belongs to the German faction, and in his heart of hearts he has never managed to reconcile himself to the ways of the Russians. They're so inconsistent. One day they're all sympathy and plead to be allowed to help you after their work, laying and weeding the lawns; another day they turn a deaf ear to all your requests and entreaties and empty a barrowload of building rubble on the same lawn that they so eagerly volunteered to help make. True, Herzl's wife is also a Russian. But Nina is unique among her countrywomen for her reserved manner. For many years she has borne the burden of managing the kitchen stores, generating a spirit of economy, cleanliness, and open-mindedness. Like her husband, she is gifted with a fine aesthetic sense. Their room, tastefully furnished in a European style, is gleaming and spotless. True, the pretty rugs, bookcases, and chest of drawers were acquired with money that Herzl received from the German government in reparation for his family's lost fortune, but he should not be judged harshly on this account. The money he received was paid over almost in its entirety to Yitzhak Friedrich. We must not criticize him for keeping a small sum to furnish his home and buy himself an accordion. What else was there left in his life? Their only daughter had died in her infancy of diphtheria.

Being childless, they naturally wanted to make the most of their modest home. It was a venial human weakness.

As rumor has it, the Goldrings are not a happy couple. Every evening they sit in easy chairs on the darkened veranda, saying nothing, doing nothing. Sometimes Herzl has to go and turn off a sprinkler; he promises Nina not to be long, and he keeps his word. Their house is quiet. The only sounds in the evening come from the radio and from Herzl's accordion. He plays march tunes, to our perpetual surprise. The Goldrings have their supper early, before the dining room gets too full. They greet everyone, strangers included, but it is impossible to engage them in friendly conversation. Herzl agrees blankly to everything you say to him, as if he only wants to be left in peace. Nina reacts with exaggerated concern, as if she is trying hard to make you think she is interested in you, whereas in fact she is only interested in making you believe that she is interested in you.

Herzl takes no part in kibbutz meetings, except to complain from time to time about the destruction of his plants. On such occasions he reddens, wrinkles his nose, and announces indifferently that if they want his resignation, he is prepared to tender it on a moment's notice. If his arguments are accepted, he goes on to say that actions speak louder than words, and leaves the meeting immediately, since the other items on the agenda are no concern of his. If they are not accepted, he states that his resignation takes effect forthwith, and leaves the meeting immediately, for the same reason. But at six o'clock the next morning he shatters the silence of the yard with his lawn mower, as usual, and makes no reference to his threat.

Every few days he loses his temper for some trivial reason and snarls an acid 'I wish you were dead' at someone, then returns to his customary politeness. Some of our young people, either because of the irritating noise of his lawn mower or for some other reason, nickname Herzl Goldring 'the dentist.' The title is not witty, and it does not meet with our approval.

Despite everything, he is a wonderful gardener, and his devotion, imagination, and taste have turned our kibbutz into a garden of delights. Thanks to him, we have none of the unsightly plots, beds of weeds, and piles of rubble that you find in the grounds of some kibbutzim. It would be even lovelier if it were not for the mischievous Russians. That has been Herzl Goldring's opinion for many years. They lack the most basic cultured instincts. Is culture a matter of booklearning and long words? No. Far from it. No, Reuven Harish, culture is a matter of everyday life, of taking trouble over details, of cultivating a general aesthetic sense. These people walk across the lawns, making ugly bare strips, dump rubbish among the bushes, trample down the young seedlings, and why? Just to take a short cut or out of pure thoughtlessness. How sad that our children, including those of the Germans, pick up this corrupt culture, this false culture. It gets worse every day. Corruption is like bindweed: if you don't eradicate it ruthlessly, it kills everything.

Herzl Goldring looks at you through his sunglasses. His look is embarrassed, not embarrassing, but nevertheless you feel ashamed, you lower your eyes, you stammer an excuse and promise Herzl Goldring never to cut his foliage to decorate your room. But you are bound to break your promise. But why the hell should a man feel ashamed of any step he takes in his own home? Is it any wonder that Herzl Goldring hates you bitterly in the hidden depths of his heart?

Every day at half past four in the afternoon the mail arrives in a red van that announces its presence with a hollow, cow-like blast on its horn. Tsvi Ramigolski gets up from his desk, over which hangs a photograph of his dead brother Aaron. 'All right, I'm coming,' he murmurs abstractedly, as if someone will hear him and stop hooting. He hurries out into the dusty square in front of the hut. Halfway there, he claps his hand to his forehead and goes back to pick up the outward-bound mail that in his haste he has forgotten. Then he presses through the impatient crowd thronging round the van, exchanges bundles, and shouts out the names of those who have letters. Gai Harish clutches the lucky ones and begs for the stamps. Oren Geva eyes the silver emblem on the hood of the van and thinks inscrutable thoughts. Herbert Segal, meanwhile, receives a new record with religious awe and scrutinizes the writing on the wrapper. Mendel Morag is here, too, to send a parcel of cakes to his relatives.

We live in a small, far-off land, in its northeastern extremity, in a small village a long way from the nearest town. Like all isolated communities, always and everywhere, we love getting letters. Let us imagine that we have the right to peep at letters that are not addressed to us and see what excitements we can espy.

Here, for instance, is a letter from Rami Rimon to his onetime girl friend. It contains no reproach and no words of conciliation. It is a very short letter: the obligatory words of greeting, then a brief description of his preliminary training. What news at home? I'm holding my own, and I've had some pieces of good luck I'll tell you about some other time. Food's not bad. Not enough sleep. One can get used to anything, though. You forget some things and learn others. I hope things on our border don't get too hot before I get there, because I want to be in on the action. Nothing else to report. If you can, say a few nice words to my mother now and then. It must be hard on her. Write to me if you feel like it.

Fruma, too, has had a letter from her son. Rami's letter to his mother is even shorter than the one to Noga. No description of his training, not even a brief one. No mention of the shortage of sleep. All he says is that he is well, that the others in his tent are all pleasant boys, though a mixed bunch, that he's in excellent health. He hopes she isn't mourning for him day and night. He'll come home on leave soon. Finally, as if after reconsideration, he remarks the cookies were lovely, Mom, and it would be nice if you sent me some more.

Fruma, of course, will bake some and send them off very soon. What a pity her relations with other people nowadays are so bitterly quarrelsome.

Dr Nehemiah Berger writes to his brother and sister-in-law from Jerusalem. He thanks them for being kind enough to invite him to stay. He is almost on his way. No, he is not afraid of the situation on the border. On the contrary, he sometimes finds Jerusalem terribly dreary. He is so bored that he is unable to concentrate on his research, so he is wasting his time on ridiculous translations that earn him his living. What a tragi-comic paradox: one earns five times as much for a mechanical translation as for original research. He's not afraid of the heat in the valley, either. Jerusalem may be cooler but it is the dry-ness that makes him ill and drains the intellectual juices that are vital for creative work. Above all, he confesses to an over-powering longing to see his relatives again. What sort of life do I lead here? No wife, no children, only painful research work, and who can say whether I shall live to complete it? Sometimes I say to myself, Nehemiah, the history of Jewish socialism is a complex structure of wonders and miracles. Who are you to try and plumb its depths? There's one thing I know, and I'll maintain it till my dying day: anyone who says that socialism is an imported plant in our garden doesn't know what he's talking about. We never dissociated our national messianic aspirations from the goal of social salvation. But to prove it one has to explore paths thousands of years old, picking up a fragment here and there, without getting lost in the details and losing sight of the fundamental thesis. It's wearisome work. And who can I talk to about it except to you, my dear Ezra and Bronka, my nearest and dearest, and your dear children? Which reminds me, how is Einav? It can't be long now till the birth. I hope and pray it goes well. Our brother Zechariah sent me a picture postcard. He may be coming over, but he doesn't give any details. Does he write to you regularly? Give my love to Oren and little Tomer – he's probably not so little any more – and to Einav. I'll be on my way to see you soon. All the best. Your loving brother, Nehemiah.

*

And what about Siegfried? Siegfried's letter is rather strange, brimming with an odd joy. Has peace finally come to your land? A curse on the enemies of Israel who do not let us find our redemption quietly. Look after yourselves. Wouldn't it be better for our dear Einav to move away from the border till she's had her child? We have a brother in the capital who would be happy to look after her. Think over my advice. Everything is flowing smoothly here. I'm doing good business and 'pouring out my wrath on the Gentiles.' I've taken on an ex-Gestapo officer as a doorman. You would be as happy as I am if you could only see him bowing and scraping. I'm so happy to have my enemies in my power. Revenge is certainly sweet. Sweeter than honey. I've got the gold and silver now, and they all dance attendance on me, with *'Jawohl, Herr Berger,' 'Bitte, Herr Berger,' 'Danke, Herr Berger,' 'Wunderbar, Herr Berger.'* When I see you in a few weeks' time I'll tell you all about it, and we can enjoy the enemy's humiliation together. There is justice in this world, that's what I say, even if our national poet Bialik isn't right when he says 'justice will be done when I depart this world.' Here am I, the son of a Polish-Jewish cantor who was burned in the furnaces of Sobibor, lording it over the son of a Prussian Junker, the grandson of a Prussian Junker, the great-grandson of the Devil himself, and he is grateful to me for paying him a couple of pence more than doormen get paid in other clubs. It's a miracle, that's what I say. Signs and wonders, mighty hand and outstretched arm! Incidentally, Hamburger has just bought another car. He's got two now, one for himself and one for his wife. What a pity that he's so blinded by wealth he can't see the wonder of it. He's also taken

171

on a liveried chauffeur. Eva will tell you her news herself. I'll leave her some room.

Eva says thank you for the pretty picture. Here in Munich the weather is cold and rainy. The rain never stops. It has a certain beauty, but I feel sad when I remember the weather in the valley. Life is quiet and pleasant here. But no life is entirely free from sadness. And all sorts of strange thoughts. Be well. Tell me how Stella is getting on at school. Do you think Reuven would be good enough to cut off a lock of her hair and send it to me via you? Would you ask him? Please. I pray that my daughter won't hate me. Yours, Eva.

Ezra Berger reads the letters from his two brothers, the one in Germany and the other in Jerusalem, and thinks them over during one of the long silences between himself and his little friend. Amazing things happen. Wonders and miracles, as Zechariah says. Father used to say to us, love work and hate power and put your heart into everything you do. But nobody could say that Father put his heart into being a cantor. May he rest in perfect peace. When Nehemiah ran away to Lvov, to the university, Father went into mourning for him. When Ezra joined the movement and came to Palestine, Father said we all have our trials to bear. When Siegfried went off and became Siegfried, Father said it's a very sore trial. Two's company, three's a crowd, little Noga. There's a great truth in that. Pour out your wrath on the Gentiles, Zechariah said when he came here in 1948. That was his be-all and end-all. I remember a terrible argument he had with Nehemiah. I'm going to go back there, he said, and be a dirty Jew. A filthy Yid. That's what he said. Yes, I said, you're right, men aren't made of myrrh and frankincense, but you're my brother and you weren't born to be a scoundrel. Nehemiah's argument was different. Stay here, have lots of children. That's our revenge. Zechariah laughed and paraphrased an old saying. Their world stands on three things, he said, murder, fornication, and greed. Those are its three legs. I'm going to smash one or two of those legs, just as they smashed me. As our dear father used to say: Hate power, hate work, hate your enemies, and you'll float like pure oil on sewage. Our brother Zechariah said this, too, that day: a true Jew, gentlemen, must pierce the darkness and eat away the rotten foundations of the earth, as our national poet Bialik puts it. If they bruise our head, we must bruise their heel, and their heels are murder, profit, and debauchery. Murder is forbidden in the Torah, but even the Devil wouldn't stop me debauching them and bleeding their money out of them. So Zechariah went to Munich, and Nehemiah lives in Jerusalem. 'It is better for me to die than to live.' 'Would God I had died for you.' Those verses may be allegorical, or something, but they're not true. That's what I think, little Turquoise. Here am I sitting under my vine and under my fig tree, as the Bible says, and my wife as a fruitful vine by the sides of my house, and where's Ramigolski now? Ramigolski is a white skeleton without a wrapping. My fate has been better than Zechariah's, better than Nehemiah's, better than my friend Ramigolski's. My lot has been a happy one. But it doesn't matter. It doesn't mean a thing. I was thinking and I happened to talk aloud, like a man crying out when he dreams. Listen, Turquoise, my brother who lives in Germany can interpret dreams. Really.

We didn't throw him in a pit and show his striped robe to our father. You don't understand? I'll explain. A: Who wears striped robes nowadays? Only the Arabs. B: Our father was burned. C: Our brother, who interprets dreams, doesn't feed the Gentiles; he pours out his wrath on them. D: Conclusion. There is no conclusion. The conclusion is that the analogy doesn't work, and it's best to forget about it, because I'm tired and it's half past midnight.

Between Ezra and Bronka there is silence. Since they live in a small apartment, they sometimes accidentally touch or bump into one another. Then they look at each other. Bronka pales. Ezra mutters:

'Sorry.'

Bronka does not ask. Ezra doesn't expect her to ask. All she ever asks is, for instance:

'Have you written to your brothers yet?' And Ezra, as if weighing her words before he answers:

'Not yet. Maybe I'll have time on Saturday. We'll see.'

Ezra spends most of his time in his truck. What little free time he has is divided between his friends the fishermen of Tiberias and his little friend, in the grove beside the swimming pool. It is surprising, in view of this, that he did not forget Bronka's birthday. On one of his journeys he bought her a pretty vase, and set it silently on her bedside table. As for Bronka, she did not refuse her present. As she buttoned up her housecoat, early in the morning, with her back to him, she said:

'Thank you. It was kind of you.'

Ezra replied tersely:

'Yes.'

Bronka said:

'Perhaps you could take the curtains down for me, too. They've got to be washed; they're all dusty.'

And Ezra:

'Why not? May I stand on this chair, or must I go and borrow a stepladder from the stores?'

Every Sunday, the beginning of the week, Bronka lays at the foot of her husband's bed a clean, neatly folded shirt and pair of trousers. Every Friday she takes his dirty working clothes, turns the pockets inside out, and puts them in the laundry bag. And every night, when Ezra gets back from his journey, he finds a cup of tea waiting for him as usual on the table, covered with a saucer to keep it warm. Every three or four days Tomer visits his parents' house to see to the little garden. Oren empties the garbage bins every three days, provided his mother reminds him and provided he is not suffering from one of the dark moods that take hold of him from time to time for no apparent reason. And Einav, on those evenings when Bronka does not feel well, brings her her supper on a tray, covered with a white napkin. Recently, Bronka has been unwell for three days running. Ezra did not give up his second daily trip, but he bought his wife a book about symphonic music in Tel Aviv to take her mind off her illness and her thoughts.

Now for an act of heroism.

On Saturday evening, when the other members were all gathered for their weekly meeting, Tomer Geva started up a gray tractor, switched on the headlights, and set out to turn off the irrigation taps in the outlying fields. On the way he thought about various things, about his father, for instance, who had still not lost his youthful vigor. A great mystery this, which impresses Arabs and women; it is the only thing that lets you live your life, and without it you're nothing. On the way he almost ran over a jackal, which was caught in the headlights and was saved only by its instincts. The creature escaped and was swallowed up in the great darkness, running in terrified zigzags across the fields to the end of the dark, where it rested and wept and laughed with madness in its voice.

The oppressive heat was still making itself felt. And the dogs howled, as dogs do on hot nights. The swish of the sprinklers clashed with the crickets' chirping. Amid these sounds, hideous and deafening, came the vicious howl of bullets close to Tomer's ear. Tomer hesitated for only a fraction of a second. He determined the direction of the shots. With a flick of his hand he put out the lights. He leaped out and landed on the rough earth. The tractor continued at its former pace but headed to the left, down the slope. The bullets pursued the tractor, and the youth was saved, though wounded, apparently, in the arm. The tractor, driverless, rushed down the slope. The bullets pierced it with fierce savagery. There was a roar, flashes rent the darkness, a dull shock, a guttural shriek, then silence.

Who else except these wretches would have laid an ambush in a wadi and opened fire at night at a range of a hundred yards? The tractor had rolled straight into the thick of them. Terrified as if it had been an armored car, they had thrown a hand grenade at it and run.

The next afternoon, after Tomer had been operated on and two bullets removed from his arm, his family and friends gathered round his hospital bed. Congratulations, explanations, and jokes assailed the patient. Even Einav's tears could not detract from the warmhearted atmosphere. We may quote Oren's words. First, the tractor is finished. Done for. The grenade smashed it to smithereens. Perhaps one or two pieces of the engine could still be used. Secondly, there was an investigation. With a tracker and dogs. You should have seen the dogs, Tomer. They ran through the vineyard. You're the talk of the whole valley. A single boy defeated a whole ambush unarmed. They found traces of blood on the way out of the wadi. They blew themselves up with their own grenade. The boy took the tractor and turned it on them. Third, Tomer, reinforcements have been brought up. On both sides. We're flexing our muscles. If we have another squeak out of them – that's what they said to the wogs – we'll smash their whole army. Now we're waiting for them to squeak. So we can smash them. If you'd been better, they'd have done it tonight. Crushed them bone by bone. Squashed them. Till there was nothing left.

Oren's dark eyes flashed with excitement. Hatred hardened the set of his jaws and his mouth. There was no smile on his face, only icy rage. Tomer lifted himself up in bed and gave his brother's chin a friendly punch with his good hand. He smiled a forced, fleeting smile, but it met with no response. Oren was not disposed to let affection interfere with serious business. Let us take a look at his face. If we interpret the signs rightly, an enthralling idea is going through the boy's mind. Despite his self-control, he is biting his lower lip. He looks excited.

17

Two Women

REUVEN HARISH is fond of stories that bring out the bright side of human nature, such as that of the well-fed, pleasure-loving businessman who is fired one day with a holy zeal and dedicates his life and fortune to the welfare of the Jewish nation, or of the difficult, repressed man who is overcome one day by a spark of humanity and self-sacrifice. Stories such as these appeal to his considered view of the world, according to which life is too complicated to be reducible to simple formulas.

It is a pity that Fruma Rominov does not seem willing to comply with this scheme and betray unexpected symptoms of love of her fellow men. Fruma Rominov does not like kibbutz life. Even her face seems to testify to her consuming sense of mortification. Her mouth droops sulkily like a spoiled child's; her tiny eyes of indeterminate color search your face as if to mock at your weakness. Her gray hair is dry, her body lean and angular under her blue dress. Fundamentally, we agree with Reuven Harish's negative view of Fruma. But there is a side to her character that merits respect and that we must not overlook in forming our opinion of her. Fruma Rominov does not believe in kibbutz life, yet she adheres zealously to its principles, because so long as the principles remain unaltered she holds that even their opponents must observe them strictly. She does not approve of compromises. She sees cant and hypocrisy for what it is. And that is to Fruma Rominov's credit.

The heat wave lasted for nine days. Then a westerly breeze whirled pleasantly into the valley and chased the *hamsin* back toward the bleak mountains and beyond them to the desert plains to the east. The cool air touched the inanimate objects and soothed their raging fury. We could breathe again. The oppressive heat had dried the very marrow in our bones. Now we could be more agreeable. We would not give up judging one another, for that is our secret weapon in our task of world reform, but from now on we could temper our judgments with a measure of charity.

It goes without saying that this does not apply to Fruma Rominov. Fruma stands apart from the general relief. It is evening time. Fruma bustles around the great baking oven in the communal kitchen. She is baking cookies. Two evenings a week the large oven is available to the women of the kibbutz for their private baking. Fruma Rominov is baking cookies for her son the soldier. A few weeks ago Fruma emerged from her shell and stealthily left a dish of little cakes on Noga Harish's bed. Fruma imagined that Noga would one day be the mother of her grandchildren. But in the meantime something shameful has happened. Her mother's lascivious blood runs in her veins. How could she have done a thing like that to Rami at such a difficult time? And I know my boy was fond of her. She doesn't deserve him. Sometimes I think there is more immorality in a kibbutz than elsewhere. It's not an accident. If only Yoash . . . Yoash would have made his way in the world. Yoash could have overcome all the obstacles. Yoash would have sorted out his life and become a somebody. He was well-balanced. He could have spat on them all. He could have been a somebody. But Rami will also settle down. After his military service they'll give him an important job, and perhaps there'll be a small room in his apartment for me. In Haifa, maybe, on the Carmel. I need to live somewhere high up, because I'm not well. I'll have a room of my own and I'll look after the children when you go out to the movies. It's a good thing, from that point of view, that he's a long way from the little hussy now. I'll bring up the children to be well-mannered. Not little savages. Don't worry about that hussy. You'll find someone better, even someone prettier. Because you're a good-looking boy. This is no place for a boy like you. This is a place for invalids. And you're so strong. You're much better-looking than she is. You're good-looking like Yoash. You'll laugh at them. You've got the kind of looks that drive girls wild. That's what I say, and I know what I'm talking about.

With a sigh Fruma bent down to look at the oven, screwing up her eyes because of the heat. The cookies smelled good.

'A few more minutes,' she said.

Einav Geva, who was also baking, said:

'I never take mine out at the right time. It's always either too soon or too late. I haven't got your knack, Fruma, of catching them at the exact moment.'

'Never mind,' Fruma answered, 'experience comes with age. That's life.'

*

How she limps. Tomer Berger, such a greasy Casanova, and he's ended up catching a cripple. Or did she catch him? You'll make such a marriage, Rami, that their eyes will pop out of their heads. Only take care of yourself. Because you're good-looking. You may not be brilliant. Not so good at talking in impressive phrases. But you're straightforward. Like me. Sometimes I'm sad when I think how straightforward people suffer in this life. Clever people don't say everything they think. But you always say everything you think, son. Always. To everyone. It's not wise, Rami, it's not always wise. But you'll develop. You have an open mind. You'll learn from experience. You won't always be the good little lamb that everyone exploits. If they want a volunteer to unload a truck-load of manure at six o'clock in the evening? Rami. If they need someone to get a dead cat out of the food store? Rami. Rami, Rami, always Rami. Don't be a fool. Don't be such a simpleton. Now they're laughing at you because your girl friend's left you and gone off with an old lecher. They don't understand that you're not a fool. You enjoyed her, and then you dumped her because she's not a nice girl for all her good looks. That's what happened. Yes, that's how it was, idiot. You don't always have to tell the whole truth. Don't be a simpleton, or they'll destroy you. They don't deserve to have you living here, because you're decent to your fingertips, like your mother. Now, now's the right moment to take them out. She limps twice as badly now she's pregnant. What a terrible limp.

Fruma removes the hot tray from the oven with an old cloth and holds it under Einav's nose.

'Sniff this. Smells good, eh?' Einav smiles shyly and says:

'You're unbeatable, Fruma.'

'Try one. Melts in the mouth, eh? Take another one, for your husband. They say he likes sweet things. By the way, when are you having your baby? You must have worked it out.'

'Next month, apparently.'

'Splendid. I'm delighted to hear it. It doesn't have to be difficult the first time. Don't let your friends frighten you. What are you going to call the child?'

'I, we thought . . .'

'What about Reuven? Reuven Berger. It would make your mother-in-law very happy. By the way, they say she hasn't been too cheerful lately.'

'Do you think . . .'

'No. I didn't mean anything specific. Just generally. You know I . . . I'm not a hypocrite. But I wanted to say something to you, something personal. It's about your leg. There's a new doctor in Jerusalem, at the Hadassa Hospital, a recent immigrant from Poland, who works miracles with orthopedic cases. There was an interesting article about it in the paper – perhaps you saw it. As soon as I read it, I thought of you. I'm always like that. I think a lot about other people, but I don't make a big fuss about it. It might be worth your going to Jerusalem to see this doctor. It can't do any harm. You never know in life what will change your luck. Isn't that right? Your leg's got worse recently, hasn't it? You don't mind me talking about it, do you? I've really been thinking about you recently. You're still young, and you ought to try to be pretty. Men are apt to behave badly when they don't find their wives attractive physically. That's life.'

Einav tries to change the subject. It's natural.

'I don't care if I'm pretty or not, at the moment. I can't think about such things just now. What does Rami have to say, Fruma?'

As if by magic Fruma's face changes. The wrinkles round her eyes vanish, the firm set of her jaws relaxes somewhat, and the corners of her mouth droop, suggesting a spoiled child about to burst into tears.

'Rami? My Rami? He writes me wonderful letters. He's getting on marvelously in the army. Rami is like me: he's so honest and straightforward and dedicated that he's well thought of everywhere. It's a very rare quality. Incidentally, I think that your father-in-law is only carrying on with Reuven Harish's daughter now because my Rami paved the way for him, so to speak. But my Rami saw straightaway that it was rotten fruit. He took a bite, enjoyed it a bit, then threw it away.' (Here Fruma wrinkles her nose in disgust. Her voice is full of venom. Her face is twisted in a cruel, gloating grin.) 'Your father-in-law picked up and sucked what my Rami threw away. It's disgusting. All in all, there are interesting goings on in your family now. If I were in your place, I'd keep an eye on my husband. I hope you don't mind me talking about it. I'm saying it for your good, really. After all, I've had a lot of experience, and I only want to give you sound advice. Now that your husband's been wounded, you'd better be all eyes. It gives them a kind of magic charm. Incidentally, they say that little Dafna's got her eyes on Tomer. These things have become fashionable now among our young girls, as everybody seems to realize except our schoolteachers. That's life.'

Einav looks down at the pastry on the table in front of her, kneading it and molding it into little cakes. She does not look up at Fruma. She wants to avoid the malice, but she does not understand it clearly. She is not glad of Fruma's company.

Unhurriedly, Fruma transfers her cookies from the baking sheet to a tin, and unhurriedly she lights a cigarette and casts a serious glance at Nina Goldring, who is in charge of the stores, dragging a sack of sugar. Isn't that just typical of the kibbutz? Typical. A woman struggling and nobody offering to help her.

'Nina, do you want a hand?'

'No, thanks,' Nina says, 'I've finished. That's where it goes. Thanks, anyway, it was kind of you to offer.'

'What do you think, Fruma?' Einav asks. 'Is the *hamsin* going to start again? I wouldn't want to have the baby in a heat wave.'

'You're quite right, my girl. That's very true. The *hamsin* drives men wild. You'll go away to have the baby, and he'll find himself some tasty morsel behind your back. Taste one of this kind, too, Einav. I put a bit of wine in the pastry. Delicious, isn't it? Does Bronka ever bake cakes for you? No? Not surprising. They say she's very busy. Teaching. It's interesting, by the way, I've been reading a novel just this week about an actress who had nine husbands, one after the other, and, then, when she was already a grandmother, she got married again to a young artist. You haven't tried these yet, Einav, the spiced ones. They're excellent. Here, take one, don't refuse an old widow. Well, then . . . What were we talking about? Yes. Imagine if your mother-in-law suddenly got pregnant by Reuven Harish. You think it's impossible? You'd be surprised if you knew some of the things that happen. There's a novel about an old man who has a child as a mistress. I read a lot now I'm all alone.

Somebody ought to write a novel some day about our kibbutz.
There's plenty of interesting material. And symbolism, too.'

Einav asks Fruma when Rami will be coming home on leave.
Fruma looks at Einav and doesn't understand for a moment
what connection there is between her question and what went
before. But she is not perplexed for long. A sour smile of complicity flits across her face and instantly vanishes.

'One day I'll show you my Rami's letters. He writes beautifully. I'm sure he's got a natural talent for writing. If only
the teachers here had taken the trouble to help him develop.
But no, they didn't do it and they never would. They're not
interested in developing talents. On the contrary. They want
to produce simple people. Just simple people, who'll work all
day in the fields and go to bed at night and make children and
grab a weapon when it's necessary and rush out to die hero-
ically in battle. *Constructive* people. Come and see me some
time, Einav; I'll give you the address of that Pole in Jerusalem.
Your cake could have turned out quite well, Einav. It's only
a little bit burned. Never mind. Experience comes with age.'

Fruma Rominov is a thin, wrinkled woman. She holds herself
very erect. Her nose is narrow and pointed like a bird's beak, her
hair is faded to an indeterminate color, her eyes are blue. Her eyes
are blue, but sometimes, when a gloating look comes into them,
they take on a vague, murky color. She is slightly built, and her
movements are sharp and lively. Her mouth is different. It frequently has an offended air, and its corners twitch tearfully. Her
movements, as we have said, are sharp and lively, and they fill
you with nervous apprehension. As if you had something to fear.

In the old days Alter Rominov's cheerful laugh moderated his wife's bitterness. Alter Rominov was a tiny man, like his wife. It was amazing that from such loins should have sprung a strapping, well-built pair of sons. The boys did not inherit their father's cramped, European-Jewish appearance. Apart from the horsy jaws, none of Alter Rominov's features was reproduced in his two sons. For obvious reasons they hebraized their surname from Rominov to Rimon.

We loved their father for his unbounded kindness. He was always in a good mood. Always trying to be funny. There was nothing sharp about his humor; his jokes, like their author, were mild, pale, and inoffensive. The kind of jokes that win a man neither admirers nor enemies. He was the principal butt of his own humor. 'Don't give me a gun when I'm on night watch,' he said. 'A man like me can frighten robbers away unarmed.' We understood him and felt a gentle sympathy for him. His name was omitted from the rota of night watchmen.

The physical work ruined Alter Rominov. Most of the founder-members of the kibbutz adapted and acclimatized themselves to the rigors of the life. The work and the climate brought out a dormant strength in such characters as Reuven Harish and Ezra Berger, and, of course, Grisha Isarov – each in his own way. But Alter Rominov grew weaker and weaker and looked more shriveled every summer. He used to wander around the camp, battered and exhausted, trying to hide his weakness with poor jokes.

'You can see that I'm 100 per cent European,' he used to say. 'You've become completely Asiatic, but I'm a European through and through. The *hamsin* finishes me off. What I need is white ducks and a topee.'

And when you slapped him heartily on the back and asked how he was, he would answer:

'I feel like a rabbinical student pressed into the Czar's service, ha ha ha.'

He was miserable, and there was always a look of shy puzzlement in his eyes, which could be quite endearing. But he also had a stubborn pride. It was his pride that made him resist his wife's attempts to persuade him to leave the kibbutz and live like a civilized human being. He listened to everything else she said, but not to this. To his sons he used to say:

'The land of Israel ought to be the opposite of the ghetto. If we want to make a ghetto, it would have been better to stay in Europe. At least there there was no *hamsin*.'

And it was during a *hamsin* that he collapsed and died. Not like his son Yoash and not like his friend Aaron Ramigolski, but like a ghetto Jew. In his last years he had been working in the laundry, but one morning he was asked to go and help Israel Tsitron in the banana plantation. Alter put on a curious hat and said:

'For the sake of the nation, let's try irrigation!'

He worked the irrigation pipes for three or four hours. When the sun began to beat down on his head, he vomited. He was told to sit down and rest. He gave one of his shy smiles and said:

'Death among the hose pipes.'

Ten minutes later he vomited again, flopped down, and said:

'I'm so hot.'

187

Israel Tsitron went off to fetch him some water. When he came back, Rominov was sitting with his back against the trunk of a gigantic banana tree, as if he were resting; but he was dead. Fruma contends that we killed him. We deny the charge gently and try to change the subject. Reuven Harish wrote a poem in his memory, which was published in our news sheet.

Two years later Yoash Rimon fell in the Suez campaign. He was commanding a parachute squadron. The two successive disasters did not break Fruma's spirit. She revealed great resources of strength. It must be counted to our credit that we do not judge Fruma with our accustomed severity. What a pity that she, for her part, judges our actions with redoubled severity. Fruma Rominov volunteered to run the kindergarten, which she does with intelligence and authority. The children love her because she does not practice favoritism and because she always tells them the truth, even the kind of truth that is not normally told to small children. The parents respect her. On the education committee she is outstanding for her consistent and uncompromising stands. On several issues she has saved us from adopting the easy way out. At one of the meetings she said:

'I am opposed to certain aspects of the kibbutz ideology. But since they exist, they must be upheld. Hypocrisy is no solution. It's very easy to pretend, but one pretence leads to another. That's life. And therefore . . .'

Such words naturally engrave themselves on one's memory.

Fruma Rominov gathers up her baking equipment and her cakes, covers the whole trayload with a white cloth, and steps briskly out of the kitchen, asking Einav on the way whether she can do anything to help her, Einav thanks her and says she can manage by herself. Fruma tells Einav that she is a wonderful girl and goes out into the night. The night stoops over her and blows vague scents in her face.

18

Menace

THE NIGHT stoops over you and blows its scents at you.

An unpleasant, sour smell wafts from the hen house. A dense vapor from the cow shed, a damp smell from the stores. Various odors drift from all sides. A wild smell from the fields. The riotous air of the mountains provides a lively accompaniment. The cascades of mingled odors excite the furious barking of the dogs, which gives way to distracted and terrifying howls.

The moon is still in hiding. Your eyes seek its pale radiance and find only the stars, conversing in a bluish flicker. The mighty, moonless sky is indifferent alike to you and to the silent, encircling foe.

Our village is encircled. Outside the fence something stirs. If only you could interpret the signs. A snarling menace surrounds the fence trying to penetrate and disrupt our tiny order. Base treason whispers already on the outskirts of the camp. Mute objects mutiny first. In the panting darkness they slowly change their shape. Take on other forms. You look at them, and they seem alien; their angles soften and curve. You look at the trusty bench half hidden, as always, among the flowering shrubs, and you find all its lines altered. You sharpen your gaze and try to put down the treachery, and it intensifies with a snicker. There are no lines to be seen. Only shapes, unconnected shapes, black within black wrapped in black. You fix your eyes on a pleasant arbor, but they seem to detect a cautious movement. Look up at the mighty sky. There, at least, things are as they were. But no. Even above you something is happening. From the top of the water tower a bluish light hits you with a terrifying wink. A spasm has seized dumb objects. They are rebeling against good order. Even the searchlight beam quivers apprehensively. Unruly shadows respond with a riotous dance.

Now the crickets. The crickets exchange secret messages. Into their concentration intrudes the distant throbbing of the refrigeration plant. The swishing sprinklers intrigue against you and join the side of the crickets. The crickets are learning your secrets and signaling your fears to their listening friends out in the hostile fields.

The mountains are invisible, but their presence broods over the valley. The mountains are there. Drunken gorges pouring down to attack us. Blocks of dark rock hanging high up as by a thread, threatening to sever their connection with the mountain. A hint of a movement, a patient, subdued murmur comes creeping. The mountains are there. In total silence, they are there. Standing like curved columns, like giants frozen in some obscene act and turned to stone, the mountains are there.

The mountains stand in massive succession. Plotting evil deep in their frozen cascades of rock. The mountains are

190

scored by ravines. The mountains are invisible in the darkness, but the stars declare their position. To the east the pattern of stars breaks to reveal a clearly defined pool of black. A massive screen blocks the stars. That is where mountains are. That is where they are silently waiting to see what will happen. It won't be long now. The night is charged.

19

The Clapper in the Bell

THE DECISION had been taken some days earlier in the highest circles. Our kibbutz was to work a small field known as the Camel's Field, at the foot of the mountain, which had been the object of bloody disputes between the two warring states. From the legal point of view the land was ours, as the maps testified. But the reality was different. For years now the small plot had been worked by fellahin who came down the mountain under the protective cover of the enemy army. After careful consideration it had been decided that the time was ripe to make the facts correspond to the theory and to assert our legal right to the land. The army, of course, was to be responsible for our protection.

Tsvi Ramigolski, the secretary of the kibbutz, said:

'We must hope for the best but be prepared for the worst.'

Nina Goldring said:

'Let's hope it all goes smoothly.'

Reuven Harish said:

'The issue may be no more than symbolic. But only fools refuse to recognize that life is made up of symbols.'

And Grisha Isarov, accompanied by a chorus of enthusiastic youngsters:

'At last!'

We were ordered to have an armor-plated tractor ready in the shed, to draw up a list of names, and to wait for the signal, which might come, we were told, at any moment between now and the winter. We had to wait twenty whole weeks for the signal to come. Things did not get under way till the autumn. Meanwhile, other events, of a personal character, took place.

Noga Harish goes into her room and turns the light on.

It's late. Ten o'clock. Where is Dafna? Dafna has gone to the basketball field to watch a game and admire Tomer's half-naked torso. The game is over by now. The voices have died away, the floodlighting is off. Dafna, as usual, has gone with the players to crown their victory with flattering remarks. A crowd of players and supporters has gathered in the dining hall to celebrate the team's achievements with bottles of fruit juice.

Noga's room is silent. Noga is stretched out on her bed, leafing through a book of verse by a young poetess. She is not reading. Her hands are turning the pages idly, while her eyes stare up at the ceiling.

Grandma Stella, Mother's mother, was a very stern woman. Uncle Isaac is Mother's cousin, and a match was arranged between them when they were children, as between kings and princesses in the Middle Ages. Then Daddy came and spoiled all the arrangements. The princess ran away with the minstrel. The kingdom was in a ferment. Uncle Isaac was a pianist. He still is. I remember when he came here, he lifted me onto his lap and he was fat and he tried to teach me to play the piano in the recreation hall. He kept kissing me. I remember his smell. It was a strong, rough smell, very hot and rather frightening. He was terribly polite. He brought me dolls and clothes for them and mechanical toys for Gai. Daddy wouldn't let us take them because we're kibbutz children and because they came from Germany, a land of murderers. What is a land of murderers? I'd like to go and see the land of murderers some day. Mother said that suffering had corrupted Uncle Isaac and that she was responsible for him and had to purify him. How do you purify a man? How does suffering corrupt? What does it corrupt? At the end of the story the princess came back to the crown prince as the fairy grandmother had decreed. A young peasant lad had snatched her away, but she went back to the palace and lived happily ever after. Now comes the question. Where am I? I'm not in the story. I must find an opening and get into the story. I'm the peasant's pretty daughter, and the princess . . . No. I'm the princess's daughter by . . . No. I'm the little daughter who stayed behind with Phalti, the son of Laish, when Michal went back to the palace to the old minstrel king David. I look like Grandma Stella. He walked behind her crying. He's got strong shoulders. They're hairy. They're bent, as if he's tired. Her mother's blood flows in her veins. In another hour or two he'll be back. Therefore shall a man leave everything and cleave to his wife and they shall be one flesh. I said to him, Ezra, it's just words. It can't be like that. One flesh is only in poetry. They're two people really. Where am I in the story? Little lunatic. Only a lunatic would throw stones into the pool at night to smash the moon's reflection to make the moon a white puddle trembling in a black puddle. One day, in a hundred years, in a thousand years' time you'll take me in your truck, and we'll go somewhere else. Perhaps to your fishermen in Tiberias. They're your friends. You're a fisherman. I'll be a goldfish. Mother used to love water. Streams and rivers and lakes. I belong to the mountains. When I was little, Daddy used to teach us a poem at school about a vulture, and I was the vulture. You're not saying anything, my big bear. You never say anything. Only proverbs. Don't talk to me in proverbs; I've heard them all before. Come here, touch me. Your hands are always so warm. Feel mine. They're frozen, aren't they? Let's see if you can say a proverb about my hands – quickly without thinking. No. Don't. Let's go for a ride in your truck, dear bear. A long way away. Now listen to a pretty thought: if you were my father, I'd be your daughter. It's eleven o'clock already. Time won't pass, and you won't come and be my daddy. My grandmother's name was Stella, and Mother's new husband is her kind of fella. You think you know who I am. I'm Turquoise Hamburger. You don't know a thing. You're just a simple truck driver. I'm the queen's long-lost daughter. I'm a little girl whose big sister took her to the desert and left her there and went back to the palace without her. But I'm going. I'm going to the palace. The murderers won't hurt me. I know a secret password. I'll go to the palace, and she'll scream with terror. She'll fall at my feet, and I'll spare her. Perhaps. Then I shall have a case to try. One man stole another man's wife, and I shall punish them both severely. The one who stole the poor man's lamb has sinned before me, and the other one will be punished because he didn't cry out or resist. Why did you give in, dear bear? You're so strong. The queen knows you're strong. After all, the queen is really your daughter. That's a secret. So why didn't you say anything? You talk, but you don't say anything. My father isn't made of myrrh and frankincense and you're not, but I am. How innocent they both are, my fathers.

You're heavy, Ezra. That's what I love about you: you're heavy. You're big but you're simple. I'm going to embroider you on a napkin, because I love you. Don't talk. A horse is a wonderful animal. It's a paradoxical animal. It can be obedient like a donkey, but it can also gallop across the plains. Don't talk proverbs. When a horse sweats, it smells of love. I get excited when I think of a horse's smell. No, don't talk. Let's travel. Let's go somewhere else. A gypsy girl and a bear. Don't talk. A galloping horse is the most wonderful animal in the world. It will gallop into the distance, and we'll hear its hoof-beats like a clapper like a heartbeat like a drumbeat in the king's palace when the gypsies come and it suddenly turns out that the girl with the dancing bear is the princess is the clapper in the bell.

20

If There Is Justice

RAMI RIMON came home for the weekend on leave. His face was thinner. His skin had shrunk a little. His jaws seemed more prominent. The lines on his face were sharper. His mother's face struggling to get out. Fine creases ringed his mouth. The sun had etched wrinkles round his eyes. Twin furrows ran from his nose to the corners of his mouth.

He was wearing an impeccable greenish uniform, with his beret tucked in his pocket. His stout boots were shod with steel at toe and heel. His sleeves were rolled up to reveal hairy forearms, and his hands were covered with little scars. He was conscious of his manly appearance as he strode slowly across the yard with an air of studied indifference. The men and women he met greeted him warmly. He responded with an offhand nod. There were traces of gun grease under his fingernails, and his left elbow was dressed with a grubby bandage.

When the first tumult of hugs and kisses, received by Rami with a wavering smile, had died down, Fruma said:

'Well, you won't believe it, but I was just thinking of you the moment before you turned up. Mother's intuition.'

Rami thought there was nothing strange in that. He had said in his letter that he would come on Friday afternoon, and she knew perfectly well what time the bus came. As he spoke, he put down his shabby kit bag, pulled his shirt outside his trousers, lit a cigarette, and laid a heavy hand on Fruma's shoulder.

'It's good to see you, Mom. I wanted to tell you that I'm really glad to see you again.'

Fruma glanced at his dusty boots and said:

'You've lost so much weight.'

Rami drew on his cigarette and asked about her health.

'Come inside and have a shower before dinner. You're all sweaty. Would you like a cold drink first? No. A warm drink would be better for you. Wait, though, the first thing is to take you along to the surgery. I want the nurse to have a look at your elbow.'

Rami started to explain about the wound. It happened during a bayonet practice; the clumsy oaf of a section commander . . . but Fruma did not let him finish the story.

'There you go dropping your ash on the floor. I've just washed it in your honor. There are four ash trays in the house and you . . .'

Rami sat down in his filthy clothes on the clean white bedspread and kicked off his boots. Fruma rushed to fetch her husband's old slippers. Her eyes were dry, but she tried to turn her face away from her son to hide the look he disliked so much. Rami, however, pretended not to have seen that strained look, as of a dam about to burst. He lay back on the bed, looked up at the ceiling, drew the ash tray that Fruma had put in his hand closer to him and blew out a puff of smoke.

'The day before yesterday we crossed a river on a rope bridge. Two ropes stretched one above the other, one to walk on and the other to hold. With all our stuff on our backs,

197

spade, blankets, gun, ammunition, the lot. Now, who do you suppose it was who lost his balance and fell in the water? The section commander! We all . . .'

Fruma eyed her son and exclaimed:

'You've lost at least ten pounds. Have you had any lunch? Where? No, you haven't. I'll dash across to the hall and get you something to eat. Just a snack – I'll make you a proper meal when you've had a rest. How about some raw carrot? It's very good for you. Are you sure? I can't force you. All right, then, have a shower and go to sleep. You can eat when you wake up. But perhaps I'd better take you to the surgery right away. Wait a minute. Here's a nice glass of orange juice. Don't argue, drink it.'

'I jumped in the water and fished him out,' Rami continued. 'Then I had to dive in again to look for his rifle. Poor wretch! It was hilarious. It wasn't his first accident, though. Once, on an exercise . . .'

'You need some new socks. They're all falling apart,' Fruma remarked as she pulled his dirty laundry out of the kit bag.

'Once, on an exercise, he fired his submachine gun by accident. Nearly killed the battalion commander. He's the clumsiest fool you can imagine. You can tell what he's like from his name. He's called Zalman Zulman. I've written a song about him, and we sing it all day long. Listen.'

'But they don't feed you there. And you didn't write every other day, as you promised. But I saw in the letter box that you wrote to Noga Harish. That's life. Your mother works her fingers to the bone, and some child comes and collects the honey. It doesn't matter now. There's something I must know: Did she answer your letter? No? Just as I thought. You don't know what she's like. It was just as well you ditched her. Everybody knows what she is. The mistress of a man who's old enough to be her grandfather. It's disgusting. Disgusting. Have you got enough razor blades? It's disgusting, I tell you.'

'Is it true they're starting to work the Camel's Field? That's going to cause a flare-up, all right. Provided, of course, the powers that be don't get cold feet. You know, Jewish sentimentality and all that. My buddies say . . .'

'Go and have a shower. The water's just right now. No, I heard every word. Test me. "Jewish sentimentality." There aren't many boys of your age with such an independent way of thinking. After your shower you can have a nap. Meanwhile, I'll ask the nurse to come here. That wound looks very nasty. You've got to have it seen to.'

'By the way, Mom, did you just say that she . . .'

'Yes, son?'

'All right. Never mind. It doesn't matter now.'

'Tell me, tell me what you need. I'm not tired. I can do anything you want me to.'

'No, thanks, I don't need anything. I just wanted to say something, but it's not important. It's irrelevant. I've forgotten. Stop running around. I can't bear it. We'll talk this evening. Meanwhile, you must have a rest, too.'

'Me! I'll rest in my grave. I don't need to rest. I'm not tired. When you were a baby, you had something wrong with your ears. A chronic infection. There weren't any antibiotics then. You cried all night, night after night. You were in pain. And you've always been a sensitive boy. I rocked your cradle all night, night after night, and sang you songs. One does everything for children, without counting the cost. You won't repay me. You'll repay it to your own children. I won't be here any more, but you'll be a good father, because you're so sensitive. You don't think about rest when you're doing something for your children. How old were you then? You've forgotten all about it. It was the time when Yoash started going to school, so it must have been when you were eighteen months old. You were always a delicate child. Here am I rambling on, and you need to sleep. Go to sleep now.'

'By the way, Mom, if you're going to the surgery could you bring me some corn ointment. You won't forget, will you?'

At five o'clock Rami woke up, put on a clean white shirt and gray trousers, quietly helped himself to a snack, and then went to the basketball field. On the way he met Einav, limping awkwardly. She asked how he was. He said he was fine. She asked if it was a hard life. He said he was ready to face any hardships. She asked if his mother was pleased with him and answered her own question:

'Of course Fruma's pleased with you. You're so bronzed and handsome.'

The field was floodlit, but the light was not noticeable in the bright twilight. The only living souls there were Oren's gang. Rami put his hands in his pockets and stood for a while without doing or saying anything. The Sabbath will go by. Empty. Without anything happening. With mother. Sticky.

What do I need? A cigarette. That thin boy playing by himself over there in the corner is called Ido Zohar. Once I caught him sitting in the common room at night writing a poem. What was I saying? A cigarette.

Rami put the cigarette to his mouth and two planes roared by, shattering the Sabbatical calm, hidden in the twilight glow. The dying sun struck sparks off their fuselage. The metal shone back dazzlingly. In a flash Rami realized that they were not our planes. They had the enemy's markings on their wings. An excited shout burst from his throat.

'Theirs!'

Instinctively he looked down, just long enough to hear Oren's confused cry, but by the time he looked up again the drama was almost over. The enemy planes had turned tail and were fleeing from other planes that were approaching powerfully from the southwest, evidently trying to block their escape. Instantly, dark shapes fell through the air toward the orchards to the north. Both planes had jettisoned the spare fuel tanks fixed to their wings to speed their flight. Rami clenched his fists and growled through his teeth, 'Let them have it.' Before he had finished there was an answering burst of gun-fire. Lightning flashed. After what seemed a long interval, there came a dull roll of thunder. The fate of the raid was settled in an instant. The enemy planes disappeared over the mountains, one of them trailing a cloud of white smoke mixed with gray. Their pursuers paused, circled the valley twice like angry hounds, then vanished into the darkening sky.

Oren shouted jubilantly:

'We hit one! We smashed one! We brought one down!'

And Rami Rimon, like a child, not like a soldier, hugged Oren Geva and exclaimed:

'I hope they burn! I hope they burn to death!'

He pounded Oren's ribs exultantly with his fists until Oren drew away groaning with pain. Rami was seized by demented joy.

His joy accompanied him to the dining hall, where a spirit of noisy excitement reigned. He made his way among the tables to where Noga Harish stood in her best dress, looking at the notice board. He put his hands on her shoulders and whispered in her ear:

'Well, silly girl, did you see or didn't you?'

Noga turned to face him with a condescending smile.

'Good Sabbath, Rami. You're very brown. It suits you. You look happy.'

'I . . . I saw it all. From beginning to end. I was up at the basketball field. Suddenly I heard a noise to the east, and I realized at once that . . .'

'You're like my little brother. You're cute. You're happy.'

These remarks encouraged Rami. He spoke up boldly:

'Shall we go outside? Will you come outside with me?'

Noga thought for a moment. Then she smiled inwardly, with her eyes, not with her mouth.

'Why not?' she said.

'Come on then,' said Rami, and took hold of her arm. Almost at once he let it go.

When they were outside the dining hall, Noga said:

'Where shall we go?'

Strangely enough, at that moment Noga remembered something she had forgotten: Rami's full name was Avraham. Avraham Rominov.

'Anywhere,' Rami said, 'Let's go.'

Noga suggested they sit down on the yellow bench, facing the door of the dining hall. Rami was embarrassed. People would see them there, he said. And stare at them. And talk.

Noga smiled again, and again she asked calmly, 'Why not?'

Rami could find no answer to her question. He crossed his legs, took a cigarette out of his shirt pocket, tapped it three times on his matchbox, stuck it in the corner of his mouth, struck a match, shielded the flame with both hands even though there was no wind, inhaled deeply with half-closed eyes, blew out a long stream of smoke, and when all this was done, lowered his eyes to the ground once more. Finally, he gave her a sidelong glance and began:

'Well? What have you got to say for yourself?'

Noga replied that she hadn't been going to say anything. On the contrary, she thought it was he who was going to do the talking.

'Oh, nothing special. Just . . . What do you expect me to do?' he suddenly burst out violently. 'Spend the whole evening, the whole Sabbath, my whole leave with my mother, like some mother's darling?'

'Why not? She's missed you badly.'

'Why not? Because . . . All right. I can see I bore you. Don't think I can't live without you. I can get on quite well without you. Do you think I can't?'

203

Noga said she was sure he could manage perfectly well without her.

They fell silent.

Hasia Ramigolski and Esther Klieger-Isarov came toward them, chatting in Yiddish and laughing. When they caught sight of Noga and Rami their conversation stopped dead. As they walked past, Hasia said:

'Good evening. Shabbat Shalom.' She dwelt suggestively on the stressed syllables.

Rami grunted, but Noga smiled and said gently:

'A very good evening to you both.'

Rami said nothing for a while. Then he murmured:

'Well?'

'I'm listening.'

'I hear they're going to start working on the hill,' Rami said. 'There's going to be trouble.'

'It's so pointless.'

Rami quickly changed the subject. He told the story of his section commander who had fallen in the water while trying to demonstrate how to cross a river on a rope bridge. He went on to say that it wasn't the poor fool's first accident. 'Once, on an exercise, he accidentally fired his submachine gun and nearly killed the battalion commander. You can tell what he's like from his name. He's called Zalman Zulman, of all things. I've written a rhyme about him:

> Zalman Zulman's full of fun,
> Always letting off his gun.

Zalman Zulman lost his grip,
Took an unexpected dip.
Zalman Zulman . . .

'Just a minute. Does he play an instrument?'
'Who?'
'Zalman. The man you were talking about. What's the matter with your elbow?'
'What's that got to do with it?' Rami asked indignantly.
'With what?'
'With what we were talking about.'
'You were telling me about someone called Zalman. I asked if he played an instrument. You haven't answered my question.'
'But I don't see what . . .'
'You're very brown. It suits you.'
'It's hardly surprising. We train all day in the sun. Of course we get brown. Listen: we went on a fifty-mile route march, with all the kit, gun, pack, spade, and all at the trot. Eight of the people in my squad . . .'
'Chilly, don't you think?'
'. . . collapsed on the way. And we had to carry them on stretchers. I . . .'
'I'm cold. Couldn't you finish the story tomorrow? If you don't mind terribly.'
'What's the matter?' Rami considered, and then asked thickly, 'What's up? Is somebody waiting for you? Are you rushing off to . . . to keep an appointment?'
'Yes. I've got to take my father his dinner. He isn't well.'

'What, again?' Rami asked absently. Noga explained that he had a pain in his chest and the doctor had ordered him to go to bed.

'Next week he's got to go and have an examination. That's all. Shall we meet here again tomorrow afternoon?'

Rami did not answer. He lit another cigarette and threw the lighted match away behind the bench. Noga said good night and started to go. Then she stopped, turned, and said:

'Don't smoke too much.'

At that moment five steps separated them. Rami asked irritably why she should care whether he smoked a lot or a little. Noga ignored his question and said:

'You're very brown. It suits you. Good night.'

Rami said nothing. He sat alone on the bench until the dancing started in the square, as it did every Friday night at a quarter past nine.

When it was over, shortly before midnight, he set off for his mother's room. He changed his course, however, because he met Dafna Isarov, who asked him if he was going home to bed already, and Rami thought he detected a sneer in her voice. So he turned off the path. His feet guided him toward the cow shed, where he had worked before he was called up. And as he walked he talked to himself.

This could never have happened to Yoash. It's happened to me, though. Women understand only one language, brute force. But, as mother said, I was always a delicate child. Hell. Now they're laughing. Everybody wants something bad to happen to someone else so as to make life more interesting. It's like that everywhere; it's like that on the kibbutz and it's even like that in the army. You're a child you're a child you're a child. You're like my little brother. Maybe being brown does suit me, but it hasn't got me anywhere. She didn't insult me for once. She didn't even call me a horse. What did she do to me tonight, how did she make fun of me? My Rami is a delicate, sensitive boy. I wish I could die. That'd show them. I can bend this sprinkler with my bare hands. That'll drive Theodor Herzl Goldring mad. I've got stronger hands than Yoash. If only he weren't dead, I'd show him. Where am I going? Walking around like some Jack looking for his Jill. Leaping on the mountains, skipping in the hills, as that filthy old lecher would say. People like that ought to be put down. Like Arabs. Punch him in the face, he raises his hands to protect himself, you hit him in the stomach and give him a kick for good measure. All over. Here we are at the cow shed. Hey, Titan, good bull. Are you awake? Bulls sleep standing up because they can't lie down because of the iron ring. If they come to slaughter you, Titan, don't let them. Don't give in. Show your mettle. Don't be a ghetto bull. Give them a *corrida*. We mustn't give in without a struggle. We must be strong and quick and light and violent like a jet fighter. Swoop and dart and turn and soar like a knife flashing through the sky like a fighter. A fighter is such a powerful thing. I could have been a pilot, but Mother.

Strange that the moon is shining. The moon does strange things. Changes things strangely. Changes the colors of things. Silver. My Rami is a delicate sensitive child Rami writes poems like Ido Zohar he loves nature hell he loves plants and animals hope they burn to death. Her father has a pain in his chest. It's because of old Berger. Dirty old man. Her father taught us a

207

poem by Bialik once, called 'The Slaughter,' where it says that there is no justice in this world. It's true. It's a ghetto poem, but it's true. He's lived his life, he's got grown-up children, he's found his niche. Why did he steal from me? What have I done to him? And she said I was brown and handsome. If I'm brown and handsome, and he's old and fat, then why.

When I die, she'll know. It'll shatter her. The moon colors everything white. Silver. Listen, Noga, listen. I've also got a pain in my chest, I'm also in pain, so why don't you. I make fun of Zalman Zulman, she makes fun of me, they all make fun of me. It shows there isn't any justice in the world, only slaughter, Titan, worse than anything the Devil could invent. That's from the same poem. The man who's being slaughtered starts thinking about justice. The man who's slaughtering him thinks only about violence. My mistake was not to use force on her. Why, Titan, why didn't I use force, do you know why? I'll tell you. Because my Rami is a delicate boy curse them he loves nature hope they burn he loves plants and animals filthy whores. That sounds like planes overhead. It's after midnight. I love these planes, roaring along without lights. There's going to be a big war. I'll die. Then they'll know.

The fish ponds. A light in Grisha's hut. A pressure lamp. I can hear Grisha's voice. In the boat. Shouting to his fishermen. He's been in three wars and he's come out alive.

Maybe Dafna, his daughter. Ridiculous. They'd laugh. What's in this filthy shed? Barrels. Sacks of fish food. The fishermen's supper. If they find me here. Grisha's belt. A pistol. It's a revolver. Fancy leaving a revolver in an empty shed. They'll be coming back to eat soon. They'll laugh, they'll laugh. They'll say I went for a walk to look for inspiration. I know how it works. It has a revolving drum with six chambers. You put a bullet in each chamber. After each shot the drum revolves and brings another bullet in line with the barrel. That's how the revolver works. Now let's see how Rami Rimon works. A trial. Without a judge. I'm the judge. Now let's begin.

Rami takes a bullet out of the leather holster, a yellow metal case containing a little brown metal projectile. First of all, he puts the bullet in his mouth. A sharp, metallic taste. Then he puts the bullet in one of the chambers. He spins the drum without looking, because luck must be blind. He puts the gun to his temple. The chances are five to one. He squeezes the trigger. A dry thud. Rami inserts a second bullet. Spins the blind drum. Four to two. Gun to temple. Squeezes. Dry thud. Maybe I'm being silly. We'll soon know, Judge. I'm not trying to kill myself. It's only an experiment. Up to five. A delicate sensitive child couldn't do this. A third bullet. Blind spin. Cold damp hand. I've touched something damp. If I can do this, I'm not a delicate sensitive child. Up to five. Gun to temple. Squeeze the trigger. Dry thud. I'm past halfway. Two more tries. Fourth bullet. Now the odds are against me. Now comes the test. Watch carefully, Judge. Spin. Slowly. The drum, slowly. Without looking. Slowly. Temple. You're crazy. But you're no coward. Slowly squeeze. It's cold here.

Now the fifth. Last one. Like an injection. Delicate sensitive child's trembling. Why? Nothing will happen because nothing's happened so far, even though according to the odds I should have died with the fourth bullet. Don't tremble, dear little delicate child who cried all night with earache, don't tremble,

think of Grisha Isarov who's come out of three wars alive.
Yoash wouldn't have trembled, because he was Yoash. Little
ghetto boy, with a little cap and a gray coat and side curls, I
want to know how many I. Not to kill myself. Four. That's
enough. Madness to go on. No, we said five – five let it be.
Don't change your mind, coward, don't lie, you said five, not
four. Five let it be. Put the gun to your temple. Now squeeze,
horse, squeeze, you're a ghetto child, you're a little boy, you're
my little brother, squeeze. Wait a moment. I'm allowed to think
first. Suppose I die here. She'll know. She'll know I wasn't joking. But they'll say 'broken heart' they'll say 'unrequited love'
they'll say 'emotional crisis.' Sticky, very sticky. Hell. Squeeze.
You won't feel a thing. A bullet in the brain is instant death.
No time for pain. And afterward? Like plunging through the
sky. An invisible fighter. It doesn't hurt. Perhaps I've already
pressed the trigger and died perhaps when you die nothing
changes. Other people see a corpse blood bones and you carry
on as usual. I can try again. If I press the trigger, it's a sign I'm
still alive. Afterward everything will be black and warm. When
you die it's warm even though the body gets cold. Warm and
safe like under a blanket in winter. And quiet. Squeeze. You've
got a chance. Like when we used to play dice when I was little
and sometimes I wanted very badly to throw a six and I threw
a six. Now I want very badly to press the trigger but my finger
won't press. Trembling. Careful you don't press it accidentally.
Everything is different when the moon shines yellow. Can hear
Grisha cursing next week we're going to the firing range that'll
be interesting I'll be top of the class I'm an excellent shot now
count up to three and shoot. Eyes open. No. Eyes closed. No.

One, two, th – no. Up to ten. One, two, three, four, five, six, seven, eight, nine, t –.

But Rami Rimon did not try his luck the fifth time. He put down the revolver and went out into the fields and wandered about till his feet guided him back to the cow shed. Grisha won't notice. And if he does, he'll have a shock. I forgot to check the most important thing. I didn't look inside the gun to see what would have happened if I'd pressed the fifth time. Better not to know. Some things are better left undone.

A new thought occurred to Rami. It soothed him like a gentle caress. Not all men are born to be heroes. Maybe I wasn't born to be a hero. But in every man there's something special, something that isn't in other men. In my nature, for instance, there's a certain sensitivity. A capacity to suffer and feel pain. Perhaps I was born to be an artist, or even a doctor. Some women go for doctors and others go for artists. Men aren't all cast in the same mold. It's true, I'm not Yoash. But Yoash wasn't me. I've got some things he didn't have. A painter, perhaps.

It'll be morning soon. Planes in the sky. Sad. Zalman Zulman's full of fun, always letting off his gun. Zalman Zulman lost his grip, took an unexpected dip. Zalman Zulman, whore like me, looking for justice in the w.c. Zalman Zulman go to bed, time to rest your weary head.

I composed the poem. I can abolish it. It's an abolished poem.

21

To Read Poems

THE SUMMER is at its height.

The school is closed. The children have been sent to help in the fields. Tractors rumble noisily to and fro. Every spare hand has been pressed into service. Time is short. We, too, are going. Be patient.

We shall leave Reuven Harish in peace. We know that he is going through a difficult period. We refer to his health, not to his family troubles. We judge physical infirmities indulgently. Gone are the days when we made a man like Alter Rominov work in the fields. Most of us are no longer young, and we know the terror of unexplained pains.

Reuven Harish had a pain in his chest, and the doctor ordered him to bed for a few days. He had two women to look after him. Bronka brought him his breakfast and lunch on a tray, and Noga brought him his supper. Noga also looked after Gai on the rare occasions when the little rascal showed up at his father's house. Relations between the two women, not surprisingly, were curt. Bronka might say, for instance:

'The bedclothes need changing.'

Noga throws her a sidelong glance, and answers after a deliberate interval:

'Yes.'

Bronka asks:

'Does he sleep well at night? If not, I've got some very good pills.'

Noga says:

'I don't know. I don't ask him how he sleeps at night.'

Bronka says:

'There are some boxes of grapes outside the kitchens. I'll go and fetch some.'

Noga says:

'Thank you.'

Bronka says:

'You don't have to thank me.'

Noga asks with a calm, calculated smile:

'Why not?'

After a few days Reuven went to hospital for a checkup. The results of the examination came in the post at the end of the week. He was not suffering from a malignant disease. The examination had revealed a slight dilation of the blood vessels that, in conjunction with instability and frequent fluctuations in the blood pressure, could give rise to a certain anxiety. Anxiety, not panic, the kibbutz doctor emphasized to the patient. There was no danger. The conclusions were self-evident: to avoid all tension, take plenty of rest, abstain from certain foods, not to give up physical work but not to overdo it. Gardening was an excellent form of exercise. Above all, not to fall prey to depression. The latest expert opinion was that depression has a direct effect on the bodily organs, and the blood vessels provided the prime example. There was no danger, no defect, certainly no cause for panic, only a temporary unpleasantness that demanded a measure of caution and restraint.

One evening Bronka called on Reuven to ask whether he would like to go to the meeting of the classical music circle. She thought it would do him good to go. It would take his mind off his gloomy thoughts. Reuven replied that music would only aggravate his recent tendency to depression. Bronka said that his isolation was encouraging unkind speculation. Reuven answered that he did not consider himself above being judged by his fellows. In any case, he added, waving a frail arm in the general direction of the window, as people grew older they must keep their eyes open. Bronka said she did not see exactly what he was getting at. Reuven did not answer. The room grew darker. Outside the lamp came on and cast a faint light through the window. Reuven groaned. Bronka asked anxiously if he was feeling ill. Reuven ignored her question and said:

'Bronka, very soon you're going to be grandmother to a dear little granddaughter. I've been thinking, perhaps . . . Perhaps you ought to tell Ezra . . .'

Before he had finished his sentence Bronka got up from her chair and came over to sit on the edge of his bed. She rolled back the blanket and laid her kind, wrinkled hand on his chest. Her voice when she spoke was full of emotion:

'Reuven.'

'Yes?'

'I beg of you . . .'

'Yes. Carry on.'

'Get up. Let's go and listen to the music.'

'You know, Bronka, I never took Ezra seriously.'

'I don't understand. What are you trying to say?'

'I hadn't judged him, if you see what I mean. Until the day we traveled back from Tel Aviv together. After what happened at the bus station. I was shattered. He didn't gloat. No. That journey opened my eyes. I saw him. I saw that he . . . that he was alive. Do you know what he talked to me about all the way?'

'The Bible? The fishermen? His two brothers?'

'No. About death. He said the important thing wasn't to die gloriously. It was to die as late as possible. You remember the Dutch colonel? You know, I told you about him. When you're ill, you connect things in your mind. I made the connection. He too . . .'

'Don't talk about that.'

'Bronka, we, you, me, Ezra, we're past the halfway mark. We're nearer to the end of the journey than the start. I've got to go back. I've forgotten something at an earlier stop. It doesn't matter. It was a line from a poem I shan't write. It's sad. There's something else I have to say. After all . . . all that, you'd think . . . I thought all that would count in my favor . . . But no. There are no reductions. No privileges. Not even for . . . It doesn't matter. I don't think the system is right. But that's not the main point. The main point,' Reuven continued after a pause, his warm, steady voice filling the room, filling the darkness, 'the main point is that we both have children, and our children judge us and they don't judge us fairly. It's dark outside, Bronka, and outside in the dark my daughter is living a wild life. How does she think of me? A tedious sermonizer. A quitter. A man who didn't have the strength to save her mother for her. A loser. A disgrace, Bronka, that's how she thinks of me. She lives a wild life outside in the dark, she hates words, Bronka. What does she think of me? She's out there now. I'm jealous of her. I'm jealous for her. She doesn't belong to me. She'll go somewhere else.'

'Reuven.'

'But I'm not ashamed. I may not be a winner . . .'

'Reuven, I'll stay here. I won't go to the music. I'll put the kettle on. We'll have some tea.'

'I may not be a winner, but I'm not ashamed for a moment. Of anything. I'm not ashamed of my poems. And I'm not ashamed of my children. Even if they go away. Even if they make fun of me. Even if they change. I'm not ashamed of anything in my world. Bronka.'

'Yes.'

'What will you do if Einav has a boy instead of a girl?'

'What a funny question. What'll I do? What can I do? What a strange question.'

'It doesn't matter. Bronka.'

'Yes.'

'I've changed my mind.'

'What about?'

'The music. I'll get dressed. We'll go.'

'We'll go?'

'Wait. The kettle's boiling. Have some tea first.'

'Coffee. I'd rather have coffee.'

'But . . .'

'And then we'll go. Together.'

And on Saturday morning, when Reuven was sitting in a deck chair in his little garden and Noga was lying next to him on the grass and asking if he shouldn't go indoors because it was getting very hot outside, Reuven answered her question with one of his own.

'Stella, you used to read a lot of poetry. Do you still have the time and the inclination to read poetry?'

'Why do you ask?'

'It occurred to me that we might . . . that it would be nice if you and I could read poems together one evening a week.'

'If you like, I've got no . . .'

'No, you don't have to. No.'

'Daddy,' Noga said, 'there's something I've always wanted to say to you, but I never know how to say it. It's that people . . . that people are people. Take yourself, for instance. You should let yourself be. Don't force yourself to be words. People can't ever be words. And you . . . You don't have to keep on proving. You're not a proof. You're . . . You're a person. I haven't said it very well, have I? You haven't understood. I can't explain. I've got to tell you. But I don't know how to.'

'So you don't want to. You don't want us to read poetry together one evening a week. You don't have to. I just thought we might, perhaps, we might start with . . .'

22

More of the Blessed Routine

WITH EYES like hawks' we observe our neighbors' actions. Our judgments take effect in a hundred and one devious ways.

Let us eavesdrop, for example, on the conversations in the communal clothes store. Here the long hot hours crawl sluggishly on, hours of ironing and mending and sorting clothes. The cupboards are divided into compartments, family by family, like the cells in a honeycomb.

Einav Geva tells Nina Goldring what she has heard from Dafna Isarov. Nina Goldring tells Einav Geva what she has heard from Yitzhak Friedrich, the treasurer. Fruma Rominov tells Hasia Ramigolski, on the authority of Gerda Zohar, who heard from Bronka Berger, the original source: Reuven Harish is worn out and depressed. Because of his illness and also because of his daughter. Apropos of which, some say that Ezra Berger has written to his brother in Germany, the one called Zechariah, who changed his name to Siegfried, and hinted in his usual apothegmatic way at the new complication.

'And what about Siegfried?'

'Well, this Siegfried is a business partner of Eva's new husband. So Eva will find out about it all. As for Eva, there's a feeling going around that she'll come back to us. And then we'll see.'

'They say her husband's bought her a car and hired her a chauffeur, and she lives like a lady in high society.'

'Still, I think she'll come back. I don't believe she's happy there. Do you really think money and comfort are everything? No, money can't buy happiness,' said Hasia Ramigolski, and Gerda Zohar was quick to agree with her.

'Meanwhile, Siegfried's on his way here. Bronka said he's coming to Israel to sign on artists for his cabaret. Anyway, Eva will find out about her daughter. If you ask me, it'll give her something to think about.'

'Blood's thicker than water. And the apple doesn't fall far from the tree, as they say.'

'There's a famous novel about an old man who was always running after young girls.'

'You think there isn't enough material here for a novel already?'

'Anyway, now that things have taken this turn . . .'

'If you think about it, from one point of view you could say that Bronka's really Noga's stepmother. In that case, Ezra's her mother's husband, in other words, her father. But from the other point of view you could say that Reuven is Ezra's father-in-law. And in that case, Bronka is Reuven's . . . You don't follow? I'll explain again. Slowly. Look:'

'I'm not surprised at the children. Ezra's or Reuven's. You don't have to be a great psychologist to see that . . .'

'I'm surprised at Reuven not making the girl stop it. A real father would have . . .'

'Yes, but don't forget that his relations with the girl aren't easy.'

'Oh, no. Definitely not. Not at all easy.'

As soon as Fruma had left, Einav Geva said sweetly:

'About Fruma, I want to tell you, they say she's wild because Noga Harish dropped her little genius. Fruma won't ever forgive her for it.'

At this Hasia Ramigolski rounded on Einav menacingly:

'It sounds to me, Einav, as if you're gloating. I don't approve of gloating over someone else's misfortunes.'

'Heaven forbid. I wasn't gloating. I was simply stating a fact. Fruma won't forgive her. She doesn't know how to be friendly. Once we were working together at the baking oven. You can't imagine the kind of things I had to listen to. Don't ask me to repeat them. She was oozing malice from every pore. She told me, for instance, under the pretence of being friendly, that . . .'

'No, Einav. You're still young. You don't understand human nature. Fruma isn't malicious. Fruma is a woman who's suffered misfortunes. And one can understand her. And if you don't understand a person like that, if you can't understand, it's a sign that . . .'

'You're right, Hasia, you're quite right.' Einav avoided the ambush that threatened to cut off her line of retreat. 'I'm not disagreeing with you about that. All I'm saying is that there's no contradiction: a woman can be unfortunate and still be malicious.'

Hasia rejected the offer of a cease-fire. She had another blow to deal, and a chance to secure much better terms of capitulation.

'You don't understand at all, my dear. But just wait a bit. You'll be a mother soon. I hope you aren't made to suffer. But if you are, you'll learn a few home truths. You'll realize, for instance, that Fruma is a wonderfully straightforward woman. Of course, you haven't had a chance to appreciate that yet. When you've had to face the disasters that Fruma's had to overcome . . .'

Einav put up a desperate struggle. Her voice took on a singsong tone, as if she was trying to teach Hasia a fact of life.

'I'm telling you, Hasia, Fruma Rominov would be malicious even without the disasters. It's in her nature. I've heard what sort of a person she was before all those famous disasters. I've heard. It's in her nature, I tell you. And you can't change human nature. It's a waste of time talking about it. By the way, Hasia, that's a lovely blue shirt your Tsvi . . .'

No. Hasia was not one to allow her victim to escape from her clutches by an old trick like that. Hasia wasn't interested at the moment in Tsvi's shirts. She was interested in crushing once and for all the shallow arrogance of these young people who consider themselves to be experts in psychology.

'No, my dear. If you want to know what Fruma Rominov was like when she was younger, you ask me. Fruma may be a difficult person. But she's straightforward. And that's a very positive combination. Before you form opinions about people, Einav, my dear, you must understand a bit about psychology. Talking casually like that, excuse me for saying so, is a sign of immaturity. But I understand you. I understand what makes you think as you do. I see exactly why you can't be objective. I won't explain now. In a few years' time, perhaps. If you still remember this conversation, I'll remind you what you were like once, and we'll both smile. You know, when a person judges someone else, he's really judging himself, without realizing it. And you can see what he's really like.'

Einav gave a last wriggle. 'I didn't mean to say that Fruma was entirely negative. You don't have to be an expert in psychology to know that there's nobody who's entirely negative. There are various facets to everybody, including Fruma. All I wanted to . . .'

'You've changed your ground now. If you'd only thought before you started speaking, Einav, you wouldn't have said things you'd have to retract later. These trousers are only good for the garbage heap. That Grisha gets through working clothes like a youngster of twenty.'

Einav, grateful for her conqueror's magnanimity, ventured cautiously:

'Have you heard what they've been saying lately, Hasia? About Grisha, I mean.'

'I've heard something, not about him but about one of his daughters. You'd better watch out, Einav. They say your husband's made friends with one of the little Isarov girls. I heard that last week, after a basketball game, the little Isarov girl dried his back for him. If I were in your place, I'd have a word with my young man before the birds start chirruping. You should always stitch that kind of seam from the back. It's stronger that way, and it looks better too. That's right, unstitch it, don't be slovenly at your age, unstitch it and sew it again from the back.'

The buried roots of a burned tree trunk.

Three small concrete bungalows with corrugated-iron roofs. Like those the British army built to house its men. Each one is divided into two dwellings by a plywood partition. In this way we were enabled to house six old people. They are the parents of the founders of our kibbutz, who survived and came here to shelter beneath their sons' and daughters' wings.

The grandparents occupy a special position here in Metsudat Ram. They are not real members, but they enjoy most of the members' rights without any of the obligations. They have voluntarily taken on certain tasks, such as knitting and darning socks.

We must admit that there is something ridiculous, even embarrassing, in the spectacle of an ancient old man bending over a worn-out sock and painfully darning it. But who compelled them to? We didn't. They offered to do it of their own free will.

Throughout the morning you can see them, a dark cluster in the shade of the spreading sycamore that stands opposite their bungalows. They sit in easy chairs, their frail bodies wrapped in dressing gowns; the knitting quivers in their hands, and their heads are bent as though they are muttering spells.

Sometimes brown-skinned children gather at a slight distance, pointing and chanting: 'Grandpas, Grandmas, dance, dance, dance.'

When we said that the old folk are lean, we were not idly generalizing. As it happens, there are three old men and three old women living here, and not one of the six is fat. The leading figure among them, known as Gospodin Podolski (the father of the Podolski who arranges the work rota), is tall and thin, but he has a hunch on his left shoulder. The other two men are short and frail; they are nicknamed respectively 'Thick' and 'Thin.' The former's head, cheeks, chin, and neck are covered with short white bristles. The latter is completely bald. His face is pink and smooth like a young girl's. His gestures are so careful that it seems as if he is moving through a world made entirely of crystal.

Of the women, one is as slender as a twisted stick; her face is long and sharp; her hair is thin and shows the skin of her scalp. The second is hunched up like a baby, with her head sunk between her shoulders. But her eyes are clear and radiate an inner light. The third is sunken-cheeked and always wears a black dress and a necklace of glass beads and a pince-nez secured by a curling red cord. She is Esther Klieger's mother and the grandmother of the Isarov tribe.

Toward ten o'clock they nod off to sleep. They look like dark statues. Even in these burning hours, they are muffled in cardigans, pullovers, and woolen caps. They seem like an expedition camping apprehensively in dangerous territory. Or like the representatives of a state that no longer exists, lingering on with stubborn pride in a strange and hostile capital.

They do not talk much. Sunbeams filter through the leafy sycamore and touch them kindly. If one of them starts to say something, he can rarely expect an answer. They speak a Yiddish dotted with Russian and Polish words. Mrs Klieger, for example, may say:

'It drives me mad. I used to be able to thread a needle with my eyes shut.'

Or:

'That beetroot soup yesterday was nothing like borsch.'

Or:

'My flower pot broke, and I planted the geranium in an old tin.'

Or:

'My sleeping pills have no effect on me any more.'

And Gospodin Podolski, after considerable reflection:

'Well, well.'

Or:

'That mouse came again last night. I found proof. It ate one of my cookies.'

Sometimes, with his eyes closed, 'Thick' may say:

'There was a *goy* in my town. Trochim his name was. He owned woods. He was a terrible anti-Semite. And he, of all people, hid a Jewish girl in the bad days. Two Jewish girls.'

And one of the women, the one with the thinning hair:

'All the rags under the stairs ought to be burned.'

The connection between this and the previous remark is dubious. But 'Thick' interrupts her accusingly:

'A diet without salt robs you of all your strength. And I mean *all* your strength.'

At this Gospodin Podolski emits an angry growl and shakes his head. He eyes his audience. Then he lays a firm hand on the arm of 'Thin,' an unusual gesture here. 'Thin' trembles. Gospodin Podolski states with conviction:

'Nowadays one may keep a small farm there. Not like in Stalin's days.'

The hunched-up woman replies:

'The Ukrainians were always the worst. A thousand curses on them. And the same goes for the Lithuanians.'

Mrs Klieger tries to illustrate this with a story.

'Back in Rovno there used to be a Jew. He was really well off. He had his own mill. And what does he do now? Now he's a carter near Haifa. But I knew him. He was a good man. A saint. He still is. Such men you don't find any more. He had three daughters. One of them . . .'

But fatigue overcomes Mrs Klieger. Her story disintegrates and evaporates in the hot air. Or perhaps she stopped because the hunched woman cut in with:

'Tea will be here soon.'

The old folk all come from the vicinity of Kovel. The parents of the German members did not survive. Some died peacefully, like Grandma Stella Hamburger, and some died violently, like Reuven Harish's parents and sisters.

Many years ago, in Kovel, when the future founders of our kibbutz were carried away by their enthusiasm for the Zionist youth movement, their parents tried to stop them, some with anger, some with taunts, and others with rational arguments. But in time the tables were turned, and they were forced to seek refuge here with their obstinate progeny. In consequence, they behave toward their sons and daughters, and even toward their grandchildren, with extreme politeness and even respect. They do not proffer advice, as old people elsewhere do. They submit uncomplainingly to all the regulations of the kibbutz. A silenced terror seems to govern all their dealings with the kibbutz institutions. If one brings them a trayload of tea, they half rise and bow, and Gospodin Podolski offers his thanks on behalf of the whole community. This is the point of the Jewish saying 'He who has been scalded by hot water blows on cold water.' In the presence of the kibbutz secretary or treasurer or sanitary officer they behave as if he represented a tyrannical Gentile authority. Every evening they shuffle weakly to their children's rooms to have coffee with the family and to look – but only look – at their grandchildren. They would never dare play with the little children or tell them stories for fear of breaking the unfathomable educational rules. When the malicious chorus chants at them: 'Grandpas, Grandmas, dance, dance, dance,' they hunch their shoulders and turn up their collars, as if against a fierce wind. After all, they have been warned time and again, tactfully but firmly, that a modern child is not to be smacked or rebuked, so as not to harm its delicate sensibilities.

Their old age is apparently protected against every want and humiliation. But they are isolated in their own quarters. They try to contract themselves to avoid being in the way. An air of sadness envelops them. How can it be helped? They have left their best years far away, their own children have got the better of them, they have felt the touch of an icy finger, and they are doomed to sadness. Even the evergreen pine trees, when a slight wind touches their boughs, let out a faint moan.

At midday the dining hall fills with hungry, thirsty people. By one, the hall is almost empty. The members whose turn it is to work in the dining hall clear and wipe the tables and start laying them ready for supper. They work expertly, mechanically, their minds free to dwell on other things. Within limits, of course. Absent-mindedness is liable to interfere with efficiency.

At two o'clock Ezra Berger signs the bill of lading, collects his thermos of coffee and bag of sandwiches from Nina Goldring, and sets off on his second trip of the day.

Shortly afterward, Fruma Rominov appears at the door of the kitchens to load her dishes with the young children's evening meal. At the other end of the kitchens Herbert Segal pants as he unloads the milk churns from his little trolley. If you walk across the yard, you will come across Reuven Harish, his shoulders slightly bowed, trailing a group of tourists. His speech is slow and thoughtful, as if he is confiding his doubts to his audience rather than haranguing them with brisk slogans. At times he attains a musical flood of enthusiasm, and his voice wavers, as if in an effort to stem a rising surge of emotion. His audience, not unnaturally, frame such remarks as:

'This is a real religious experience.'

Or:

'A truly Biblical figure.'

Later, at four o'clock in the afternoon the time-honored rest; deck chairs on the lawn, the whisper of the wind in the trees, the scent of roses and of coffee, the clicking of knitting needles, evening papers, reading glasses, the twilight glow, answered by a blaze of light on the mountain-tops to the east, Herzl Goldring's accordion, Herbert Segal's violin, the spray from the sprinklers. Even the sight of Oren Geva and his friends stealthily climbing up to the observation point at the top of the water tower for some unknown purpose cannot dispel the calm.

*

Every Saturday evening the kibbutz assembly meets. Tsvi Ramigolski puts on his glasses, beats the table top with his hand, rebukes the knitters, appeals vainly to the cluster gathered around the new week's work roster.

Occasionally, a dispute arises, but it is always good-tempered. The practical-minded propose practical solutions, while the theorists swoop on their solutions and produce a dozen proofs to show that what seems good in the short run will produce appalling results in the course of time. Tsvi Ramigolski guides the dispute skillfully toward a compromise between the demands of idealism on the one hand and realism on the other.

A report on security from Grisha Isarov. Grisha's delivery is gruff, but his news is good: the grim prophecies have been proved wrong. Things are quiet. No worries. Still, no one can tell what will happen tomorrow. Or even tonight. I'm no prophet. Especially when the word comes through about the Camel's Field. Meanwhile, as I said, things are quiet. Still, things were calm in '36, just before the troubles. I remember once, that winter, I was in Beer-Tuvia at the time . . . Yes, well. There's one other thing I have to say, comrades: this place is a hive of rumors. And that's bad. Very bad, indeed. Like the story about the shepherd who always cried wolf, wolf, and when the wolf came – you all know the end of the story, comrades. I think the moral is clear to us all. So a bit less talk. That's it.

On Thursday evenings the various committees meet. Their atmosphere is not favorable to grandiose theories; practical details are the order of the day. In the financial committee, Mundek Zohar bargains with Yitzhak Friedrich for the erection of a special building for the regional council, which is housed at present in a tumble-down shack. Mundek thinks it is high time to put up a small building. Isaac Friedrich thinks that the time is not right yet or, rather, that there are not sufficient funds available, the current year being a lean one.

In the cultural committee, the news of Dr Nehemiah Berger's impending visit is considered. This would be a splendid occasion to organize a series of lectures on the history of socialism. The matter will be discussed.

In the educational committee, the pressing problem of delinquency is aired. The subject is fiercely debated, and a far-reaching decision is taken: to send Oren Geva to a consultant psychologist in Tel Aviv who is employed by the kibbutz movement. This decision is to be kept a close secret.

On Thursday night, an hour before midnight, Einav Geva felt the severe labor pains that frequently accompany the birth of a first child. Tomer, perturbed and somewhat irritated, drove his wife to the hospital. He made every effort to drive the dusty truck as smoothly as possible and to avoid the potholes in the road, so as not to cause his wife unnecessary pain.

Einav entered the maternity ward at close to one o'clock. Tomer stayed for a few hours, time enough to smoke eight or nine cigarettes and joke a little with a tall, dark-skinned nurse. At four o'clock in the morning he asked the night nurses to tell his wife that he was going home now, but that he would come back that afternoon. He had to go and supervise the work of getting in the cattle fodder. He had already turned to go when the night nurse's voice stopped him.

230

'Congratulations it's a boy.'

Tomer gaped at her in amazement.

'What, she's . . . she's had it already?'

The nurse barely looked up from the papers on her desk.

'Congratulations it's a boy.'

Tomer blanched and leaped toward the desk. Seizing the nurse's elbow, he asked shyly:

'Excuse me, is it a boy or a girl? Which is it?'

'Congratulations it's a boy I've told you five times already.'

Tomer groped in his pocket, drew out a cigarette, put it to his lips and forgot to light it.

'When am I allowed to see it?'

When she answered that he had best come back in the afternoon, he clasped his large hands and said:

'Tell her congratulations. Tell her I'll come back this afternoon. Tell her I'm not allowed to see her before then, and anyway I can't because we're getting in the cattle fodder, and I've got to be there because otherwise they'll cut the wrong field, the one by the bananas, and . . . never mind. Tell her I'll be back in a few hours' time. Yes. So it's a boy you say. That's very good.'

Something else happened that same Thursday night.

Turquoise went out, as usual, to wait for her older friend. Titan, the bull, watched her through the bars. He breathed heavily. His breath was warm and moist. The girl saw the bull and pulled a face. Titan's eyes were bloodshot.

Behind the cattle shed were the outlines of the tractor shed. It was cold, and she shivered slightly. From the cold and from

231

boredom she jumped lightly up and down on the balls of her feet. And then it happened.

At twenty-five past eleven that Thursday night, in the middle of a light jump, Noga Harish felt a pain. A terrible pain. A pain in her abdomen.

She stopped jumping and put a shaking hand on the spot. The blood drained from her cheeks. Her mouth fell open. Her heart froze. In a moment of sudden, fierce comprehension other, earlier signs fell into place. No. Yes.

Mo-ther, she murmured, her eyes bulging. The cold turned to a raging fever. The blood that had drained from her face flushed back into her skin. Mother.

Then suddenly a strange thing happened. The beam of the searchlight on top of the water tower collided with another light. The yellow ray of the enemy searchlight.

The two powerful lamps pointed their jets of light straight at each other's eyes, as if trying to dazzle the other to death.

Opposite loomed the disjointed forms of the mountains, lit by a garish reddish-purple glow.

The two beams of light remained locked in a furious embrace, piercing each other's eyes, bitter and stubborn, like knives poised for murder or like drunken lovers.

23

Simple Fisherfolk

SHE LOOKS up at the starry sky. Old queen Stella. The princess. The clapper of the bell. Gypsies. Him.

'Drive to Tiberias. To your fishermen. With me. Now.'

'Are you out of your mind, Turquoise? Get out. Why did you get in? It's almost morning.'

'I wish you dead, Ezra. I wish you'd drop dead. Right now.'

Ezra tugs at his cap. His face is twisted in an expression of stupefaction. His mouth is set firmly. He does not know yet. His grandson is struggling to be born. He does not know. Noga does not know what she is saying.

'Get moving, I said. I said drive to Tiberias. Right now.'

And after a moment's pause:

'I wish I were dead. You don't understand anything anything anything. You're so thick, great bear. What you've done to me. You don't care you don't care about anything great rough sweaty bear what you've done to me.'

He looks at her. Tired. Reaches out to touch her cheek. Changes his mind. Starts the engine. Turns round to face back along the dead road. His face is blank. Numbly he squints at her and asks:

'You mean . . .?'

Noga does not answer. Ezra shakes his head a few times. In a furious undertone he says:

'No.'

And again, after a silence, after a grinding of gears:

'What have I done to you?'

Turquoise suddenly gives an ugly laugh, fraught with something that is not laughter.

'Well? Shall we get married? It's usual to get married in such cases, isn't it?'

The man does not answer. His lower jaw drops, though, in what looks like a yawn, but isn't. His face in the dark wears a hangdog air. Noga looks. Sees. Still in the same tone that sounds like coarse laughter:

'Fool. Silly fool. You're a bad man. My father will kill you. My Rami will kill you.'

Suddenly he brakes, steers to the edge of the road, lets go of the wheel, grabs her shoulders and plasters her face with rough kisses. Lets her go. Lights a cigarette. He starts driving again, slowly, as if the truck were heavily loaded. His head hunched into his shoulders.

Close to two o'clock, at the approach to the sleeping town, Noga was overcome by nausea. She put her head out of the window and vomited.

The air inside the restaurant smelled of smoke and grilled fish. The fishermen nodded to Ezra and his girl. They showed no sign of surprise. They did not exchange smiles. Abushdid himself in his stained apron approached their table and inquired how they would like their coffee. Ezra said that the girl would have the same kind of coffee as he drank. With cardamom.

The others smoked in silence. Asis remarked, not to Ezra Berger in particular, that a bent oar had cost them two broken pressure lamps. Kabilio said that at today's prices it would cost sixty pounds to replace them if it cost a cent. Asis thought it wouldn't cost more than forty. Forty at most. Ezra asked whether Babadjani had been let out yet. Yes, yes, Abushdid said happily. Babadjani's been let out. He had a stroke of bad luck. He's out now. You never know what you've got coming to you. Your luck hides away in a dark corner, and suddenly it jumps out and kicks you in the teeth.

Ezra inquired where Babadjani was. Babadjani's on the water, Asis said. He might look in later. Or he might make straight for home. You never know what a man'll take it into his head to do.

Noga asked softly why the fishermen here worked with rowboats and not with motorboats. Gershon Saragosti smiled for a moment, then stopped smiling and said:

'We're just simple folk, sweetheart.'

The coffee was strong, with an intoxicating smell of spices. Abushdid explained to Noga that the smell came from the cardamom.

An easterly breeze blew off the lake, bringing with it a rich black fragrance. A night bird's call sounded. Gershon Saragosti was smoking a strong-smelling foreign cigarette. Ezra asked if he could have one. Saragosti apologized for not offering. He was too tired to think straight. Anyway, he'd had all sorts of pains in odd places these last few days. This is no life, God knows. It's no life if you're not healthy. You must know what the Bible says about that, Ezra. When you're not young any more, you're not happy. Doesn't it say something like that in the Bible? Here, have a cigarette. Take one for your daughter, too. Or don't you let her smoke yet? Too young? Take one for yourself. So what does the good book say?

' "His life abhors bread and his soul dainty meat, his flesh is consumed so that it cannot be seen, yea, his soul draws near unto the grave, and his life to the destroyers"; that's what it says in the Book of Job, and there's a great moral. Listen, Kabilio, you listen, too. It says that a man mustn't complain. Why should we accept the good and not accept the bad? I say this not as a religious man, Saragosti, but quite simply; you have to take the tough with the smooth. One day you're licking honey, the next you're chewing onions, as they say.'

'You're right, Ezra, by the holy Torah you're right. It's a hard life. Is this your daughter, Ezra? She doesn't look much like her father. She's got a very beautiful mother, I should say.'

Noga said yes, her mother was very beautiful. And the fisherman, draped in a rough overcoat, his cheeks sprouting stubble, asked, if her mother is so beautiful, why her father wanders around the world like a man with no place to go.

'My father,' Noga said with a sidelong glance at Ezra, 'my father is a very special man.'

'A very special man, by the holy Torah, by my life,' said Abushdid. 'A simple, uneducated man but he knows the Torah and he knows life. He's a wise man.'

'A wise man has eyes in his head,' Ezra said slowly, 'and where are my eyes? In hell, that's where my eyes are, Abushdid.'

'Why do you say such wicked things, Ezra, why do you curse yourself in front of your daughter? You shouldn't do it. That's the way to bring bad luck on yourself, it is, Heaven forbid.'

'My daughter knows. My daughter's not a child any more. She's old enough to see. The fool sees with his eyes, but the wise man sees straight to the heart. Isn't that right, Turquoise?'

'Whatever you say is always right, Daddy.'

Ezra asked Noga if she was happy here. Noga said of course she was. She'd never been anywhere like this before. Ezra asked if she felt better now. Noga replied that now she didn't feel anything. Gershon Saragosti smiled at her and said again:

'We're just simple folk.'

And again he smiled. His face seemed made to smile.

Silence.

Asis began to tell, from his corner, the story of how two pressure lamps that were as good as new were broken. Kabilio helped him when necessary by supplying forgotten details. Abushdid dozed at his counter. Gershon Saragosti, too, was asleep, slumped over a table some way away. Turquoise rested her head on her daddy's shoulder. Ezra thought she was asleep. But Noga was awake. Her tears caressed his shoulder through the dusty shirt.

Through the doorway opposite a stretch of water showed. The lake. Black and vaguely chilly.

Abushdid woke up and turned on the radio, fiddled with the knob and found a faraway station broadcasting dance music. A sharp eye could make out the shapes of the mountains beyond the dark lake. Yellow lights flickered there, hovering mysteriously between the water and the stars, inexplicable unless one was aware of the presence of the mountain which was reflected on the black water. It was three o'clock in the morning.

237

Saragosti and Asis rose to leave.

'No Babadjani,' said Kabilio.

'We can't wait for him till morning,' Gershon Saragosti said.

'Any message for him?' asked Kabilio.

'No message. Only to steer clear of bad luck,' said Asis.

'And you stick to good luck, the pair of you,' said Abushdid.

The murmur of the easterly breeze. Ripples stirring on the water. The roots of the mountains hidden in the sea bed. Nothing intervenes. The moon has set. In the silent deep live the fish. Breathing through gills. Some swim in shoals; others prefer solitude. Vast expanses of dark water open up before them. They are free to wander as they choose. The air is damp. A report sounds. Noga asks what that strange sound was. Ezra stares at her as if he has difficulty in recognizing her. He pauses for a long while, as if he has forgotten, as if he will never answer. At the end of his silence his speech is blurred.

'Sound of oars. Asis and Saragosti are out on the water.'

Softly Noga murmurs:

'Now.'

PART TWO
The Clapper in the Bell

24

An Undesirable Character

SIX WEEKS later the last signs of spring died away. The corn-fields turned gray and dry under the white light. The luxuriant vegetation gave way to skeletal brambles. A deadly pressure seemed to flow down from the mountains. Long blazing blinding dazzling days. But for three days a false autumn reigned.

Such false autumn days occur occasionally in our summer. In the morning a blessed coolness blows from the west. Dark clouds like a band of strolling players come between us and the fearsome light. A gentle breeze murmurs in the foliage and in the pine needles, and a cool dampness bears witness to the new regime. Deep breath expands the chest. Even the cramped muscles of the eyelids relax somewhat, free from the terror of the cruel glare. Everyone relaxes and gulps in the welcome freshness of the autumn air.

But these low clouds, these faithless nomads, are deceptive. In the morning they court us, but at midday the feigned mask of kindness falls away, and they display their true ferocity. Dampness and oppressive heaviness beat down mercilessly, and the familiar leaden grayness returns to the sky. Soon the white light is back, clear and bright and savage.

Early on one of these false autumn days, at breakfast time, a long yellow taxi drew up in front of the dining hall. A dark-suited man wearing a purple tie got out, holding a small blue case in his left hand. For a moment he inspected his surroundings, closing one eye and opening the other wide, and pensively rolling out his lower lip. His face suddenly contorted into what looked like a forced smile. He put down his case, produced a green handkerchief, and carefully wiped his forehead, his chin and both his hands. Then he lit a cigarette and waved his arm casually to the driver, who was watching him through the car window. The driver understood his meaning and settled back in his green leather seat for a long wait.

The man betrayed no sign of haste. He stood as if rooted to the spot, inspecting his surroundings. Men and women passed close by him, on the path that circles the dining hall, and cast him curious but friendly glances. The newcomer returned their looks and even nodded politely, but he did not address anyone. Eventually, he caught sight of a green bench half-hidden in the shrubs at the edge of the lawn. He picked up his suitcase and walked over to it. His step was light and bouncy. Evidently the case was not heavy. He sat quite still, smoking with an absorbed look, as if trying to extract every particle of taste from each mouthful of smoke. Once or twice the thumb of his left hand, which was holding the cigarette, rose to scratch his eyebrows, an intriguing gesture that conveyed no hint of embarrassment but only absent-mindedness or else concentration – and a certain anxiety, since for an instant the burning tip of the cigarette almost touched his black hair.

The stranger's face was full of folds and wrinkles, as if he had too much skin, so that instead of being stretched over the bones of his skull it hung from them in limp abandon. On his upper lip there was a tiny, shapeless mustache, around which a curious movement could be detected, as if his nose and its surrounds were forever twitching with some mysterious life.

Finally, he pinched the stub of his cigarette until the remaining tobacco spilled out; he stood up, picked up his case, and walked across to the door of the dining hall. He walked with a slight stoop, like a man walking into a strong head wind.

It seems that it was Podolski, the co-ordinator of the work rota, who greeted the stranger and asked if he could help him. The latter replied in well-phrased, musical Hebrew and in a somewhat hoarse bass voice, and inquired where he might find Comrade Berger. Podolski asked whether he was referring to Ezra Berger or to his son Tomer. The stranger smiled, in such a way as to arouse distinctly uneasy feelings in the other. He was looking for Comrade Ezra Berger, the father. Podolski shook his head and replied:

'Ezra? He's out on a trip. He leaves at six in the morning. But Tomer is in the dining hall. I'll call him.'

The stranger apologized for any inconvenience he was causing, but said that he would prefer, if it was not too much trouble, to see Comrade Bronka Berger first.

Podolski suggested that he go into the dining hall and have something to eat and drink, and meanwhile he, Podolski would go and look for Bronka. The stranger replied that he was impressed by the hospitality for which kibbutzim were famous, but that he preferred to wait over on the bench. There was no need to hurry. He was not a busy man. He had plenty of time. There was something he would like to know, he added, adjusting his purple tie as he spoke, even though it was not out of place, he would like to know, well . . . how to put it . . . whether . . . whether there was any news in the Berger family. He knew, of course, about the arrival of dear little Danny, but . . . what he wanted to know was . . . how matters stood generally in the family, because, er . . . he was himself a member of the family and . . . he would like to know the facts before he met Bronka. Naturally, his interlocutor was not obliged to answer.

Podolski reflected for a moment, then said:

'It seems they still have problems. If you'll excuse me, I'll go and tell Bronka you've arrived.'

Ten minutes later Bronka appeared, wearing working trousers and a white apron. Zechariah embraced his sister-in-law and kissed her very properly on both cheeks. Bronka, her wrinkled face all smiles, asked when he had arrived in Israel and when he had got to Metsudat Ram and which way he had come and whether he found the heat oppressive and why he hadn't sent a telegram to say he was coming and what his plans were and how he was. Above all, what a pity, what a terrible pity it was that Ezra hadn't known that it was today that. As she spoke she seized his suitcase and began to lead the way. Here am I wearing you out with my chatter, and you must be tired out from the journey, and hungry and thirsty besides.

Zechariah took the suitcase from Bronka and placed his hands firmly on her hips.

'Excuse me a moment,' he said. 'There are some more cases in the taxi. I must pay the driver and dismiss him. There are some presents for all the family, too.'

It turned out that Zechariah had arrived at dawn on an SAS plane and had already been in touch with various people in Tel Aviv by telephone. He had intended to spend a day or two first in Tel Aviv to deal with some urgent business matters. But while he was passing through customs he had been overcome by such strong feelings of nostalgia that he had thrown everything to the winds and hurried straight here, to his beloved family. What is more important than one's family, my dear Bronka? Nothing in the whole wide world. So here I am, bursting to proclaim, 'I am your brother Joseph.' You must excuse this emotional outburst, Bronka, but that's the way with emotion; it carries one away, ha ha, yes, that's the way with emotion.

When they were inside the shuttered room Zechariah hastened to unwrap some of his packages. Before he would touch the glass of fruit juice that Bronka offered him, he insisted on showing her the presents.

'Look at this material, Bronka. Feel it. Isn't it magnificent? Yes, Bronka, it's for you. You can make it up into a beautiful dress. Lovely cloth for a lovely lady. In this case is a tape recorder for the young couple, and there's a complete woolen outfit here for dear little Danny – how I long to hold him and kiss him and cry over him; the electric shaver is for my own beloved brother Ezra, and I haven't forgotten our dear Oren, either – he's sure to like this model railway. Look, Bronka, it works on its own electrical circuit, and it's just like the great railway system of Europe. No, I haven't forgotten about the principles. I'm a man of principle and I respect the principles of others, including the collectivist ideology of the kibbutz. Of course, of course. But all the same, can't I give some small, purely token gift to the people I love? Please, Bronka, let's hear no more about it. Not a word. If you don't want my presents, that's a sign you don't want me, either. I'll leave right away. Surely you don't want to offend your dear brother? That's enough, Bronka. I've already heard all your arguments. You're not saying anything new. Look, Bronka, look, look at this tape recorder: it's the latest model, three tracks, four speeds, extra-sensitive microphone; you can record the most complicated music. God rot those filthy Germans in hell – but there's nothing wrong with their industry. This is the most famous make in the world. Oh, Bronka, my dear, they make marvelous machinery!'

While Zechariah poured out his persuasive arguments without letting his sister-in-law get a word in edgeways, his thin, hairy fingers ran over the objects taken out of their packing cases and boxes. His movements were as skillful and dexterous as those of a traveling salesman, and his voice held the insistent tone with which traveling salesmen hector their stunned victims into buying.

Bronka poured him a glass of ice-cold juice. Zechariah pursed his lips and sipped it delicately. His eyes filled with forced joy. He wiped his lips with his green handkerchief and replaced it instantly in his pocket with the skill of a prestidigitator.

'It's cold,' he said, 'and refreshing for the weary soul.'

Bronka asked if he would like a shower. Zechariah refused with a spate of polite phrases. Not at all, not at all, he must be disturbing her terribly, she had her work to do, she could leave him and get on with it, he wouldn't steal or break anything, she could trust him.

Bronka burst out laughing.

'No, I don't have to go back to work. We'll go to the nursery to see Danny, and on the way I'll look in and say I shan't be doing any more work this morning. We don't have a visitor like you every day, after all. It's so many years since we last met. Yes. You came in '48 as a refugee, and you left us after a year. Still, let's not talk about the past now. Ezra will be sorry, of course, that he wasn't here to greet you. But it's not his fault. It's your fault, because you decided to surprise us. You're the guilty party, Zechariah.'

'Yes, I'm the guilty party.' As Zechariah spoke, he scratched his eyebrows and his little mustache with his thumb. After a slight pause, as if recalling his duty, he smiled.

Bronka did not enjoy his smile. It exposed all his teeth, upper and lower; the sight was not a pretty one. It was even slightly frightening.

Her visitor removed his dark jacket, tucked his shirt well into his trousers, and loosened his tie. Then he went out with Bronka for his first stroll in the kibbutz grounds.

As they ambled along, he took out a cigarette and lit it with a gilt lighter. As he did so he remarked that he had given an identical lighter as a present to his brother Ezra. All in all, he continued, despite the distance that separated him from his brothers, he always felt, deep down in his heart, very close to them both. Their troubles pained him as if they were his own. That was the way with emotion, he said; it overcame distances.

Bronka decided to change the subject. She indicated a white building and said that it was the nursery. They would go in and take a look at little Danny. Danny was asleep, a pink skull with a covering of dark down, a tiny clenched fist thrust into a soft cheek.

Zechariah's face suddenly wrinkled, and he looked like an old man in tears. But perhaps it was just the sudden transition from bright sunshine to the dark interior that contorted his features.

They went outside.

Zechariah-Siegfried Berger said:

'Father's first great-grandchild, God rest his soul. I'm not saying a word against your customs here, but I'd have thought he should have been named Naphtali-Hirsch, or Naphtali, or at least Tsvi, if you want a more modern equivalent. But, of course, the younger generation must do as it pleases. They look forward, we look backward. That's the way it is. Not the other way round.'

Bronka said:

'That's the stable over there. Horses.'

Zechariah's mouth fell limply open, and for an instant Bronka had a vague impression of a reptile, or a frog. But the image was dispelled at once, as he exclaimed enthusiastically:

'Horses! Horses are splendid. I didn't know they were still used on kibbutzim. I love horses.'

Bronka said nothing. Discreetly, her visitor lavished courtly attentions on her, stepping aside to make way for her, bowing slightly, offering her his arm, or taking hold of her elbow at every obstacle. Bronka was flattered but felt slightly embarrassed. Was it merely foreign good manners? Surely it was nothing more. They walked around the kibbutz for another half-hour, Bronka in her blue working trousers and white apron and Siegfried with his shirt and tie. Outside the playground he grinned and interrupted his hostess.

'Swings! That's magnificent!'

'The children play here unsupervised for hours; their social habits . . .'

'Bronka, do sit on the swing. Let's swing together. Please. I feel as happy as a sandboy.'

Bronka ignored the strange request, and they strolled on together. They came to the recreation hall. They inspected it inside and out, and Bronka described the cultural life of the kibbutz.

Zechariah said:

'I have regards and some small gifts from Eva to her previous family.'

Bronka:

'Is she happy over there?'

Zechariah:

'Happy? What is happiness? I can tell you that Isaac Hamburger takes good care of all her needs, both physical and intellectual. Is that high fence electrified? No? I thought, perhaps, for security . . . Excuse my ignorance.'

Bronka gave a brief account of how Tomer was wounded. Zechariah struck his hands together and groaned aloud, as if acting the part of a terrified woman.

'Good God, what a miraculous escape. Damnation on the enemies of Israel, who never let us live in peace.'

They strolled on.

*

Back at the house, Bronka suggested that he lie down and rest until lunchtime. Ezra would be back at half past one, and needless to say he wouldn't be making his second journey today. It was not easy to explain why it was that his brother had voluntarily decided to do the work of two drivers.

Bronka suspected that Zechariah already had an inkling of the situation; she preferred him to know the true facts, and so she tried to hint at them.

Zechariah took off his shoes, lay back on the divan, and lit a cigarette. He extinguished the lighter flame with his finger. Bronka let out a surprised sound. Zechariah showed his teeth and said that he always did that: if he felt drowsy, he touched the flame and woke up. Bronka's eyes widened, but her voice was calm and controlled as she said:

'But . . . why? You can take a nap. It would be good for you. Ezra won't be back till half past one.'

Zechariah replied:

'I don't want to sleep, but if you don't object I'll keep quiet. I want to think about dear, sweet little Danny.'

Silence.

Bronka served cakes and fruit and coffee. Zechariah closed one eye and opened the other wide. He looked at her as though he were seeing her for the first time. Eventually, he said:

'Dear Bronka, I feel completely at home here.'

Silence.

Bronka said to herself: I still don't know this man. On the one hand, there's something of Ezra in him. What is it? Ezra is a silent man, and this one talks a lot. Perhaps they share a kind of forced cheerfulness. On the other hand, they are not alike. I can't like this man. He's very polite, it's true. But his politeness seems to be a screen for a kind of coarseness underneath. I wonder what Reuven will have to say about him.

A little bird spread the news, or perhaps it was Podolski. A visitor from Germany had arrived, Ezra's brother. From the amount of luggage he had brought with him it looked as though he was planning to stay a long time. In the clothes store, in the kitchens, in the laundry rooms, tongues wagged. Some said the family's problems were about to come to an end. Others said that, on the contrary, they were only beginning.

As soon as Ezra stopped his engine and got down from the cab, he was told that his brother had arrived. Not the one from Jerusalem, the one from Germany. He had arrived at breakfast time, suddenly, in a yellow hired car. It was Podolski who had taken him to Bronka, and he had brought a lot of luggage with him.

Ezra doffed his dusty cap, slapped it twice against his knee, and hurried to his house. Curiously enough, of all the emotions he might have felt, it was a sudden absence of mind that came over him.

At the sound of heavy footsteps on the steps leading up to the veranda, Zechariah leapt up with an agility that was out of keeping with his age and position in life. The door opened, and the two brothers met face to face. Zechariah saw the grease stains on his brother's clothes. Ezra noticed his younger brother's mustache, which was an innovation. Surprisingly, in that instant he also noticed the nervous twitching of the mustache.

For a moment they continued to look at each other. Then they fell in each other's arms, thumped each other on the back, gabbled in Yiddish, parted only to return to the bear hug.

Bronka let them savor their pleasure for a few minutes. Then, choosing the right moment, when the hugging had stopped and a look of embarrassment was appearing on her husband's rugged features, she handed him his clean clothes and suggested that he have a shower right away. Ezra was grateful. He made his excuses to his guest and went out to the showers. He would have to return, of course, in a quarter of an hour, but in the meantime he could collect his thoughts. Bronka's consideration and understanding had come to his rescue yet again. He had to admit it.

In the afternoon they all sat out on the lawn.

Bronka filled and refilled the fruit basket and the cookie dish. Ezra borrowed an extra deck chair from his neighbor, Mundek Zohar. The talk flowed easily. They talked, for instance, of world politics. Bronka said that the situation in Israel depended on the relations between the great powers. Ezra thought that in the modern world a large-scale war was no longer a possibility. Not because the prophecy had come true and the wolf was lying down with the lamb – he didn't want to be taken for a simpleton – but because there were no lambs left. They had all been eaten by the wolves. The vision had been fulfilled: the wolf was lying down with the wolf. He wasn't just being witty. Nation would not lift up sword against nation, simply because they had all studied war, and they would go on studying war.

Bronka said that one single madman could destroy the whole of mankind.

Zechariah agreed with alacrity and surprising enthusiasm. He added that the next war would be an exciting spectacle. It is uncertain whether he was being serious or not.

They also discussed the principles of the kibbutz. Bronka protested about Zechariah's presents, which she found embarrassing. Zechariah repeated solemnly that he respected the principles of the kibbutz, because he himself was a man of principle. But he had a right to demand that his own principles be respected, and he regarded the right to make small presents to his family as a matter of principle. He was, he might say, a wealthy man now. And a wealthy man had a moral obligation to share his wealth with his relatives, because family bonds were sacrosanct. Moreover, he still recalled how when he had first come to the country in 1948, naked and penniless, his dear brothers Ezra and Nehemiah had not hesitated to share all they had with him.

Zechariah then described life in the new Germany. The leading thinkers spent all their time in self-mortification. Humanity oozed from their every pore. Even if we envisaged Germany as an old whore playing the young virgin, we could still enjoy their embarrassment and laugh wholeheartedly at their clumsy contortions.

At about four o'clock Einav and Tomer arrived, and brought Danny with them. Zechariah, without the least embarrassment, played with the baby and lavished signs of affection on Einav, complimenting her on her good looks and those of her baby. Danny had inherited, he said, his mother's fine features. He was a fortunate child to have such a beautiful mother. The baby's smile was the spit and image of his mother's. And he could claim some expertise in the matter of beautiful women, if they would pardon his lapse from modesty.

Tomer was taken aback when his uncle asked him, with a shrewd, piercing glance, whether he believed in the survival of the soul after death.

Before he had recovered from his surprise, Oren arrived. He was introduced to his uncle and was confronted almost at once with the same curious question. Did he believe in the survival of the soul?

Oren frowned and looked down at the ground as he answered that 'soul' was just a literary word and that he, Oren, hated literature. Zechariah smiled till the pink inside of his lower lip showed. Then he offered Tomer, Einav, and Oren the presents he brought them, saying that they were a token of his fondness for them. Bronka said:

'That's not settled yet.'

They drank coffee. Zechariah complained that he was being gorged with food and drink. Bronka said he was probably used to finer fare. It's the thought that counts, Zechariah replied. Feelings were more important than food. He had been intending to go to Tel Aviv first, but at the airport that morning he had been overcome by nostalgia and postponed his business. Tomorrow, though, or the day after at the latest he would have to go to Tel Aviv. *Force majeure*. He had come to find Israeli artistes. The public was crying out for piquant novelties. The Germans were eager to taste the choice fruits of the land, the piquant flavor of the new Israel. They were excited by men with breasts, singing fish, white Negroes, and Israeli Jews – non-Jewish Jews.

Bronka and Zechariah disagreed about the nature of the new Israel. Zechariah maintained that the new Jews were the opposite of the old Jews and that even the moronic Aryans were aware of the fact. Bronka admitted that there was a difference between the Jews of the Diaspora and the Israelis, but claimed that the new Israel was the logical outcome of Jewish history. Zechariah objected that logical terms were neither alive nor dead. Tomer then made an outspoken contribution to the discussion:

'Thanks to the might of Israel, even the Diaspora Jews can hold their heads up high.'

Zechariah turned to face him. He brought his face close to Tomer's strong tanned features, and his nostrils and mustache quivered as if he were sniffing the boy's flesh.

'Hold their heads up high? Anyone who holds his head up high is no longer a Jew.'

Einav said:

'What a strange idea. I don't agree at all.'

Tomer said:

'A Jew is a man, and a man is someone who holds his head up. A proud Jew never stoops.'

'Anyone who never stoops is not a man,' Zechariah said. 'He is more than a man: he is a superman. Like you, my dear nephew. I've heard all about your exploits. But I was talking about ordinary Jews. Heroes are different.'

Tomer thought for a moment, then answered:

'Zechariah, you talk as if "Jew" and "hero" were opposites. And that's not true.'

Zechariah scratched his bushy eyebrows with his thumb and said:

'We mustn't quarrel. I'm heavily outnumbered, and anyway I'm your guest.'

And they all laughed out of politeness.

Einav lifted Danny out of his pram.

'Danny says good night. Danny's going to have his supper and go to bed.'

Bronka and Ezra said good night to their grandson, Tomer whispered something to Einav, and Zechariah was allowed to kiss the baby. He also kissed Einav on the forehead and on the cheek. Tomer, as he watched, said to himself that it would be best for the man to leave as soon as possible. A man like that was capable of anything.

A quarter of an hour later Oren, too, left, without saying a word. The visitor had given him an idea, and he wanted to think it over for half an hour or so, somewhere else.

As for Tomer, this was the time when he had his daily swim. He asked to be excused. We'll meet again. Perhaps we'll meet again. Yes, we'll meet again perhaps. Perhaps after supper.

Siegfried surprised his hosts by asking Tomer if he could go with him. He was fond of swimming, even if he was not a great swimmer. If Tomer could wait five minutes, he would unpack his swimming trunks and join him.

Tomer was taken aback but managed to smile and say:

'Why not? Do come. I'll bring you back here afterward.'

Zechariah nodded to his brother and winked at his sister-in-law. Bronka was startled for an instant: it was a wink of complicity. What was he up to? Nonsense. It didn't mean anything.

On their way to the swimming pool Tomer explained, out of politeness, about the buildings they passed. After each description Zechariah thanked him and clapped his hands for joy, as if he had learned some great new truth from Tomer's terse words, which were spoken in fact to forestall an awkward silence or an embarrassing remark from his uncle.

'That's the clinic. One of the first buildings to be built here. It's about thirty years old.'

'Thirty years? That's a long time.'

'Over there they've dug a shelter, in case of shellings or air raids.'

'Oh!'

'That's the memorial to Aaron Ramigolski. One of the founders. He died in the course of the work. It also commemorates the other victims.'

'Thank you. Thank you for your kindness, dear Tomer.'

But Tomer's efforts failed to have the desired effect. Siegfried did say something embarrassing. Taking advantage of a pause, he said:

'Tell me, my dear nephew, how do you manage to solve the problem of women?'

'What?'

'The problem of women. I mean variety, adventure. I mean –
you understand – you're a healthy young lad. Well? Do you go
into town sometimes? Or perhaps you manage to amuse yourself here on the kibbutz? Forgive my curiosity. I'm speaking to
you as man to man.'

Tomer:

'Here . . . Here we have different customs. We . . .'

Siegfried:

'Customs may differ, but men are the same everywhere. You
surely don't mean to tell me that here on the kibbutz you vigorous young men keep your hands idly in your pockets, to use
the old Hebrew phrase? No, I can't believe it. Can it really be
that men here look at their neighbors' wives morning, noon,
and evening without anything happening? It's impossible to
believe. Come on, I can't believe it. I can't imagine it. After all,
we're modern men.'

Tomer:

'Well, there may be the odd incident. But by and large . . .'

Siegfried:

'And you?'

'Me? I don't.'

'Never mind. You don't owe me anything. I tried to ask
you freely, as a man. But naturally you don't have to answer.
Cigarette?'

Tomer hastily nodded. They smoked. They reached the
swimming pool and changed. It was evening. The water reflected a distorted image of the pine trees. Slight ripples disturbed
its surface and shattered the image. Tomer explained that the
water was clear because it was changed every three days. It

was linked to the irrigation system. Zechariah expressed exaggerated enthusiasm, as if this were an exciting technological innovation.

Silence. There were not many swimmers. High above there were signs of twilight, and in the west the sun was setting in a riot of colors. Soft light sparkled on the water. Some girls were playing opposite, jumping off the top diving board and splashing each other. The spray caught the light of the setting sun, like a string of pearls scattered through the air, or sparks from fireworks soaring and falling back into the water. The visitor rubbed his eyes and sighed.

'Ready?' Tomer said. 'It'll be getting dark soon.'

'How beautiful it is here. Such a pure silence. I almost feel an urge to pray.'

'Yes. It's nice here.'

The two men stepped forward and dived. Tomer, if the truth be told, was apprehensive. Could the old boy really swim, or was he just fooling? Better watch out.

Zechariah-Siegfried quickly allayed his nephew's doubts. He plowed through the water with precise, economical strokes. His white body capped with black hair cut a perfectly straight path through the ripples. Tomer swam the width of the pool, plunged, and surfaced in the opposite corner. He cast a glance at his uncle, either to calm his inner fears or to seek his admiration. Zechariah was floating almost motionless on his back, supporting himself with rapid, precise movements of his legs.

Tomer shook his head and said:

'You *can* swim.'

Zechariah, still keeping his gaze fixed on the darkening sky, murmured:

'Some day your uncle will tell you a story about gypsies and a dog. Not now. Now we're swimming. Some other time. You don't look like your father, Tomer. You're an Israeli. Sculpted with a firm chisel. What were we talking about? Yes. Gypsies and a dog. I'll tell you some other time. We're going to make a fine pair of friends, my lad.'

After a few moments he added:

'The water's marvelous. Warm and caressing like a woman. Swimming in water like this is like petting. It arouses one's desire.'

Tomer said nothing. Disgusted, he swam away from the visitor. He struck out across the pool and climbed out. Logically, Zechariah ought to have followed his lead. But Zechariah did not act logically or take the hint. He slowed the movement of his legs. For a moment he lay motionless on the water, not breathing, corpselike. Suddenly his body began to sink. Tomer saw the water distort the lines of his strange head, the eyes unclosed. At first he thought he was just playing. But the motionless body continued to sink until it was lost in the murky depths. The young man was alarmed. His heart had told him from the start that the stranger would bring disaster. Now his heart beat violently. He tensed all his muscles, filled his lungs with air, dived into the water and plunged to the limit of his breath. In the dark depths he felt all around him, but his hands touched nothing solid. He returned to the surface. Panic overcame his presence of mind. Even on the night he was wounded he had not felt so frightened. He filled his lungs and prepared to dive again. Like a dark arrow at that moment at the other end of the pool the man shot out of the water, waving, breathing deeply, smiling at Tomer with his hideous smile, which displayed the inside of his lower lip.

'You frightened me,' Tomer said.

'I'm sorry. I'm very sorry.'

'It's time to go home. Let's get out.'

'Just a little more,' Zechariah pleaded. 'Just a little longer.'

There was a flirtatious pleading in his voice, like a woman or an obstinate child.

They swam for a little longer.

Zechariah did not repeat his earlier action. He swam slowly, rhythmically, savoring each stroke. He let the water wash over his face, then raised his head. He raised his head and spread out his legs. His legs moved like a pair of powerful pistons. Firm muscles rippled beneath the white skin of his back. Tomer was surprised: covered with clothes that body gave no hint of its true character.

Suddenly, in the center of the pool, his body rose, his back curved like a bow, his arms outstretched, and he turned an elegant and spectacular back somersault in the water.

At that moment, in the midst of the magical feat, as the setting sun softened the lines and brought out the massivity of the scenery, Noga Harish first caught sight of Zechariah-Siegfried Berger.

She was standing at the edge of the pine wood, which ran down to the pool. She had wandered here in the course of a pensive evening stroll. Gossip had informed her of the brother's arrival. But at first glance she mistook him for someone else.

She saw Zechariah-Siegfried, and her thoughts were confused. So confused that for a split second she was on the point of dashing across to the edge of the pool to see and to be seen. But the urge died away at once. The girl stood without moving and looked at the man. Eventually, when the visitor, responding to Tomer's signals, climbed out of the water and toweled himself dry, Noga Harish turned and disappeared once more into the wood. She returned home by another route.

Tomer and his uncle set out for the Berger's house. It was already night. The first crickets had started their mournful song. A breeze was stirring the tops of the pine trees, which, as usual, gave out a soft, sad moan.

'If we don't hurry, we'll miss the supper. I don't usually stay in the pool longer than ten minutes.'

Of course, of course, Zechariah did not want to upset the routine. He offered Tomer his heartfelt apologies for causing the delay. No one knew better than he did the importance of time. Every moment was precious. 'Incidentally, when I got out of the water, there was a beautiful girl standing on the other side, looking at me. I can always sense it when a beautiful woman is looking at me. It's an instinct. Who was she? Didn't you see her? Pity. A real Oriental beauty. In my opinion, my dear Tomer, this land produces stunning beauties. They're not like the blonde, blue-eyed Nordic women. But, of course, that's a matter of taste. What do you think? What's your opinion?'

Tomer's opinion was very definite. He didn't approve of his uncle. Tomer's opinion of Zechariah-Siegfried Berger was adverse.

25

You're One of Us

To clarify the true nature of what is to come, let us address ourselves briefly to Hasia Ramigolski. We might have turned to Esther Klieger – Esther Isarov, that is – or to Nina Goldring or to Gerda Zohar, or even to men such as Israel Tsitron or Mendel Morag, all hard-working people who eat their bread in the sweat of their brows and judge both themselves and others severely. We have chosen Hasia Ramigolski, not because her husband is the secretary of the kibbutz – a fact that counts neither for nor against her – but because we have seen her and exchanged words with her. Words, however, that any member of our kibbutz might have spoken at the time.

Hasia is no foolish young girl. Hard years have etched their mark on her face and in her heart. Experience has taught her simple truths, such as it is the exception that proves the rule. Life is not governed by rules. Life is made up of numerous small acts, and it is by these that even great men are to be judged. Hasia also knows that the hours of sadness, anxiety, and routine outnumber those of joy and pleasure, though life is not all bitterness, and there is also joy and contentment.

Admittedly, Hasia does not express her thoughts in this way. She is not given to voicing truths or coining slogans. But that is what we are here for. That is why Hasia works her fingers to the bone while we – to our shame – rest our hands on our arms and our arms on the desk and watch her out of the window, scratching the air with our pen, doing nothing. We are here to express things. We do not shirk our task. We express for Hasia what Hasia herself does not express. But our heart is bitter. We are uneasy. For once we shall let her speak for herself.

'A man should always try to be completely fair. It isn't always possible, but there are some people who try and some who don't try. And the harder it is, the better you see what kind of a man he is, or if he's a man at all. If at least he makes an effort, then he's a man. If he behaves like a swine, then he's a swine. Personal example, my dear, that's what's important. At least with me. Take Reuven Harish, for instance. Before all this business he was really a somebody. I don't mean he didn't have his faults. Of course he did. I've known him for years, and I understand all his facets and all his problems. He's not a simple man. And he's had to go through a lot. But he was a somebody. He set an example. At least, he always tried to be fair. When Eva left, for instance. But now? He's reaping what he sowed. All the complications started because of him. I'm not blaming. Things like the goings on between him and Bronka happen, of course. A man of his age is still a man. But not when he's got an adolescent daughter. It's a very difficult age. As a teacher he ought to have realized that. That's how it is. Once you lose your head, that's it. You lose all restraint – whether you're an intellectual or not. And another thing – you should always know whom you're getting involved with. We've known for a long time that Ezra is a bit strange. What did they think? That he didn't know? That he didn't care? Isn't he a man, too, and a complicated character at that? Last winter already, believe it or not, even before Noga began, I said to my Tsvi that Ezra would do something that would make us all sit up and take notice. Not that he would commit murder or suicide. No, he's not the violent type, even if he is pretty massive to look at. But to start something with the girl – that's his form of revenge. You could tell. Last winter already I had a premonition. Do you remember the film we had here a month or two ago? That French film, with Françoise Arnoul. Remember? There was exactly the same thing there, with the general who carried on with the lieutenant's wife, and the lieutenant took his revenge with the general's daughter. Exactly the same. People are the same everywhere. The next day, after the film, I said as much to Nina in the kitchens, you can ask her, even though she didn't agree with me at the time. She said it wasn't the same. Of course, it's not exactly the same. I don't say that situations repeat themselves exactly. But people feel the same things everywhere, always. Actually, though, that wasn't what I wanted to say. I wanted to tell you something completely different. You get this triangle in lots of novels, too. And especially in a situation like this, with a girl like Noga, who takes after her mother. You know what I mean. I think heredity is very important. You can't change: if you're born like that, that's the way you are. All right. Up to there I can understand it. Even that she's pregnant from Ezra doesn't surprise me in the least. I said as much to my Tsvi at Shavuoth; I said that Ezra would make her pregnant. She doesn't know anything; nobody's ever taught her. That's another thing, incidentally, that'll have to change here: sexual education is very important for adolescents, because it's a difficult age. And Ezra isn't exactly the type to take precautions. All right, what's done is done. It's happened before in other kibbutzim and even here. It's not so long since Einav got married when she was four months gone. Of course that was entirely different – different age, different circumstances. Still, these things do happen. But that wasn't what I wanted to say to you. So far it's easy enough to understand. Not to condone, of course, but to understand. But there's one thing I can't begin to understand. I simply can't comprehend it. They say the girl absolutely refuses to have an abortion. What an idea! She has all sorts of romantic notions. And how she refuses! Reuven's gone completely to pieces, and she doesn't give a damn. And Ezra, of course, is just a shadow of his old self. He goes about quoting verses from Job and Ecclesiastes like ... I don't envy him now. Even Bronka – imagine! – went to plead with the little so-and-so to go and have it. But nothing does any good. Her mind is made up. She says it's her child, and she won't budge. She's been taken out of school, even though Herbert Segal said she mustn't be victimized. I'm really surprised at Herbert. Usually he's much more strict and much less sentimental. All right. That wasn't what I wanted to talk about. She doesn't go and see Reuven. She hides from Ezra, or maybe he's hiding from her. So who's she got left? You'll never guess. The tourist. Ezra's brother, who's been here for two or three weeks now. Of course he's already stuck his nose deep into the dirt. I have a feeling he's the type that's fond of dirt, you know, a nihilist or an extrastentialist, some kind of a beatnik, and he's become Noga's spiritual father. Do you realize how far it's gone? And you know what they're saying about him? They say he has exactly the wrong influence on her.

He's urging her not to do it. I mean to go ahead and have the child. Do you understand what's going on? Do you? If I were Bronka, I'd kick him out. Let him find somewhere else to stir up trouble. They're all the same, those Jews who went back to Germany after the war. They're up to no good. All kinds of underworld figures. You can imagine. To cut a long story short, when a man starts to go off the rails, and stops trying to be fair, you never know where it'll end up. Do you suppose Reuven ever dreamed that his affair with Bronka would lead to this? Believe me, if that child is born on this kibbutz – I won't work another day in the nursery. I'm only human, too. You know that I always try to be fair. But if they don't throw that tourist out, even if he is Ezra's brother and the Bergers' guest, then I tell you I really don't know what I'm doing here. Everything has its limits. He has a terrible influence on the girl. It's he who's urging her on to this madness. I won't be surprised, you mark what I'm saying, I won't be surprised if all this ends up in some catastrophe, Heaven forbid. I only hope I'm wrong. And, believe me, it hurts.'

Ten days after her nocturnal visit to the fishermen in Tiberias, Noga informed her father of her condition. Reuven was unable to control himself and shed some tears in her presence. Noga, too, wept. Then Reuven summoned his last reserves of courage and said that something must be done. Noga made him totter and seize the back of his chair when she informed him icily that she did not intend to agree to 'do anything.' She would never consent to it. She would have the child. Why? Just to hurt and get her revenge? No, only because she must accept her

267

punishment and her responsibility. She must suffer. Suffering would purify her. Silly little girl, they're just words, just the words of a dreaming girl. Dear Daddy, pure Daddy, you're the little boy, and I'm the grown woman. You'll never understand, Daddy. You're like . . . you're like a good little boy. Like Gai. You always think the world's made of words. You always always always want it to be good. Why should it be good? Why should it? Why shouldn't it be bad? Why not? Yes, bad. If it's worse, then it'll be truer. More (live, I tell you. But you can't see what I'm saying, dear Daddy, you're too pure and good. Don't cry, big boy, don't cry. Look at me. I'm not crying. Let's not cry. All right? Don't try to tell me that I'm bringing a miserable little bastard into the world. I've thought about that. Yes, I have. Are you surprised? Don't be surprised, Daddy. If you don't suffer, you don't live. If you're not a miserable bastard, you're sterile. Empty. I'm not talking about you. You're suffering now. My poor little girl, you can't know what . . . It'll be terrible, Noga, terrible . . .

Noga Harish kept up her stand. The kibbutz was up in arms. All except Herbert Segal, his eyes hidden behind his round tinted spectacles, who repeatedly stated to the education committee: we mustn't destroy her. But at the moment there was nobody else who would accept his opinion.

Reuven Harish – incredible to relate – called on Ezra Berger. He found him in the garage at a surprising time: six o'clock on a Saturday morning. They stood face to face, not looking at one another. Reuven muttered:

'I, er . . . I happened to be passing.'

Ezra stammered:

'The fuel supply is blocked. That is, I thought it was. I opened the hood and . . .'

Reuven considered, then suddenly frowned and said, in a strange voice:

'What's going to happen? Tell me. What's going to happen?'

And Ezra, his face deathly pale:

'I . . . I've begged her. Pleaded with her. What more can I . . .'

Reuven, oddly calm, asked:

'How . . . How could you . . . How could you have . . .'

Ezra said nothing. Suddenly, as if neither of them had spoken, as if they had not even seen each other, he rolled underneath the truck and started fiddling furiously with the engine, covering himself with black oil in his frenzy. As if Reuven Harish were not there. As if he did not exist.

Reuven left.

Bronka went to Noga's room. She spoke to her at some length.

She said she was speaking to her just as she would have spoken to her own daughter, if she had had a daughter. She had always dreamed of having a daughter. From now on, if Noga wanted it, they would be mother and daughter. Time would heal everything. Time and love. It would be as if nothing had happened. From now on everything would change. Even between her and Reuven. 'You're not to blame, Noga dear. How you're suffering, how you suffered, and I never knew. I'm to blame for everything. But now it'll all be different. If you'll only realize that . . .'

And Noga, when she had been speaking for a long time, wearily:

'Listen, Bronka, I'll need an older woman to help me when the time comes. You know what I think? I think you could be the woman. I think I want you to be the woman. Will you help me in . . . in a few months' time?'

'But Noga, dear . . .'

'Will you? Will you?'

Zechariah-Siegfried Berger had been to Tel Aviv on business and also made a trip to Jerusalem to see his brother Nehemiah. He had not stayed long; he had hurried back to the valley, to Metsudat Ram, because his other dear brother was in trouble. How could he not hurry back to help him? 'But if you'll listen to my humble advice, Ezra, it's better for you not to get mixed up in the business. That is to say, it's better for us if she does what she wants. Seen objectively, it's not a disaster. A peasant girl is going to have a bastard child, that's all. It's happened before, to thousands of girls in thousands of villages. And from the subjective point of view, dear brother, we derive a clear advantage. The community will reject the miscreant, and she will disappear for good, together with her baby. Maybe her father will go after her. Leave the financial side to your brother Zechariah. The money won't make any difference to me. I'm not thinking of her but of us. We'll get out of our difficulty and heal the rift in the family. A man must do everything he can for his family. And my family, brother dear, is you and Bronka and Tomer and Einav and dear little Danny and Oren and our brother Nehemiah. I'm a lonely man, Ezra. I haven't got a soul in the world except for my family. I want us to be happy. And our happiness will be complete when the little whore and her bastard are thrown out of here. Then, my dear Ezra, we shall return to our senses and be a happy family again. You and Bronka and your children and grandchildren, like olive shoots round your table, as the saying goes. Yes.'

To Noga Harish Siegfried addressed different words. You must stand firm to the last. You're an intelligent girl. Don't be ruled by those sheeplike gossips. Respond to the call of the blood. Not a soul of Israel may be killed, because to kill one Jewish soul is tantamount to killing the whole of mankind. Even if that soul is still a fetus. You must bring the life that is taking shape within you into the world, because there is no joy like the joy of motherhood. What's more, to stand alone and proud against the hostility of the mass is the finest and noblest stance there is. By the way, that is what your mother thinks, too. I wrote to her and asked her what she felt about it. She feels as you do. Your mother loves you deeply, and she prays every day that you won't hate her. You can trust me. I'm her close friend and confidant in her new home. But that's not the main point. The main point, my sweetheart, is this: you must come with me, with your dear uncle Zechariah, to your mother. To your mother's house. There are forests and lakes there, and golden leaves and low gray clouds, and green dreaming hills. Calm death dwells there, and we are in his arms. There your child will be born. You will belong there. You don't belong here, dearest. You must come with me to your mother. You don't belong here. You belong with us. You're one of us.

26

A Wintry Type of Person

ZECHARIAH-SIEGFRIED Berger concluded his business in Tel Aviv. In the course of three or four days he signed on a troupe of dancers who danced Biblical dances, shepherds' dances, and pioneers' dances, and also a poetess who wrote in the language of the future, a daring patchwork of words from different languages, selected for their sound rather than their sense. She would read – or, more accurately, perform – her poems for Siegfried's clientele.

He also found three beautiful girls who neither sang nor acted, but they were fair-haired and pale-eyed and powerfully built. He signed them on to appear in khaki uniforms in his cabaret in Munich. They would be armed with submachine guns and portray scenes from the life of the Israeli fighting woman, such as the capture of a fort or the interrogation of a captured Arab officer.

Anyone who wants to succeed in the entertainment business, Zechariah said to Noga, who stared fixedly at his tiny mustache, must understand secret urges and hidden desires. If I am to stand up to the competition of my professional rivals and attract the public into my den, I must aim at the depths. I'm no match for Munich with clowns and acrobats and strippers. But if I bring along a subtle excitement, then I can bowl Munich over. The son of a murdered Jewish cantor takes Munich by storm, Noga my sweetest – you can't conceive of

272

the poignancy of it. Imagine: a girl, a Jewish girl, a pretty, well-built Jewish girl standing on a suggestively lit stage, holding a submachine gun and trampling on an enemy soldier in a torn uniform who writhes and grovels and kisses her feet. It'll send them wild.

Zechariah concluded his business in Tel Aviv in time to pay a visit to our ancient and holy capital city, to see his beloved and erudite brother Nehemiah. The visit was not a success. The brothers began by exchanging memories. The memories upset them. They turned to present-day national problems and promptly quarreled. Nehemiah suspected his visitor of praising Jewish socialism in a mocking tone. He lost his temper and voiced his suspicions aloud. Zechariah was deeply hurt and answered bitterly:

'I love socialism and I love Judaism and I hold myself to be a zealous humanist. But if brothers stop believing what their brothers are saying, then the whole world reverts to chaos. Just think of Cain and Abel.'

Nehemiah replied that the world reverted to chaos because of nihilism. As he spoke he smiled, as if to say, 'I'm dropping a hint.'

Zechariah agreed at once. He even repeated his brother's remark word for word. Then they discussed Ezra and reflected together on the complicated family situation. They both came to the conclusion that the purity of the family is the most important thing, both for the individual and for society. Zechariah explained that he was thinking of persuading the girl to go to Germany with him, to her mother. She had made up her mind to have the child. The social position of the child would be very awkward. He couldn't live at Metsudat Ram, whereas in Germany, of course, the atmosphere was completely different. He himself would handle the formalities and the other troublesome details for the sake of our dear brother Ezra's happiness.

Nehemiah suggested a short tour of the city. Zechariah agreed. But the friendship between the brothers was disrupted once more when Zechariah hailed a taxi and continued to ply his brother with costly amusements. Nehemiah was annoyed, but he did not manage to deprive Zechariah of the dominant role that he had discreetly usurped. At the end of their tour, Siegfried announced that our capital was a spiritual, poetic town, with very picturesque quarters.

Nehemiah suggested that his brother stay the night with him. To their mutual relief, however, he had to return to Tel Aviv the same day on business. And from Tel Aviv he intended to hurry straight back to Metsudat Ram. He had already decided to stay there until he had brought the problem to a satisfactory conclusion and rescued his brother Ezra. The two brothers parted with an embrace. They kissed each other on both cheeks. Nehemiah urged his brother to act straightforwardly and wished him luck. His heart, needless to say, was heavy.

Zechariah returned to Metsudat Ram, having completed his business and fulfilled his obligations to his elder brother. We were not pleased to see him back. The man was planning something. We suspected his motives. He did not inspire us with confidence. He lacked frankness. There were some who considered that he was not here on his own account, but that he had been sent by our ex-comrade Eva. Fruma Rominov, as usual, gave pointed expression to the general feeling:

'The man reminds me of a pimp.'

Ezra Berger had resumed his double burden of work. He now spent almost half his hours in the cab of his truck. He also spent some time with his friends the fishermen in Tiberias. He no longer saw Noga. Perhaps he was avoiding her, or perhaps she was hiding from him. Or perhaps Herbert Segal was right when he said that they were kept apart by a common sense of guilt.

Noga worked five hours a day, as was the rule for boys and girls of her age during the school holidays. She helped Herzl Goldring with his gardening. Herzl Goldring is a bitter man, given to outbursts of fierce rage. But he treated Noga Harish with remarkable gentleness. He was not even strict about the hours she worked. If she arrived late or left early, Herzl saw and heard nothing. As they bent together over a shrub that needed trimming, he would try to amuse her with stories of her childhood. Herzl's daughter, who had died in infancy of diphtheria, had been born at the same time as Noga. He remembered the two girls when they were a year old sitting in a playpen, playing with colored bricks. He recalled the scene with complete equanimity, as if he were seeing it in the present, as if nothing had happened since. His way of recalling scenes from the past wrung Noga's heart. He remembered the colors of the bricks. He had painted them himself. A blonde head pressed against a dark head, curls touching curls, two beautiful little girls,

Noga, two very special little girls. But how could you possibly remember Asnat? You've forgotten.

One day in July Fruma Rominov stopped Noga Harish outside the clothes store and said to her:

'You're beginning to bulge. Which month are you in? Third? fourth?'

Noga turned to leave.

'Wait, wait a moment. You haven't heard what I have to say.'

'Not just now, please, Fruma.'

'Be patient. Wait just a minute. You can't go and see your father at the moment. Right? No, of course not. So where do you go to have your afternoon tea? You don't? That's bad. You must look after yourself now. Plenty of fruit, plenty of fresh vegetables, plenty of dairy produce. Do you like cream cheese? You need to take in a lot of calcium. Yes. You know why I'm saying this. I thought, I wanted to suggest, perhaps you'd come and have tea with me in the afternoons. I'm always alone. I could make you a snack, the sort of food you need. For example, I can get hold of some malt beer. I'll explain to you some time why beer is import-ant when you're pregnant. You could listen to the radio, too, with me, and even play the recorder. I'm not musical, but I've never been averse to listening to a tune or two. You mustn't give up playing the recorder. Men may betray you; things are always faithful. That's life. So come around five o'clock. If you like, you can help me with the ironing, too. For your sake, not mine.'

Noga thanked Fruma, but declined her offer. She preferred to sleep all the afternoon. She felt very tired these days. It must be the heat. Anyway, she would bear in mind what Fruma had said. Hurriedly, she turned her back, because her eyes were brimming. She had always been taught that warmheartedness and consideration were the opposite of malice, as day is the opposite of night. And now Fruma.

Herbert Segal held a meeting of Noga's class to discuss the matter with them. I want to consult you as people with experience of life. I haven't come here to make a speech. I've come to exchange ideas. I want you to know that I have called this meeting on my own initiative, without consulting the education committee. Our discussion will remain strictly between ourselves. You won't embarrass me. I trust you. I know a hint will suffice. Good. Let's begin. Our subject is the predicament of your friend Noga. No, that's not right The predicament is *your* predicament. Our predicament.

To express what he had in mind, Herbert had to explain two notions. He explained to the children the meaning of 'tragedy' and the meaning of 'tact.' With the aid of these two terms he initiated a subdued, rather solemn discussion. The conclusion was voiced by the children. Herbert accepted it. Noga must not be victimized. We must not behave like a mob gloating over someone else's distress. The solution was not artificial sympathy. That kind of sympathy was more hurtful than outright insults. But she must not be victimized. Whether or not she was responsible for her fate, she was suffering. We must be sensitive to her suffering. We must, in Herbert's phrase, exercise tact. And in his opinion, incidentally, the question of responsibility was not, generally speaking, a simple one. It was a philosophical problem.

*

Herbert Segal is a remarkable man. His words took effect. There were no more scornful or sarcastic comments. Perhaps Oren's serious remarks helped to damp down the general feelings. Dafna Isarov treated Noga as if she were ill. She walked on tiptoe in their shared room. It was not everyone who had the fortune to live with a girl who could be the heroine of a sad novel. Dafna was conscious of the responsibility that Herbert had impressed on the group, and especially, of course, on her.

As for Oren, he got into a fierce fight with an older boy, who was serving in the army, because the latter had dared to say to him sarcastically that the Berger family was about to celebrate a happy event, the birth of a new uncle for little Danny. Oren did not give a virtuoso performance. There was no exhibition of feints and subtle stratagems. He fought straightforwardly. He went straight to the point, to the disappointment of his supporters and detractors alike, and delivered a brutal kick to the most sensitive point.

He did not hate Noga. We need not weary ourselves with explanations. One day he slipped her a note folded up into a small wad, which said: *Noga you're right if thats what you feel then you must do it because you must do what you feel not what other people feel your friend OG*

Either because he felt like it, or prompted by dark influences, Oren drowned Mendel Morag's favorite cat. With an army dagger he removed the skin from the body, salted and dried it, replaced the eyes by green marbles, and made it into a soft, furry rug for Noga's bedside. Needless to say, the girl rejected the gift. But it must be added that Oren bore her no grudge.

*

Again, at sunset, on one of the benches in the garden, the girl in a blue skirt and bright blouse and the visitor in a white shirt and an orange tie, with the picture of a well-known movie star printed on it.

Those who passed by pretended not to see them, either because their power of judging had reached saturation point or because the community, at the end of a subtle and complicated process, had formed its final conclusions. About Reuven Harish they said:

'He's withdrawn completely into himself.'

'She never goes to see him.'

'He's not the type to collapse at a single blow. But he's yielding, he's bending. It's horrible.'

About Ezra Berger:

'Gradually he'll go back to Bronka. They'll meet each other halfway. There'll be a period of melancholy, but he'll go back. It's bound to happen.'

'Time. That's all. Time heals all wounds. Winter will come. He won't go on driving day and night. There won't be anywhere for him to go day and night. The nights will get longer. And he'll go back to Bronka. Last Saturday he played on the lawn with the grandchild. Twice he laughed aloud. And that evening he was seen on Grisha's veranda, playing chess with Grisha. Time doesn't stand still. He's only got to get rid of his guest. He has a bad influence on him.'

The man stared fixedly at the cigarette he was holding. The girl was sitting curled up at the far end of the bench. Her little belly made whoever looked at her realize how slender, how long her legs were. (But nobody looked at her for long. They looked away quickly as if burned.)

The leaves rustled on the trees. Starlings performed a hysterical dance in the air. They settled on the electric wires, then flapped gently toward the water tower, but changed their minds halfway and with a sudden unanimous decision headed instead for the tin roof of the cattle sheds.

Zechariah went on smoking.

A small branch from one of the bushes nudged Noga's shoulder. She played with it. She pushed it away and, like a spring, it came back and poked her again on the shoulder.

Zechariah observed her game. He chuckled.

Noga said:

'That's not a smile; it's a grimace. You can't smile.'

Zechariah told her about an ill-fated woman who had said something similar to him many years before.

Noga asked what had happened to the woman.

'She must be dead by now. What of it?'

Noga said she was sure he must have seen a lot in the course of his life.

Zechariah started to describe Eva Hamburger's present life. Noga did not press him for details, nor did she interrupt him. He stopped talking. Stabbed out his cigarette. Lit another.

'I shan't press you to speak,' he said. 'I know who you are. You're one of us.'

'It's getting dark,' Noga said. 'Let's go and have supper. If we're late . . .' She did not complete the sentence. Apparently she was not concentrating.

Zechariah stood up and offered the girl his arm. Noga did not take the hint; she refused to be supported. She walked beside the man, not touching him even lightly.

After supper Noga went to her room. She got into bed. Nowadays she spent twelve or fourteen hours every day asleep. A great tiredness came over her all the time.

Zechariah sat in his brother's house. Bronka would not hint that he should leave, even though she wanted him to. She served him one cold drink after another, because he was not used to the climate. His throat was always parched. Over and over again, Bronka told him to feel at home and help himself to a drink whenever he felt like it. Zechariah claimed that it tasted better when it was poured out for him by Bronka. Sometimes he told her strange stories. She listened to them because he was her guest and her husband's brother, but she did not answer him much because she did not like the man.

He told her, for instance, about the early days in Germany. It had been in 1950, or at the end of 1949. He had come to squeeze some reparation money out of them, and while his claims were under examination he was penniless. So he had to find work, any work. Those were difficult days. Everything was still in ruins. He found a rather strange job, but one couldn't afford to be choosy in those days. He was taken on as a temporary worker in the municipal health department in Hamburg. He worked at night, in a team of displaced refugees. Their job was to round up stray dogs. They were paid according to the number of dogs they caught, and at that time there was an ever-increasing multitude of strays. Some of them still showed signs of a pedigree, but the purity of their line had become contaminated during the war years. We used to fool the authorities. We would catch the dogs, present them to the official in charge, get an officially stamped receipt for each dog, all in accordance with the strictest German efficiency, and then we would take them to the municipal rubbish dump to poison them. And, thereby, as you will have guessed by now, my dear Bronka, hangs the tale. We didn't kill the dogs. We used to let them go. Within an hour or two they had reappeared in the suburbs. We dutifully rounded them up again the next night and once again received good German money for each and every dog. There were some dogs we captured and released twenty or thirty times. The authorities were alarmed at their extraordinary proliferation. The more they harassed them, the more they multiplied. As for us, we made friends with our mangy four-legged breadwinners and even gave them names – Heinz, Fritz, Franz, and Hermann. They used to give themselves up of their own free will, because they were fond of the journey to the municipal rubbish dump. Sometimes they found good food there. A stray dog's life is not a happy one, both from an economical and, more especially, from a psychological point of view. A dog needs to be loved. He needs a name. Needs to be recognized. We used to stroke them and tickle them behind the ears and call each one by its name and nickname, Fredi, Hansi, Rudi-Rudolfi-Rudolfini. After all, they were strays. A dog will sacrifice himself for a single sign of affection. A dog needs to belong. I'm sure you realize, Bronka, my love, that we didn't spare the lives of the mad dogs. We weren't criminals; we did have some sense of moral respons-ibility. Anyway, eventually, as you know, my claims received official approval, and then, beloved sister-in-law, then, new horizons opened up before me. But I fear I am not succeeding in entertaining you with my stories. Thomas Mann, in *The Magic Mountain*, describes a bore who is always badgering people with his trite moral tales. But his disease was tubercu-losis. He was consumptive. You don't have to listen to me. I love you, my dear Bronka, even when you look at me with dis-gust or boredom on your face, because we both belong to the same family, and I love my family regardless of how they treat me. A man like me will go to the ends of the earth for a sign of affection. And a family is not a limited company. A family is a destiny. A man must always love his destiny, because he has no choice. Would you be kind enough to pour me another glass of orange juice? It's my throat. My throat's so dry. I don't stop talking. And I'm not used to the Asiatic climate. I am a – how shall I put it? – no, not a European, I'm a – let me put it this way – I'm a wintry type of person.

27

Bells and Sadness

REUVEN HARISH was housebound. He had no teaching to do. It was the summer holidays. He should have been spending his time preparing his lessons for the coming school year. He tried to, but the words danced around on the page.

He sits down at his desk and opens a book. The words do not form sentences. He opens another book. His head drops onto the desk. He gets up, washes his face with cold water, sips a cup of coffee, returns to the desk, and once more his hand pushes the book away, and his glance starts wandering. The coffee is supplied by the generous Nina Goldring. Nina has good-naturedly taken on herself the task of caring for Reuven Harish. Now that neither Bronka nor Noga sets foot inside his room, Nina gladly performs the errand of mercy. Reuven is not well. His shoulders seem to droop, his birdlike profile has become sharper than ever. Even his bright green eyes become blurred at times. He looks like someone who is exhausted from lack of sleep. This is far from being the case. Reuven is given to long, dreamless stretches of deep sleep. Just like his daughter. For no apparent reason his face is sometimes bathed in hot sweat, and giddiness lays him out on his bed. On bad days he is forbidden by the kibbutz doctor to make any effort. Seated in a deck chair on his veranda, he picks grapes from a large bunch until he suddenly dozes off in the heat of the morning sun and sleeps for several hours.

Sometimes he recalls a nocturnal journey, in a truck battered by icy jets of furious rain. In his hallucination Reuven hears a voice, and a pale hand with delicate fingers softly touches his knee. Along with the hand come visions. Large birds, evening twilight, bells of distant churches. Within the shrouded image lurks something pure and crystalline, something that cannot be named. Reuven wonders and feels sad. What is it, dear God, what is this thing? Far far away it shows, with the rain and the sound of bells.

*

284

We were pleasantly surprised at this time by young Gai Harish. He had changed for the better. We are no tyros in matters of education, and we do not expect miracles. But this boy had become quieter and more serious. Even his manners had improved. Credit must go to the modest Herbert Segal, who had taken it on himself to speak to the boy and explain to him straightforwardly the meaning of tragedy and the importance of tact.

Gai looked at Herbert out of his warm dark eyes and inquired whether the baby would belong to the Berger or the Harish family. Herbert sighed and replied that the baby had no chance of being happy, because it would have no real family. Neither the Berger family nor the Harish family would be able to offer it a loving home.

Gai silently considered the matter. Finally he declared that he could love such a baby, because that kind of baby especially needed to be loved.

Herbert blinked shortsightedly. He fidgeted with his fingers, as if he were feeling the boy's words. Gai added that his mother, too, had fallen in love with a stranger, and that was why he and Noga had grown up without a mother. He was not angry with his mother. But inwardly he had already made up his mind never to fall in love. Falling in love always leads to disaster.

Herbert uncharacteristically looked down at the floor, taking care not to meet the boy's gaze. With a certain hesitancy he explained that this was not always the case, that love sometimes made people happy. Gai agreed as far as love between men was concerned, the way that he loved his father or Tomer loved Oren. But one should never get married. Or even fall in love with a woman. One should live like you, Herbert. Without any woman. Because you're a wise man. Herbert Segal said nothing.

Gai asked who, in Herbert's opinion, was to blame: father or mother, Noga or Ezra.

Herbert explained simply that life is sometimes complicated. There are some situations in which you cannot say that X is the guilty party and Y is the victim. Much to Herbert Segal's astonishment, Gai replied that the conflict between Jews and Arabs was an example of such a situation. Both sides say that their ancestors lived in this land and both sides are absolutely right. What is the moral? The moral is very simple. The moral is that might is right.

Herbert deferred answering immediately, hunting for a simple but crushing argument that would refute Gai's strange conclusion. At the last moment he remembered that his duty was not to defeat the child but to encourage his friendship. He therefore refrained from exercising his right to have the last word. As they parted on the doorstep, Gai looked straight into Herbert's gray eyes and made two promises. One, that he would not talk to his father or to Noga or to anyone about what had happened in the family. And, two, that he would call on Herbert from time to time for a chat or an argument. Herbert also tried to persuade Gai to let him play him some music, because music soothes the emotions and stirs up thoughts, which are our true property in life. Gai did not reply at once; he pondered and finally said that he sometimes had thoughts at night before he fell asleep. But in the daytime? In the daytime he thought only when he had to. He shook hands and left.

As he walked away, Gai said to himself that from now on it was his duty to take care of Daddy, because Daddy had problems. The thought excited him. Herbert was thinking about the boy's warm dark eyes. He came to the conclusion that the child was very mature for his age and that it would be wonderful if he could become his spiritual father. Herbert Segal was fond of Gai Harish.

The summer lost some of its earlier exuberance. The discerning eye could see the signs. True, the heat still tyrannized us with the obstinacy of an old man striving to conceal his waning vigor by means of continual bitter outbursts. It was clear, however, that the days were growing shorter. The hours of darkness, the gentle hours, lengthened. The power of the incandescent light was ebbing. The twilight became richer.

Day and night, in three shifts, tractors turned the soil in preparation for the sowing of the winter crops. Golden fields yielded to the plow and turned over to reveal their dark innards. In the orchard activity was at its height. Exhausted men filled the dining hall in the evenings. Inside the rooms the air was stifling for most of the night. More and more adventurous souls chose to sleep outside on the verandas, or even on the lawns, with white sheets wrapped over their heads to protect them from the fury of the mosquitoes. At dawn you could see a kind of scattered army of ghosts lying about, swathed in white shrouds. But the appearance is illusory. The night watchmen nudge the sleepers awake with the first glimmer of daylight.

The shrouds unwrap to disclose live men and women, tired men and women, grumbling, liable to occasional gossiping and virulent petty quarrels. We must not judge them severely. The season imposes exhausting labors on them all, while we do – what? Only those whose eye is alert to the movements of the birds and the minute changes in the color of vegetation can take a certain comfort. Faint signs, like secret messages, herald the onset of other powers.

Zechariah-Siegfried Berger extended his stay at Metsudat Ram, not without pressing on the treasurer, Yitzhak Friedrich, a monthly sum to cover his keep. Ezra's complaints and Bronka's sarcasms had no effect, I am a wealthy man, and it is right and proper to dip one's hand into a rich man's pocket. If I'm not allowed to pay, I'll take offense and leave at once. Do you want to drive me away?

In her heart Bronka did indeed pray that he would pack up and go. So did many other members. But Ezra prized his brother's company, as did one of our young girls, condemned to solitude because of an embarrassing accident.

Zechariah's decision to stay was open to a number of interpretations. His own account of it was that the company of his relatives was dearer to him than that of anyone else in the whole wide world, and he loved being here because here he could observe the building of our old-new country.

Others claimed that a sordid scheme was hatching in his mind. Who could say what its object was? Perhaps he was here on Eva's instructions to persuade Noga Harish to go back to Germany with him. Such was Bronka's opinion. Or perhaps he desired the girl and wanted her for himself. So Tomer thought.

Fruma Rominov held to an even more unpleasant explanation: his behavior was that of a cunning pimp, who takes a helpless girl in trouble under his wing, helps her to bring her bastard child into the world, and acquires absolute power over her body and her soul.

One's first impression of Zechariah-Siegfried would be that of a scoundrel, if one did not know about his background and outlook and his attachment to his family. It is my love of my family, he explains to Ezra, that makes me undertake the unpleasant task of resolving this girl's doubts and persuading her to go to Europe. But there is also a question of principle: her place is with her mother. She is delicate and spoiled, and she will develop better in Europe than here in the front line of battle. Moreover, if we can see the matter from Eva's point of view, how marvelous it would be for mother and daughter to have the joy of bringing up the child together. It would give Eva a purpose in life. As for my bosom friend Isaac Hamburger, I am sure that the artistic side of his character will forge strong bonds of love between him and his new daughter, and with his prospective grandchild. And I can reveal, by the way, that the most recent letter from my friends indicates their wholehearted approval of my plan.

Unless you suspect the truth of Zechariah-Siegfried's words, you must admit their logic, even if this only becomes apparent on deeper reflection.

Zechariah's behavior, too, is logical and systematic. He seeks the company of Noga Harish. Sometimes he manages to arouse her curiosity. For the most part, she listens to the sound of his voice, but the words elude her. His voice soothes her.

When he is with her, she is relaxed. He pins cautious hopes on her silence. He is convinced that he has the girl in his power. He does not realize that in fact only a gentle torpor keeps her with him. But even this is illusory.

Zechariah also attempts to win the friendship of Gai, as befits a friend of the family. Gai does not respond to his advances. We must wait to see the effect of a Schweigermann bicycle that is at the moment on its way from Munich to Metsudat Ram, having been ordered by Herr Siegfried Berger as a present for his admirable young friend Gai Harish.

Naturally, Zechariah does not overlook the father. He is the principal obstacle. The girl will not be able to withstand his collapse. A tear or two, and the whole careful edifice will tumble like a house of cards. The matter demands careful consideration. Reuven Harish is adamantine. His sympathy cannot be bought for the price of a modest German edition of his selected poems. Vulgar methods will not succeed with him. There is a clash of principles, like the clash of iron on iron, or the conflict between mountain and valley, to borrow our dear pioneer's own favorite metaphor. His friendship may be won gradually, of course, by flattery. But that course demands a protracted effort, whose outcome is far from certain. On the other hand, this Harismann is suffering from a complaint, whose details deserve careful attention. Certain illnesses, under unusual circumstances, can dispose of a man at a blow. And in case of any disaster, the girl passes legally into her mother's care, and that puts an end to subterfuge. And besides all these possibilities, there are other courses of action open. We can bring the law round to our side. That is the proper way for decent, law-abiding citizens. Perhaps what we really need is an intelligent lawyer. Let's go over the facts carefully: a couple have two children. The parents have been divorced for some years. Both are in their right mind. Both are financially capable of supporting the children. In such a case, legal common sense suggests that the father should have custody of the son and the mother of the daughter. That would be an equable solution in the true sense of the word. The fact that the mother has so far taken no steps to exercise her legal right detracts in no way, of course, from the legal validity of that right. And especially, gentlemen of the jury, since the father has by his own actions sacrificed both his moral and his legal right to the custody of the children. We deeply regret having to publicize the fact that he has embroiled himself in a personal scandal, the details of which my client can supply without any difficulty, and the harmful effects of which on the minds of the children will be attested by the eminent psychologist whom we shall call in due course. The mother, on the other hand, is happily remarried and her morals are above reproach. To this, likewise, we shall bring incontrovertible testimony. The conclusion, gentlemen, is logically inescapable: it is the mother, and not the father, who is entitled, on both legal and moral grounds, to have custody of the children. My client, however, is prepared to display outstanding generosity. She does not insist upon invoking the full rigor of the law. She is prepared to settle for a reasonable compromise, disregarding the father's misdemeanors and general conduct. Our offer is straightforward and exceedingly generous: he may keep the son. But on my client's behalf let me warn him that if he dares to reject our offer, considerate and magnanimous as it is, we shall challenge his right to the son as well, and he may find himself the loser on both counts.

The case rests. But this course must be a last resort. We want the deer unwounded. Netted, not shot. I haven't come to drag the girl away kicking and screaming. I want to get Harismann's blessing. And get it I will. He is a man of ideals. I shall use his ideals to break through his defenses. He will give his blessing, and I shall deign to accept it, as a favor. I shall accept out of humanitarian motives. He'll beg me to take her.

Needless to say, the visitor's thoughts were not outwardly apparent. His appearance was neat and smart. He radiated a smell of luxurious grooming. He divided his time between his brother's family and theoretical lectures to Noga, between dear little Danny, who provided him with much entertainment, and the swimming pool, which also saw a great deal of him and became accustomed to the unexpected power of his muscles. Once a week he traveled to Tel Aviv or Haifa, returning the following day. Bronka and Ezra did not know the purpose of his trips, just as they were uncertain of the purpose of his stay. But to Tomer, in consideration of his youth, Siegfried spoke frankly.

'I go to enjoy myself. Just once a week – no one can accuse me of excess. Surely I'm not expected to live entirely without a woman. When you finally decide to join me, my dear Tomer, I'm at your service, ready and waiting to shower you with delights.'

*

Noga was attentive to her body. Never before had she been so clearly aware of the independent life of her muscles or the warmth of her flesh. She lay on her back with her eyes closed and listened to the sounds of her body. The gentle throbbing of the blood at her temples and wrists, the inner gargle produced from time to time by the digestive juices, the rhythm of her breathing, which was linked to the rhythm of her thoughts, the tender stabbing deep inside her belly.

Previously, Noga had not liked her body. She disliked the coarseness of tangible reality. There was no difficulty in escaping from the body to a dream world of colorful disembodied forms. It was enough to press gradually with two fingers on the eyeballs for bright spirals of color to sweep you away to another world, a world of bells, bells whose tongue you are. Now the pleasures have changed. Now it is into the body, not away from it. To get inside yourself. The same wild dream every night: to be a fetus inside your own body, to curl up in the enclosed warmth.

The posture demanded by this mood: sitting on the floor, at the foot of the bed, knees raised, head between the knees, arms folded round it. Or another possibility: lying on your back and gently, slowly stroking your breast.

Herzl Goldring did not overburden Noga with work. When she left early, he pretended not to notice. If he thought he heard a groan or saw a twitch of nausea on her face, he insisted that she put down her hoe and go and lie down. Once, without any preamble, he said in an acid tone:

'Listen, you don't have to have the baby.'

Surprised and half-amused, Noga asked:

'How do you know?'

'Nina thinks so too. So do other people. Lots of them.'

'Are you suggesting I should put it to the vote in the assembly?'

'Oh, no, heaven forbid. Of course it's a personal matter, completely private; nobody else has the right to decide.'

'Now you're right, Herzl, absolutely right, and when you're right, no one can argue with you.'

'Argue? Perish the thought. I wasn't trying to argue. But I feel I ought to apologize.'

'You? Apologize? Why? What have you done?'

Herzl was tongue-tied. He concluded:

'Oh, I'm very sorry, I'm really very sorry, Noga. Very sorry.'

Needless to say, Herzl Goldring did not repeat his mistake. He never raised the subject again.

Kind people like Herbert Segal took great pains discreetly to influence the general mood of opinion and to surround Noga with an atmosphere of tolerance and friendliness. Not because Herbert justified her behavior, but because reason and compassion led for once to the same conclusion. The girl was facing a strong temptation to leave the kibbutz and the country and to join her mother. Those who took that course never returned. Moreover, Reuven Harish was dear to us all. His troubles were our troubles. We could imagine what would happen to Reuven Harish if his daughter went to live with her mother. When the moment came, we should have to meet and decide on the fate of the child. But we would not crush the girl. We would defer passing judgment and treat her tolerantly. Herbert Segal came to this conclusion early on and did a great deal to impress it on others. He expressed it in various ways, but the fundamental idea was the same.

The echoing chorus would come:

'She's not to blame. After all, she comes from a broken home.'

'Her determination to have the baby is a sign of her strong character.'

'Throw her out? Then what about Reuven?'

'We mustn't react emotionally. It needs thought.'

The direction of the public mind in our kibbutz is an extremely subtle process. You cannot stand up and preach to a community of mature, sophisticated men and women. You have to talk to individuals. You have to choose wisely whom to talk to. This delicate task modest Herbert Segal took upon himself. His first move was to call a meeting of Noga's classmates; he brought them to an understanding of the situation without exercising his authority. Oren Geva did not stand in his way. Next, Herbert turned to Gai Harish and sealed a secret compact with him. Then he discreetly stimulated the maternal feelings of the older women. Not with high-flown phrases. He played on their sympathy with hints and asides. He quenched their blazing moral fury: nothing was easier than to expel someone from their midst to keep the camp pure and free from taint. But what would happen afterward? Would we be able, as a community, to look ourselves in the eye? Easy solutions were a sign of weakness. Were we to counter the weakness of a poor, confused girl with our own collective weakness? No, we mustn't be governed by weakness. Otherwise, we would lose our moral justification and our right to judge the girl. She was a victim, and so was her father, and we must not forget it for a moment, because we were responsible for the happiness of each individual among us, and because Reuven was one of us, and his daughter was one of us, too. We must not treat her as a dangerous example or a corrupting influence. Such notions were alien to our spirit. She was neither an example nor an influence; she was a sixteen-year-old girl. We must not react like ignorant, prejudiced peasants. Could you imagine this girl thrown out on the street?

A flood of compassion broke over our kibbutz toward the end of the summer. The women competed in good works and acts of kindness toward the straying lamb. She was surrounded by sympathy and warmth. Sincere invitations to come round and talk. You're so lonely. Why don't you come and have tea with us, come and have a rest, take a shower, look at pictures, pour out your troubles? The women in the sewing room acted beyond the call of duty. After complicated calculations they managed to ascertain Noga's current measurements without an embarrassing fitting. They made her a set of maternity clothes, and Einav Geva smuggled them into her room.

Esther Klieger presented Noga with a brightly wrapped book, saying:

'For you. Read it. No need to give it back. Keep it. Only make sure my Dafna doesn't get hold of it.'

'But . . . why? What is it?'

'Look and see. Very useful book. Do you feel all right, my dear? Yes? You can always turn to me. Even in the middle of the night. Don't be too shy. You're like my own Dafna to me. Grisha feels the same way as I do. For us you're Dafna's sister. Yes. Take good care of yourself, my dear. And don't forget to come.'

Noga unwrapped the book. A guide for the expectant mother. Blushing slightly, Noga thanked Esther Klieger. Esther was delighted.

Within the next few days the following books were collected and handed over to her: *Childbirth Without Tears*, *Introduction to Sex*, *Bringing Up Your Child*, and also two identical copies – one from Hasia Ramigolski and the other from Gerda Zohar – of *The Happy Mother*.

Even in the dining hall, Noga was treated to dainty tidbits – chicken liver, dairy produce, raw carrot, malt beer, and sweets normally reserved for babies and small children.

Stubborn soul. How she must have suffered in her short life, that she rejects the generous kindness of the women and prefers the solitary company of a rather shady tourist who is visiting the kibbutz. Furthermore, she spends an undesirable amount of time sleeping.

Fruma Rominov approached the health committee with the suggestion that Noga Harish should be sent to a private nursing home in Haifa for the next few months. In the first place, psychologically she needed a change of atmosphere. Second, physically the girl was underweight. Her hips were too narrow. She needed to put on weight before the birth, which might be a difficult one. Third, which ought to be first, really, she ought to be removed from a certain harmful influence. Fruma's suggestion was not adopted. The committee accepted the arguments of Gerda Zohar, its secretary: the girl should stay here, since she needed constant care – not medical care but social care.

Every Thursday the women go to the laundry and hang out the washing that is not done by machine. Once, Fruma Rominov arrived early and hung out Noga's washing. Fruma, we must bear in mind, had not been well lately. She had been complaining of dizzy spells and constant lassitude. Although the doctor had discovered no physical cause, Fruma had stopped working. She had never done such a thing before. For three weeks she had not left her room. Even her meals had been brought to her on a tray by a member of the health committee. Fruma declared that the doctor had sided with those who wanted to see her dead. It wasn't his fault. He must have been put up to it. She relied on her intuition, which had never let her down. She had sunk all her life into this place. She had sacrificed her husband. She had sacrificed her son. She would sacrifice herself. That, after all, was the easiest sacrifice of all. If only one of the officials of the kibbutz could at least take the trouble to get Rami recalled on leave, so that he could be with his mother in her last days. But no. Who would do that for her? The Pogolskis or the Ramidolskis? Huh. Fruma announced to all and sundry that her end was near. She had even dreamed of her death twice recently. The dream could not be ignored. The proof was that poor Alter, too, had dreamed of his own funeral four days before they had sent him into the banana plantation and killed him. But I won't say anything. I haven't said anything all my life. I won't say anything now in my last days. Another month or two. After my funeral, all your Golskis and Dolskis will be able to do everything they're capable of, because there won't be anyone left in this kibbutz to make them feel ashamed. Noga? Noga doesn't prove a thing. I understand her. I understand her better than anyone. If you haven't suffered yourself, you can't understand others who suffer. You might think that what has happened to her is a punishment for what she did; if my Rami weren't such a sensitive boy he could tell some terrible stories about her. But I'm not crowing. I can sense when people are really suffering. There's a saying: Don't laugh at your enemy's downfall. And, by the way, I don't like to boast, but I might add that I've also done my bit for her. And long before everybody started chasing after her with love and kisses, because the fashion changed. No, it was weeks ago, when she was treated like a mangy bitch. Neglected. Despised. Abandoned. Fruma was the one who went up to her and said 'My house is open to you.' I wouldn't tell anybody else this. Except for you, Herbert, because you . . . It doesn't matter. You'll be the one to deliver the funeral address for Fruma Rominov. I don't want any Dolski-Golskis. I want you. You can start getting your speech ready. I won't keep you waiting.

One Saturday night Reuven Harish went for his usual walk. His steps led him along the path that ran behind the cow shed and down to the fish ponds. He stopped by the water pump. He breathed deeply. He saw birds. He heard the wind. He recalled a long journey in Ezra Berger's truck. Iron rods. He saw some small stones in the dust. He stooped and picked some up. Aimed at a rusty cart shaft. Missed. Breathed deeply again. Suddenly he decided to go and see his daughter. He hadn't set eyes on her for seven weeks. Go to her room. Noga-Maris.

What shall I say to her? She's not mine any more. I'll say I've come to see her. I'll say we don't have to talk. Let's sit and say nothing. You don't mind? You can say no. Then I'll leave. I've simply come to be. Here. Not to talk. May I?

Noga said yes. Sit down, I'll stay here on the bed, because I'm tired. No, I wasn't going to sleep. Sit down, do. I'm . . . I'm glad you've come.

'Are you?'

'Yes, I am.'

Silence.

Distant laughter. Sounds of singing. In the wood. A strange melody. The air is hot. The electric light is very yellow. A bird shrieks close at hand. A moth hurls itself at the mosquito net in the window frame, making drunkenly for the light. Again and again it dashes itself against the netting, thudding lightly, in stubborn desperation. Beams of moonlight, too, try to penetrate into the room. The net does not halt them. They filter through it with ease. They have no body, not even a tiny one. They are here, inside, with us. It's only because of the electric light that they can't be seen. Here they are. Familiar smell. Painful. Father's smell. Her eyes are veiled. Perhaps a lump in her throat. Darling. Child. You're like Gai, Daddy. You're a big child. You could be my little brother. Don't be sad, Daddy, don't be sad. Won't do it again. Ever. Promise. Don't be sad. Everything will be all right. Don't worry, Daddy. Don't be sad. It'll be all right. I can't bear to see you sad. Don't. I promise. I've promised.

'Daddy.'

'Yes.'

'Were you asleep?'

'No.'

'Nor was I.'

'I know.'

'Daddy.'

'Yes.'

'Let's go away.'

'Where to?'

'Let's go away tomorrow. With Gai.'

'Where to?'

'Somewhere far away. To the end of the world.'

'Where to?'

'On the way we'll stop and collect her. Not without her. The four of us.'

'Where to?'

'Somewhere else. Somewhere quiet. Somewhere safe. Just us.'

'You're hurting me, Stella.'

Silence.

Dafna Isarov cautiously opened the door, saw Reuven, muttered something, and shut the door again.

'Daddy.'

'Yes.'

'What are you thinking about?'

'Nothing in particular.'

'What about?'

'Wiesbaden.'

'What?'

'Wiesbaden. It's a place. A town. In Germany.'

'What is there there?'

'Hot springs. When I was a child I saw . . . Never mind.'

'What did you see?'

'Never mind. I didn't come to talk.'

'No, go on. Talk. I want you to.'

'Hot springs. Steam gushing out of the ground.'

'What made you think of it?'

'They took me there. I was four. Five, perhaps. My father got a job there. In Wiesbaden.'

'Was it a nice place?'

'I can't remember.'

'Why were you thinking about . . . that place?'

'Wiesbaden. Because of the geysers. The hot springs.'

'What?'

'I was frightened. Terribly frightened. I can remember. Steam gushing out with an awful hissing sound. I was only a child. Everything shook. Perhaps it was only me shaking. No. The earth shook. Everything.'

'Like in an earthquake?'

'You know, Stella, for years and years I used to have terrible dreams about Wiesbaden. And now . . . now they're coming back.'

'When?'

'Now. Last night, perhaps the night before. Several times. It's a nightmare.'

'What did you dream? Tell me.'

'I dreamed it was gushing. Under my feet. Right where I was standing. Something suddenly moved under my foot, a little crack in the ground, white steam came out, a bigger crack, a fissure. I run, it widens, steam and seething vapor, it chases me, it . . . it scalds. I scream. It's black. Roasting like burning oil. In the dream it's not always in Wiesbaden. It can be anywhere. Wherever I happen to be. All of a sudden.'

'I . . . Daddy, I'll go there. I'll go and see the place you mentioned. Is it very far from . . . Never mind. I want to. I'll go there.'

'Stella, don't look at me like that. I don't . . . I knew you'd go. Go.'

'And you?'

'No.'

'Never?'

'Never.'

'But how can you . . . all alone?'

'I don't think I can.'

'Daddy, what sort of a country is it?'

'Where?'

'There. Germany.'

'I was born there.'

'Yes.'

'Pretty. It's a pretty country. Mountains, forests, wind, lakes, rivers, old towns, inns, peasants, thick beer, castles. And Wiesbaden.'

'And the people?'

'I don't know. All the people I knew, all of them, either killed or got killed. But a strong wind blows. Filling the sails. You can hire boats on the lakes and sail, as your mother does. The sun isn't too bright, either. Or perhaps my memory is confusing it. Like twilight all the time. Less tiring for the eyes. Less light.'

'You'll hate me.'

'No, I won't.'

'Yes, you will hate me.'

'No. I . . . I've always hated hatred. I only hate . . . I don't know how to say it. Only Wiesbaden.'

'You'll live.'

'Yes.'

'How?'

'I'll teach. Read books. Bring up Gai. If Gai decides to stay.'

'Sad.'

'Perhaps not. Perhaps not so sad. Perhaps like . . . like Herbert, for example. Living along one long groove. Dead straight. Calmly. Clenched teeth. Living drily.'

'What else do you remember? Tell me more about it. Everything.'

'I can't remember everything. I try to forget. But I can't forget Wiesbaden. I'm frightened. I can remember a little. I can remember bells, for instance.'

'Bells? Did you say bells?'

'Yes, bells. Every Sunday. In the evening. At twilight. Endless fields, dark plains, black mountains in the distance. Great valleys. Forests. Little towns among the forests. Sounds everywhere, everywhere the sound of bells. Not a man in sight, not a breath of wind, not a bird in the sky. Bells. As if everything were dead, and only the bells were alive and singing, singing and alive, ding-dong sleep, ding-dong die, done ding-dong, die down dong. I'm frightened, Noga, I'm frightened at night, I'm frightened now.'

28

The Golden Dagger

E ZRA BERGER gave up his extra trip.

One evening he went to see Podolski, who was in charge of the work rota, and said:

'Podolski, I'm only going out once tomorrow. And the same from tomorrow on.'

'Has something happened?'

'Nothing's happened. I'm just tired. "Is my strength the strength of stones?"' he added jokingly. But he forgot to accompany his joke with a smile. His decision may have been due to exhaustion, or perhaps rather to the blessed influence of Zechariah-Siegfried. Zechariah had long conversations with his brother. His purpose was apparently to reforge the link between Ezra and Bronka. Obviously, the attempt was made indirectly. It is doubtful whether Ezra himself was aware of his brother's secret aim.

Bronka treated Ezra with discreet consideration. She treated him as one treats a man who has newly arrived from distant parts. Once, at dawn, they both happened to wake up together, and without a word they resumed the relations that had been severed for a long time.

Now that affairs between husband and wife and daughter and father were resolved, it was evident that Ezra did not bear a grudge or seek revenge.

Somehow, like a tree insensibly growing a rough scab over a wound, old routines were re-established in the Berger household – the glass of tea together at bedtime or Bronka's patient massaging of Ezra's stiff right knee.

After the afternoon tea, for instance, Siegfried took the baby for a walk in its pram, and Tomer and Einav went to the swimming pool or the basketball field, leaving Bronka and Ezra on their own like a young couple.

Ezra came home from his journey around two o'clock every day, had a shower and lay down on his bed for a siesta, just as in days gone by. Once, Bronka said that she wanted them both to go away for a holiday after the New Year but that if Ezra objected she wouldn't press him. Ezra sleepily consented.

Sometimes they met by chance, in the dining hall or on one of the lawns. They nodded to one another and looked away. Strangers. Not embarrassed, not bitter, just strangers. Surprisingly enough, Noga, attentive though she was to her own body, hardly associated her baby with Ezra Berger. Ezra had walked out of her thoughts. Noga saw the thickset, coarse-featured truck driver, and as she did so she felt as if he ... as if the man were familiar from somewhere else. It was as if her mind's eye were blinded. It was not that she had forgotten the facts. But the connections between the facts had ceased to exist.

Something similar had happened to Ezra. Sometimes he sat at the table in the evening and read aloud from the Bible in a colorless voice, shuddering suddenly at an outburst of mad howling from the jackals and asking himself, what did I do, when was I, ages ago I was. But he tried to skirt it. To isolate himself from it. Get back to the Bible. Sometimes he inflicted on his memory a protracted, minutely detailed torture. To his surprise he discovered that memories were wearing rather than painful. The memories were disintegrating into heaps of words that did not belong, that had no life, that . . . had no connection.

This is not easy to understand. We had thought they were in love. But no. Perhaps they were using one another. Perhaps – hard though it is to say it – perhaps Noga and Ezra had been holding onto one another as one holds onto an instrument or a weapon. Now, with the goal achieved, the tool had dropped from the tired hand, and all that was left was the urge to rest.

Slowly, as if with great weariness, Ezra came back. There were moments when Bronka dreamed of a dramatic reconciliation. She suppressed her dream. It seemed that there was a deep truth in the words spoken by Ezra to Podolski: I'm tired. I haven't got the strength of stones. I'm tired.

Bronka did not set her course out of weariness. There were still times when she missed Reuven. With determination she snapped the thread. Her eyes were opened. She saw how far. And she was a strong woman.

The scars turned pink, then gray, then faded. Perhaps because Ezra and Bronka had never hated one another. Even during the bitter days there had been a dim, whispering sympathy between them. Only they had been remote from one another. Now they had come back to each other because they had an urgent need to lean. They leaned.

One day Siegfried pinched Einav's cheek and whispered gleefully:

'Look at them, my lovely, look at those two old lovebirds. He's reading the Bible to her; she's taken off her glasses and is looking at his lips; they're both relaxed; it's a real honeymoon. She's taken him under her wing and become his mother and his sister, as our national poet puts it. Hm?'

There was a certain amount of truth in the visitor's remark, even if it was exaggerated and full of lascivious glee. There was no honeymoon. But there was – we use the term with some hesitation – a brotherly feeling. There were still long intervening hours of gray, dreary silence. It seemed as though they would last right up to the end. The big, clumsy clock would go on ticking. If they did not take care to turn the tap off properly, it would go on noisily dripping.

Zechariah had an idea. To invite his family out for a friendly evening together, somewhere pleasant, somewhere else. The change of air and the intimacy would be a balm for worn-out feelings.

He ordered a taxi to take them to Tiberias at eight o'clock, after supper and little Danny's bedtime. They were a full taxi-load: the elder Bergers and the younger Bergers, the guest playing the host for the evening, and, at Ezra's request, Grisha Isarov too. Ezra and Grisha had become close friends recently. Three or four evenings a week they sat together in Grisha's room, playing dominoes or chess. Grisha told wonderful stories, and Ezra summarized the morals of the stories in Biblical verses taken out of context.

Zechariah wore a dark suit and a flower in his buttonhole. Ezra and Tomer were in white open-necked shirts. Grisha – for

308

a change – put on a pair of shorts that displayed an enormous pair of hairy legs. Einav, for her part, wore the low-cut dress that she reserved for special outings.

They started the evening with a couple of hours in the bar of a large hotel by the Sea of Galilee. There was a small orchestra. Grisha twirled his mustache and bawled his orders at a cowering waiter.

Zechariah bowed to Einav and invited her onto the blue-lit dance floor. The saxophone was laughing and crying. Einav leaned on Zechariah's shoulder and felt a new woman. They danced together for a long time, while Bronka and Tomer glared at them angrily, though each for a different reason. Zechariah attracted admiring glances. He danced effortlessly but with amazing precision. Painted tourist women tried to lure him with smiles, but he remained faithful to his beloved Einav. Her face was radiant, and her limp had disappeared.

Ezra and Grisha engaged in a good-humored drinking contest. Zechariah, in the brief intervals between dances, outdrank them both and made fun of them, although – needless to say – his jokes never exceeded the bounds of friendly good manners. The drink did not get the better of him.

But Ezra and Grisha were carried away by the change of scene and the drinks. Around midnight they burst into spirited song, attracting the cheerful attention of the other occupants of the bar.

Tomer, who was not a drinker and was not fond of the old songs, said nothing, but glowered furiously at his wife's legs. Bronka followed his glance and announced that she was tired. Reluctantly, the others acceded and rose to leave. The wealthiest member of the party, of course, settled the bill.

They strolled for a while by the lakeside. Grisha and Ezra strode ahead, arm in arm, conversing hoarsely. Then came Zechariah and Einav, he with his arm round her waist. Bronka and her son meekly brought up the rear.

It was a warm, clear night, with a full moon. The water rippled and flashed. The outline of the mountains showed opposite. The lights of the town shone yellow. A breeze was blowing. Grisha and Ezra exchanged memories of the good old pioneering days. Bronka intruded an occasional remark. Zechariah described to Einav the latest European fashions. A subdued quarrel brewed up between Einav and Tomer, but they controlled themselves so as not to disrupt the cheerful mood of the evening. Zechariah and Grisha argued about an incident in the fighting in the Western Desert during the Second World War. On logical grounds Zechariah was right. Grisha produced a crushing retort: I was there and I saw it with my own eyes.

Zechariah gave in with a sigh:

'Conclusive proof. You win.'

Grisha was delighted.

Eventually, they turned toward the main street of Tiberias in search of a taxi. Suddenly a voice assailed them from behind:

'Hey, Ezra, what's up with you, then – here you are and you don't look in and see us?'

'Gershon Saragosti!' Ezra exclaimed.

They were all forced to go to Abushdid's together. Ezra introduced his friends to his family and his family to his friends, and they were welcomed with coffee, the like of which was not to be found anywhere else in Tiberias. Coffee that was as black as night and as strong as iron, as Yosef Babadjani put it.

'What's up, Ezra?' Kabilio asked in amazement. 'Where's your daughter, your lovely daughter, what a lovely daughter, where is she, why haven't you brought her with you? She's not ill, heaven forbid?'

Ezra grabbed Kabilio's elbow and whispered:

'Shut up Kabilio.'

Kabilio's eyes opened wide. He looked at Ezra as though he did not understand. Then at once he understood. His expression changed; he let out a long breath, winked at Ezra, and whispered with a grin:

'Of course. I see. Now I see. I won't breathe a word. Your wife . . . and that sweetie you said was your daughter . . . I see. Of course I'll shut up. Like a clam I'll shut up. You can trust me.'

So they sat, talking to the fishermen, for half an hour or so.

Grisha Isarov, who was himself a fisherman, won his hearers' hearts in the first five minutes. There was already a wager on between him and Babadjani, the stake being a bottle of arak; the subject of the bet only a fellow fisherman could understand.

Gershon Saragosti was overcome by Einav's beauty. He put his feelings into words. Einav blushed, smiled, and hastily smothered her smile. Tomer bristled and muttered to the fisherman, Shut up or . . . Siegfried woke up to the situation, and interposed a string of lively definitions of female beauty. There was a general round of laughter. Siegfried boasted that, just as some men were wine tasters, he was a professional woman taster. Again everyone laughed, except for Bronka, who had dropped off to sleep. Einav thumped the table with her little hand and shouted, Disgusting! You're all disgusting! But Tomer found himself among the laughers. There are two kinds of women, Ezra began. Zechariah interrupted him: There are three kinds – the two you were thinking of and . . . Siegfried named the third kind. There were helpless guffaws. Einav blushed again, and remarked sadly:

'That wasn't a nice joke.'

Ezra chuckled.

'I've got another one. A nice one.'

He told it. Needless to say, the fishermen all refused to be outdone. Grisha too. Even Tomer stuck his neck out and tersely told a story about a woman and an express train. Ezra was merry. We have not seen him merry before. Even in his merriment there was nothing rowdy or ill-mannered. Ezra may be only a simple truck driver, but he knows one thing his brother will never learn: how to keep things within bounds. Eventually Grisha began to tell an amazing story from the war. We shall keep our promise to him and reproduce it here verbatim, apart from one or two understandable omissions:

'Once I had in my possession a gold-plated dagger, inscribed in Gothic letters with the name "Ludendorff," and underneath, in square capitals, FROM ADOLF HITLER, WITH SALUTATIONS, TO MARSHAL GRAZIANI. You see this hand? All of you? Touch it.

312

This very hand held that dagger. A historic dagger. I imagine that Ludendorff used it as a paper knife and that in the days of the Nazis they took it out of the museum and gave it to Hitler, and Hitler presented it to the Italian Fascist Marshal Graziani. There are two fantastic stories about that dagger. One: how it fell into my hands. Two: how it was taken out of my hands.

'After the defeat of Italy I lost my unit. I simply went off on a short *after-duty,** and when I got back they'd moved on without me. To tell you the truth, I wasn't sorry. Those were great days in Rome, and I wanted to stay there. How did I live? Partly with the British, partly with the Americans, mostly with the Italian girls. Oh, those Italian girls! Once I went for a walk with one of them outside the city. We came to a magnificent villa, which was guarded by American soldiers. I was in Palestinian uniform. I was a staff sergeant. Now I'm a captain. That is, I was a captain. In our army. But nowadays we haven't got an army, only a lot of chocolate-cream soldiers. So I don't use my rank any more. All right. So, we see this guarded villa. I joke a bit with the sentries. Of course they're drunk to a man. I tell them I work for the *secret department of the British Intelligence** and that I'm on a special mission. They inform me that the stores for two divisions are housed there. I point to the badge on my arm and say I'm in the *Jewish Corps of the Top Secret Service, searching for all kinds of war criminals.** They tell me that this was Graziani's villa. They're tight as ticks, and pretty impressed, but they still won't let me

*English in original.

past without papers. So I pull out my union card and show it to them. It's all written in Hebrew. They call their officer over. Now, if *they* were drunk, their black officer is pissed out of his mind. He's almost crawling along on all fours, in his pajama trousers. Believe it or not, he's taken in by the card. He fingers it, sniffs at Ben Gurion's signature, takes a good look at the doll who's with me, and says, I salute you. He even has a go at saluting.

'Well, in we go, me and this girl, and we walk around the gardens for a while. We see some prisoners looking after the fantastic flowers, and I shout at them to pull their socks up, and they're not too impressed, but they smile like good little kids; *si signore, si signore.* Then we inspect the house for *war criminals** What a house! Words can't describe it. We find Graziani's bedroom. All done up in blue. Like a dream. We lock the door and commit a little *war crime** And there, in the bedroom, I suddenly spot this golden dagger lying on the dressing table, minding its own business. I pick it up, look at it, take it over to the light, turn it over. I see LUDENDORFF, HITLER, GRAZIANI. Grisha, I say to myself, Grisha, you're taking this with you to show your grandchildren what sort of a man their grandpa was. So I took it.

'Now I'll tell you an even more fantastic story. How I lost it.

'I lost the dagger in Rumania in '47, when I was sent there for the illegal immigration. I mean, as you can guess for yourselves, I didn't lose it. It was stolen. And how was it stolen? You'd never guess. It was a work of art. I was supposed to meet a member of

*English in original.

314

the Communist government in Bucharest. Yes. I was the chief representative of the Hagganah in Eastern Europe. That is, one of the chief representatives. Well, I was invited to the house of this minister. We talked about this and that. It turned out he'd been a member of the anti-Nazi underground. Anyway, that's what he told me. We became friends. I spent about four hours in his apartment. I told him about the Jewish struggle. I thought to myself, You've made a good friend here. He told the dirtiest jokes of any man I've met. Anyway, for some reason I pulled the dagger out of my briefcase. (I used to take it with me everywhere. I was young in those days.) I showed it to him. He was amazed. He said he just had to show it to his wife; she was also an anti-Nazi, partisan and all that. All right, I say, why not? Please do. I hand it over to him. He goes into the next room. After a few minutes he comes back. Hands me the dagger. I put it away in my pocket. When I get back to my hotel, I look at it, and what do I see? It's not the same dagger. The so-and-so must have swapped them while he was out of the room. What could I do? Kick up a rumpus? Out of the question. Don't forget we had interests to look after. Incidentally, I've still got the Rumanian's dagger. I'll show it to you some time to prove that Grisha tells the truth. But what's it worth? Pennies. If I show it to my grandchildren, they'll say, What a fool grandpa was even when he was young. It's not for nothing there are all those jokes about Rumanians being thieves.'

They exchanged stories about thieves and thefts. Ezra told the joke about 'find' and 'found.' Then he told the one about Solomon's bed and the sixty valiant men. Everyone laughed.

*

315

Close to three o'clock in the morning they woke Bronka, called a taxi, and went home. It was a riotous journey. Everyone, Ezra, Zechariah, Tomer, Grisha, the pot-bellied driver, joked noisily. Only Bronka and Einav could not keep awake. They dozed on each other's shoulders.

Zechariah eyed his brother, and said to himself:

Good. Very good.

29

Herbert Segal Fights Back

THE SUMMER broke up.

Three weeks before the New Year there were five successive days of false autumn. The temperature dropped sharply, the sky was overcast, the treetops rustled in the breeze. Five gentle days. On the fifth day Fruma Rominov died. She died at seven o'clock in the morning. She had gone out to look for the sanitary officer. She wanted to tell him that a certain kind of worm had appeared on the pine trees that could cause inflammations of the skin and eyes in young children. The trees must be sprayed with an insecticide that would kill off the worm but not harm the children.

The sanitary officer promised he would come before lunch. Fruma said she wanted to see it done with her own eyes.

She started back toward the nursery. On the way she saw a yellow kitten playing with a ball on the lawn. She stopped and watched. She felt a quiet sorrow. Living creature with gentle movements. Agile. Supple. Light. The sight of it surprised Fruma. She smiled a bitter smile to herself. But the ball, why didn't I notice sooner, the ball belongs to the little children.

Fruma bent down to pick up the ball. As she did so, she heard a fine grating whistle in her ears. She turned her head to see where the sound was coming from. As she turned her head her body turned too. She sank down on the grass, and her face ran with sweat. She tried to wipe it off with her apron. Her hand shook, and fell. Fruma summoned all her strength and tried to get up, because she could see someone coming toward her and she was ashamed to be seen lying on the grass in the early morning. She let out a hollow sob. She collapsed. Ido Zohar hurried up to her and asked if she felt ill. Fruma's face was crumpled and angry. Her eyes were damp. Ido felt he was disturbing her. He turned to go. After ten paces he changed his mind and tried to lift her. Fruma's body was heavy. Ido was embarrassed to be clasping her arms in his. He shouted. Fruma's lips whispered. Now her eyes began to run, and big tears licked her bony cheeks. Her breathing was heavy and uneven. Suddenly her lips parted, and all her teeth showed. Ido was alarmed and shouted again. Running footsteps sounded. Dafna Isarov, trembling, came up and asked what was wrong. Ido hissed twice: the doctor, fetch the doctor. Dafna flushed. Fruma fixed the boy's face with a chill gray piercing look. Ido had an idea and asked if she wanted some water. Fruma said nothing. The look with which she held Ido's face was not alive.

Later, as if through a gray mist, Herzl Goldring and Mendel Morag appeared and carried Fruma off. They put her frail arms round their shoulders. Held in the two men's embrace, Fruma was taken to the surgery. The doctor tried an intracardiac injection and prolonged artificial respiration. He said to Herzl Goldring:

'There's hope yet. Run and get a car, quickly. To the hospital.'

The concerted efforts seemed to have had some effect. Fruma's face quivered slightly, the muscles of her jaw relaxed, her mouth opened, and her fingers slowly clenched. The doctor checked her pulse. Finally, he shook his head and said faintly:

'Only a reflex action.'

Herzl Goldring burst in to announce that the car was waiting. The doctor said it would not be needed. For some reason he added:

'Thank you very much, Herzl.'

At two o'clock in the afternoon Rami arrived. Herbert Segal led him to his room and sat him down in an armchair.

Rami said:

'So suddenly, they told me . . . suddenly, they said, suddenly.' Herbert covered his round glasses with his little hand and said: 'It can't be helped.'

Rami fixed him with a tired look. After a moment he muttered:

'What a terrible thing. So suddenly.'

Herbert touched Rami's shoulder,

'Be brave, my boy.'

The remark was meant to encourage him, but in fact it had the opposite effect. Rami dropped his head onto the table and began to sob. His voice was loud and strange, almost like stifled laughter. Herbert gave him a glass of cold water. Rami opened his eyes and looked at Herbert Segal as though he did not recognize him. His eyes were dry. He reached for the glass and took a sip. Then, with sudden resolution, he pushed the glass away. Herbert stood up, went over to the window, and closed the shutters. Rami asked hesitantly if he could see . . . her. Herbert answered firmly: No. Not now.

Silence.

Herbert broke the silence to ask if there were any relatives who should be informed. For a moment Rami had difficulty in remembering. Then he said that there was Mother's sister in Kiryat Hayim and also Father's nephew's family in Rishon-le-Tsion. We haven't seen them since the last funeral. Yoash's. A moment later he added:

'Mother doesn't like them. They're very selfish. They think only of themselves.'

Herbert said:

'That doesn't matter now.'

Rami suddenly noticed the clothes he was wearing, and sobbed:

'I . . . I've come straight from training. Look, Herbert, my clothes are filthy. It . . . It isn't possible . . . So suddenly . . .'

Herbert repeated:

'It doesn't matter. It's not important now, what you're wearing.'

Suddenly Rami, as if recalling an essential formula, asked how the accident had happened. When. Where. Herbert answered each question with extreme brevity. Rami did not seem to be listening properly. He leaned back heavily in the armchair. Closed his eyes. Crossed his legs. Then he changed his mind, and stretched them out in front of him.

Herbert went out for a few minutes on urgent business. When he returned, he found the boy unnaturally calm, as if he had had a long sleep in the meantime. Unnaturally calmly he said:

'Summer will soon be over. I'll be sent on a course to become a corporal, and Noga Harish will have a son.'

Herbert looked at Rami long and hard. At that moment an exciting idea occurred to him. As usual with him, his lips tightened to a narrow straight line.

Mourning descended on Metsudat Ram. No one except Herbert Segal stopped working, because mourning does not interrupt work. But everywhere people worked silently, almost sullenly. Tsvi Ramigolski took Mundek Zohar with him to dig the grave. Tsvi had already telephoned a notice of the death to the newspaper of the kibbutz movement. Now he picked up a spade and went with Mundek to the cemetery. For a long time Tsvi had not done any physical work apart from gardening. His hands blistered, and he panted. He was fat, and his shoulders sagged slightly. The soil was hard, dry, and stubborn. The spades clanged. The cemetery was on the edge of the pine wood. There was a continuous moaning from the pines.

Should Fruma's grave be dug next to that of her husband Alter, or by that of her son Yoash, in the section opposite. Mundek Zohar refused to offer an opinion. Tsvi pondered with his eyes closed. Finally he said:

'Of course, next to Alter. That's right. Husband and wife together. I hate death,' he added suddenly, in an uncharacteristic outburst of rage.

The soil, as we have said, was hard. The spades gave out a metallic sound. And the stones gave out a stony sound.

That evening the entrance to the dining hall was draped with black crepe. Without any prior arrangement all the members of the kibbutz assembled after supper in the dark square outside the hall. Little was said. Faces were serious. At seven o'clock a small group, including Reuven and Bronka, Gerda and Mundek, went to Herbert Segal's room to keep the orphan company. Rami was still sitting in the same armchair; only his feet were propped up on a small stool that Herbert had thoughtfully provided. They sat down.

Reuven Harish sighed and said:

'Remember, Rami, you're not alone. You have a home.'

Rami nodded and said nothing.

Gerda said:

'Have you eaten anything?'

As the boy did not reply or even look at her, she turned to Herbert Segal and asked him:

'Has he eaten?'

Herbert made a worried gesture as if to ask her to leave him alone.

Tsvi Ramigolski remarked hesitantly:

'Winter is coming. A decision will have to be made about the Camel's Field. We're in for a difficult time.'

After a short silence Rami observed:

'Those twenty-three dunams aren't worth all the fuss.'

Herbert half smiled at Tsvi Ramigolski, as if to say: Well done, the boy's talking at last. Keep it up. Tsvi took the hint and continued:

'We must never give in over land. Land is the most important thing in the world.'

Rami asked for a cigarette. Mundek Zohar hurriedly offered him one. The boy took a drag and extended his jaw. He drew the smoke down into his lungs and closed his eyes. Without opening them, he said:

'I used to think that once, too. Now I think there are more important things in the world than land.'

Herbert raised his eyebrows and noted the words in his memory. The others were a little perplexed. Was it proper to start an argument at such a time? Actually, why not? He needed to be distracted. Reuven Harish replied:

'You're quite right, there are more important things than land. But without land they can't exist.'

Rami interrupted abruptly to ask whether they had arranged for someone to sit with his mother. She mustn't be left alone all night. He shivered. Herbert eyed him sternly through his steel-rimmed spectacles and said gravely:

'That's all right. Don't you worry about it.'

Rami, having apparently forgotten his question, asked Reuven Harish how Noga was. Was she feeling O.K.? Reuven answered with a faint yes and lowered his eyes. Rami said that he admired Noga immensely for her decision. He considered that she was doing something exceptional.

Herbert made a mental note of this remark, too. The others, Reuven, Bronka, did not dare take issue with him.

Three or four younger members arrived, among them Tomer and Einav. The new arrivals were pale. They had been amazed to hear sounds of conversation coming from the room. Rami greeted them as if he were host.

'Come in. Sit down.'

Herbert added:

'Come and sit down over here.'

Einav said:

'Rami, I'm really so sorry.'

Then, following a hint from Herbert Segal, the youngsters began to discuss the sowing of the winter crops. They said that the system of crop rotation was not planned as it should be. There was a dangerous disregard of the natural order of the crops. Bronka and Gerda went to the cooking alcove and made tea. Herbert whispered to them not to badger Rami or force him to drink. But Rami interrupted him and said to Bronka:

'No lemon for me, please. I hate lemon.'

Herbert Segal was alert. He was full of a new sense of responsibility. He had been studying the boy for several hours. He had changed. Not because of his mother's death. The shock had not had time to register yet. That was not the source of the change. His whole attitude had altered. The lad went off to the army full of blazing ambition. Now I can see a different quality in him, a kind of contraction of the desires. Now one notices – what's the best way to put it? – a kind of sensitivity and attentiveness. One can see the signs of a responsible man. Of course, it's still in an unformed state, but giving him a sensible hand will go a long way to help. I used to think he was doomed to become a rigid, arrogant dolt. I was wrong. He's got the makings of a responsible man. Maybe Fruma was right when she used to repeat so obstinately that he was fond of animals and plants. Fruma was a perceptive woman. But you had to be perceptive yourself to realize how perceptive she was.

Herbert Segal's senses were alert. His new sense of responsibility coursed rhythmically through his veins. He looked kindly on Rami Rimon.

The next day we buried Fruma.

Rami Rominov, leaning on Herbert's arm, walked behind the coffin. At times it seemed as if Herbert was being supported by Rami, since Rami was so much taller than he. The whole kibbutz community followed them in silence, men, women, and youngsters. There were, we recall, three or four jet fighters circling over the valley throughout the funeral, shattering the silence. They soared, wheeled, and plunged. Their roaring provoked the air until it shrieked and howled like a living thing.

At the open grave side Herbert Segal spoke as follows:

'My friends, Fruma is no longer with us, and our hearts refuse to believe it. Perhaps I was somewhat closer to Fruma than the rest of us. But you all know as I do that her life was not an easy one. Not an easy one at all. Perhaps she could have made her life easier, but she was not the type to look for an easy life. She had to bear two successive blows of fate within a few years. First she lost Alter, and soon afterward she lost Yoash. And, I ask myself, who else could have withstood such blows as she did? Fruma, my friends, had great reserves of strength. She knew how to look fate straight in the eye. And that's not easy to do. Only strong people, very strong people, can look fate straight in its terrible eye and not be broken. Collapse, as we know, lies in wait for all of us. And our defenses are very frail. Fruma was a strong woman. She had something of that blazing determination that is the mark of heroes. No, Fruma was no hero. Not in the accepted sense of the word. She did not set her sights high. But there was something heroic in her self-control. In her determination to carry on. Her severity toward us, and her even greater severity toward herself. None of us will ever forget how she helped her husband during the difficult years. Fruma was endowed with a stubborn, uncompromising honesty. I remember, my friends, how once, at a meeting of the education committee, Fruma said with her customary piercing frankness that she rejected certain aspects of the collectivist ideology. And immediately she added very simply that as long as principles were principles we should follow them. No, my friends, there was nothing compromising in Fruma's nature.'

Herbert paused for a while to allow the jets to whip angrily past and looked down into the open grave where the bare coffin lay. Suddenly, he took off his spectacles and revealed a delicate, innocent face that he had kept hidden from us for years. With his eyes closed and in a stifled tone of voice he continued:

'Fruma, our friend, you didn't know much happiness in your life. You suffered. You were always suffering. And we didn't always . . . we didn't always notice . . . what friends ought to . . . forgive us . . . we are only human. We shall miss you. I . . . do . . .'

The air was once more rent by a savage howl. The planes appeared, swooped, turned, and flew off. Herbert waited for them to vanish. When all was quiet again, he hesitated, his lips quivered; suddenly, he took two steps backward, hid his face behind his spectacles, and disappeared into his audience without finishing his address.

The earth thudded. Rami closed his eyes. A fly landed on his forehead. Rami did not brush it away but dropped his head onto Nina Goldring's shoulder, stamped childishly, and cried. (There was also a schoolboy there, by the name of Ido Zohar, who could not contain his tears, because he always responded to sadness. But his tears do not belong to our story.)

Two hours after the funeral Herbert Segal went to see Noga, to ask her whether she felt like coming to his room to keep Rami company. Noga asked him if he really thought that . . . that that was a good idea. Herbert said he had given the matter a good deal of thought. You ought to come and see him. He's asked about you twice.

Noga cast a sharp green look at Herbert Segal. Herbert did not look away, but his wise gray eyes stared steadily back. Simultaneously, the shadow of a smile touched both their eyes. Noga said:

'Why not? I'll come.'

Herbert answered:

'I didn't doubt it for an instant. I was sure you would.'

Rami Rimon was stretched out on Herbert Segal's bed. Someone had thrust a newspaper into his hand. It fascinated him strangely, as if every headline was meant for him alone. But the context was beyond his grasp. As soon as he saw Noga come in, he leaped up, leaned on the table, and stared at her body. He did not look up at her face. Noga followed his gaze and asked:

'Have I changed much?'

Rami said vaguely:

'You haven't come. It's Herbert. Herbert sent you. I know he did.'

'Sit down, Rami. You're tired.'

Rami obeyed her.

'Now stop looking at me like that. I don't like it.'

'I . . . didn't mean to. Sorry, Noga. I'm sorry. I . . .'

'Hang on, I'll make some coffee. Let's have some coffee. I'm sure Herbert won't mind me using his things.'

'No, Noga, I shouldn't drink coffee at a time like this. This is no time for drinking coffee.'

'Yes, you are going to have coffee. It's all ready. Don't argue.'

After a nicely calculated interval Herbert Segal returned to his room. He found the two young people deep in an argument about the planets. Rami argued that Venus was the planet closest to Earth. Noga insisted that Mars was much closer, because there were intelligent creatures on it, who dug canals. They both produced decisive arguments based on things they remembered well from school. Each accused the other of remembering badly and confusing the facts. Rami accident-ally touched Noga's stomach with his elbow, and his face turned scarlet. Their argument was not a bitter one. A certain friendliness animated it. If it weren't for the time and the place, Herbert Segal said to himself, you would think it was brotherly love. Herbert did not forget for an instant their respective conditions. At that moment he was suddenly conscious of the weight of his own loneliness. He wanted music. He longed for a tune as an alcoholic longs for wine. He controlled himself. Now that things were taking a turn for the better he should be feeling satisfied. No. He stared in front of him in silent dismay. He seemed to see Fruma, and he said to her: Fruma. He bit his lips and tightened them to a narrow line. He ordered himself to be clear-headed. He obeyed the order. He mustered the image and dismissed it.

Rami said:

'This little girl behaves as if she knew everything.'

Noga said:

'Don't be ashamed to admit you were wrong. It's nothing to be ashamed of. To err is human.'

Herbert explained gently that Venus is usually closer to Earth, but that in certain rare conditions Mars is nearer. On the other hand, Mars is closer to Earth in its outward appearance. Both Noga and Rami accepted Herbert's verdict. Neither had really wanted to win the argument. Herbert told them what he knew about the nearer planets and gave an account of the unsolved mysteries surrounding them. He went on to explain the differences between astronomy and astrology, a difference that symbolizes the contrast between the two great streams of human intellectual life, Myth and Logos.

The conversation continued. Herbert thrilled and amazed his guests. Early in the evening Nina Goldring arrived with a tray of food. Noga and Rami were so absorbed that they did not give her a glance. Nina left in a state of stunned amazement. She needed to share her amazement with one of her friends. She happened to meet Hasia or Esther. And a little bird did the rest.

As for Herbert and his guests, an almost palpable bond of sympathy was forged between them.

30

The Credit Side

RAMI ROMINOV stayed with Herbert Segal for the seven days of mourning. Herbert went back to his work in the cow shed, but he spent his free time sitting with Rami and talking to him about music. If it had not been for the rules of mourning he would have played him some examples. His descriptions were so vivid that Rami could almost hear the music.

Even when Herbert was working, Rami was not abandoned to solitude. Noga kept him company. On the third day she offered to read him some of her favorite poems. Rami supposed that that would be inappropriate. Noga replied that grief was a matter of feeling, not of rules and customs. Rami agreed.

By the end of the third day they had reached the point where Rami asked Noga when the baby was due. Noga stared out of the window toward the mountain, softly touched her belly and answered dreamily that it was due at the end of the winter. She was longing for winter to come. Summer was flat and empty, winter was dark and deep and alive.

Rami went on to ask gently what she intended to do, that was to say, what . . . what were her plans. Noga admitted that if it were not for her father she would have decided long ago to go to her mother, to have the baby far away, to live there for a few years, and get a taste of a different life. But it was difficult for her to decide what was better for her father, for her to go or to stay. It was madness. But she did not explain which of the two alternatives seemed to her to be mad.

Rami said:

'At first, my mother hoped that we'd get married. So did I. Then she hated you, and so did I. Specially that Friday – remember? – when I came home on leave for the first time, and there was that air battle and you were rude to me. I nearly . . . I nearly did something terrible that night. I'll tell you all about it some time. Down by the fish ponds, in Grisha's hut, I stood there and . . . I was very upset. Because of you, Noga. It was your fault. But now I don't . . . I mean, I want, I wanted to tell you that . . . now I respect what you've done. Maybe respect isn't quite the right word, but I really do. Terribly. That you've decided to have the baby. I really do.'

Noga seemed pleased by Rami's speech. She reached out and touched his cheek. She withdrew her finger at once. She was not smiling.

Rami told her about the course he was going to go on, for which there was a complicated preparatory training. 'Once I thought I'd be a great soldier. Now I think I dreamed too much of being another Yoash. Now I think people aren't the same.

Not all exactly alike. I mean there are different kinds of people. People have different kinds of character. Don't laugh. You won't believe me, Noga, I . . . for instance recently I've been reading some books about art. Don't laugh at me. Yes, you did smile.'

Noga, naturally, had not laughed at Rami.

It seemed that Rami was making a quick recovery. Even Nina Goldring noticed. And of course Herbert Segal kept a watchful eye open. Herbert was full of quiet pride. Needless to say he controlled it and did not reveal it to anybody.

On one occasion Gai Harish came into the room carrying a basket full of strawberries sent by Reuven from his garden. Who was tending the garden now? Gai himself. Gai did not give in when his sister begged him to stay and talk to her and Rami. He had to go back to Daddy. He had promised to paint the table on the veranda blue. And he was in the habit of keeping his promises.

Noga kissed him on his pointed chin.

On the fifth day renewed gloom settled on Rami. He wanted to go to the cemetery. Noga joined him without asking. Beside the mound of earth with its flimsy wooden marker, the boy stood for a few minutes, his mouth tightened by sadness. His face bore a surprised expression, as if he had forgotten why he had come.

On their way back they crossed the wood by the swimming pool. The dead pine needles that whispered beneath their feet awoke memories in them. Rami said:

'It seems like years ago.'

Noga agreed.

*

When the week of mourning was over, Rami rejoined his unit. Two days later Noga had a long letter from him, couched in emotional language. Next day Herbert Segal, too, had a letter from his protégé, giving a detailed account of his life, except for those details that are not allowed to be told to civilians. From now on Rami wrote to Noga almost every day. To Herbert Segal he wrote regularly twice a week. At Rami's specific request, Herbert took out a subscription to a literary and artistic magazine for him. He asked Rami to write and share his impressions of the magazine. Rami did so.

Needless to say, the course of events did not escape our watchful eye. Opinions were divided. Some said:

'It's in bad taste, to say the least. Fruma must be turning in her grave. How could he, even before the week of mourning was up . . . And who with? With a girl in that condition . . .'

Others said:

'Herbert is pulling the strings. He has plans of his own.'

And others again said:

'After all, they're both unhappy. So they have something in common now. In fact, it may all be for the best. What's wrong with it, after all?'

The time that Noga spent with Rami in Herbert Segal's room she had not spent with Zechariah-Siegfried Berger. To be more precise, she had stopped seeing him. On the other hand, we cannot deny that she longed to see him and to listen to him, and especially to hear the sound of his voice. On one occasion Zechariah-Siegfried had told her with a curious smile that he was here as the emissary of a distant power. Noga considered that she found him fascinating because he was strange and full of surprises. Now that she re-examined his remark she discovered a touching poetical meaning to it.

Sometimes at night she woke up in a fever of wanderlust. She sat up in bed, stretched her arms out in front of her as in a dance, and whispered: Take me, gray uncle, take Turquoise somewhere else, far, far away, take her to her mother, into the darkness, into those dark forests of yours.

One morning, as she was getting dressed, she felt a gentle spasm inside her. She felt herself anxiously. The spasm stopped, and did not reappear for several days. That morning she had meant to go and look for Zechariah. Her experience made her change her mind, and decide not to see him. But she was unable to explain the connection between cause and effect. She did not try very hard. She went to her father's room instead.

She found Reuven lying in bed, surrounded by pills and medicines, reading an old German book. She stayed with him for a couple of hours. She asked him to tell her about Fruma Rominov as a young woman. Reuven complied willingly, but he spoke in a tired voice.

Alter Rominov had never been a well man. Yet he always refused to see the doctor. We always used to see Fruma running along next to the doctor pressing him with questions and complaints. Fruma and Alter, despite the difference in their characters, were always devoted to each other. Alter gave in to Fruma, though, in almost everything. Fruma was a determined woman.

*

The change that had taken place in Noga did not escape Zechariah's attention. On one occasion he shared his inner-most thoughts with Tomer in the way that one jokingly talks a foreign language to a child. He spoke as follows:

'You and I, as men, may find it hard to understand what's happening to her. I was hoping that she would go with me to the place where she belongs. Sometimes the pious missionary and the sly pimp use very similar means of enticement. But the resemblance is only superficial. The Jesuits were well aware of the similarity, but they were equally aware of its limits. Only a fool would confuse Jesuits with pimps. It would be better for your father, too, by the way. As you are well aware, my dearest Tomer, the baby will confront your father with a very difficult decision. And I was about to – you see, my friend, a woman is not a man; that's a cardinal principle in life. I have a special feeling for those remarkable creatures. It doesn't matter now. Incidentally, you, too, if you only took the trouble to broaden your experience . . . But that's beside the point. I knew before-hand that she would kick and struggle. I thought about her father, too. Of course I did. By the way, from a strictly legal point of view . . . Never mind, that's also beside the point right now. You see, Tomer, my beloved nephew, there has been a recrudescence of pure childhood love, full of compassion for the poor, lonely orphan. Innocence, decency, and progressive education have brought about a sudden relapse. You know what a relapse is, my boy, don't you? No? I'll explain. Actually there's no need. That's not the fly in the ointment. What is? The fly in the ointment is a man by the name of Segal. He appears suddenly like a *deus ex machina* and earnestly tries to unpick the whole delicate fabric that has been so skillfully woven by your dear, devoted uncle, Zechariah, namely me. Do you know what *deus ex machina* means? No? Wait, I'll explain. Actually, that's also superfluous. I can use a different sort of illustration. An exposed flank. You know, my dearly beloved friend, what an exposed flank is, do you not? Yes, of course you do. You're a real live officer in our new Jewish army. Of course. I like that look you're giving me, as if I were a madman or a clown. That shows me I'm making you nervous. And that, my boy, gives me a special pleasure, a multiflavored pleasure, each flavor sweeter than honey, a pleasure that you can never taste, because . . . because of the difference between us, my dearest nephew. Yes. Well. Never mind. That's beside the point. We were talking about Segal. Segal *ex machina*. I spin my web, he spins his. I break up one match, and the pander makes another – if I may be permitted to use a metaphor taken from real life. And so my hammer has met its anvil, as our national poet Bialik puts it. A war between spiders, or should we say, rather, two fairies clashing over an innocent soul. The good fairy is Segal, and the wicked fairy is your funny uncle, Siegfried, namely me. The good fairy appears *ex machina* and supposes that I am already lying bound and gagged at his feet. Forgive me for boring you with my chatter; I get very much attached to my cleverness sometimes. But there's one thing Segal doesn't know, namely that his humble opponent has already defeated greater challenges than him. His opponent knows what Herr Herbert cannot grasp, because he lives in a world of make-believe. He knows that the *machina* itself has dismantled and is of no further avail. *Machina*, by the way, comes from a Greek word, from which the word 'machine' was stolen, and the two words mean the same. Still, that's beside the point. Are you still hesitating whom to put your money on? O man of little faith. Put your trust in your loving uncle. He will get the girl. And not by force. Herbert Segal's plans will be frustrated, because he is a man of progressive principles. I shall win her with signs and wonders. But not by force. I hate force, Tomer my angel, because force is blunt, whereas we must be sharper than needles.'

Zechariah interrupted the spate of his discourse, lit a cigarette, sniffed the lighter flame for a moment, then blew it out loudly. His face quivered; flaccid folds of flesh hung from his cheekbones. He looked ridiculous. He looked frightened and frightening. Tomer took advantage of the pause to ask perplexedly:

'Herbert Segal? What's Herbert Segal got to do with it?'

Siegfried flashed him a grimace that was meant to be a smile and announced pensively:

'Force is something very powerful. An ocean. A universe. A law. Like . . . Never mind now. Tomer, my own dear son, how would you like to come to Haifa with me tonight? Would you? Come with me, my Tomer, and get a taste of life. I shall gladly bear the burden, and I shall shower you with pleasures. Open your mouth, and I shall fill it with delights. Come, O fairest of men. Come, and let us go together to meet the beloved. How about it?'

Tomer refused.

Tomer was disgusted by his uncle. One fact, however, was gradually dawning on him: Zechariah was planning to leave and to take Noga Harish with him. And that was all to the good. To that end it was worthwhile bearing the trouble-some presence of the wandering Jew a little longer. From the whole long speech he drew one conclusion: the old lecher was going to Haifa that evening. If he was going to Haifa, then he wouldn't be there in the evening, and that, Tomer said to himself with a feeling of relief, was on the credit side. There are two sides to every coin.

31

A Withered Tree

CAN ONE omit mentioning the model electric railway, worked by remote control? No, certainly not. It was a splendid and fascinating toy, designed as a perfect scale model of the European railways. Zechariah-Siegfried had brought it with him two months previously as a present for his younger nephew, Oren. It seemed as though the donor was no less thrilled with it than the recipient. Oren and his uncle spent hours on end playing with the train. At first, however, the boy had refused to touch the gift. But Zechariah tempted his nephew. He laid the track out on the floor of Ezra and Bronka's room, set up the signals, connected the controls, and played with the train on his own, while Oren stood chewing sweets and watching him with a patronizing smile on his face. Finally, Siegfried tricked the boy. He took off the front wheels of one of the engines and pretended not to be able to put them back. Oren silently picked up the engine and with two skillful movements snapped the wheels into place. His face wore an expression of contempt. Zechariah showered him with compliments and declared that Oren displayed extraordinary technical skill. Oren bent glumly over the control panel and fiddled with the insides with a bored expression on his face. Within five minutes the two of them were racing the trains. The toy responded to their fingers and revealed its hidden possibilities.

Zechariah and Oren had long hours of leisure during the summer. They took over the secret space between the pillars that supported the Bergers' house, and there Siegfried constructed an intricate network of lines running over hills and down valleys, through tunnels and across bridges. There were junctions and stations and gradients and branches laid out with rich imagination.

Oren was not tall, but his body was broad and solid, his face broad and compact. His hair was close-cropped and rough. Siegfried often said:

'What a masculine appearance. What an air of manhood. Enough to overpower the most fragile and delicate women, with pure, transparent skin and slender bodies. They'll fall for you. You're tough.'

Oren noticed a dirty smile fleeting like a shadow beneath his uncle's bushy eyebrows, accompanied by the closing of one eye and the opening wide of the other, as if in absent-mindedness, or the opposite.

The space between the pillars of the house was cool and dim. It was a secret hiding place. The garden plants hid it from the path that led to the steps up to the veranda. True, neither

Siegfried nor Oren could stand up straight here. But they had no intention of standing up. They bent over their flashing toy, holding handles and levers and electric switches, their heads extended and their bodies curled. They hardly spoke. Even Siegfried suppressed his usual cheerful chatter. Sometimes he smoked as he played. On one occasion Oren dared to ask him casually for a cigarette. Siegfried grinned happily and said:

'Certainly not. I can't let you smoke. You're too young.'

Oren agreed earnestly:

'Yes. Because it's wrong.'

Zechariah curled his lower lip, displaying its pink inside.

'Yes, wrong. Improper. Not allowed.'

Oren said:

'Against the principles.'

Siegfried said:

'Corrupting.'

Oren said:

'And very nasty.'

Siegfried said:

'It harms the innocence of youth. And nothing is more precious than youthful innocence.'

Oren said:

'Nothing in the world.'

Siegfried let out a low chuckle. Oren did not echo it. They smoked in silence.

Let us watch them, the man and the boy, racing the engines toward one another until they collide with a dry bang. Yellow sparks flash from the line. If they continue like this they will soon end up by destroying the fascinating toy. If it had been given to us, we would have hidden it away in a cupboard and played with it when no one was looking, in an entirely different way. We would not have been carried away by the thrill of destruction. We love system and harmony.

First of all, the control panel, with its different-colored switches, red and green and black. From here you can govern the whole complicated layout with two fingers. You can operate the junctions and raise and lower automatic crossing gates. You can make a train go faster, or stop it in mid-course. You can even work a shunting engine in one of the tiny stations and detach a wagon from one train and connect it to another. That is not all. By means of an intricate clock mechanism you can set the whole system, with its various levels and junctions, to run automatically. All its operations are co-ordinated according to an accurate timetable. But by doing this you take all the fun out of the game.

The shape of the engines is strictly rectangular; they convey a striking impression of restrained power. Through the windshield you can see the tiny figure of the driver, with his peaked cap, and the assistant driver with a bushy mustache. Little passengers peep out of the red carriages with their German inscriptions, respectable gentlemen with hats and suits, businessmen in gray raincoats, ladies in traveling clothes, even the bags and suitcases have not been forgotten. They are neatly stacked on the shelves above the seats.

Is there any thrill in the world to compare with the thrill of complete mastery, fingers running lightly over the control panel and deciding numerous fates? But, alas, we can also see how even this noble pleasure can degenerate in the hands of unscrupulous adventurers in insatiable quest of the unusual, the fascinating, and the unnatural.

Siegfried and Oren run the trains head-on at one another and enjoy the crash and the sparks. At times Siegfried rests his arm on Oren's shoulder and says affectionately:

'My orphan. You're strong and tough. Don't give in to them.'

And Oren, with a strange gleam in his eye, replies:

'No, I won't give. I'll take. It's a pity you're going away. You and I could. Yesterday I exploded a hand grenade in the wood. I threw it into a fire. It smashed the fire.'

Zechariah:

'Put out this flame. No, not by blowing. The way I do it. With your finger. That's the sign.'

'I want you to tell me why you came. You tell lies. You're ugly.'

'No, my boy. You can count on me. I shan't leave before I'm finished. I shan't abandon my agents.'

'I can wire up the veranda railings. Electrify them.'

'No, there's no need to do that. You mustn't. Someone might get hurt.'

'Suppose you go away and I'm left alone.'

'My orphan. You can manage on your own. You're tough. Gentle women love tough orphans.'

A few minutes later, as Oren laid a gray freight car across the track to derail a fast-moving train:

'Hey, Uncle, what's the matter with you? Are you a clown Are you ill?'

Siegfried, with supreme seriousness:

'Hush, I am ill. I'm seriously ill. Cancer. I'll die again soon. Actually, I came here to die in the Holy Land. Our poor brother Zechariah, may his memory be for a blessing, may his soul be bound up in the bundle of life, was a strange man but an interesting and original one. Peace be upon his ashes, saith Herbert Segal.'

Oren, his eyes screwed up and his jaw protruding:

'When? How long?'

'Oh, my silly little orphan, I was only kidding. I'm not a sick man. I'm still alive. I shan't die here. I shall die in the forests in enemy territory. I came here to honor thy father and thy mother.'

'You're like my father, only much more.'

'You, too, son. Both of us. I'm not my brother's brother, and you're not your brother's brother. Cain and Abel. You're a bad apple. You'll fall off the good tree.'

'No, I'll infect them. All of them.'

'Firm and clean on the outside, sweeter than a good one inside. Juicier. Sweet decay, the essence of rottenness.'

'You're mad, Siegfried. That's what my mother says.'

'Your mother has an excellent eye for character.'

Sometimes the waves throw up a rotting plank on the beach. To and fro the water tosses the blackened object, alternately dashing it on the sand and dragging it back with a melancholy rhythmic ebb and flow. You would suppose the plank would go on being wave-tossed for ever. To and fro, to and fro. But you can't trust water. Suddenly it abandons its baby, leaving it high and dry. From now on it belongs to the desolate sands, to the yellow vengeance of the scorching sun, a solitary black spot.

Afternoon again. Once again the lawn offers its gentle slope. The leafy trees once more filter the slanting rays, which pattern the green with nervous spots of light.

Einav and Tomer, clad in white shorts, are playing tennis. Einav is fair, with a broad face and gently molded figure. Tomer is dark, with thick hairy arms, and his movements are economical. The ball arcs elegantly from one racket to the other. The players are so skillful that their motions are hardly perceptible. A slight twist of the hips, a short sharp wave of the arm, a glance to follow the ball's flight.

Two or three children watch the couple play, exchanging covert giggles and whispers. Far off to the west a busy motor chugs. The distance softens the sound. A powerful smell of coffee fills the air. Herzl Goldring is working in his own garden. His plot is trimmed in amazingly rectangular forms. His wife Nina looks on from the veranda, wearing her reading glasses. She is busy writing a letter, or an article for the kibbutz newssheet. Reuven Harish comes out for his evening stroll. He will be back in twenty minutes, as usual. Grisha Isarov and Ezra Berger, their heavy bodies stripped to the waist, are sitting over a chessboard set up on an overturned box. Mendel Morag stands over the game, offering jocular advice. Ezra is smoking a cigarette, and Grisha is sucking on his unlit pipe, which is elaborately carved.

In Fruma Rominov's house the windows have been taken out of their frames. The furniture has been removed, and through the open door the painter's ladder is visible. One of the younger couples is due to move in soon, chosen on grounds of seniority.

Our own dear Stella Maris appears from the bushes and settles herself on the green bench in the shade of the trees. She has a small leather case in her hand. She rests it on her lap and drums on it with her fingers. Ezra looks up from his game and eyes her as if he recognizes her. Noga notices his glance. She chews her upper lip, and closes her eyes. Grisha Isarov raps the box with the back of his hand. Ezra starts, takes a deep breath, and returns to the game. With three long strides Tomer recovers his ball, which has run away down the sloping lawn. Einav wipes her damp face with the hem of her skirt. Her limp gives her an additional charm. She has a striking figure. Nina Goldring calls to Herzl to come and have his coffee. Coffee's ready; if he doesn't hurry up it'll get cold. Herzl puts down his shears, dusts his hands, and climbs the steps to the veranda. Noga opens her leather case, and takes out a folded sheet of paper and a red pencil. She unfolds the paper but keeps the pencil clasped between her teeth. She closes her eyes again. Grisha must have said something funny: Ezra gives a coarse laugh. Herzl Goldring throws him a reproachful look. From the direction of the recreation hall Bronka appears, wheeling Danny in his stroller, his arms and legs waving. She asks Einav and Tomer if they want to go on playing. They can carry on; she'll be happy to have Danny for a little longer. Danny and she are having a lovely time together; they've just had a nice long walk, and now they're ready to start again.

From the hidden space underneath the Bergers' house a lean man with a thin black mustache emerges. He comes up on Noga from behind and casts his shadow on the sheet of paper spread out before her. Noga's eyes are closed. The man reaches out and strokes the air near her hair, which is done up in a bun now. His shadow responds by moving across the paper.

Without surprise the girl's eyes open, and she slowly turns her head. He bares his lips in a smile. Noga indicates the place to her left and says:

'Sit down. Don't stand behind me, sit down. I don't like people standing behind me.'

Zechariah sits down with an exaggerated effort and says:

'Bless you, my dear. You're kind to an old man. The old man is touched and moved by your kindness.'

'Wait. Stop. Tell me what countries are on the way.'

'Well, you can choose, my sweet, you can choose an exciting route. All borders are open. Everything is possible. What would you like to see: Italy? Switzerland? France? Scandinavia?'

'I haven't said yes yet. I'm still here.'

'And that's just what your wonderful mother has written to me. I had a letter from her yesterday. You can't imagine how much happiness your decision has brought her. And yet, despite her longing to see you, she, too, suggests we shouldn't go by the most direct route. No, you must see the world. That's what dear Eva writes. You must show her beautiful places. Take your time. I can hold on for another two or three weeks before I hold my daughter in my arms, even though my heart is aching. I can't sleep at night. We've got a lovely room ready for our own Stella Maris, in the attic, with windows on three sides, with Munich at her feet. A panoramic view, the lake, the forest, the big park. Ulrich, the gardener, has even been told to put up a hammock for our dear one at the bottom of the garden, among the whispering fir trees. Even Isaac is excited. He can hardly wait. We spend whole days making plans. But we can wait. You must take our girl on a long tour, Siegfried. You must show her the world. And in the winter, after the happy event, we shall leave the baby with old Martha, who was cousin Isaac's nanny as well as mine, and we'll all take off for Spain. We have reservations for the spring in Majorca. Tell my child all about Majorca. Kiss her for me on her forehead and on her sweet chin.'

'I still haven't said yes. I'm not yours yet,' Noga said in a flat tone of voice.

'You know, my dear, there is an expression I am very fond of: "The president-elect." Think about it, my sweetheart. He doesn't hold the reins of power yet, but at a certain definite, publicly known date he will enter into office. Meanwhile, he can roll it round his tongue and savor it. It's his for certain. He knows it. Everyone knows it. Like a sweet that you slowly unwrap. Like a bottle that you don't uncork at once. But it's yours. Even more so than when the drink goes down your throat. Like making love, when you delay the climax. Anticipation is so sweet. Like a big flame that's still locked up inside a matchhead, and you roll the match between your fingers. By the way, are you going to let me?'

'Let you what?'

'Carry out your mother's instructions.'

Before Noga could say a word, Siegfried had leaned over and kissed her on the forehead and on the chin, as Eva had written, and gently stroked her hair. Noga mechanically touched the places that his lips had touched, as if the skin had been burned. She spoke in a whisper:

'Leave me alone now. I haven't said yes.'

'No, you haven't, my little saint, but your heart has spoken the word, and I have heard it. I've heard it, my little Stella; one heart has heard another.'

'Go away now. Don't be here.'

'I'll go. Right away. I wanted to talk to you about clothes, but I'll come back another time. Your mind's elsewhere. You're dreaming about him.'

'What clothes? About who?'

'New clothes, special clothes for our great trip, summer clothes and winter clothes. But you're not concentrating now. You're dreaming about your young knight with the horse's teeth. Have I guessed right? Yes? Yes, of course I have. Seek and ye shall find. Herbert Segal has handed the little soldier over to you. And you have accepted the responsibility. You're sorry for him. Mark what I say. You're sorry for the soldier, but it's not easy for you to remember every moment of the day that you've got to feel sorry for him. So you have to keep reminding yourself what a poor little colt he is.'

'Go away, Siegfried. Go away.'

'You've got a generous heart, my girl. A kindly, devoted heart. Even at difficult times you think of others. What a wonderful heart you have, my child; you're a lonely, hated outcast, hounded by the Herberts, and just the same you over-come your suffering and force yourself to think of others. To live for others. To help them. To serve them. To sacrifice your-self and your desires and your happiness for your father, your father who didn't spare you a moment's thought when he went out looking for a mistress. To give up your future for a con-fused, repulsive orphan, who kicked you yesterday and who will kick you again tomorrow, because he's not crazy enough to marry a girl in your condition. You're a saint, my child, you're choosing to sacrifice yourself for people who don't love you. You're a real saint.'

Here, in a strange, exaggerated gesture, Siegfried went down on his knees before his young friend, and two thin streams of tears ran down his cheeks.

The onlookers, Tomer and Einav and the Goldrings, stared at him in horror and amazement. Nina said to Herzl:

'What a clown.'

Tomer said to Einav:

'He's mad. Crazy!'

Einav said:

'That's it. That's the word I was looking for. That's exactly the right word for him.'

Noga stood up and left the spot with quick, small steps. She did not look back. Zechariah got up, bowed politely to his audience, fingered his mustache and shrugged his shoulders.

Grisha Isarov and Mendel Morag exchanged a hurried glance. Grisha laid his hand on Ezra's arm and said gently:

'Play. It's your turn.'

Ezra stared glassily, slowly passed his hand close to his fore-head, and finally muttered:

'What? What? Yes. That's right. Of course. Quite right. It's my turn. Yes.'

Meanwhile, Siegfried had disappeared. The scene calmed down. Tranquillity reigned once more.

Bronka decided to speak frankly to Zechariah. That evening she went to his room. (He had been given a room in one of the huts on the edge of the kibbutz, though not before he had pressed another check on Yitzhak Friedrich to cover his board and lodging and any inconvenience he might have caused, as he put it.)

Zechariah received his sister-in-law reclining on a camp bed, wearing a nylon vest. His lean, powerful body gleamed with perspiration, because it was very hot inside the hut. It was Bronka's first visit to the room. Ezra, on the other hand, had been there a few times, to play dominoes and engage in general philosophical conversation. And at other times Oren had spent an hour or two here for some purpose or other.

Zechariah said:

'What a pleasant surprise. Please sit down. I'm sorry I can't receive you as befits your dignity. I've nothing to offer you except some dry biscuits and German magazines.'

Bronka, ignoring his invitation, did not sit down on the bed. (There was no chair in the tumble-down hut.) Her face was grim and determined. She stood to attention by the door, her feet together and her arms held stiffly at her sides.

349

'I've come to say that your behavior today was the last straw.'

Zechariah nodded sympathetically. There was a gleam of understanding and concern in his eyes. To increase Bronka's embarrassment, he made no reply beyond his sympathetic nod.

'I'm talking about the scene you made on the lawn this afternoon.'

Zechariah nodded agreement once again, as though waiting for her to continue, as if so far she had said nothing to explain her surprising visit. Bronka's confidence was somewhat shaken by his silence. She hesitated. She frantically hunted for something she could say that would draw him out of his silence.

'It was . . . it was absolutely impossible.'

Siegfried's face suddenly lost its expression of tolerant sympathy and a crooked, gloating smile appeared in its place.

'Well.' He spat the monosyllable out harshly.

'I insist that you explain to me frankly and openly what you are here for.'

Instantly, Zechariah's expression changed as though one dramatic mask had been magically substituted for another. Astonishment spread over his features. His voice when he spoke was that of a man who has been viciously insulted.

'But Bro-nka . . . *Gott im Himmel*, what an extraordinary question. Ex-traor-dinary . . . You know I've come here to be with my beloved family. What else have I got in the whole wide world. I'm a lonely old man, Bronka. I've come in out of the cold to warm myself at your hearth. But of course if I'm in the way . . . No question about it, at once, tomorrow morning, tonight even. No question about it. At once.'

As he spoke, he sprang to his feet as if he had made up his mind to pack his bags immediately.

Bronka apologized. Perish the thought. She hadn't meant to hurt his feelings. He wasn't causing any inconvenience. On the contrary, they were glad to have him. Hadn't they said so often? All she had wanted to do was to ask him one specific question, about his . . . his rather peculiar relations with Noga Harish.

'Ah, so that's all you came about,' said Zechariah, and he sighed an enormous sigh of relief, as if it were only now, at last, that Bronka's true purpose had been revealed and as if the discovery had taken a great weight off his mind.

'This afternoon . . . on the lawn . . . You . . . I mean, I'd like to know just what your intentions are toward her. You understand, forgive me, I'm asking you as . . . as your hostess, if you prefer to see it in that light.'

'But of course, Bronka, of course, there's no question about it, of course I owe you an explanation. The explanation is very simple, my dear Bronka. I've got nothing to hide from you. Far from it. So let's talk about it. Let's speak up quite frankly. Agreed?'

'Yes, quite frankly,' Bronka echoed, without questioning the reciprocal frankness that Zechariah demanded. What secrets could he ask her to reveal in exchange?

'Agreed,' she added.

'Fine,' said Zechariah, leaning back against the wall as if in preparation to deliver a long lecture. 'Well then. Item one. In the course of my work in the Diaspora I happened to meet a wonderful woman, the wife of an old friend of mine.

I refer, of course, to Eva Hamburger. She requested me to take advantage of my visit to my family in Israel to make the acquaintance of her daughter, who, as it happens, lives in the same kibbutz as my own relations, and to give her her mother's love. At the same time, I was requested to inform the mother reliably about the girl's condition. I complied with the request, met the daughter, and wrote to the mother informing her of her unfortunate condition. Is there anything wrong with that?'

Bronka shook her head mechanically.

'Item two. By return mail the mother asked me to convey to her daughter her feelings of apprehension, of guilt, and of remorse. This mission, too, I fulfilled to the very best of my limited ability. I was also requested to tell the girl that her mother earnestly entreated her to come back with me to live with her mother and her stepfather, Herr Isaac Hamburger. They were eagerly looking forward to seeing her. They were both convinced that in view of her predicament a change of environment and way of life would be good for the girl. That, moreover, both from a social and from a financial point of view the proposed arrangement was preferable to her present circumstances, which could be described without exaggeration as intolerable. True? You see, my dear Bronka, I am revealing all my secrets to you frankly and openly, and I expect you to repay me in kind.'

Bronka recovered from the barrage of words and asked sternly:

'But what need is there for a go-between? Perhaps you can explain that to me. Why can't Eva write to Noga directly? And why was it necessary to ignore Reuven Harish and get at his daughter behind his back? After all, isn't he her father, and doesn't decency demand that he be consulted about such a decision?'

Zechariah smiled happily, as if Bronka's questions were meant to help him make his point more clearly.

'You have asked three important questions, Bronka my dear, and all three of them go straight to the heart of the matter. First of all, the go-between. As you well know, the human mind is a complicated thing. Not at all simple. Our Eva is smitten by feelings of guilt and remorse, as I believe I have already stated quite frankly. She is afraid that her daughter reproaches her for abandoning her. It is only natural that she should take advantage of the visit of her old friend, in whose tact and experience she places generous – perhaps overgenerous – confidence. As for the girl's father,' Siegfried said, instantly wiping the smile off his face, 'he belongs to the next item.'

'Go on. I'm listening.'

'I shall now have to take advantage of the agreement we made to speak perfectly frankly, as I have something to say that may not be very pleasant. Noga's father complicated his life with . . . how shall we put it? . . . with a late-flowering love affair with a married woman. Everyone is entitled to complicate his own life as much as he pleases. But this selfish man also complicated the lives of his children. And his children are Eva's children, too. True, Eva was not faithful to him, either. But she left her home, went into voluntary exile, and sacrificed the joy of living with her children, all to protect the children and avoid damaging their impressionable minds. The same cannot be said of the father. Both he and the woman who deceived her husband to gratify their mutual lust, both of them ignored their children. They indulged the desires of their flesh, and neglected their children, who are their real flesh and blood. We consider – both the Hamburgers and yours truly – that this was an appalling crime. And the main victim was the adolescent girl, who in her desperation ruined her own life almost beyond repair. Eva, her present husband and their closest friend all believe – although with sorrow and pain in their hearts – that the father has lost all moral and legal right to decide his daughter's fate. If the father had not done what he did, the daughter would not have been driven to the course she took. The proof is easy enough, because the man whom the girl used as a means of ruining her life is closely related to her father's mistress. Forgive me, Bronka, for setting the facts so plainly before you.'

Bronka smiled despite herself, and said:

'You astonish me. You would make a great lawyer. You find it so easy to argue black into white.'

'I'm color blind, my dear. Colors just run riot in front of my eyes.'

'Everything you say is put so tactfully, and yet behind it all I can sense a terrible rudeness, as if . . . as if you were filling in an official form.'

Zechariah chose to ignore the critical remark. He leaned toward Bronka and picked his words carefully.

'Now for item four. As far as the previous items are concerned, the mission entrusted to me by the mother and the harmful influence of the father, I was only a spokesman. A kind of roving ambassador. But item four concerns me myself. Now, if you will forgive my rather formal preamble, I propose to dispense with formalities and make a personal confession.'

Bronka widened her eyes and murmured:

'Yes. Yes.'

Zechariah sighed, closed his eyes, reopened one of them, and said:

'A very personal confession. I am, as is well known, a lonely old man. No home, no wife, no children. A few memories of my childhood, a few scars left by my sufferings, that's all my possessions. Who or what have I got in the whole wide world apart from my brother and his family? I came to you to . . . to pick up a few crumbs of your happiness, a happiness that has never fallen to my lot.' (Zechariah's eyes – for the second time that day – filled with tears.) 'I came to . . . to find warmth. To draw some wistful satisfaction from the contentment of my dear brother Ezra. That is why I didn't go to stay with Nehemiah, Bronka, my love: Nehemiah, like me, is a withered tree. So, I came here to pick up some crumbs of happiness. I am a parasite, a creeper clinging to the oaks of the forest. I am no more than what our enemies accuse me of being. But what did I find – to my horror – when I arrived? A tragedy. An appalling tragedy in my brother's family. The last solid rock on which my life was founded, the last mainstay of my crumbling hopes, was being carried away and destroyed. My beloved brother was the victim of a faithless woman, the plaything of a wanton little girl, cast out from the bosom of his family. How could I help being shocked? Was my heart made of stone? So I said to myself, you, who have never had a home, who will never have a home, if you can manage to restore the ruins of this one home you will be able to say on your dying day: I have not lived in vain. I may have been a rotting tree, but my decay enriched the lives of others. What I mean is – forgive my rhetoric, emotion is blocking my throat – what I mean is, I undertook – without asking your permission – to do whatever lay in my power for you. For many nights I thought the matter over. I came to the conclusion that if I could only persuade the complex-ridden little creature to quit my brother's life and disappear from here for ever, it would open the way for a reconciliation between husband and wife. Then, and only then, Uncle Zechariah could pack his bags and leave behind him a job well done. He would not expect any gratitude. He would go back out into the cold dark night. But deep down in his heart he would carry with him wherever he went a secret pride, a worthwhile reward for all his labors. Was that a sin? Did I do wrong, dear Bronka? I was only trying to help you . . . To rid you of the little hussy. To take away with me the abscess that is poisoning your lives and your happiness. And also to teach the errant wife a lesson, so that she would always be faithful to my brother. Besides – I openly admit it – gratifying my modest pride. Was that a sin?'

And as he spoke, Siegfried went down on his knees before Bronka, just as he had done a few hours previously to Noga, and his face was tear-stained.

Bronka whispered:

'I don't understand it at all. I'm afraid of you. You're strange. You're sly.'

356

Siegfried groaned desperately.

'Don't try to understand, Bronka, don't try to understand, it's not understanding that's needed, it's feeling. You're right. I must go. But not alone. I must take little Eva with me. For your sake, Bronka. For my brother's sake. For Oren's sake. For Noga's sake. For Eva's sake.'

Suddenly, in a vehement outburst, he added:

'Will you help me? Will you help me?'

And without waiting for her answer, he compulsively pushed her toward the door, bowed a servile bow, smirked, sobbed, declared that this time he had truly revealed all his secrets, pleaded once again for Bronka's sympathy, and slammed the door shut behind her.

Bronka went out into the night with a heavy heart. She tried to control herself and put her thoughts in order. She was still convinced that the man was a scoundrel and a clown. And yet, as she reached that conclusion, she had a feeling that her judgment was somehow unfair to him. That feeling, like all her other feelings at that moment, was sharply defined.

Zechariah threw himself down on his bed, drew a small flask out from under his mattress, and took a few swigs. Then he sneezed twice. Then he slowly perused a German magazine. And after that, unbelievable though it may seem, he cried.

32

Come, Let's Go

FROM REUVEN Harish's last poem:

When far to West the crimson sun has set
And night falls swiftly, like a sudden blow,
When heart is tired of pleading, 'No, not yet,'
Then sounds an ice-blue whisper: Come, let's go.

33

Dim in the Night

DIM IN the night comes the sound of enemy soldiers singing on the slopes of the mountain. Round their fortified positions they have lit small camp fires. Their faint undulating song comes down off the mountain to howl outside our windows.

Wistful yearning fills the night. The points of fire hover in the sky, since darkness hides the mountain range from sight. They may be singing with joy, but the night tends to distort the sound and fill it with simmering sadness.

What are they plotting? Autumn is near. Every morning white-robed workmen gather there to dig trenches and build concrete defenses. An officer stands over them holding what looks like a thin stick. Fragments of his orders make their way down to us. Deep pits are dug at the edge of the Camel's Field. The heaps of fresh-dug earth mount day by day. Pickaxes clang against rock. A constant procession of clumsy flat trucks, with a lively, arrogant jeep darting in and out. Soldiers with steel helmets watch us every hour of the day and study all our movements. The squat fellahin who used to work the Camel's Field are no more to be seen. Grisha Isarov's juicy curses meet with no response. Their men seem to be under new, stricter orders. At times their slender jet planes appear and fly low over the mountain. They steer clear of the sky above our valley. High above the roof tops of our little bungalows our own planes flash in pairs.

Eight days before the New Year festival a military patrol set out at twilight along one of the forsaken tracks, right under the noses of the enemy positions. We can hardly deny that this was intended to tempt them into an early engagement. In our defense we can say that the patrol did not cross the disputed line. The time was carefully chosen so that the setting sun would be shining straight into their eyes. Before the patrol set out we were instructed to take the children down into the underground shelters. But the operation passed without incident. The enemy let the patrol pass within a stone's throw without firing a shot. What were they plotting? We, for our part, if we may be forgiven, experienced a thrill of anticipation. Something was about to happen. The rhythm of our lives was about to change.

True, there were those among us who were not free from pangs of sadness. Ido Zohar, for example. Ido climbed, alone, to the observation post at the top of the water tower. There he found a filthy old mattress with its innards spilling out. The boy lay flat on his back and looked up at the slight late-summer clouds. From time to time he addressed himself to them. He had a question to ask. But why should late-summer clouds linger to listen to a dreamy youth? The clouds eye him and pass silently on their way. They seem not to be moving, in the absence of a wind. But a closer examination reveals their secret. In reality they are slowly drifting eastward, and others take their place. These, too, are at the mercy of powerful forces. They have no fixed shape. Are they the ghosts of primeval monsters? Which is the most subtle of the beasts of the field? For whom does the autumn speak? And what is the mission of the birds?

Three days before the festival, the kibbutz assembled to elect its new committees. In a number of cases we could not avoid bringing public pressure to bear on those who refused to accept the burden of office. The community can neither exercise brute force nor hold out promises of material gain. Our system compels us to rely entirely on moral sanctions. The formation of the new committees was completed in the course of two general assemblies. The members of the various committees can expect to receive no material advantages. On the contrary, they have to shoulder an additional burden of difficulties and frustrations. Despite this, suitable candidates were found and consented to stand.

Herbert Segal was elected secretary of the kibbutz. That is not to say that we had anything against Tsvi Ramigolski, who had fulfilled his duties to the very best of his ability. Nevertheless, we were pleased at Herbert's election. People are not made identically, like coins coming from the mint. On the basis of long acquaintance with both of them we are convinced that the best of Herbert Segal's ability is better than the best of Tsvi Ramigolski's. Tsvi, incidentally, did not escape the burden of active responsibility: he was to succeed Podolski as co-ordinator of the work rota, so that Podolski could take over from Yitzhak Friedrich the office of treasurer. Mundek Zohar, naturally, continued to serve as chairman of the regional council. The vacant chair of the education committee, which had recently lost two of its leading members, Herbert Segal, the new secretary of the kibbutz, and the late Fruma Rominov, was left unfilled until after the festival. Many members supported the candidature of Bronka Berger. We, for reasons best known to ourselves, preferred Yitzhak Friedrich, the ex-treasurer.

A decision would also have to be taken about the case of Grisha Isarov. It had been suggested to Grisha that he spend two years away from his family helping an emerging African country to build up its armed forces. Grisha had difficulty in concealing his enthusiasm and excitement. Some of his opponents said that he was incapable of staying in the same place for five consecutive years. If we let him, he would spread his wings and flit from one adventure to another. Others objected to the proposal on the grounds that there was no one to replace him in his work at the fish ponds. Our own objection was founded on different considerations. Esther Klieger's life would be hell if she were left to bring up seven unruly children on her own. And a man ought to accept responsibility for his family.

*

The day before the festival, Rami Rominov came home on leave. The arduous training had left his face lean and weather-beaten. His resemblance to a certain quadruped had become so marked that it was no longer amusing.

Out of his meager earnings as a soldier Rami had bought Herbert Segal a book titled *Israeli Society and the Challenge of Our Times,* and for Noga he had bought a small box of water colors.

Rami left his bags in Herbert's room and went to the dining hall. He made a detour to avoid passing his mother's room. That same morning a young couple had moved in. Rami did not want to see the changes; he was afraid of the sadness. But the sadness crept in in a different way. The women who were serving lunch showered special tidbits on him. They were trying to make him happy. They failed, because he saw through their motives and only felt more miserable.

Toward evening, just before the festive meal, Rami and Noga went for a short walk together. Noga said to Rami that he looked nicer out of uniform. Rami agreed. They did not talk about army life. She did not ask, and he was not eager to tell. The conversation turned on a different topic: whether people's characters could be changed. Rami did not deny the effects of heredity, but he believed in the power of education, and even more so in the power of personal determination. Noga thought that the poet whose name she had forgotten was right when he had said that man was merely a reflection of the landscape of his birthplace. She interpreted the phrase 'landscape of his birthplace' broadly,

THE CLAPPER IN THE BELL

to mean inherited characteristics. 'Birthplace' is something in our blood, not just a geographical location.

Rami was inclined to disagree but changed his mind and said to Noga that she was not an ordinary sort of girl. Noga smiled at him gratefully. Her smile made him shiver, and this Noga noticed. A feeling of pride ran through her. She leaned toward him and kissed him as if he were her brother Gai. Rami went pale. He reached out and squeezed her shoulder roughly, studiedly, as if he had been rehearsing the gesture in his mind. Suddenly he asked her hoarsely if she would be his wife. Noga smoothed her skirt. Both their gazes fixed on the same spot. Noga was the first to raise her eyes.

'Why?' she asked.

Rami's lips curled and he muttered:

'What do you mean "Why?" I . . . That's not an answer. I'm asking you a serious question.'

'You shouldn't have asked.'

'Yes I should. I had to.'

Noga said:

'You're sweet, Avraham Rominov.'

And in her voice there sounded that long-forgotten tone in which as a child she had always addressed people much older than herself.

The dining hall is brightly lit. There are white cloths on the tables, and brightly colored plastic dishes. A large banner with the cheerful message: RING OUT THE OLD, RING IN THE NEW! The portrait of Aaron Ramigolski, may God avenge his soul, looks down on us: a young man with an unruly mop of hair, an open-necked shirt and an attempt at a mustache. His features resemble those of his brother Tsvi, though they are somewhat softer. Aaron's face is Tsvi's face without the harsh imprint of the years. What is he thinking as he looks down at us? We teach our children to try to live up to his memory. We tell ourselves the same thing. We look at him. He looks back at us without a trace of rancor. The company bursts into song. Latecomers walk on tiptoe. Nobody looks askance at them. Their neighbors wish them a Happy New Year, and they reply, a happy and prosperous New Year to you. A sharp ear can isolate some familiar voices: Grisha's bass rumble, Einav's soprano, and our guest Siegfried rushing shamelessly ahead of the rest. To all outward appearances, Siegfried has become one of us. He has abandoned his jacket and tie and now sits wearing a white shirt with the sleeves rolled up above his elbows. You can tell he is happy, because he is beating time on the table with his cup. The singing is followed, as is our custom, by a sequence of readings. Some of them are taken from traditional texts and some from our newborn folklore. Herbert Segal, the new secretary of the kibbutz, reads: 'Send us dew and rain in their due season.' Ezra leans toward his brother and whispers:

'Our ancestors were clever peasants. Did you notice: they didn't pray for a certain quantity of rain. They asked to have it in its due season. At the right time. And that's the really important thing.'

Zechariah smiles delightedly at this exciting piece of exegesis and says:

'Yes, yes, that's right.'

Now, according to custom, the heads of the various farming activities rise in turn to give an account of the achievements of the past year.

Dafna Isarov gives a spirited reading of the poem 'In the Fields,' by our national poet Bialik. Rami casts a sidelong glance at the Harish family. Noga is sitting between her father and her brother. Herbert Segal, Rami's neighbor, intercepts his glance and makes room for it in his tightlipped ruminations. Perhaps another eye is watching Herbert watching Rami. But no. It seems certain that the adversary has temporarily abandoned his barricades and is wholeheartedly enjoying the celebrations.

Grisha thunders (from notes):

'Let us drink to the new year. Let us drink to working men and women wherever they may be. Let us drink to a year of plenty, a year of joy and peace. *Lehayim*, comrades. A Happy New Year!'

Bottles are opened, and red wine is poured into plastic teacups.

The hubbub of the meal.

Herzl Goldring and his wife Nina enter, very late. They look for a place to sit. Gerda Zohar, in a black skirt and white apron, seats them at the last table. She smiles. Herzl mumbles:

'Yes, yes, Happy New Year, that's right, Happy New Year.'

Outside all is silence.

The bungalows and nurseries are in darkness. The yellow lamplight falls in murky puddles.

Tomer, who, as his luck would have it, has to serve as night watchman on this festive night, leans on his rifle and scratches his head. It would not be true to say that he is thinking: truer rather that he is fuming. Beyond his post is a slope. At the foot of the slope is the swimming pool. Next to the pool is a pine wood. Behind the pines are graves. Beyond the graves are fields. At the end of the fields are mountains. If the mountains have eyes, then surely we and our New Year and all our old years must seem like grasshoppers to them. But high above the mountains the stars look down contemptuously on the mountains' haughtiness. What are the mountains when viewed by the stars? Heaps of shifting dust, here today and gone tomorrow. There is a terrible threat of arrogance in the stars. But when we look at them we see no arrogance. Only repose. Perhaps a faint flicker of mockery. Perhaps a watchful slumber. Perhaps some other quality, which we cannot grasp. Weariness overcomes us. Our hand drops. We shall drop with it. Our lives cascade from gulley to gulley till they drain away into the sand for a fleeting sensation in our hidden parts. If only we had the weight of massive mountains, the peaceful arrogance of stars, the calm of solidified lava, a magical key to unknown gardens, away from curse and blessing, hope and fury. Our flesh, our blood subject us to cruel humiliations. We cannot rid ourselves of the humiliation, but we are free to protest. Of course, the mountains will ignore our protest. But they are mountains, and what are we.

We cower at the foot of the mountains. What is beyond them? Vast desert plains, twisted canyons at the mercy of dry scorching winds. Anti-Lebanon Hauran Golan Bashan Gilead

Moab Arnon Edom, a long grim mountain wall. Beyond them there is no enchanted garden. There is a land of lizard viper asp and fox. And beyond that are more mountains, more dreadful than ours, stretching away to the east. Beyond them is the plain of the two rivers, held in the jaws of the mountains. And further beyond, fresh mountain ranges spread to infinity, with peaks of permanent snow severed by knife-gashed valleys, where black goats furiously tear the scrub tended by shepherds as black as they are. And everything is tyrannized by the dread light of a merciless moon. We do not belong here. Our place is in cool shady gardens. But which is the way back?

'Happy New Year, Harismann,' Ezra said, when the festive meal was over. The younger people were dancing in large circles, the older ones clustering at the windows.

'Happy New Year, Ezra,' said Reuven, with a faded smile.

'So how are you, Harismann. How are you keeping?' Ezra continued, putting on a cheerful face.

'So-so,' Reuven answered, with a weary shake of his head. Suddenly he exclaimed furiously:

'Why ask? We're old men. There's no point in asking.'

'Keep well,' Ezra concluded. 'Look after yourself, Harismann. Take care.'

'We're old men,' Reuven repeated with a curious persistence.

Ezra turned away to look for his wife and his guest. He had the feeling he had spoiled something. Now he wanted company. He suddenly recalled his nocturnal journeys and relished the memory of roads swathed in drifts of white mist.

Reuven retired to his room. He washed, and glanced through the newspaper over a glass of tea. Dimly he heard the sounds of dancing. He heard the drone of the crickets. He got up and turned on the radio. A feverish voice speaking a strange language. No, it's not Dutch yet, Colonel, it's not your language yet.

He switched off. Swallowed a pill and washed it down with the remains of the tea. Turned restlessly in bed. Kicked the blanket off. Rolled himself up in the sheet. More sounds. He groaned. Thought about distant water. Felt a stabbing pain in his shoulder. Finally, sleep came over him. He dreamed of a plain full of wild horses. There were gigantic men, and women, too. The place and the people were strange. In his dream he tried to formulate something. A faraway shout shattered the picture and the words. Dim in the night came the sound of enemy soldiers singing on the slopes of the mountain. Their song howled outside Reuven's window and leaped into his dreams. Somebody cried far away. Reuven was flooded with a blackness in which abandoned boats were carried by the tide with broken masts. A bird screeched. Then fell silent. A new dream came, full of a pale finger not attached to any body, full of the sound of drums beating out a dim rhythm.

34

My Brother's Keeper

REUVEN HARISH woke up. The drums had not died down. Their faint rhythm had become stronger. The air was charged with sound. The shutters opened, and he saw, with wide eyes, the jagged flashes of machine-gun fire. It had started.

For some weeks now the fellahin had abandoned the Camel's Field. They had stopped coming down to it in their dark robes. Our patrols had been skirting its edge in the evenings, when the setting sun was shining into the loopholes of the enemy fortifications. The men inside had refrained from firing. Both camps seemed to be breathing deeply, tensely. If the rains had come a few days sooner, the Camel's Field would have remained uncultivated. In the spring it would have sprouted thistles and briars and colorful wild flowers. Perhaps even the dead might. But the rains chose to come later.

It happened that same morning.

Opposite Reuven Harish's window strode the large figure of Grisha Isarov, in olive-green army clothes and enormous boots. A heavy black pistol hung carelessly from his army belt.

'Get down to the shelter,' Grisha shouted. 'Right away. Quickly. This is no time for the Muses.'

At five o'clock in the morning, when the mountaintops were wreathed with an enchanted halo of purple light, the tractor had been started up. Its cab was heavily armored with steel plates. A large plow was coupled to it. The blades gleamed. The engine rumbled and roared hoarsely.

Twenty minutes before the sun burst through the mountain screen, the tractor had crossed the invisible line, put down a marker, and dug its tusks into the soil of the Camel's Field. As the sun rose, furious machine guns began tickling its steel ribs.

Reuven Harish leaned out of his window and addressed the myrtle bushes outside:

'Welcome, Colonel. I knew you'd be back. And here you are.'

He was half-asleep. For the moment.

It was a limpid blue morning. The fish ponds received the sunlight, transmuted it as water does, and sent out brilliant flashes.

The tractor pivoted on its tracks and began to cut a second furrow, parallel and close to the first. The bursts of machine-gun fire did not affect it. Such pinpricks were beneath its dignity. Solemnly, steadily it proceeded on its straight course. Reuven continued to stand at his window. He bit into an apple. Grimaced. Someone called out to him again to go to the shelter. Reuven asked why. Mundek shouted that everyone was in the shelter, the children, the women and the men who were not on duty.

'What are you waiting for?' he added.

Reuven asked himself the same question but could find no definite answer. He laughed aloud and threw the rest of the apple into the myrtle bushes.

Polished, resplendent, wearing a hat and a spotted tie, and equipped with a walking stick, Herr Berger the tourist stood outside the secretary's office and surveyed the scene about him.

One after the other, the pair of them, Reuven from his window and Siegfried from his vantage point, saw two balls of fire blazing in the Camel's Field. One landed under the nose of the indifferent monster. The other whizzed past and shattered far away, at the edge of our vineyard. At once there was an answering whoosh. White lights flickered on the mountainside opposite. Now we unleashed our pent-up fury. A thick, dark column of smoke rose among the trenches and slanted northeastward, betraying the direction of the wind.

The tractor absent-mindedly, as though absorbed in philosophical speculation, continued on its course. Its pace neither increased nor slackened. It remained, as before, solemn and steady.

The firing grew faster and heavier. All around the armor-plated reptile bubbles of dazzling light burst, raising clouds of earth, smoke, and stones. Was the haughty machine protected by an invisible magic cordon?

Now that things were coming to a head, Reuven experienced a powerful surge of excitement. He felt a physical disturbance at the sight of the enemy shells falling wide of their target. The haughty indifference filled him with optimistic foreboding.

The world shattered into one great scream. A shell plunged into one of the fish ponds and raised a plume of muddy water. Another shell singled out the pine wood, smashed through the trees and blazed red black yellow orange. A third shell, quiveringly close, sliced off the roof of the tractor shed. A foul scorching smell assaulted Reuven Harish's nostrils. He leaned out of his window, held his head and vomited into the myrtles. He was still feeling happy. That powerful feverish flush that grips weak men when they suddenly have a ringside view of violent fighting. Let the struggle wage on to the utter end of its final destiny.

Reuven stood at his window, his mouth open wide to scream or to sing. But his innards rebeled and he vomited again and again. Herr Berger heard his retching. He came and stood on the other side of the myrtles. Calmly, politely, he asked whether he could be of assistance. A gun silenced the howling of the wind. Shells screamed here and in the enemy camp. The pine wood blazed with fire, and fire had taken the enemy's strongholds. Another fire raged in the tractor shed. A stench of burning rubber. The blood-curdling bellow of a wounded cow.

Reuven Harish:

'Come in, my dear sir, I have been waiting for you to come.'

Siegfried, still calmly polite:

'I'm coming, I'm on my way, I'll be with you directly.'

Columns of dust rose from the slopes of the mountain. Dark men shot out of a dugout, running here and there with arms raised, like puppets whose strings have snapped.

A sound like a cord snapping close to the eardrum, followed by a menacing howl. The shell crashed into the wall of Fruma's house, the house that had been Fruma's in days gone by. The roof tilted, faltered, clung to the rafters with its fingernails, and finally gave in and collapsed with a hollow groan, raising a mushroom of dust.

Now from another point of view: the fire smoke howling sound and fury are mere illusion. Deception of unreliable senses. What is all the running of the tiny bouncing figures? What is their dark fear? The mountains stand as always.

At last an armor-piercing bullet penetrated the tractor's defenses and shattered its haughty pride. A blurred manikin shot out and zigzagged blindly across the field, falling and getting up, clasping his stomach, beating his chest with his fist as though swearing a powerful oath, leaping and flailing the air, as if the force of gravity had been momentarily weakened, caught his foot in a hole and collapsed on the ground, still kicking his legs in the air as though the whole universe had risen against him. Then, realizing the futility of kicking against empty space, he stretched his legs out, rested, made peace, lay still.

Reuven sits facing his visitor. A bowl of rosy-cheeked apples separates them. Slight disorder reigns in the room. The proper place for books is not on the floor. The packet of pills should have been put away in a drawer. The sour smell of vomit is not pleasant to breathe.

Siegfried:

'I have come.'

373

Reuven:

'So I see.'

Siegfried:

'You're not well.'

Reuven (why?):

'Thank you.'

Siegfried:

'You're not cheerful.'

Reuven:

'I'm ready.'

Siegfried:

'Yes, you're ready. With your pure soul and your innocent mind you're ready for a Syrian shell to turn you into yet
another Ramigolski, another plaster saint.'

'My dear sir, try to tell me something new. Your cleverness
has a rotten smell. You're playing the part of a grand-opera
executioner. You're a dead man. I'm not afraid of you. So,
you're laughing, Mr Berger. But you're laughing at the wrong
place. You're confused. That's not where you're supposed
to laugh. Why did you laugh? Go and learn your part. You
laughed in the wrong place.'

'That's enough, Harismann. You have no strength left.
You're tired out. Look at yourself. You're flushed. You're pale.
No, don't look out of the window. You haven't got an alibi.
You did flush. You did go pale. Your hand is shaking. You're
all hunched up in your chair. You've lost her. You're ashamed
to cry. You're holding back the tears. You're biting your lip.
Don't deny it. You're gritting your teeth. Don't be ashamed.
Cry. Let the tears flow. She's mine. You're mine. You're taking

over the bank, but you've lost everything. That's not right, my dear pioneer, that's not the way for an honest man to behave. You want me to disappear. To be a bad dream. A nightmare. Feel me. Touch me. I'm not a ghost. I'm here, with you. In you. I'm real. I'm your humble servant. Your daughter's suitor. Your brother. Your best friend. Kiss my hand, Harismann. Beg for mercy. You're mine.'

'Go away, sir, go away. Don't stay here.'

'I'll take good care of her. I'll be gentle. I'll love her for you, too.'

'Tell me, sir: she's beautiful, isn't she? Beautiful, quiet, dreamy – isn't she? She's . . . she's a miracle, sir. Isn't she?'

'Oh, how we love her, Harismann, you and I. In her we are one flesh. Why are you getting up? Sit down. Or rather lie down. Don't move. Movement now can be fatal. Lie still on the floor. Don't try to get up. It's dangerous. Lie still. Relax. Perfectly still. I'll fetch you some water. Here are your pills. No, you mustn't struggle. Relax, I said. Don't make any effort. Rest. It'll pass. The doctor's busy now with the wounded, but when it's all over he'll see you, too. I'm here by your side. You're not forsaken. You're in reliable hands. No, don't pull a face. Close your eyes. You're a good-looking man. High, clear brow. Don't be afraid. There's a friend at hand. Can you still hear me? A bosom friend. Don't move. Unclench your fist. Don't chew your lip, obstinate man. Take care. Be sensible. Don't put a strain on your heart. Stop gurgling like that. Here, I'll sit next to you. On the floor. Give me your hand. Pulse too fast. Perhaps I'll stroke your hair. I'll sing you a German song if you like. A lovely, sad children's song. I'll tell you an old

story, too. Perhaps you'll go to sleep. Think of water. A little
spring on the rocky mountainside. A stream trickling through
the forest. An innocent little girl meets a wolf. Now a wide
dark river. The water is cold, unchanging, gliding into the arms
of the sea. Sea. Little waves. A dark jetty. White foam. A man
and his daughter sailing together to the end of the sea. Go,
pure man, go quietly, go in peace. Don't think about operatic
executioners. Don't think darkness. Darkness is a tunnel from
light to light. The transition is not difficult. Go to another
place. Go across valleys and over mountains. See the roads
that are forbidden to me. Who are you now, pure man. You're
me when I was alive. I love you. I love you in your daughter.
We were brothers. I loved you very much.'

At dawn on the day following the festival of the New Year an
armored tractor from Kibbutz Metsudat Ram began to plow
a piece of land that had previously been worked illegally by
the enemy. At first light the enemy artillery opened fire. The
work continued, and the fire was not returned. The enemy
proceeded to shell the civilian settlement indiscriminately with
recoilless guns. The population took to the shelters. Our forces
retaliated with heavy artillery fire. When approximately one-
third of the disputed plot of land had been plowed, the tractor
received a direct hit and its driver was killed. The engagement
lasted some eighty minutes. Firing ceased only with the total
silencing of the enemy positions, which sustained a large number of direct hits. With the exception of the tractor driver, our
forces suffered no casualties. A member of Metsudat Ram,
Misha Isarson, aged forty-four, was wounded in the arm by

shrapnel. His wound was dressed on the spot, and he continued to discharge his duties as superintendent of the civil defense of the kibbutz. It is reported that during the shelling a member of the kibbutz died in his room. He was known to be ill at the time. Houses, farm buildings, and agricultural equipment suffered serious damage.

After the investigation and before the funeral, Ezra and Bronka, in agreement with Herbert Segal and others, decided to ask Siegfried to leave. Nobody suspected him and nobody blamed him, but we had received no clear explanation of the circumstances of his presence in Reuven Harish's room at the time of the tragedy. Noga's calm but insistent demand that he leave immediately tipped the balance against him.

The request was put to Siegfried firmly but politely, and he responded with an indifference bordering on meekness. For pedagogic and other reasons Herbert Segal refused to allow him to see Noga. Siegfried replied that he understood and accepted Herbert's reasons. He offered Herbert a considerable sum of money for a library to be named in memory of Reuven Harish. When Herbert declined it, he burst into tears. He repeated the outburst when he took his leave of his brother and his family.

He left the country on a night flight. From the airport he sent a telegram to the secretary of Kibbutz Metsudat Ram expressing his gratitude and sympathy.

Siegfried left, and the rain came. Cruel drops. Monotonous complaint. Grumbling gutters. Dry dust turned to thick mud.

Wet wind dashing against shuttered windows. Continuous howling of battered treetops.

On a dark, rainy morning Reuven Harish and the tractor driver, whose name was Mordecai Gelber, were laid to rest. Because of the rain there was only a short address. There was a symbolic link between the two deaths, as anyone with any sensitivity would appreciate, said Herbert Segal. Reuven Harish had been a pure man. We mourned his passing.

. . . Ever After

THREE MONTHS passed.

Noga Harish was in the last three weeks of her pregnancy. On a stormy midwinter's day we saw her married to Avraham Rominov. There were no celebrations. Herbert Segal kissed both the orphans. Rami kissed Noga. Someone, Hasia or Nina or Gerda, perhaps all three, stifled a sob. Oren Geva scratched a pattern of wavy lines in the plaster on the wall with his fingernails. Ido Zohar took refuge in the empty recreation hall and composed a poem. Bronka made some curtains for the couple's room. Grisha dug a trench outside their window to carry off the rain water.

A fortnight went by. Gai Harish caught a cold. The good women looked after him. He was moved in the evening from the children's house to the Bergers' home. Bronka gave him tea with honey. Noga and Rami came to keep him company.

Bronka stroked Noga's hair. Rami played checkers with the patient. Then he played chess with Ezra. Then the young couple left. Bronka turned the light out. In the night Gai's temperature went up, and next morning it came down again.

Gossip has informed us that Einav is pregnant again. Danny can crawl now. He plays with bricks. Tomer likes to throw his son up in the air and catch him in his big hands. Danny screams with joy. Einav screams with fear.

Ezra needs to wear glasses. In the evenings he reads aloud from the Bible in a cracked voice. Bronka sits facing him, knitting, listening or not listening.

Herbert Segal, in his room, puts a record on the record player and listens alone to the sound of the orchestra and the sounds of the wind and the rain. Sometimes he makes tea and mutters to himself, like many lonely people. Sometimes he gets out his violin and plays a simple tune or two.

What about Israel Tsitron, Herzl Goldring, Mendel Morag, Tsvi Ramigolski, Yitzhak Friedrich, and their wives, and the other members of the kibbutz? Now that it is winter and there is little work to be done they sleep a lot. Some of them read to broaden their minds. Some of them take part in study groups organized by the cultural committee. Others are content to withdraw into themselves. As we do, too, at merciful moments, when it does not gnaw at us or waft a cold deadness in our face.

The rain comes and goes. Dark clouds roll overhead and hurl themselves against the mountain wall. But they do not break it. The slopes sprout wild plants. Turbid water pours down the gulleys. The fishermen have removed their nets from the stormy lake. I am tired of the masquerade. I shall unmask. Perhaps, I, too, shall go to Abushdid's and huddle in a dark corner. Sip coffee and stare at the damp walls.

On the day of the spring festival Noga gave birth to her daughter. She named her Inbal, meaning the tongue of a bell. The baby was underweight, and her head was slightly flattened in the difficult delivery. Look at her face. Do all those other faces meet in it, Grandma Stella's, Eva's, Noga's, Siegfried's, Rami's, Ezra's, Reuven's? Her features are still unformed, though. True, she has blue eyes. But the color may well change in a few weeks' time.

The mountains are as in days gone by. I turn my eyes from them. I shall take my leave on a Friday night, at the Bergers' house. Outside the wind may howl and the rain beat down. The house is like a bell. Ezra is seated, wearing his glasses, which make him look old and resigned. Bronka and Noga confabulate in the cooking alcove. There is a warmth between them. Stella Maris. A paraffin heater burns with a blue flame. On the rug, as always, are two babies. Dan and Inbal. Tomer and Rami discuss the news peacefully, amicably. Herbert Segal, who is visiting, drinks a glass of tea in silence, keeping his thoughts to himself. Einav drops off to sleep with a newspaper over her face. Gai and Oren are here, too, standing at Ezra's desk, heads together, dark hair touching fair hair, their joint stamp collection spread out in front of them.

The armchair in the corner is ringed with light. No one is sitting in it. Do not fill it with men and women who belong elsewhere. You must listen to the rain scratching at the windowpanes. You must look only at the people who are here, inside the warm room. You must see clearly. Remove every impediment. Absorb the different voices of the large family. Summon your strength. Perhaps close your eyes. And try to give this the name of love.

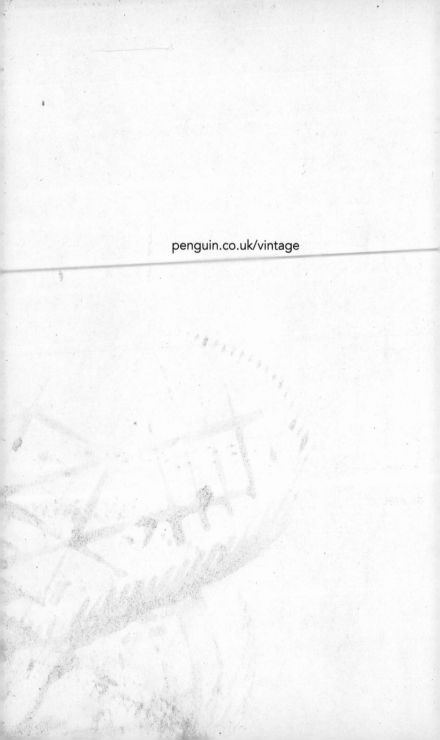

penguin.co.uk/vintage